That Hurt Thing

March 03

That Hurt Thing

For Chris & Karen,
May all you wishes
come true!

Fara Spence

Fara Spence —

HaWK Publishing : Tulsa

Published in the United States by HAWK Publishing Group.

HAWK and colophon are trademarks belonging to the HAWK Publishing Group.

Printed in the United States of America.

LIBRARY OF CONGRESS CATALOGING IN PUBLICATION DATA
Spence, Fara
That Hurt Thing/Fara Spence–HAWK Publishing ed.
p. cm.
ISBN 1-930709-34-X

1.Fiction–Canada
2. Fiction–Oklahoma

I. Title
[PS3563.I42145R4 2000]
813'.54 80-52413
CIP

HAWK Publishing
www.hawkpub.com

H987654321

In memory of my father, Kenneth Spence.

1936 – 1977

And for my courageous students at
Thunderbird Youth Academy—
Remember your heart!

ONE MILLION THANK YOUS TO:

Bill and Kirsten Bernhardt; my editor Jim Vance; my agent Mary Sue Seymour; Connie Jodrey, Karen Bagnell; Marie Muirhead; Jeff Kolker; Dr. Kim Murray; Dr. Chris Kolker; Terry Aylward; Judea Cassyn; Chris Pauley; Steve Richard of Big Sky Studio One, Halifax, NS; Robert van Nostrand; Ron and Marjorie Kolker; Ellen Diem; Ruard Wallis de Vries; Marie Green; Olivia Ingraham; Les Davis and Kelly Brown of Key Funeral Home; Rick Stephens of Stephen's Funeral Home, Pryor, OK.

AN EXTRA MILLION FOR:

Sheldon O'Brien.

P.S. My mother, Betty Spence, has something to say: I always worried about Fara, locking herself up in her room for hours, making up lies and writing them down. It's a bit shameful, if you ask me. Hope some good comes of this.

If any readers would like to contact me, please send email to
fsmail@faraspence.com, or visit www.faraspence.com.

chapter one

Nick stared at the dead body on his bed.

It wasn't real. Was it?

He took a step closer and peered down.

Stats: White female, late twenties, black hair, tight black dress and heels. Pretty female, too.

His towel fell away and Nick clutched at it as if she could see him naked. His hair was still wet and when he leaned closer, drops splattered against the girl's forehead. The wolf pendant he wore around his neck wagged over her face, throwing little wobbly shadows.

He extended a hand toward the phone and hesitated. Maybe I should wait, he considered.

Wait for *what?*

For her to become even more dead?

He paused to think logically about the situation. He'd driven twelve hours in the rain from Halifax, Nova Scotia and arrived in Montreal at four. He'd eaten a couple of burgers in a greasy French diner. Then back to motel room nine where, emerging from the shower, he'd discovered a body on his bed.

Instead of the phone, he grabbed the book on the night stand. The odd book that had brought him to this time, this reality.

He glanced at the phone again, stepped toward it — and then went into the bathroom, shut the door and stood there panting. He couldn't report a dead woman on his bed while he was naked. It just wasn't right somehow.

And think of the questions: *Why were you undressed when you found her? You didn't notice her lying there before you went to shower? What are you, blind?*

Shivering from wet hair and adrenaline, Nick put the book along the edge of the sink and dressed in his blue corduroys and jean shirt.

He turned to the mirror and combed his blond hair to the side, the way Chloe said she liked it. Good ol' Chloe.

What would his dearly beloved say about this?

She'd probably tell him to call the cops or the front desk, anything other than standing around looking stupid and finding comfort in the book.

And that's why you aren't picking up the phone, isn't it, Nick? Because of the book. Because the book offered you an adventure; the book said this would happen, that a mysterious woman would appear and —

"Didn't think she'd be dead!" Nick hollered into the mirror. Sure, he had wanted an adventure, but he hadn't really taken the book seriously. It'd been more of a lark, something to offer a diversion.

He gathered the book from the sink's ledge and followed the letters with his fingers.

That Hurt Thing.

He'd found the book in the discard box of a secondhand bookstore on Brunswick Street. It's true that a book's cover speaks first, because Nick was immediately drawn to the foil cover's illustration — or was it an original painting? — of a black tulip slashed into two pieces. Between the halves, a black scorpion held its curved tail high as if aching to strike.

Inside the front cover, someone had scrawled: *'Call unto her and she will heal that hurt thing.'*

Brown stains smeared the first few pages and Nick, in his yearning for something new and bigger than his life, hoped it might be blood. The book drew him in effortlessly, like an old friend who whispers in your ear and makes you swear not to tell a soul what he's about to say.

That Hurt Thing

Do you dare summon me, Oh weak and weary of soul?
Do you long to taste the wolf's blood gone cold?
Be certain, for the scorpion goddess knows only rage,
For those who hold mockery upon my page.

Follow borders two from your place of birth,
Come willingly with courage and merry mirth.
Careful what you wish for I will grant it to thee
Without thought or pause or mediocrity.

Nick wasn't sure if it was the bad poetry, or pure curiosity that made him turn the page:

Once you arrive you will await my form,
And dark and light will mingle with storm.
Be worthy of disturbing my sleep and time,
There is no turning back once I make you mine.
Now put me away and do not read more,
Until I greet you in my purest form.

Now who could resist a book with that lure?

After he'd purchased it for a mere two dollars and fifty cents — it was a write-off, the bookseller declared — Nick took the book to his apartment and spent the next few nights deciphering it.

Not that there was much to decipher. From what he understood, if you followed the instructions, a scorpion goddess — whoever that was — would show up and grant a few wishes. Like a genie in a book; a *novel* idea.

Follow borders two from your place of birth.

That sentence was too easy. Borders two would take him out of Nova Scotia, past New Brunswick and into Quebec. And as everyone knows, the only city worth seeing in Quebec is Montreal, the colorful, noisy city of obsessive fashion and midnight bistros and theater of the absurd.

Now put me away and do not read more, until I greet you in my purest form . . .

As per the last two lines instructed, Nick hadn't read ahead. While he wasn't sure if he would ever take the chance, he didn't want to rule it out, either. Like a man who's unsure about God, he doesn't confirm his doubt *just in case.*

And then he and Chloe had argued about her needing more space, and hell, she didn't know how unnecessary that made him feel with her chronic game of *Push and pull; c'mere and go away; yes and no.* Usually he just took it. Took it and withdrew into himself or his schoolwork, but this time was different. Labor Day weekend was approaching and grabbing the book, he thought: What the hell, live a little. Skate on the edge of comfort.

That edge had taken him to Montreal.

And here I am, Nick thought. In a motel room and there's a dead women on my bed. Could this be the greeting in the *purest form*?

Don't be dramatic, he told himself. However this woman got in my room, it has nothing to do with the book. Speaking of which, he'd best deal with the situation. Time was a-wasting and the law didn't appreciate delays when cadavers were involved.

He turned from the mirror, closed his eyes and took a deep, deep breath as he stepped out of the bathroom. What was the big deal with a dead body, anyhow? He'd helped his father with the mortician business since he'd been a boy. Death was part of the cycle, a little answer to the big riddle —

When he opened his eyes, the girl was gone.

She couldn't be gone. Dead people don't get up and walk away. Sometimes limbs flinched when rigor mortis relaxed but they didn't do anything as blatant as really move. They just lay there —

"Hello, Nick."

Nick felt his shoulders jerk upward so quickly it hurt, and he scanned the room without moving his head. He felt his eyes strain to the far left and stop. His head followed.

She sat in the cheap wooden chair beside the window, legs crossed and a cigarette dangling from the corner of her lip. He glanced to the bed, saw the dimple in the brown bedspread where she'd been lying.

Be worthy of disturbing my sleep and time,

There is no turning back once I make you mine.

Nick rolled his tongue along the front of his teeth. "H-how do you know my name?"

A little giggle. God, she was beautiful. The kind of beautiful you associated with bitchiness and money. The kind of beautiful that had never bothered with him.

His guts danced inside.

He couldn't place this woman exactly, couldn't pinpoint her race. She was a mixture, of course. The most beautiful people almost always are. Maybe a blend of Italian and Korean and hell, a dash of Betty Page, and Veronica from the Archie comic books, too.

Her body was long and lean and she knew it. She wore her confidence like a pair of comfortable Gucci shoes. There was no posing this way or that to bring out her best features. There was no need.

The tip of one ear peeked through a curtain of black hair, and even that single detail was enticing. Her face was square, a perfect canvas for the fleshy red lips and wide, exotic eyes.

Nick began to sweat. "You didn't answer my question," he told her.

Her next breath lifted her torso as she stood and smiled. The hem of the tight dress clung to the tops of her thighs. "Nick, are you hurt?"

"Hurt?" He glanced down at the book in the crook of his arm. "Well . . . no." His voice was raspy and he cringed at how childish he must seem. "No, I'm not . . . hurt."

She dragged on the cigarette, letting the blue smoke curl into her nostrils. Nick didn't like smoking; it was distasteful, dirty. So why did she make it seem sexy, even wholesome? Amazing how much influence a beautiful woman could have.

She stood with her back to the window so that her face was shadowed. Was she smiling? Streams of sunlight pushed past the curtains and caught the smoke, illuminating it.

In one smooth gesture, she stubbed the cigarette in the ashtray by the window and moved out of the smoky web toward him.

Her lips separated and with a tiny moan, she knelt at his feet. Her head bowed, her long black hair splayed over her shoulders like liquid plastic. "Master," she said simply, "what is your wish?"

"Master?" Despite his nervousness, Nick laughed. Okay, this had to be a joke. "You've got to be kidding. This is Ralph's doing, right? You're a friend of Ralph's?" God knows his best friend was capable of anything.

She lifted her face upward. Her hair creased in the nape of her neck; her green eyes widened. "Master, why did you seek me if you weren't sure?"

Now she wasn't making any sense at all. "Get up." He touched her shoulder. "C'mon. Get up. This is crazy."

On her feet, she met him at eye level, easily five nine. Her hands dangled at her sides.

"How'd you get in here?" he wanted to know.

She blinked and touched her throat. "I . . . I . . . didn't."

"What do you mean you didn't?"

"That hurt thing," she said.

Nick shrugged and put the book on the night stand. Why was she reading the book's title to him? Was this some freaky game she liked to play, like those people who read every road sign aloud and make words out of license plate letters?

She walked to the night stand and dabbled her long red fingernails over the foil cover. "The book," she announced. "I think it's time you moved ahead, turned the page. It's only polite."

A chill whipped along Nick's spine. It was really happening, just like the book said, *honest to God!* Then again, she'd been here alone with the book while he'd been having a few burgers. Maybe she'd found the book and wanted to confuse him.

She could even be a prostitute, Nick considered.

She probably had a master key and shared the profits with the manager; after all, it wasn't like the motel was the classiest of joints. When he'd checked in, the scraggly man behind the counter looked up from his car and boat magazine and asked if Nick wanted the room on a nightly or hourly basis.

"Well?" She jiggled the book.

Nick sighed. "Okay, I'll play your silly game."

He reached for the book, perhaps too impatiently, and it slipped to the carpet. As he leaned to retrieve it, he caught the glint of silver. A knife. Sunshine girl holding a knife. Where the hell did that come from?

He jerked upright again. "W-what're you doing with that?"

She stood quietly, the blade pointed toward his chest. It was a switchblade, with a smooth black handle that caught the light. Though he knew he might be in serious danger, Nick couldn't help but marvel at how beautiful the weapon was in her hands. Had he ever seen such lovely hands?

"Nick?" She moved toward him. "Oh, Nick"

He shuffled backward so quickly he hit the bed and landed on his backside. God, how naïve he'd been. He should've known she was some crazy chick lying in wait to rob him. But he'd been taken off guard by the situation, by her beauty.

She was a small woman and if he had to, Nick was pretty sure he could wrestle the knife from her. But who knew how crazy she was? And crazy people had all kinds of crazy strength.

Nick swung his legs over the bed, but one foot caught in the blanket and he fell flat on his back. He lay there, staring up at the crazy woman and feeling as vulnerable as a baby.

She dangled the knife between her fingers like a cigarette. "Turn the page, Nick." She tossed the book beside him on the bed. "Read."

Leaning on one elbow, Nick glanced at her warily, and thenlicked his thumb and turned the page.

He read: *Kiss her or kill her.'*

He blinked. There had to be some mistake. She'd altered the book. This didn't make any sense at all. Oh, she was keen, he had to give her that.

"Nick," she said simply. "Please decide."

"To kiss or kill you?" He bolted to his feet, strode across the room and swung open the motel door. The doorknob thunked against the back of the wall. Sunlight suddenly filled the room, so bright it hurt his eyes. She stood there, a glaring contrast with her black hair and black dress.

He could run now, get the hell away from the girl and her knife. After all, this whole scene was really nuts. He glanced at the book on the crumpled bed.

And dark and light will mingle with storm.

Storm's a good word, he thought, because he'd never felt so unsettled in all his life. Her hands were on her hips now, and her smile, wide, perfect. She moved her eyes over him and settled on his face.

Nick said, "What's your name?"

"Lyra."

"Lyra? That's a constellation."

She nodded.

"This is insanity, Lyra."

"Nick, it isn't. I know you."

"You know me?" He shook his head. "What can you possibly know?"

She counted on her fingers. "Nick O'Brien. Twenty-four. In your last year of honors chemistry at Dalhousie University. Next year you hope to be starting medical school. You live in an apartment at the top of your father's house. Your mother died when you were eleven. A teenage sister, Paula. Your family runs a funeral parlor. Best friend is Ralph. And then there's Chloe, who you'd desperately love to get into bed."

She smiled. "See, I really do know you."

Nick slumped to the bed and put his head in his hands. Frankly, he was amazed. "H-how do you know all this?"

"Oh, come now. You make it sound like it's a bad thing."

A man and woman passed by the open door and glanced in. The woman, an overweight redhead dressed in plaid pants, grinned as if she thought it cute, the lovers' quarrel. When they entered the next room, Nick closed the door and crossing his arms across his chest, turned again to Lyra.

"I don't understand," he admitted.

She grinned. "Well? Kiss or kill?"

He put up a hand. "You're a hooker, aren't you? A hooker playing a part and this is Act One. Maybe Ralph somehow planned this, and now you're going to play the mysterious femme fatale and seduce me."

That had to be it, he decided. How else could she know all those details of his life?

"Would you like that, Nick?"

"What I'd like is for you to put down the knife."

"All you have to do is ask." Gently she put the weapon on the table beside the ashtray and presented her palms. "There, that wasn't difficult, was it?"

"Now the truth."

"The truth." She chuckled and for an instant, seemed much older than he'd originally guessed. Her green eyes chafed against his own. "Let's get real here, Nick. You summoned me."

"Summoned you?"

"That's right."

"You afraid I'll tell Ralph I figured it out?"

"This, my dear Nicholas, is only between you and I."

"Ralph had nothing to do with it?"

She crossed her fingers. "Girl Scout promise."

Somehow, she didn't strike Nick as the Girl Scout type. But if Ralph hadn't planned this, who did? And how did she know so many things about him?

Nick sawed down on his back teeth. "What do you want from me?" It was a dramatic question and under any other circumstance, he might have laughed. But this was no laughing matter. There was a freaky woman in his room with a knife and spouting nonsense.

She licked her lips and sighed. "I want you to decide."

"Look, don't be stupid, okay? I'm not going to kill you —"

"Then it's kiss me?"

"*Kiss you?*"

Lyra moved across the room then, and put her lips against his.

chapter two

This wasn't just any kiss.

Nick knew right away that he was dealing with something wicked, something *dark*. But he was too attracted to her, and maybe to the darkness, to think rationally. He wound his arms around her waist and she gave a little sigh that was, despite it all, endearing.

Her lips were plump and generous and when they pressed into the hollow behind his earlobe, Nick felt as if he were falling away from life and into himself, into a dimension that left no room for logical thought.

It seemed as if a lifetime passed between them as they explored and tangled thought and presence. It was like inching toward the first hill of a roller coaster. He realized the plunge downward was inevitable, but felt powerless to stop it.

Not that he wanted to stop it.

Not even when evening passed and Lyra lay asleep in his arms and he realized that this was a scene right out of surreal central.

It was just past midnight. How had so many hours passed without his realizing it?

The influence of a beautiful woman, of course.

This had to be the strangest thing that had ever happened to him. Was he really in bed with a slinky woman who claimed to be a genie he'd summoned?

And her name, Lyra. Named after a constellation? Why, that had to be made up. Had to be part of the darkness she carried with her like a scent.

Seeing Lyra now, it was hard to believe there could be anything sinister about her. She looked so innocent, her black hair falling into the crevices of her shoulder blades, a touch of pink on her pale cheeks.

It should have excited Nick to feel so lucky, and it did, but there was a low voice he couldn't quite hear, a whisper that murmured of evil and decay.

"Lyra. Wake up." Nick gently pushed her shoulder. She smiled and opened one eye, then buried herself deeper into his arms.

Hell, what a mess.

Nick was pretty sure Chloe wouldn't agree to this scene — after all, he didn't even know this Lyra person.

He thought of Chloe and how many times she'd dismissed him. Women didn't realize how deep their subtle rejections went for a man, how it hit right at the spot that spoke of manliness.

He began to feel angry.

Angry that Chloe could be so cold; angry that she took his feelings for granted. He moved closer to Lyra, soaked up her acceptance of him. To hell with Chloe. To hell with it all.

Lyra moaned in her sleep and Nick hoped she'd wake up and want him once more — after all, she seemed pretty *energetic.* He fondled her breast and then dragged his hand to cup the tight fullness of her backside. She gave a little grin and kicked the blankets away, but she didn't wake up.

What was that?

Nick leaned on one elbow to get a closer look. A tattoo at the base of Lyra's spine. Interesting; why hadn't he noticed it before?

Maybe because it was tiny. Or maybe during the blur of tearing their clothes off, examining her body for marks had been the last thing on his mind.

A scorpion.

A small black scorpion curled as if ready to spring into assault. It was peculiar and erotic. Nick touched it. Smooth. And what a coincidence that both Lyra *and* the book's cover bore a scorpion.

Is it a coincidence, Nick? Is it?

A wisp of fear nudged him.

He pushed it aside and kissed Lyra's shoulder. The tattoo was exciting. In the same way that this weekend was exciting. He couldn't imagine a more perfect character for a crazy fling than Lyra with her mysterious, exotic presence. He just bet she was one of those women you'd always be learning things about, even if you knew her for a million years.

He closed his eyes and nestled closer. She turned on her side and they snuggled like spoons in a drawer.

Outside, gentle rain sprayed the window.

Yawning, Nick thought about the scorpion again. The way he lay against Lyra, the tattoo was directly in line with his crotch.

Somehow, there was something funny about that.

Three black scorpions scuttled over the sand.

Nick dreamed on.

He was in a desert and the scent of smoke and something like cinnamon hovered in the hazy air. A wind came up, spraying sand into his face and hair. Squinting, he shielded his eyes with one arm. The wind died as quickly as it began.

Near his feet, the scorpions made a smacking sound which didn't seem right at all. But he'd never seen a scorpion in real life. They could've mooed and he wouldn't know the difference.

In fact, there was little about this scene that he recognized. The scorpions moved slowly toward a sandy hill, and Nick, uncertain what he should do, followed.

It was hard to climb the sand mound with bare feet and the thick white robe that swished between his ankles. At the crest of the hill, he wiped a line of sweat from his brow and struggled to take a deep breath. It was deadly hot; even his toes were sticky and moist.

The scorpions faded then. Just faded into the color of sand until they'd completely disappeared. Nick searched the ground, feeling more and more lost and alone. The big bugs might be creepy, but they'd at least offered a little direction.

What would he do now?

Where would he go?

Nick turned to see a walled city shimmering in the haze of heat. It was just how he'd imagined an ancient Middle Eastern city — probably in Egypt — would look, if indeed this was the Middle East. That was the thing with dreams — they didn't have to make sense.

Wherever it was, it was an impressive setting. Palm and sycamore and fig trees hovered near buildings the color of butter and clay. Wooden pillars held in place square roofs that were garlanded with flowers of pink and yellow and white.

Lifting the robe slightly so he could move easier, he walked toward the arched entranceway. It was further away than he anticipated, and he stopped about half way to lean against his knees and take several deep breaths.

God, the heat. Unbearable.

As he got closer, he heard the sound of a crowd jeering, and then four men scurried past him toward the city.

Nick hesitated. A jeering crowd could mean anything — jugglers, a sports competition or something darker, something *dangerous.*

In fact, it might be dangerous for him to go prancing into an unknown city like this, and he tried to remember what he'd read of ancient Egypt.

From what he remembered, the Egyptians had been reasonable people, though a teacher in high school had once explained that soldiers who spilled military secrets could lose their tongues.

Oh well, no secrets will I spill, he thought with a grin.

Besides, I'm dressed like those men that just passed by, he told himself. I could be a local, or a visitor from a nearby city; no one will notice me. Besides, this is a dream. Isn't it?

Isn't it?

Two naked boys played ball near the entrance; they scarcely gave Nick more than a passing glance. He felt more confident, even grateful for the unplanned dream sequence into Egypt.

A man rushed by wearing a blue kilt. Nick blinked; wasn't that supposed to be Scotland? Or maybe this guy was an ancient freak, not unlike the freaks of today. Even Halifax had the infamous man who wore skirts and high heels, claiming that it was simply more comfortable. Heels comfortable? Somehow, Nick doubted it.

Inside the city, he followed the sound of the crowd which brought him eventually to an open courtyard filled with people.

The focus of the crowd was a wooden pedestal. Empty, except for a box that measured about three feet by three feet. After a few moments, a man climbed the pedestal and was met with applause.

He gave a curt nod, and rubbing his hands together, walked toward the box. He wore a black headdress and a cloak that floated over a white robe; Nick guessed that he was an authority or religious figure.

It was odd, all this attention drawn to a large square box.

Was there something inside it? He couldn't remember much about Middle Eastern rituals, but perhaps someone was to be married and the box would hold the bride until she jumped out to her groom. Maybe that explains the origin of a woman popping out of a cake, he considered half jokingly.

A sharp squeal caused Nick to turn to the left and he pulled back as a naked woman was pushed harshly up the steps to the pedestal.

Definitely not a bride . . .

Stumbling ahead, she squinted at the crowd. She was bold, but it wasn't serving her well now. When the man grasped her arms, she looked as if she might spit at him.

He lifted his hand then, and slapped her face. There was a cracking noise and she slumped to her knees with a gasp. The people shouted their approval and shook their hands. A little boy began to whimper and the mother hurried off with the child, as if she didn't want to disturb the fun.

She was being punished, this woman on the pedestal. That much was obvious.

And what a shame. Not only was she lovely, but her expression reflected softness and intelligence, too. Whatever had she done to deserve such public humiliation?

Her head had been shaved, and a dark bruise darkened her thigh. Had they beaten her?

Her eyes peered into the crowd and they settled on a man standing beside Nick. With a tiny shrug, she mouthed something to him. The man nodded and with a frown, turned away.

Nick turned to him. He was familiar, somehow. "Do . . . do I know you from somewhere?"

The only response was the crowd's swelling cries, and then they chanted a single word again and again — in Arabic, he supposed. While Nick didn't understand what was shouted, he felt sure the crowd called for the woman's death.

Only the man who'd turned away was silent. Nick stared at him, feeling again as if he knew him. In fact, it was as if the entire scene had been played out before.

In one sudden gesture, the man on the pedestal seized the girl, lifted her as if she were a child, and dropped her feet first into the box. Her head was thrown back; her jaw clicked open and closed. The executioner put a hand between her shoulder blades and pressed her down into the box.

She didn't fight or protest. In fact, she seemed to welcome the release her pending death would bring.

A plump woman near the front wrung her hands and when a heavy lid was placed on the box, two young men threw their arms around one another's shoulders and began to sing.

It didn't make sense to Nick. None of it. Not only the joyous mood over the woman's death, but how were they going to execute her? Put her in the box and what? Keep her there until she died of starvation?

Then he saw the torch.

"No . . . "

A thick hush waved through the crowd. Surely these people couldn't be so cruel? Why, this was inhumane, downright evil. They wanted to burn her *alive.*

Instinct caused Nick to rush forward, but then realizing the futility of his actions, he stopped. Another man came up from behind and slapped Nick's shoulder. "Don't concern yourself about the likes of her. She's a whore."

"They mean to burn her!"

"She's a *whore.* Caught on her back with another woman's husband."

Nick glared. "And the man, where is *he?*"

"He's had a beating, don't you worry!"

"So why's she being put to *death?*"

The man smoothed a dark mustache. "No fear. You haven't seen the last of Serqet. Named after the scorpion goddess, cursed from the start, she was."

"But they're going to kill her!"

"She's brazen, see?" He wiped the corners of his lips; his eyes were bulbous and bloodshot, as if he'd been drinking. "She said she's proud. Proud of lying on her back. A whore! Like I said, boy. You ain't seen the last of her. Not with *sin and smoke and flame . . .* "

Nick shook his head. He turned to find the man who'd been familiar, the one the woman had sought with her eyes and then he realized that the person beside him had spoken English.

Nick snapped his head to the right again. "How can you —"

But the man was gone.

The girl's first cry was more of a whimper, but it drifted across the crowd like sand. Smoke wiggled from the top of the box.

Nick shouted out his protests, but no one seemed to understand, or care.

Nick screamed again, but it was lost in the zealous screams and animated waving of arms. Good God, the people actually enjoyed this show of brutality.

A woman was being burned to death in front of him and he could do nothing about it. Her screams which started as distinct stabs of pain now ran together like an enraged opera. Nick put his hands over his ears to block her cries.

He pictured her inside the box, mad with pain and terror, the flesh burning away from the bone.

"Oh God!"

Slowly, slowly, the dark cries subsided and the people, as if they'd participated in a religious orgy and were now spent, stood quietly praying.

Then smoke . . .

Blue-black smoke that unfolded against the white sky. Nick watched it spiral and shift and begin to take form. He made out hair first, long flowing hair that moved as if beneath water. Then a face.

Lyra's face.

Her mouth deepened into a frown and her eyes peered down upon the crowd first with confusion and then rage.

The executioner on the wooden stand looked upward. He didn't seem alarmed by the form in the sky; neither, for that matter, did anyone else. It was as though burning women and having them reappear as clouds was an everyday occurrence.

The executioner held up an open book. A book? Nick leaned ahead — was it *That Hurt Thing*? He couldn't be sure.

The crowd clapped when the book was held skyward. Only the woman in the clouds didn't seem as keen, for she writhed and her mouth gaped, reminding Nick of Edvard Munch's painting "The Scream."

"Good God . . . " Nick whispered beneath his breath. Just what kind of people were they?

Your people, Nick. They are you . . .

Chanting now. Chanting, and what did this have to do with the book? And then the book was slammed shut and Nick felt himself falling *into* the book which didn't make any sense, but it was as if he were living the experience through the womanly figure in the clouds —

He awoke with such a start that for a few seconds he didn't know where he was. He lay there panicked, until it all came rushing back: Montreal, a beautiful stranger, weird dream.

The lamp beside the bed had been left on and Nick clicked it off. The darkness of the room seemed to squeeze him, shape his thoughts. As if it were a living thing that strangled what he knew and believed. A car turned into the parking lot, its lights pulling through the thin curtains. Lyra turned on her side; he could smell wine on her breath.

"Stupid dream," he mumbled, the sound of his own voice not reassuring him nearly as much as he would've liked.

He thought of the woman in the box again, recalled the way her jaw shivered and the way her eyes clung to the one man who'd turned away. Had that woman been Lyra?

He rubbed the area between his eyes; his hand trembled.

He was being too serious.

It was just a dream. A dream about a burning woman who happened to resemble the eccentric Lyra.

No big deal on either count — the dream or Lyra's eccentricity. *Perhaps if Lyra were more normal, she wouldn't have anything to do with me.*

It was an uncomfortable thought.

Nick hunched his shoulders and let them fall with a breath. "I'll just go with the flow . . . " he whispered back to the voices that haunted him.

His mood was lighter and he imagined himself to be the James Dean of the modern world. With a little swagger, he got out of bed and crossed the dim room to the window.

Another car pulled into the parking lot. Nick closed his eyes against the glare and then realized that the driver could see that he was naked. He pulled the gauzy yellow curtains shut and turned to see the book between his feet.

The red eyes of the scorpion watched him.

Lyra touched the back of his neck. Leaning his head against her, Nick was startled to turn and find that she was still asleep — and hadn't touched him at all. Something black flickered in the corner of his eye and his head snapped in the direction of the window.

His breaths fell heavy.

Be certain, for the scorpion goddess knows only rage,

For those who hold mockery upon my page.

Nick stared down at the book. He'd been so taken with it and now . . . now he wasn't sure he even wanted to touch it.

How'd it get between his feet anyhow?

He dragged in a deep breath. He'd probably knocked the book to the floor when he and Lyra were occupied with more *pressing* matters.

He walked toward the lamp, caught his toe on the edge of the box spring, felt pain rip through his foot. He stumbled toward the light, found the stem, brought his hands up to the metal tab, turned it.

Yellow light scoured the darkness. Lyra's eyes moved beneath her lids, but she didn't wake. She lay with one hand splayed against the pillow, her fingers stiff, as if she pointed to the book on the floor.

Nick made a fist, clenched and unclenched it. His eyes were drawn to *That Hurt Thing*. Should he read more?

Maybe.

Maybe not.

He touched his wounded toe. Saw how the very tip was flushed. *The book, Nick, the book.*

It was amazing how an inanimate object could provoke such thought and emotion. He thought of his favorite sculptor, Auguste Rodin; it was amazing how Rodin breathed such life, such energy into his creations. "The Kiss," for example, could hardly be called just a chiseled hunk of stone.

Not that Nick could compare the book to Rodin. It was just a book, after all.

No, that's wrong, he corrected himself. It's more than a book. It's almost as if it's alive, a character unto itself. For instance, right now I'm supposed to read the next part . . .

God, was he having this conversation with himself?

He stood up, chewed the skin along the inside of his lip, stared at the book. It was a beautiful cover, brightly colored and in your face. Like Lyra . . .

Sweeping it up with one swift motion, Nick sat on the edge of the bed and spread the book against his naked lap.

Flipping to a random page, he read: *'Go with the flow . . . '*

The rest of the pages were blank.

chapter three

Go with the flow?

In disbelief, Nick quickly flipped through the pages. Wasn't that what he'd said aloud moments ago?

Go with the flow.

Suddenly none of this was funny anymore.

He didn't want to go with the flow.

He wanted to go home.

Nick grabbed up his knapsack, stuffed his sweater inside, realized that he was still naked and plucked at the clothes he'd thrown over the back of the chair. His toe throbbed — he'd probably broken it — as he pulled on socks, underwear and pants. His jean shirt smelled sweaty but he put it on anyhow. What did hygiene matter when this insanity was going on?

As for his toothbrush and shaving kit, he'd leave them. He could buy more in Halifax; it would be one less reminder of this weekend. He just needed to get out of there.

Sweating, he flung open the door and stood there, feeling like five and twenty blackbirds flapped against the inside of his stomach.

"Nick?"

He heard the bed creak behind him. "I'm leaving," he said.

"Nick, look at me."

Slowly he turned to face her. She leaned against the cheap headboard, one arm across her forehead. A sleepy grin crossed her lips. "Nick, what're you doing, huh?"

He didn't answer.

"Nick, don't be afraid." She tucked the white bed sheet around her and crossed the floor toward him. A cool wind rattled past them and lifted the curtains. "You having a hard night or something? Is that it?"

"I think it's best if I just go home."

Lyra tilted her head to one shoulder. Seeing her like this, with her little smile, it was hard not to trust her. Especially when she put her lips against his ear and whispered, "Nick, don't leave me. It's only just begun."

"I had a crazy dream," he blurted out. "About you . . . and me and some familiar guy I couldn't quite place. You were —" Nick swallowed; even now he could hear the woman's raspy screams. "You were burned alive and you ended up in the sky and then drawn into a book and . . . " He rolled his eyes. "Like a genie in a *book* instead of a bottle. You must think I'm crazy."

"It wasn't a dream," she whispered. *"It was a memory."*

"Don't jerk me around, okay? It was really weird."

She shrugged. "Sorry. You can't leave me."

"I can do anything I want! I'm going." His voice sounded sulky, he knew, a sulky boy's voice. He looked across the way toward the blue Toyota. "You can stay the night here, and tomorrow too. The room's paid till Sunday morning."

"Nick," she implored, "I don't think you understand. I'm who you summoned. *You* invited this adventure."

Nick threw up his hands. "Look, I'm a broke college student, ya know. A boy compared to you. This was fun, but now . . . well, now it's getting too much like something out of a shadow box and how . . . how old are you, really?"

"Does it matter?"

"Well, yeah, it does. Does to me."

"Twenty-eight." She lifted a corner of her mouth. "A whole *planet* away from twenty-four."

"Don't be sarcastic."

"Oh, Nick, you don't have to make it so difficult."

"Have it your way. I'm going."

He threw his knapsack in the back seat of the car and started the ignition. Lyra stood in the open doorway, her arms crossed, watching him. The blue neon vacancy sign swayed in the wind on creaking chains.

"Good-bye," he said, though the car windows were up and she couldn't hear him. He waved.

She smiled and gave a little wave, too.

Nick pulled out of the parking lot and turned in the direction of the highway. Traffic was lean and for that, he was grateful. The French drove like maniacs. He always felt like he went from one near-miss to another. God, it'd be a long night, driving back to Halifax with precious little sleep.

But as the motel got further away, Nick found himself missing Lyra. Crazy! How can I miss her when I don't really know her? He turned up the radio and tried to put her out of his mind. But like an annoying itch, she came back.

And back. And back.

Images were already warm memories: her thick laugh; the way she said his name; the little mole on her shoulder; her vulnerability, her mystery . . .

He changed radio stations. "L'amour est un pilule aigre," the announcer said. *Love's a bitter pill.* He spoke of the title of a song by a new rock band.

Oh, ain't that the truth, Nick agreed with a sigh.

His highway exit approached; he slowed. He thought of Lyra in the doorway, her hair blowing around her shoulders as she clasped the sheet against her.

There was water on the exit ramp and the car skidded for a few seconds. Nick guided the car out of the skid. Moments later, he was merging with the highway. A transport truck whined past him, throwing up rain that had collected on the road.

Nick, don't leave me. It's only just begun.

He took the next exit off the highway.

When he pulled into the parking lot of the motel, Lyra's outline curled against the window. She was hunched slightly, her hands against the glass, as if she'd been waiting.

Nick rushed from the car and she disappeared from the window to open the door. The black number nine glinted in the blue glow of the neon light.

Lyra fell into his arms. "I missed you," she whispered.

"This is insanity," he declared. "A bitter pill."

He kicked the door shut with his foot, James Dean style.

The weekend was theirs.

Nick forgot about the book and the crazy dream as he and Lyra kayaked along the river, picnicked overlooking the city, walked hand in hand along St. Catherine's street, took a carriage ride through Old Montreal.

Lyra's French was perfect. And when Sunday morning came, Nick decided that Lyra was perfect for him.

With one reservation: he knew practically nothing about her. She was like a three dimensional mystery.

They'd talked a lot over the weekend — well, *he'd* talked a lot about his life. Now it was her turn. He smoothed her hair and softly she awoke.

"Hi there." He kissed her mouth.

She smiled. "Sleep good?"

Nick laughed. "Have we actually done any of that?"

"You look troubled," she told him.

He hated how easily she read his mood. Then again, he'd always been easy to read. When he was a kid, he'd stolen a pack of playing cards from Canadian Tire and his mother had known immediately from his expression that he was hiding something.

"Not troubled, exactly," he admitted. "More like perplexed."

Lyra yawned. Her skin was moist and smelled faintly of the cocoa butter she'd sampled at a boutique on St. Catherine's. Nick imagined how delicious it would be to shower with her.

"Lyra." He drew a finger along the mole on her shoulder. "What's this all about?"

"Us?"

"Yeah, us."

She leaned up on her elbow. "I have such strong feelings, Nick." She touched her heart. "Right in here. It's like it's all trapped inside me and I'm only waiting to let it out. It's been this way for a long, long time."

Nick rubbed her head. This is good, he thought, she's opening up. "Did you have a bad childhood or something?"

"Let's just say that I once loved a man who turned me away."

"So it's not easy to trust again?"

"Not easy at all."

"What was he like?"

"Sort of like you in a way. Oh so handsome." She sighed. "But married —"

"Married?"

"Don't be smug!" She closed her eyes and pulled in a breath. "You're judging me."

He shook his head. "It's not that. I'm thinking of that odd dream again. You were put to death because . . . "

"I was caught with him," she finished the sentence. "My married lover."

"How'd . . . why do you say that?" Had he told her that detail? He couldn't be sure.

"Just a guess?"

"Lyra, c'mon, be serious. How could you know what I dreamed about?"

"Oh, Nick." She kissed his arm. "Don't be dramatic."

Nick put his hands behind his head and stared at the ceiling. "Things in my life just seem to happen all at once," he told her, touching his necklace. "You know, I found this wolf pendant one day, and *That Hurt Thing*, the next." He laughed. "Then I meet you and have a dream that seems to bring it all together."
"Bring what together?"

"I dunno. Nothing, I suppose." He shrugged. "Anyhow, tell me about this married guy."

"What's to tell? I lost him." She took a long breath. "Nick, you don't know what it's like to lose someone . . . "

"I lost my mother," he said, surprised to hear himself say it. He never talked about his mother; it was easier that way.

"Nick, that must've been so hard."

"Sometimes I still miss her. You still miss this guy?"

She nodded. "I sure do."

"Ever think of contacting him?"

She clawed the sheets into a fist. "His family is in the way. No sense. Not yet."

"You mean his wife and kids?"

"I mean that it's not fair." She hunched her shoulders forward. Her pain was evident; it was hard not to feel sorry for her. "We had such good times. He took me everywhere, to fancy dinners, to ski slopes, even to the zoo. Anyhow, it doesn't matter now." Her voice lowered. "He's gone . . . nothing matters . . . "

"I'm sorry," Nick said. "His loss."

She seemed to like hearing this. "You really think so?"

"I do. Look at you, you're gorgeous. Good company, too."

"Oh, Nick." She snuggled in closer. "You're so good for me, for my self image."

"Well, my mother used to say that we attract the energy we send out."

Lyra brought her dark brows together. "What does that mean?"

"Well, Mom was a parapsychologist. It was one of her whacky theories." He laughed. "She believed that there are energies all around us, and our thoughts pull in whatever energy that matches what we're thinking."

He grinned. "I don't really buy into that whole metaphysical bit, but yeah, it's fodder for thought. Then again, if my mother was so enlightened, why'd she kill herself?" His voice rattled. "I thought she was happy . . . "

"She probably had to die."

He pulled his head back. "What did you say?"

"Oh, Nick." She ran her hands through his hair. "I mean that life was probably more than she could bear. But it's sad for you to be left alone."

"I'm not alone. I have my father, and my sister, Paula."

"I bet you look like your dad."

"That's what everyone says. He's a great guy. I work with him at the funeral home. Sometimes he's a lot of fun."

"Fun in a funeral home?"

Nick turned on his side and draped an arm over her waist. "That's the thing, Lyra. Everyone expects morticians to dress in black and whisper as we're preparing the bodies. It's not like that. We listen to the radio, we laugh. Dad has some real good dead jokes. But he's respectful, compassionate, not only with the bodies and families, but with everyone."

"He's an amazing man. You're very fortunate to have him."

They were quiet for a moment and then Lyra added softly, "Nick we both know what it's like to lose someone we love. Maybe that's why we get along so well."

"It's true." He touched his lips to her neck. "Because this sure feels right, Lyra."

"Why don't you take off the pendant, Nick?"

"Huh?"

Lyra pointed with an index finger. "It looks so heavy."

He touched the cool pewter. He hadn't expected her to say that. They were sharing intimacies, for God's sake.

"Nick, let's be completely naked."

Whoa! What was up with this woman? He glanced down at himself. "Lyra . . . we *are* naked."

"Those eyes are watching me."

"The wolf eyes?" Nick scratched the underside of his chin. He hadn't shaved in a couple of days and it was beginning to itch. "It's not real, Lyra."

"It's spooky."

He found her reaction a little spooky, too. The necklace was unique, but that was what made it interesting. He couldn't imagine anyone really getting upset over it.

She touched it lightly. "Where'd you find it?"

"It's an odd story. When my father had the apartment built for me at the second floor of our house, I found it stuffed in an old grate."

"Peculiar."

"Yeah. And . . . " He hesitated.

"And?"

"It was wrapped around this doll, like a voodoo doll. Our house is old. God knows how long it was there. Another thing is that my sister always said that part of the house spooked her."

"Maybe she inherited her mother's psychic stuff. Wow, a voodoo doll." She cuddled closer. "When was this?"

"A few months ago. Like I said, only a day before I found the book —"

"Take it off, Nick." She flicked her green eyes over him in that way that meant some *real serious business might be happenin'*. Nick fingered the silver chain. What could it hurt to take it off? Hell, he'd take his fingernails off if it'd put her in *that* kind of mood again.

He felt her fingers pressing into his shoulders. It was amazing how sexy she was, sexy and magnetic. She made him feel like a million bucks and change.

He threaded his fingers through her hair. A car horn sounded in the distance. He couldn't think of anywhere he'd rather be right now than kissing Lyra's shoulders and neck and chin . . .

"Nick," she whispered. "Take it off, please . . . "

"Forget about it, Lyra."

"*Please*, Nick."

Still kissing her, he reached for the chain, pulled at it — and then stopped. He didn't want to take it off. He just didn't. It didn't make sense, but there it was.

"No, Lyra. It stays put."

She pulled away and her mouth turned down. "Don't you want to please me?"
"I don't take orders from women."

God. Nick wanted to laugh at how ridiculous that sounded. Yeah, like he hadn't been a lap dog for Chloe all these years. There were men who had that aura of *Don't screw with me*, but Nick certainly wasn't one of them.

"Okay then." She threw her arms around him and pulled him closer. "If that's the way it has to be."

He chuckled. "I'm the master, after all, right?"

"Abso . . . " She curled her hands along his backside. " . . . lutely."

After they made love, Nick realized that he had to be leaving. He hated to leave Lyra. He missed her already. But this fantasy weekend couldn't spill over into reality, as much as he might like that.

If only he knew more about her. As they drove along St. Catherine's Street toward a bistro Lyra recommended for brunch, he realized that once again, she'd evaded answering any direct questions about her life.

The restaurant was full and noisy, quite a contrast to their hushed morning together. Food softens reality, he told himself. Maybe Lyra would divulge more about her life. If they were to continue what they'd started, he needed to know her basics like hometown, occupation, last name — the sort of information lovers take for granted.

Holding her hand across the table, he said, "Lyra, I want to thank you for this wonderful weekend. I'm going to miss you."

He worried that his words were too formal. That was the thing with infatuation; you could never figure out the right mix of tones. "But," he continued, "like you said, it's only just begun."

"I agree." She moved her thumb along the top of his hand. Her black dress was wrinkled and there was a small tear near the shoulder. She hadn't changed her clothes in days. "Lyra, I bet you'll be glad to get home, too. Do you live far from here?"

"Don't worry about me, Nick."

"I want to see you again. You have e-mail?"

This made her laugh.

"How will I find you?"

"You won't have to."

He wrote his name and number on his napkin and handed it to her. "Here, if you need to find me . . . "

She crumpled it and threw it down. "Nick, it's That Hurt Thing —"

"You don't want my number?"

"Don't need it."

The waitress approached them, and Lyra ordered for them in perfect French. Good thing, too. Nick had struggled with French all his life. Once, driving through Quebec, he'd stopped in a small diner and ordered *juice de pomme de terre* — potato juice, instead of apple, his original intent. Three men sat at tall stools along the counter and each one in turn, stared up at him, grinning.

Nick glanced to the crumpled napkin and picked at his eggs. "You don't want . . . to see me again?"

"But of course, Master."

"Do me a favor? Don't call me that anymore. It's getting too weird —"

"Master!" She dug her fork into his hand.

"Hey!" He yanked his hand back and shook it. "What are you, *nuts?*" There were four prong marks near his thumb. A couple of people at the next table stared at them. Nick felt himself blushing.

"You are not appreciative," she snapped. "You summoned me and this is how you treat me."

He leaned back in his seat and stared at her. How could someone so beautiful be so crazy?

"You don't get it," she told him, her voice soft again. Tears shimmered in her eyes, and though Nick reached across the table to touch her hand, the tears didn't move him as they would have minutes ago. "Nick, I only want to make you happy, to serve you as the book instructs."

"Let me get this straight." He took the fork from her other hand and held it, thinking of how she'd held the knife in the hotel room in a similar fashion. "You're saying that when I bought the book and followed the directions, I inadvertently summoned you?"

"Big word *inadvertently*, but yes, that's exactly it. Nick, we already discussed this. Why won't you accept it?"

He thought of his dream, saw the executioner holding the book to the sky and then slamming it shut. "So you're like a genie in a book instead of a bottle?"

She just stared at him.

"Lyra," he continued. "Does the fact that I found this necklace one day and the book the next . . . well, is there any connection?"

"I don't even *like* the wolf pendant."

"I know you don't, and that in itself is curious."

She snorted. "Hey, I thought your sister was the one with the psychic vibes."

His affection toward her wavered. Sure, the weekend had been great, but he wouldn't carry it further. Lyra was a gorgeous girl. Lots of fun. Just a little short on neural transmission. He felt fickle, too. Just this morning, he would have done anything to carry on with her.

This act she played was annoying. Humiliating even, for both of them. She was probably into S & M and liked being the submissive one. Which was a contradiction, as she seemed anything but passive or timid.

"What are you thinking, Nick?"

"So you're tying to say you'll do *anything* I tell you?"

"You have three wishes. Use them wisely." She took her fork from his hands and began to eat again. Her expression was so serious it was hard to believe she was anything but sincere.

Nick smirked. "What if I asked you to kiss my feet right here in the restaurant?"

"Making it difficult again." Lyra tucked her hair behind her ears and stared at him. "Must I prove everything? Why can't you just *believe?*"

"Didn't think so." He rolled his eyes. What a cracker! He scanned the artwork on the walls. A painting of a woman with a large red umbrella; another of a sleeping cat curled into the head of a lion

He felt an affinity with the cat. Had he been naively close to danger all weekend? That was the classic story, wasn't it? You fall in lust with someone and only later do you learn that you'd danced with a con, slept with a murderer.

Lyra could even be an escapee from a mental hospital.

Scary.

Something touched his foot. He flinched.

And then realized why.

Lyra had slipped beneath the table. Kissing his feet just as he'd requested.

chapter four

Nick couldn't speak at first. The bistro was full; people glanced their way. He pulled his head back and whispered harshly, "Lyra!"

She looked like the cat in the painting, leaning on her haunches, her small hands plucking off his shoe. The woman at the next table gestured to her companion and then toward the floor where Lyra kissed Nick's stocking foot.

"Regarder la femme, la bas. Mon Dieu!"

Look at that girl. My God!

Lyra's head touched his sore toe; he winced. His hand went to pull her up and he hit his glass. Apple juice slopped from the glass and soaked the white linen.

"Lyra, get up now. Stop it. Get *up!*"

She unfolded from the floor and perched on the edge of the chair. She seemed oblivious to the other customers who gestured her way, whispering. She gathered her hair at the back of her neck and continued eating as if nothing unusual had just happened.

"Lyra, what're you, nuts? I didn't mean it."

She dabbed at her lips with the napkin. "Then you shouldn't say it, *mon amour'*. By the way, that was a practice wish. Next one's real."

"It was a *joke.* Do you know what a joke is, Lyra, or is that too difficult a concept?"

She touched the juice stain with her index finger. "Quite a mess you make when you don't focus."

"Lyra, what's going on here? Why would you say you'd do anything I asked? I mean, what's it all about?"

She shrugged. "Aren't you going to eat your breakfast?"

He shook his head. How could he eat when everyone stared at them like they were both crazy? Not that they were far from hitting the truth.

Lyra was crazy and he wasn't far behind. After all, how many sane men would spend a weekend with a woman who kissed their feet in public and called themselves a genie?

The waitress asked if he wanted another glass of juice; he declined. He had a new focus — getting the hell out of there and away from Lyra.

"So humor me here, Lyra. You're a genie who'll fulfill my every desire?"

She nodded. "Pass the pepper, please. That's the thing with these places, no spice."

He put his hand over hers. She looked up, made a face. "Anything?"

"Three wishes," she repeated.

"Just three? And after that?"

"Then my duty is done and I am free." She leaned close to him. Her smoky green eyes were still. Nick thought about his dream again, thought about the dark eyes in the clouds. "Just be careful what you wish for, Nick."

He looked away. "This is bull."

But what about the dream, Nick? Is that bull, too?

He grasped his wolf necklace and thought of Chloe, who, unlike Lyra, didn't find the pendant a bit spooky. He missed Chloe, felt guilty over the way he'd planned on tossing her aside for what? A roll in the hay with a crackpot. God, what had he been thinking?

"So what will you wish for?" Lyra asked. "I bet you want lots of money."

He grinned. She seemed to really believe what she was saying. "I bet everyone asks for money."

"Not everyone. This man I loved, the married man. He didn't want money."

"So you were his genie, too?"

"At first. But then I became much more. After awhile, we decided to make our own magic."

"Hey." Nick grinned. "How about if I ask you to mess up my chemistry professor, Dr. Sampson. Would you do that?"

She tilted her head to one side and peeled her lips back from her teeth. "Mess him up real bad." She frowned. "Why? You don't like him?"

"Oh this is a good game we're playing here. Listen to this now. I was late handing in one paper and the guy gives me a D! For one lousy day! That brought my average way down."

Nick shook his head. Every time he thought about it, it made him furious. "Can you imagine applying to medical school with less than perfect marks?"

"Sounds dreadful."

"Yeah, Sampson's not my favorite person these days." Nick put a twenty dollar bill over the check. "Anyway. Let's get out of here." As they were leaving, he said, "So anything I want, huh?"

She nodded.

"You're a good little genie, Lyra, but I'm not going to make any wishes."

"You won't play the game?"

"I'll stick to chess." He winked.

Nick found himself anxious to be on his way. How had he ever considered Lyra to be more than a fling? Still, part of him already missed her. This is what *bad love* is, he thought.

They sat in his car. Earlier, Nick had been embarrassed that the inside of his car was messy with empty soda cans and a bag of Oreo Cookies he'd brought with him for the long drive.

Now, he didn't care if she thought he was a slob, didn't care one bit.

Still, Nick didn't want to just leave her there, but Lyra insisted that she didn't need a drive. She probably lived in the city, which would explain why her French was excellent.

He kissed her good-bye. Despite it all, the kiss was sweet and inviting, and he found himself kissing her and kissing her — and kissing her.

"Nick, let's go home," she breathed into his ear.

It took a moment for Nick to realize she'd spoken. "Home?"

"Back to the room. To *our* room."

The car windows were fogged from their heat and breathing. Nick turned on the ignition and defrost. "Lyra, I need to go to Halifax. Tomorrow is a holiday, but I have school Tuesday. I can't miss school. Don't you have something you need to do?"

"Stay the night. One more night."

"Drive twelve hours on Monday and go to school the next day? That's a lot to ask." He didn't add that Chloe's birthday was next week and he wanted time to buy her a present. It felt good to think of Chloe again.

Lyra squeezed his knee and moved her hand to his thigh. Her face was flushed from his beard rubbing against her. Her eyes held only him — it was a heady acknowledgment. If only she weren't so gorgeous. It made ignoring her neuroses far too easy to do.

If he got on the road at six in the morning, he could be home just after dinner that evening —

"This is crazy to even consider," he announced. It was incredible how his emotions flip-flopped. Lust, indifference, lust, indifference, lust, *lust* . . .

Nick drove back to the motel and to his surprise, they were given the same room. Inside, Lyra turned on the radio and fidgeted with the curtains, as if returning home from a long journey.

"You look happy, Lyra."

"I am." She climbed on the bed and jumped up and down like a playful child. The springs creaked and groaned and dust was thrown up. Nick watched her with a smile, feeling that James Dean thing happening again.

Atmosphere couldn't be underestimated, Nick realized. In the restaurant, he'd been short with her, anxious to get far away. And now in this shoddy motel room number nine, he couldn't stop watching her, *wanting* her.

He thought of a song he'd heard once though the title evaded him, a song about *making love like a woman but breaking like a little girl.* Lyra was such a creature.

Delicate and tough; exotic and innocent.

If he didn't get away from her soon, he'd be doomed. Doomed to what, he couldn't say for sure, only that it would be dark and saturating.

"Who are you?" he asked.

Lyra slumped to the bed. She gathered her hair in one hand and held it. "C'mere and let me show you."

"Seriously."

"I am being serious."

"Why are you so secretive?"

"Am I?"

"And you answer all my questions with questions."

"This room needs a plant, something to liven it up." She examined the dingy brown carpet.

"Shouldn't you let someone know where you are or at least get some other clothes?" Nick didn't want to be mean, but she hadn't changed her clothes in days.

She flicked her head up and smiled. "I just need you, Nick."

"How'd you get in my room that first day?"

Lyra shrugged. "Did I frighten you?"

"I thought you were dead. It wasn't a good feeling."

"I'm sorry."

"I just don't get it. Don't get you."

"You've got me." She tutted. "I'm right here. Are you making things difficult again?"

He didn't mind that she argued with him. At least it felt *normal*, something everyday lovers did. It was the genie crap he found nauseating. He'd never liked people who acted like their existence was bigger than life.

In his first year of college Chloe had taken a fleeting interest in this jock named Paul. Whether it was jealousy or revenge, Nick had asked his Biology lab partner, a girl named Laurie, to dinner.

On the way to the restaurant they'd found a twenty dollar bill stuck in a water grate along the sidewalk. Scooping it up, her brown eyes sparkling, Laurie announced that this was a sign that they were destined to become lovers.

Over dinner, she talked about the significance of his being a Gemini and she a Pisces, and that she bet his Venus was in Aries, but they could get around that because the universe would send them only most excellent vibes.

After dinner, they went to her dorm room where, despite his inclination that Laurie was one nut short of a pecan pie, Nick helped her undress and they fell into bed together.

Between the sheets, however, Nick's excitement died.

It didn't seem to matter how pretty she was. All Nick could think about was her flaky inferences. She reminded him of one of those cult people who sell you flowers at airports, the ones with the big smiles who smell like incense.

Nick turned to Lyra. He threw up his hands. "I don't much care for secrecy. I find it frustrating. Why won't you just tell me about you? I don't even know your last name."

She yanked the hem of her dress upward in short, teasing stutters. "Then let me reveal *all*, my sweet master." Humming, she stood on the bed as if it were a stage and she, the major attraction.

"Stop it, Lyra."

She pulled the straps of her dress off her shoulders. Despite it all, Nick felt himself becoming excited.

This was like his own private strip show. He tried to imagine Chloe being so naughty, and chuckled. Chloe's version of naughty was kissing with the lights on.

Lyra kicked off her heels and paused, her black hair framing her face. "I'll reveal all," she repeated. "And then I want you to take a *good, hard look*."

Nick liked the sounds of that. Especially the good and hard parts. Maybe she just needed a little coaxing. Maybe she just needed a little *lovin'* kind of coaxing.

He moved toward the bed. "C'mere," he said. "C'mere and we'll talk."

Sometime during the night, Nick awoke and called his father.

Though he had told Ralph the name of the motel where he'd be staying, he hadn't told anyone else. It would only be right to let Bruce know he'd been delayed.

Sitting on the edge of the bed, he peered at his watch. Two in the morning. Not a great time to call. But after one ring, his father answered.

"Dad. It's me. Still in Montreal."

"Hi, Nick. Just thinking about you."

Lyra opened her eyes and put her arms around his waist. Nick turned to face her. "Who you talking to?" she mouthed.

"My father," he whispered.

"What's that, Nick?"

"Ah, nothing, Dad."

"Son, do you have someone there with you?"

"Ah . . . no. The television, that's all."

"So when are you getting home?"

"Tomorrow," Nick replied, rubbing Lyra's hair. "How's everything at home? How's Paula?"

"Everything's fine. Tonight Paula and I went to the Fringe Festival. Pretty good. So why didn't you leave today? Paula was hoping you'd see a play with us."

"I don't know, Dad. Just wanted an extra day, I guess."

"Can I hear his voice?" Lyra whispered, sitting up. "Your father's voice?"

That's an odd request, Nick thought. But he held the phone out as Bruce spoke for a few seconds and then brought it back to his ear. "Well, I'll see you tomorrow, Dad. Tell Chloe I'm running late if she asks."

"Sure will." A pause. "You sure someone's not there with you?"

"Gotta go. Talk to you later," Nick added and hung up. Maybe he shouldn't have asked about Chloe in front of Lyra. But it wasn't like there was any future for them. After all, she'd crumpled the napkin that he'd written his phone number on.

"Lyra, so are —" He stood up quickly. "Lyra?"

She was crying. Her head tucked into the pillow, her back shivered. He knelt beside her and put a hand on her shoulder. "Lyra, what's wrong?"

"Never mind." Her voice was muffled by the pillow.

"Hey, hey . . . " He gathered her into his arms. She resisted at first, and then clung to him, her arms around his shoulders, her head pressed against his neck.

"What is it?" he asked again. "Lyra, what happened? Did you not like the sound of my father's voice?" The last line was said to try make her laugh. It didn't work, for she just sobbed harder.

Finally, she looked up and wiped her tears away. "Nick, I'm sorry."

"I don't understand," he admitted.

She moved out of his arms and went to the window and peered into the dark parking lot. Her skin looked cold in the dreariness of the room. "I guess when I heard your father's voice . . . " She turned around. "It . . . it made me realize how alone I am. You're so lucky." Her bottom lip trembled. "Lucky to have him. Have a family . . . "

"You don't have a family, do you?" He crossed the room and led her back to bed. "C'mon, Lyra, let me cuddle into you."

She felt limp in his arms as he stroked her hair and whispered that everything would be okay. It was obvious she'd not known a lot of love.

Still, her reaction was peculiar; had seemed to come out of nowhere. It was an awful admission, but he'd be glad not to have to deal with her problems.

"Nick?" Her voice was sleepy now.

"Yeah?"

"When you get home, give your father a great big hug. Appreciate him. You don't know how lucky you are . . . "

"Okay," he whispered, though he had no intention of hugging his father. Sure, they were close, but physical affection was a rare occurrence, reserved for birthdays or other special occasions.

Speaking of birthdays, he thought of Chloe. He remembered the silver locket he'd seen in a store in Halifax. At the time he considered it too expensive, but now, he made a point to purchase it. After this weekend, he had a whole new appreciation for her.

Nick woke just after dawn, his body feeling strangely exhausted and refreshed at the same time. He'd been dreaming of Halifax, but couldn't remember anything more specific than that. It didn't matter. He was grateful not to have had the odd dream about Egypt again.

He turned to Lyra and saw that she was awake, watching him.

"Hi," she said.

He kissed the mole on her shoulder. "Feeling better?"

She nodded. "You were mumbling in your sleep again."

"Was I?"

"You sounded so unhappy. Are you ever lucky I came along when I did."

Soft morning light eased past the curtains, giving the room a sleepy, drawn feel. Nick yawned. "I've got to get going soon. Long drive ahead of me."

"Poor Master."

That word again. He gritted his teeth, but said nothing. Despite it all, they'd had a great evening. He wanted it to end on a good note. Not with this genie stuff.

Easing himself out of bed, Nick pulled on his tee shirt and pants. It was a little past seven; he was already late getting away. The wrinkled bed looked inviting. God, he needed sleep, but it would have to wait.

"Can't put it off any longer," Nick announced with a long stretch. "Time to go." He watched for Lyra's reaction; there was none. Just as well, he supposed.

The air was cool in the parking lot. It had rained earlier and the pavement was damp. Lyra huddled against him. He rubbed her bare shoulders. "Get in the car, I'll take you somewhere."

"I'll be fine," she insisted.

"I can't just leave you here like this. Get in."

He unlocked the passenger door and Lyra folded into the car. Nick started the ignition and cranked on the heat. "You really must be a genie to go around without a coat. It's cold."

She stared ahead, expressionless.

"You were pretty upset last night," he said.

"It was nothing . . . just a mistake."

"Oh, Lyra."

"Forget it," she said sharply.

"Okay, sure. Oh, here, take the book, too." Nick chuckled and reached into the back seat to snatch *That Hurt Thing*. "I won't need it. Besides, it's like your bottle, isn't it? Where you live?"

She clutched the book to her stomach and smoothed it with both hands. The foil letters glinted back at them.

"Lyra, you sure you'll be okay?"

"Absolutely."

"Please let me drive you somewhere."

There were dark circles under her eyes and Nick had that sensation again of her being older than she claimed. "You like Montreal?" she asked.

"Yeah, it's nice to visit. Ever been to Nova Scotia?"

She simply smiled.

"We had a good time this weekend. Thank you."

Lyra nodded. "It's amazing how good we are together."

Nick adjusted the rearview mirror. "I don't want to leave you here in this parking lot. Doesn't seem right. It could even be dangerous."

"There's no danger," she assured him.

"What will you do?"

She reached for the handle and pushed the door open a crack. "What I always do."

Nick knew she wasn't about to elaborate on her answer, on any answer. He kissed her hand. "Well. You take care, okay?"

"I love you, Nick."

He blinked, startled by the ill timed declaration. This was their good-bye. It wasn't *Seeya round*, or *Talk to you later*. It was *over*.

Lyra hunched her shoulders forward and she frowned. "Don't you love me, Master?"

"Hell, Lyra . . . I dunno . . . ah, yeah. Sure." Nick hugged her across the seat with one arm. A drop of rain splattered against the windshield. "Sure, Lyra. I love ya lots."

chapter five

Getting into a school routine after such a wild weekend was difficult for Nick. He found he couldn't stop thinking about Lyra. He saw her everywhere and nowhere. It was like she'd put a spell on him.

Sure, she was crazy, but she'd been sweet, too. Not to mention beautiful and good in bed. He remembered her erotic strip show, and the way her eyes sparkled. Maybe it was the intimacy he missed, the way she'd held back nothing. Nothing except any personal information.

"Hey, Nick!" Chloe poked his ribs with her finger. "What's up with the glum face, huh?"

He flinched, surprised at how jumpy he'd been the past few days. Last night he'd helped his father in the *kitchen* — what they endearingly called where the bodies were prepared for the funeral — and Nick had dropped the nozzle of the tube that would fill their client, Mr. Beltz, with enough embalming fluid to keep him from stinking up his farewell party.

Nick pulled a book from the top shelf of his college locker and turned to Chloe. "Don't you have American Lit now?"

"Got canceled. Thought I'd walk you to class."

They'd arranged their schedules so they could commute to and from college together. The few moments they spent between classes usually perked Nick up, but today he felt numb and disinterested.

He sighed. "Come sit in class with me, Chloe. It's a lecture, not a lab."

"Okay. I can look over my notes." She touched his arm. "Don't you think it was weird to go off by yourself to Montreal? Weird to have a holiday?

"It's not like you to just take off without telling anyone where you'd be staying. Montreal's a big city."

"I told Ralph," he said with a shrug.

"So what'd you do there?"

He took a pen from the magnetic shelf attached to his locker, clicked the ink point open. "Not much. Stuff."

"What kind of *stuff?*"

He hesitated. Should he be honest and tell Chloe about Lyra? After all, it wasn't like they had an actual relationship. Still, he didn't want to extinguish all hope, just in case.

One more *just in case* added to the growing list . . .

"Well?"

"Kayaked a little, read, hung around the motel room."

"No entertaining French women?"

Was she hoping he hadn't? Hoping, and maybe a little jealous? "Just me and my shadow."

"An odd thing to do," she repeated, "just leave and go off all alone."

"Well." He closed the locker and snapped the combination lock closed. "If we hadn't argued the day before, I might not have left."

She crossed her arms and looked away. "So it's my fault?"

"No one's fault." He pinched her elbow. "Absolutely no one's."

The fluorescent hallway lights flickered, then went out. Chloe squinted and touched his arm. Dalhousie University was an old school and in the dim light, the long narrow halls were more spooky than Nick liked to admit.

"What's going on, Nick?"

"Power failure, I guess."

Dr. Sampson walked toward them. The window light silhouetted his form. Nick thought about his wish to Lyra: *If I ask you to mess up my chemistry professor, Dr. Sampson, would you do that?*

"May as well go on to class, folks," Dr. Sampson instructed, rubbing the top of his head. "Might be temporary, the lights." Chloe always said Dr. Sampson looked like a troll, short and wide, always flicking his suspenders — who wore suspenders anymore?

"Oh, I don't need this today," Nick murmured as he pushed his way into class. As he took his seat, Ralph slapped his huge hand on his shoulder and said, "How was Montreal, pal?"

Nick glanced toward Chloe who took a seat beside him. "Okay, I suppose."

"Let's go for a beer after classes this evening." Ralph chuckled and brushed back his black hair. There were only two narrow rows of windows located at the back of the room and in the dim light, Ralph's dark features looked surreal. "You can go too, Chloe."

"Generous of you," she joked back.

"You must be bored, to sit in on Sampson's class." Ralph hunched his wide shoulders. "Any more exciting and the man would be anemic. Well," he gestured to Nick again. "beer later?"

"Can't. Got to work in the kitchen with my father."

"It's odd, calling it a kitchen. What do you do there, make pizza?"

"Nah, we order out."

"Gross," Chloe added.

"Tonight we're dealing with a double suicide. Not looking forward to it."

Those were the worst kind, the young suicides. Not only because the pair were teenage sisters who'd made a death pact, but because of the waste. The waste of thought, of energy.

"Listen, O'Brien." Ralph clapped Nick's shoulder just as the lights flooded back to life. He pointed at the row of lights. "Hey, I'm good, yeah?"

"God, now we have to look at your ugly mug, Ralph."

Students still walked past the open door of the classroom. Dr. Sampson stood in the doorway, waving his arms and hollering that class wasn't canceled and "Let's get inside, people."

Then he flicked his suspenders and walked to the lecture podium. He reminded the students that their papers were due tomorrow and added, with a quick glance toward Nick, that late papers resulted in an automatic D.

Nick clenched his jaw. It really ticked him off that his average was almost halved because of Dr. Sampson and his cement code.

Nick caught something from the corner of his eye and turned to the doorway to see Lyra —

Lyra?

Nick blinked, not believing, not wanting to believe it was actually her staring at him, that sinister, sexy smile like wire stretched across her face. She still wore the same black dress. His eyes went to the mole on her shoulder. It was like she'd never left him.

Maybe she hasn't.

Chloe was saying something, but it didn't register. The noise of the class garbled, like he was sinking beneath water. He gripped at his throat, feeling a tightening sensation that made him swallow and swallow without clearing it.

Lyra seemed a long way off now. It was as if he were looking down a long tube that constricted to a narrow opening and he could see just her face and then just her eyes —

He was drowning. Suffocating.

Didn't anyone see what was happening to him?

He gripped the sides of the desk and rocked forward with panic. His cheeks were sucked inward as he tried in vain to get even a sliver of a breath. Once his cousin Dawn had locked him in a coffin and he remembered the panic as he desperately sought a line of light. It was the same way now, that same sense of riding a fine line between realities.

Nick, you make everything so difficult.

His fingers stung with heat; his eyes felt as if they were being yanked from their sockets.

You're not appreciative of me, Master —

"Nick! What's wrong?"

Like being plunked on his backside back to reality, Nick shook his head and focused on Chloe. God, what had just happened?

"Chloe." His voice trembled. "D-did you see someone in the doorway?"

"What?"

Nick looked to the doorway. Empty. "I feel sorta stomach sick." He pressed his palms above his eyes. "I need the bathroom."

The bathroom was empty and he sat on a closed toilet seat, his head in his hands. Could it be he had imagined seeing Lyra? After all, no one else seemed to notice her. But it had felt so real. As real as when he'd been stuck in the coffin listening to the sounds of Dawn's cackling laughter echoing in the viewing room.

Was this like a flashback? But that didn't hold logic, either. His weekend with

Lyra had been good. Well, an odd sort of good, but nothing he could call traumatic. Surely people didn't have flashbacks from too much sex, did they?

He went to the mirror and leaned so close that his focus muddled. Exhaustion. That must be it, he decided, drawing back to study his grim expression. His blond hair was greasy and there were strings of red in his eyes; he hadn't had a good night's sleep since Montreal — or *during* Montreal. Lyra and sleep didn't even fit in the same sentence. *Worn ya thin*, that's what Ralph would say if he knew. But he didn't know. Lyra was his very own little secret.

Tonight he'd help his father and then go right to bed. Sometimes a good night's sleep cured a myriad of problems. Maybe he was coming down with something. Sleep deprivation put stress on the immune system, not to mention what it does to circadian rhythms.

Yeah, that's it, O'Brien, he told himself *Don't make a weekend fling into more than it. Don't let the genie scare ya.*

Genie.

He laughed. The more he thought of Lyra the genie, the more ridiculous it all seemed.

Genie, yeah, right.

The lights flickered then, and died.

In the blackness, Nick heard the bathroom door open and then softly, softly close.

He was no longer alone.

Nick felt the hard coolness of the sink beneath his hands and he clung to it, fearing that any second he'd have that drowning sensation again. It was terrifying, not trusting that he could stay on this side of sanity.

He took a breath. "Hey, who's there? Ralph?"

"Nickeee . . . " came the whispered response."

Nick move closer to the wall. It was so black; he felt weightless.

Don't be dramatic, he told himself. Just walk toward the door and open it and leave. It's that simple.

But when he moved, he heard snickering and beyond that, a hissing sound. He backed up, hitting the sink against his backside just as the scent of cinnamon reached him.

He sniffed the air.

Good God. Lyra.

He'd been stupid to leave the classroom. Stupid to think he could let down his guard. He remembered the way she held the knife against him in Montreal, the ease with which she said, *Kiss or kill?*

Was she here to take revenge for the cool way he'd handled their final morning together? What did she expect? Roses and candy?

But she's not dangerous, not really, another voice said. All she wants is your attention. Just a little love, just to serve you. Serve her master.

"Who's there? Who the hell is there?"

Whispered snickering. A breathy giggle.

His shoulders hunched, Nick shuffled along the wall until he came to the corner.

If only the lights would come on again. If only this; if only that. Think logically, stay in the now. Bide your time. You can't see her, so she can't see you —

But a genie can see anything.

Anywhere.

She's not a genie!

He heard scratching then. The noise seemed to get closer. Nick flattened against the wall. Swallowed. He squinted toward the door for a line of light, but there was only darkness.

If he could just reach the door and yank it open.

His teeth chattered and he bit down hard to still the sound. He peered into the blackness and imagined that he saw the shape of a head. He thought of drawings he'd seen of aliens, imagined their large eyes watching him squirm in the dark room.

Nick forced himself to take a deep breath. He wasn't thinking straight. Darkness is only the absence of light. The bathroom isn't any different than it was twenty minutes ago under fluorescent lighting, and just when have you heard of assault in a college bathroom?

It touched his pant leg first.

Nick gasped and clenched his teeth together. Something cold touched his knee, then the upper part of his thigh. A dull sound left his mouth. He trembled.

"Who . . . who's jerking me around?" His voice quivered.

He moved toward the door with a new desperation. Hearing whispered voices was one thing; quite another when something's grabbing at your legs.

His head met with cool metal; the condom dispenser. The sharp edge of the machine poked him in the chest. Nick took a noisy breath.

The dispenser was beside the entrance. He felt the frame of the door, brought his hands down and found the handle, grasped it. But then he was pulled back, harshly now, pulled toward the back of the room.

Nick swung out a fist; it made a wide arc and struck the mirror, shattering it. He cursed in pain. Glass sprayed over him. He felt it in his hair and on his shoulders.

His guts shuddered.

He held up his fists again, his head jerking back and forth. "Okay," he whispered. "C'mon, you son-of-a-bitch. C'mon!"

More laughter. And then a buzzing sound like electricity and light glutted the bathroom.

Ralph slapped his knee, laughing.

Ralph?

His dark head jiggled with the motion. "Oh, man, that was good. You were *losin' it!* Hell, that was . . . "

Ralph's words dissipated as his eyes lowered over Nick and back to his face. He bit the corner of his lip. "Geesh, Nick . . . "

Nick didn't have to look down to know that he'd wet his pants.

He slumped against the wall and closed his eyes.

chapter six

Dr. Gerald Sampson lived a life of contradictions.

No one knew just how much. There was a purity in this secret; it permitted Gerald to realize how truly special he was.

Not even his wife Holly knew what really went on in his head, or just how much he lived there, walked the rooms of secret thought, examined, shaped, considered.

By day he was a chemistry professor. A damn *fine* professor. But his job was a cloak that hid the true guts of Gerald Sampson. Holly worked as a waitress four nights a week from three to eleven, so when Gerald got home, he was alone. Oh, how magnificent were these four days. That's when he took off the cloak — no, ripped the cloak from his body and shivered with the anticipation of what lay ahead.

Digging into the very back of the closet, Gerald indulged his senses one at a time, beginning always with scent. Eyes closed, he lifted silk and smooth cotton and crushed it against his nostrils.

Gerald liked to dress in women's clothes.

He liked to parade in hose, panties, skirt, blouse, heels, the whole enchilada. There were no limits, oh no. What he needed, he took. There were restrictions in other walks of life but not here, no sirree bob.

He looked good, too, of that he was sure. Especially when he wore a hat that covered his balding top. His only regret was that he hadn't started indulging earlier, when his gray curls were still black luster.

Sometimes after he'd dressed and pressed powder and lipstick to his face, Gerald drove past his affluent neighborhood into the north end of Halifax where he would sit in a cafe, just sit there being womanly and trying to catch the eye of another woman.

He didn't like it when men noticed him, but they rarely did. What he wanted was a friendship with another woman, just to talk and complain and hear her stories. Women had stories that men never heard and oh, how Gerald yearned to be in this secret girls' club.

Tonight he felt especially good. The power failure at the university had upset the balance just enough that there was an extra surge of adrenaline waiting to be used.

Gerald chose his weapons. Tonight called for lavender, though he'd heard Holly say that any shade of purple was for spring and summer. He didn't care; he prided himself on being his own fashion statement.

He chose a lavender dress suit. He liked this suit because the skirt fell past his knees so he only had to shave the lower part of his legs. That saved time. A silky white blouse lay beneath his outer clothes, as did his Victoria's Secret sporty underwear.

A close shave and foundation followed by mascara and lipstick and the man was ready. Ready!

"You're a babe," he said, shaking his shoulders at the mirror. "A *snaaake!*"

Gerald didn't have a matching purse to go with the outfit so he rummaged through Holly's things and found a square plum purse with a large silver buckle. It wasn't ideal, but it would do.

In the garage, he put a white scarf over his head and then a hat over the scarf. It looked a tad ridiculous, but fancy, too. The sort of fancy only the very rich would dare try.

The air was heavy as he pulled his Ford Explorer into traffic. The thought occurred to him that he should've taken a taxi in case someone recognized the jeep. Maybe next time.

Excitement sluiced through his pores and he took deep breaths so he wouldn't sweat and ruin his make-up. Parking the Explorer several blocks from the Lizard Cafe was effortless — a good omen — and within minutes, he'd entered the smoky restaurant and was seated facing the door, his favorite location.

He ordered coffee with cream — the only time he drank cream was when he dressed up; another little secret. The hose itched but he ignored it, just like he imagined a woman would.

The cafe was busy, but no one gave him more than a passing glance. Gerald began to feel a little discouraged and he thought of how others would see him if they knew.

Maybe they'd laugh. Maybe they would say it was stupid, even sick, to dress like he did in women's clothes.

"Excuse me, may I sit with you?"

She was tall and thin with black swinging hair, everything a young woman would want to be. She looked cold, though, with only a thin black dress that hiked almost to the top of her thighs.

Gerald set his coffee cup down with a clunk. He regretted for an instant that he couldn't flirt with her as a man. But this was his big debut, and he'd not ruin it, no, by God.

She leaned a hand against the table. Her nails were long and painted a deep red. "There are so few seats."

"Please, ah . . . join me."

Gerald hadn't thought far enough ahead to practice his womanly voice and it crackled at first. If the girl noticed, she didn't comment. Gerald looked down at his dirty nails. He'd forgotten the nails again.

"What's your name?" she asked.

Gerald stammered. He hadn't thought of a name, either. "Ah, Holly. Yours?"

"Nick . . . ole. Nicole."

"Nice to meet you."

She nodded and reached into her purse for a cigarette. She extended one to

Gerald who declined; she scratched a match against the side of the matchbox.

"Love your hat, Holly." She held the flame and watched it. The whites of her eyes looked milky and pale. "It suits your complexion."

"Th-thank you."

She moved the match to the long white cigarette and inhaled. Smoke cradled her chin and faded away. "Holly, I'm new in town. Think you can show me around?"

Gerald couldn't believe his ears. Show her around? "Of course," he told her, his heart beating a million beats a second. "Where you from?"

"Oh, here and there."

It was an odd answer, but perhaps he was being too personal. "Well, there's lots to see in Halifax. The Titanic graveyard?"

"The Titanic graveyard is here?"

He smiled. "It sure is."

"Well, Holly." She waved a hand. "I'm not really into graveyards. I was hoping for something a little more *alive*."

Oh, well there's Citadel Hill . . . the old fortress."

Nicole made a face.

"And nightlife . . . if you're into that scene."

"Now you're talking. Oh, I just know we're going to have lots of fun together. I so like to have fun, Holly." She took a deep drag on the cigarette and blew a wobbly smoke ring. Her mouth looked like a shiny red poppy. "Everything else is just icing on the cake."

There is something untouchably lovely about death.

So thought Nick as he examined the silent faces of the two sisters who'd chased a bottle of Valium with a bottle of tequila.

Lying side by side in matching coffins, their identical upturned noses and shiny brown hair making them look more like porcelain than human, Nick couldn't imagine what could have been so bad that they'd take their own lives.

Their names were Olga and Anna Basha, the only children to a family of immigrants from Lebanon. Had the girls' adjustment to Canada been that severe?

It was always hard to deal with young people in the funeral business. People expected the elderly to die. No one understood the untimely passing of a child or a teenager. It was like being cheated somehow, taken out of the game before halftime.

Nick turned away. The viewing would be in less than an hour, and his father wanted him to ensure everything was ready. When people mourned, the tiniest of details were magnified. As a result, you couldn't be too meticulous.

He found his father in the office and announced that everything was ready. Bruce wore his typical blue suit as he stood in the mirror adjusting his tie. People often commented on the similarity between the two of them — the same yellow hair and blocky build.

"Shame about those girls, isn't it?" Bruce said. "If anything bothered you that much, you'd tell me, wouldn't you?" He met his son's eyes in the mirror.

"Dad. Nothing would bother me *that* much."

"Promise?"

Nick nodded. Was his dad worried that he might want to follow in the footsteps of his mother? Nick knew that Bruce had never really gotten over losing his wife. A decade later and the man hadn't been on a single date.

Bruce was a good looking guy, too — all his own teeth and hair. He'd have no problem finding a woman to hang on his arm.

"Why you watching me like that, son?"

"Do you . . . do you miss Mom?"

Bruce turned from the mirror. Clearly, he hadn't expected the question. "Do I miss her?" He seemed to say this more to himself. "You know I do."

"I think Mom would want you to move on, you know."

"Move on?"

"Go on a few dates, stop working so hard, that sort of deal."

"I hardly meet anyone I like."

"Dad. You never go anywhere to meet anyone!"

"I'm a busy man." Bruce chuckled, but it came out sounding hollow. He straightened the framed Renoir print on the wall with one hand.

"There's something you need to understand about me," he continued. "I'm a singular man. I loved *one* woman. Whether or not I meant it to be this way, I can't say . . . "

"You know," Nick interjected, "that's the biggest bunch of bull I've ever heard. You don't give anyone a chance. What about Miss Jamrod? She liked you."

Miss Jamrod was Nick's English teacher who'd dropped by their house, apparently to deliver a homework assignment to Nick during his senior year in high school. An attractive woman with a nice attitude — and legs — she'd flirted with Bruce who simply sat there quietly eating potato chips and ignoring her.

Bruce rolled his eyes. "She had funny ankles."

"That's an excuse. She was *very* pretty." Nick picked up a pen from the desk and chewed the top of it. "Think Mom would want you to be alone like this?"

"I don't know," was the serious answer.

"It's like you're punishing yourself," Nick said with a shrug.

His father just stared at him.

"What, you think it's your fault about Mom? Dad, you don't?"

"It's just not that easy, Nick." Bruce bit down on his lower lip.

"What's not that easy?"

"I guess I feel responsible about her death to some degree."

"But why? You had a good marriage, didn't you?"

"I . . . I guess so. I wasn't a perfect husband. I made some bad mistakes."

"Dad, you're not making any sense. Is there something I don't know?"

Bruce hesitated. "No, nothing. Look, can we talk about this later —"

"It's not your fault what happened to Mom! It was her choice to leave us like she did."

"You're right, Nick. And I'll think about what you said, okay?"

Nick nodded quickly. He'd taken a thermos of apple juice from the house and now he took a long swallow. Wiping his lips with the back of his hand, he said, "Well, if I can't make you see the light, think I'll be on my way, if that's okay?"

"Go ahead." Bruce smiled. "You're a great help here, you know. Still think you should stick with this business instead of medical school."

Nick laughed. "I promise to send you patients I can't fix. Anyhow, I'm meeting Chloe. She's helping me with English."

"The obligatory Shakespeare course, eh?"

"Oh yeah. I need all the help I can get." He touched his pocket. "I want to give her her birthday present, too."

"I thought you were celebrating this weekend coming up?"

"Yeah, but I want to give her the present today."

Bruce grinned. "You feeling guilty about something?"

"Of course not."

"So what's the present? Something from Montreal?"

"Nah. A locket with the initial C on the outside, and N on the inside." He grinned. "Isn't that special?"

"And you think *I'm* stuck on one woman . . . "

Nick chuckled and left. Their house, two blocks from the funeral home, was a large three-story home, the top level being a full attic. College was expensive and to save money, Nick's father had partitioned part of the second level so Nick could have a small apartment there. It was an excellent arrangement that gave him privacy and the right to raid his dad's fridge — the best of both worlds.

Chloe was waiting for him on the front step. She lived next door — and yes, they'd heard all the jokes about the stereotypical girl next door. She had her own key to his apartment; he wondered why she hadn't used it. But that was the thing with Chloe. Sometimes she could be unpredictable.

There were two doors that led to his apartment, one inside the house and another that could be reached from the outside. They walked around back and used the outside entrance.

Nick unlocked the door and let them in. Chloe slung her jacket over the rocker in the living room. "Strange not to hear Paula's music coming from downstairs," she said.

Nick smacked his lips in disapproval. "She's probably with the loser boyfriend."

Chloe rolled her eyes. "You're too hard on Brad. I know he's a bit odd, but

Paula likes him. She hasn't had a lot of boyfriends."

"That's what worries me. She takes this too seriously."

"Nick, she's had enough teasing in her life. It's not easy being overweight."

He agreed. Paula had always been a chubby child; by the time she was ten, she was nearly a hundred and fifty pounds. As a result, she had few if any friends, and spent much of her time reading in her room and listening to old Elton John records.

That was before Brad came into her life.

"You know, she's not feeling well today and instead of staying home tonight and resting up, she's gone with that loser."

"Well, Brad loves her," Chloe added, as if wanting to reassure him. "That much I can tell."

"Please. What does he know about love?"

Chloe chuckled and took her anthology of Shakespeare out of her red knapsack. "Any old fool can love, Nick."

They spread their books on the carpet. Nick had struggled with Shakespeare all term. He didn't see the allure in Shakespeare's *use-a-thousand-words-when-ten-would-do.*

He was studying *Othello* for a quiz. Chloe disagreed with his interpretation that Desdemona was a metaphor for all that was wrong with the world.

She thudded her fingers on the page. "She was an abused gal. There are just boundaries that women have and obviously Othello didn't respect those of his wife."

Chloe certainly had no trouble asserting her boundaries when they fooled around, Nick thought. While he respected her for it, it was frustrating, too. How many women twenty-four and over talked about only serious commitment coinciding with sex?

Good ol' sensible Chloe. Always thinking ahead, always so tidy and nice and mature.

Not wild and free like Lyra. He thought about how she'd kissed him in the parking lot of the bistro, how warm her hand felt on his thigh, how she'd whispered, *"Let's go home."*

What would it take for Chloe to be so uninhibited? Would she need to be convinced she was a genie, too, or was something so kinky too imaginative?

"Are you listening to me, Nick?"

Nick looked up. "No, not really."

"You want to pass this test or not?"

He put his hand against the rocking chair and pushed it back and forth. The old chair creaked against the floor. "Chloe, can I ask you something?"

"What is it?" She closed the book slowly.

"It's a crazy question." A pause. "But what do you know about genies?"

chapter seven

Chloe frowned. "Genies? What's this got to do with Othello?" Her blue eyes darted over his face. "This a serious question?"

"I . . . I was reading a story about genies," he lied, "and thought maybe being an English major, you might've read something about the myth of the genie."

She laughed. "Is the science man thinking about the metaphysical?"

"What if I am?" Did she think he was incapable of creative thought? Sometimes arts majors got on his nerves with the way they acted like they were the only free thinkers around.

He remembered the joke about what English majors say when they finish college: *Will there be fries with that, Ma'am?* It was a nasty joke — and not original anymore, but he resisted repeating it.

Chloe touched his hand, as if to apologize for making fun. "I know a little, why?"

In one way, Nick would've loved to tell Chloe everything; he was accustomed to confiding in her. But he couldn't tell her about Lyra. He couldn't admit that while he wanted him and Chloe to get together, he'd been sleeping with someone else.

He might not know a lot about women, but he did know that they didn't understand that sort of logic.

Chloe picked up his pen and shook it. "Genies, or the *djinn* are sort of like fairies. Didn't you see *Aladdin?*"

"Ah. The Disney djinn. Now how reliable is that?"

She chuckled. "Well, it is true about giving the master who catches them three wishes."

"Just three?"

"Then their service is done."

"How are they caught?"

"In a bottle."

"Or a book?"

Chloe made a face. "Don't know about that. I know they come from the desert. Apparently, people who die a sinful death are transformed into genies. They're trapped between worlds, and so they spend their time playing tricks and whatnot. They can even take on different forms."

"Like what?"

"Cats, snakes, scorpions."

Nick swallowed. Scorpions? He thought about his dream again and about the tattoo on Lyra's spine. As for the sinful death? He bet adultery counted as pretty sinful back then, not to mention Lyra's admission to having a thing for married men.

So maybe she *was* a genie.

No, that's not possible. She simply *believed* she was a genie. Anyone could read up on this stuff and act it out. That's what crazy people did all the time, they simply believed they were Napoleon or part ape or something equally strange and then tried to convince the rest of the world.

Even the guy who murdered John Lennon believed that he was the *real* John Lennon. History's full of these delusional crackpots. Why, there had even been a student at Dalhousie who was kicked out because he tried to convince others that he was Jesus Christ. When other students kept a safe distance, he'd taken a bat to class to beat the *non-believers* into submission.

Chloe chewed on the top of her pen. "So why all this interest in genies?"

Nick sniffed. "Can't I be interested in anything other than chemistry without drawing suspicion?"

"Just seems strange," she admitted. "But good to see your brain extends past atoms and synaptic transference."

"Synaptic trans*mission*."

They both laughed.

"How do you know all this stuff, anyway?" he said.

"Read about it in a course somewhere, I guess." She shrugged. "General knowledge."

"Yeah, genie mythology's right up there with the first prime minister." He stretched out his legs. "So these genies are free to roam without anything stopping them?"

"Well," Chloe added. "They do have one enemy."

"Let me guess, priests or other religious figures?"

"The wolf."

"The wolf?"

"That's right."

"That doesn't make sense," Nick said.

"What can I tell ya? I didn't come up with this stuff."

Nick touched his wolf pendant. How incredibly . . . odd. He thought of how Lyra had wanted him to take it off; how she said it spooked her. Then again, that was probably part of the genie act. She'd obviously rehearsed.

Chloe gestured to the way he held the wolf pendant. She giggled. "So is that your genie protection?"

Nick forced a grin just as Chloe stood up and said she needed a drink. From the kitchen she hollered out, "So why'd you leave Dr. Sampson's class the other day after inviting me to go with you? You went to the bathroom and didn't come back."

"I . . . I wasn't feeling well."

As close as they were, there was no way in hell he'd tell Chloe he'd wet his pants.

"You could've told me you weren't coming back." She returned with a glass of water and sat down again. "Ralph left and he didn't come back, either. I smell bad or something?"

"I should've let you know. I had to rush home . . . I guess I was too embarrassed."

"You were that sick?"

There was a poster of Einstein on his wall above the couch. Nick glanced at it, wondered if Einstein had ever wet his pants.

"Chloe, please. I don't want to go into it."

"Fine. We should get back to Willy, anyhow." She pointed to the book and grinned. "Maybe you should find yourself a genie and get them to change that D to an A. That, or really punish Dr. Sampson for being such a jerk."

Oh, that's not even funny, Nick thought. Still, he laughed. He didn't want Chloe to know how much her mini djinn lesson had spooked him.

Everything she'd said coincided with what he'd dreamed and noticed. Everything. Even if it were all coincidence — and it was — it was just unnerving enough to pick into his comfort zone.

Be careful what you wish for, Nick . . .

He watched Chloe. Lovely Chloe with the pale skin and quick wit, the woman he'd loved practically all his life. God, how close he'd been to blowing any chance with her. Lust was certainly a powerful tool in the hands of the foolish, that's for sure.

"Hey, wait a second. I have something for you." He retrieved the present from his pocket and handed it to her. "It's your birthday present. Early, I know."

Chloe opened the box and held up the necklace. "Ah, it's so pretty. Thank you so much."

"Happy Birthday," he said.

The chain was long and she slipped it over her neck. The locket nestled between her breasts. She smiled down at it and then pulled him into a hug.

"I like silver." She gently pulled away and pointed to his wolf pendant. "Now we match."

He grinned. "Oh that we do, m'dear."

She outlined the C on the locket. "It'll be my good luck charm." She paused. "Nick . . . I have something to tell you."

He waited.

"Connie and I talked about getting our own place."

Connie was Chloe's best friend; a sharp woman who was so intelligent she made Nick feel stupid. Nick always had the feeling that Connie simply tolerated him.

"Well, this is news. But . . . you have free rent with your folks," he reminded her.

"I know, and they're great, but . . . " She shrugged. "You don't think it's a good idea?"

Nick didn't like to think of Chloe living any further than next door, but he nodded anyhow. "Whatever makes you happy."

"You could visit me."

"That's what I like to do, visit you."

She stared at him. "Is that sarcasm?"

"No," he lied.

There was a small silence and then she said, "Let's just get back to Shakespeare, okay?"

Nick nodded. "Okay."

When it was time for Chloe to go home, Nick walked her down the back exit and all ten steps from one doorstep to another.

"Thanks again for the necklace," she said. "Early birthday present, huh?"

"Sure. You think I have an ulterior motive?"

Chloe laughed. "No. My locket is almost as nice as your wolf pendant."

"You really like the wolf pendant?"

"Oh, yeah. It's great. What'd you ever do with the doll you found it wrapped around?"

"I don't know. Must be around somewhere."

"You think it was a real Voodoo doll?"

Nick rolled his eyes. "I doubt it."

"That's such a weird story. Who do you think stuck the doll and necklace in the grate?"

"Who knows? Our house is nearly a hundred years old. It was probably some kids messing around and forgot about it. You driving into school with me tomorrow morning?"

"Oh, I forgot. I don't have to be in until third period. Connie said she'll pick me up."

He nodded. "Sleep well then."

"You, too," she said hugging him.

Nick turned his head to kiss her and she backed away. A flash of anger lit inside him; he instantly dismissed it.

She touched his face. "Nick . . . "

"No need to explain," he said, backing away and feeling as wanted as nuclear waste. Would he ever learn? "I'll talk to you later."

"Nick, I'm sorry. C-can I give you another hug?"

Before he could answer, her arms came around him and Nick willingly moved into the embrace. It was pitiful how he took whatever crumbs of affection she threw him.

Love pigeon, that's what he was.

A pathetic love pigeon.

"Please turn the music down," Paula told Brad the next morning.

She rolled her eyes and pushed the sofa cushion behind her back. Did Brad think playing the Rolling Stones full blast would do something to help her stomach flu? The point of staying home from school was to rest, after all.

"Hey, sure, babe." He adjusted the volume and came to sit beside her on the couch. He scratched his brown beard. "The greatest rock and roll band in the world, ya know."

"They're sorta before my time. Actually, yours, too."

He bobbed his head to "Mother's Little Helper." "That song says so much about life. About what it takes to go against the grain."

"By taking drugs?"

He laughed and slapped his knee. "Gotta get with the groove. You wanna dance, babe?" He grabbed up her Tarot cards from the desk. "Or, hey, why don't ya read my cards for me?"

She just watched him. Sometimes Brad really got on her nerves. He was nineteen, but when he acted like this, she felt like she was baby-sitting.

"I told my brother I'd try to rest as much as possible. Especially since I was sick last night and I went out anyway."

"What does he know? He's not a doctor yet."

"It doesn't take a doctor to know you should rest when you're sick," she pointed out. She knew he was just saying that because he didn't like Nick.

Nick didn't like Brad, either. Nor did her father, for that matter, and at times like this, she could see why.

"Babe, I hate it when you're not tiptop." He put his hands on her shoulders. "You're too beautiful to be down." He made a dramatic sweep of his hand behind her head. "Hey, what's this?" He held an envelope up and shook it.

Paula grinned.

"Hey, it's a letter. Addressed to Paula O'Brien! Who's that, I wonder?"

"You wrote me another letter?"

"Me?" He moved his head to the music and shrugged. "You want it? Huh? Huh?"

"I want it."

"It'll cost ya, babe." He puckered up and Paula kissed him, and then he dropped the envelope in her lap.

Paula smiled, her annoyance gone. He really did care about her. She loved it when Brad wrote her letters. Sometimes he wrote her poems, too. He was so talented.

She ripped open the white envelope and unfolded a sheet of lined paper.

For my Babe, Paula O'Brien.
You are so sweet, you smell like limes,
I want to make you all mine, all mine.

You are a fish and I'm a fisherman above,
the blue sea shaking worms down to catch love.

"Well, whatcha think, babe?"

"Ah . . . it's really beautiful."

"It's a song, ya know," Brad announced, nodding. "It ain't finished, of course. I was thinkin' of entering it in a contest."

She kissed the paper. "Do I really smell like limes?"

"No, but I couldn't think of anything else to rhyme with mine."

"I didn't know you wrote songs."

"I'm working on another one at home. It's called 'Taxi drivers got big hearts even when the fare is a dog.'"

"Catchy title. A dog?"

"Yeah, a dog." He kissed the top of her head. "Read my cards for me now?"

"Okay," she said reluctantly. "Shuffle them."

"It's amazing how you can do all kinds a stuff." He shuffled them carefully. "Where'd ya learn this kind a groovy talent?"

She shrugged. "Dunno. Dad says I inherited it from my mother." She gestured to the cards. "Cut them three times."

"You do got vibes, dontcha?"

"I guess so." She flipped up the first three cards. "The Lovers; the Queen of Cups; and the Three of Swords."

Brad smiled and rose a brow. "The Lovers, that's us, huh?"

"Well, I hope so." She tilted her head. She didn't want to tell him that The Lovers card was reversed; not a good sign at all. In fact, the cards were all reversed.

"Well, babe. Whatcha see?"

"Interesting. Queen of Cups . . . deception, a warning to watch your back."

Brad didn't like to hear this, she could tell.

"Oh, it's not so bad," she said. "Maybe a woman who'll try to run out of your taxi without paying."

"Told ya women are the most ferocious of the sexes." He laughed. "And the other card?"

That card always gave Paula the creeps. Trauma and loss and disappointment. But she didn't say this. Not only because she didn't want to upset Brad, who could take these things too literally, but also because sometimes it was easier to just focus on the positive.

"Well?" He stroked his beard.

"Oh, that's just . . . a party or something."

"Not much of a party, some guy with three swords."

She reached for the next three cards and stopped, then shuffled them together and put them on the coffee table. "Brad, honey, I'm just not in the mood for a reading today. Is that okay?"

"Ah, babe. It was just gettin' good."

"It's only a pack of cards," she said, more to herself. "Not like they're really written in stone."

"Guess you're right, babe. Hey, can I get you something, babe? You need a Diet Coke from the fridge?"

"No, I have everything I need right here. You're the best boyfriend in history, you know that?"

If only her brother and father could see the other side of Brad. The side of him that was sweet and tender.

Sure Brad was a bit immature. But he was open-minded. Unlike Nick, he didn't laugh at her Tarot readings. He didn't judge her for her size; he said there was just more of her to juggle. How many guys had made fun of her over the years? Pointed at her and laughed. She'd never had a date before Brad came along. Why couldn't her family see that?

And so what that Brad was three years older? If she were forty, it wouldn't matter a hoot. Nick was just using that as an excuse. What Nick really didn't like was that Brad drove a taxi for a living. So what? If someone didn't do it, what would you do when you needed to get to the airport?

"Sure I can't get you something, babe?"

"I'm fine. I feel a lot better." She sighed. "This morning was weird, though. I felt really weird."

"Like you had a mother's little helper?"

"Actually, yeah. I was at Nick's apartment and he cooked me breakfast. I was fine and then things felt pretty spaced and sorta unreal. Then I got stomach sick."

"Want me to cuddle you?"

"That would be great." She liked it when Brad cuddled her. It made her feel safe and warm, like a squishy bug.

She giggled. "Squishy bug," she said.

"You're silly."

"Silly squishy bug."

They both laughed.

There wasn't enough room on the sofa for both of them. But dear Brad, instead of stating the obvious, suggested they sit on the floor so she could lay her head in his lap.

It wasn't as good as a real cuddle, but it would do. Especially when he stroked her hair with his big hands. In a way, Brad was as much a freak to society as she was. He was short for a man, only about five-four, and so thin that Nick said if Brad turned sideways, he'd disappear.

And his hands.

They were so big they reminded her of paws. But tender paws that knew how to touch her and make her feel safe.

It still angered her that people saw her as some sort of monster just because she was fat. Didn't they know how their words hurt her, made her feel like dog turd? I mean, was it illegal to be fat?

"Whatcha thinkin' bout, babe?"

She looked up and put away her thoughts. "About you, and how squishy you make me feel."

His blue eyes widened and then narrowed. "Ya know, we could go to my place where we can cuddle in private."

Brad had recently moved into a basement apartment. While Paula would've liked not having to worry about Nick or her dad coming home, she found Brad's place a bit of a dump.

Maybe it was a guy thing to let the dishes pile up for days and not to wash his sheets or empty the garbage. In fact, sometimes she wished that Brad would wash *himself* more.

"Can't we just stay here?" She kissed his wrist.

"You know if your brother comes home, he'll start raggin' on me. He don't want me here."

"He won't be home."

"But he knows you're sick."

"He *won't* be home."

"He hates me."

Paula didn't respond.

"He's a snob, your brother," Brad continued. The muscles in his arm tightened. "I get people like him all the time in the cab. They sit there, so damn snooty, ya'd swear they never farted in their life!"

"Nick's okay," she said. "He's a brother, typical stuff."

"Why don't you just move in with me, babe? We can tell them to go to hell!"

Paula began to feel uncomfortable. She didn't like it when Brad talked like this. She didn't want to tell her family to go to hell. They weren't that bad. "C'mon, lighten up, Brad."

"It'd be perfect." The hand that had been stroking her hair stilled. "You won't even have to talk to them again."

"Brad." She leaned up on one elbow. "I'm only sixteen, remember? And I *like* my family."

He made a funny noise with his mouth. "They got ya brainwashed, babe."

"C'mon, Brad . . . "

"Makin' you one of the slaves." He thudded his fingers against his chest. "Breaks my heart. *Breaks* my heart."

She wanted to tell him not to be so dramatic. The way he exaggerated how everyone was against them was, well, annoying.

But as much as she hated this kind of talk, she hated the thought of losing him even more.

Instead, she sat up and put her arms around his neck. "I'm only your slave," she said playfully.

His posture didn't soften into her embrace. "Babe, this ain't no joke. There's a government conspiracy going on, dontcha know? Surely you know."

"Yes, you told me —"

"You gotta watch yer back. Us real people got to insist on being emaciated!"

Paula was sure Brad meant *emancipated*, but she didn't point this out. When he started raving about government plots, she'd learned that it was best to nod and agree, and then he'd run out of anarchist steam.

"Brad, you still want to go to your place? I can be ready in a few moments."

"Ain't you interested in what I'm sayin'?"

"Yes, of course," she lied. "But let's go. Here, I'll just leave a note —"

"Leave a note?" Brad gave a sarcastic laugh. "What for? Ya 'fraid they'll think I kidnapped ya?"

"Forget the note then. Let's just go." She struggled to her feet, embarrassed that it could so difficult for her to move around. Skinny people didn't realize how lucky they were to be able to do the littlest things like getting up without a strategy.

Brad didn't help her as he usually did. She put her hands against the floor and pushed, using her knee for leverage. Sweat dampened the back of her neck.

"Hey, you want some help, babe?"

She shook her head, embarrassed. "I'm fine," she said when she was finally standing. "See?"

Brad watched her carefully and Paula was certain for a moment that he viewed her in the same way as the rest of society: as a fat nothing. Part woman, part whale. A freight train with a head. A big Mac truck with training wheels.

She felt the muscles in her stomach tighten. She wanted to wipe the sweat from her neck, but that would only make her look fat *and* greasy. Dirty, even.

A dirty, greasy slob.

"Hey, hey . . . " Brad lifted her chin. She could see that he was confused. No wonder. She was practically on the verge of tears.

"Hey, I adore ya, babe." Brad's eyes were soft and kind. "What's up with this, huh? Ya think I don't love ya or some stuff like that, huh?"

She wiped her upper lip with her sleeve. "Don't know . . . "

"Hey." He pulled her into his arms. "Hey, you're my babe. *My babe.*"

"Am I?"

"Sure, sure . . . Life is gonna be roses, babe."

Paula pushed herself deeper into his embrace, and thought about the Three of Swords card again.

chapter eight

Nick got home just after dark to find the house empty.

His father had a meeting and wouldn't be home until late. Good thing, too. Bruce wouldn't be impressed with Paula missing school and then going out.

He bet Paula was at Brad's place. Oh yeah. That's probably where the sick girl was.

He opened the fridge door and just stared. He was sure that men throughout the ages solved problems the same way, by staring into the fridge to ensure the food hadn't done anything stupid in their absence.

It wasn't like Paula not to at least leave a note.

He grabbed the glass jar of apple juice, uncapped it and took a long drink.

He didn't have Brad's phone number, even though the guy had been living in his apartment for a month now. How convenient for Paula not to leave that information around.

Nick fell into the rocker and flicked aimlessly through the television channels. His stomach growled, reminding him that he hadn't eaten dinner.

If Chloe were here, she'd say he was overreacting, that Paula wasn't a child. She'd be right, too, she was always right.

Nick hesitated, and then decided to check Paula's room one last time to see if he'd overlooked a note.

When he opened the door that led into the rest of the house, he tripped over the book.

The book.

That Hurt Thing.

He stared down in disbelief.

Oh, Nick, it's only just begun . . .

"What the . . . "

He picked it up, using only his thumb and forefinger. How could this be? He'd entered through this door not fifteen minutes ago. Anyhow, he couldn't be seeing the book. He'd left it in Montreal, given it to Lyra —

How the hell was this happening?

He groped for a logical explanation: Lyra could've thrown the book in the back seat of his car and he hadn't noticed. Or maybe Paula found it in his car, had been curious enough to bring it into the house and had accidentally dropped it outside his door. In his worry for her, he might've just stepped right over it. Or maybe the Tooth Fairy found it while visiting Santa Claus.

With a sigh, Nick closed the door and locked it. He put the book on the coffee table. Was it a threatening find? Could it really be explained logically?

Of course. Everything can be explained logically. Everything.

Nick, are you making things difficult again?

The air in the apartment felt suddenly stale and he threw open a window and stared up into the sky. It was barely dark and the stars were just coming out.

He examined the patterns of the stars. He didn't know exactly where the constellation of Lyra was, but he felt as if that gathering stared down at him, taunting him.

When he turned around again, the book was no longer on the coffee table. It was on the floor. Open.

Folding his arms tightly, Nick looked down and read: *Things are not what they seem. Release control.*

A shudder as thick as molasses moved through him.

What the hell?

In Montreal he had read *Go with the flow . . .* and the remaining pages had been empty.

He peered closely to see if words had been written or typed in. It was hard to tell for certain.

Release control?

"No," he whispered to the book. "No."

He licked his thumb, went to turn the page and stopped. The book *wants* me to turn the page. It wants to control me. It wants . . .

Nick raced down the steps and out the back door to the large field behind their home. His feet rustled over the thick grass and when the land met the edge of the swamp, he felt cool water seeping into his sneakers.

With a grunt, Nick threw the book into the swamp. As it whizzed out of his hands, his entire body felt lighter.

The book was evil.

Lyra was evil.

And had she followed him to Halifax?

Followed him and broken into his house to leave the book on the landing outside his door —

Everything can be explained, remember?

Thinking on it logically, there was no way Lyra could have followed him. Halifax was a fairly large city; finding him would be next to impossible.

He was being paranoid. Again.

"Paranoid, paranoid . . . " He repeated this like a mantra as he made his way back toward the house. Anyhow, it didn't matter. The book was gone now. There'd be no more reminders of *That Hurt Thing.* No more reminders of Lyra.

When he got close enough to the house, he saw Paula peering at him through the upstairs hall window.

So she'd made it home after all. About time.

He shook a disapproving finger, hoping she could make it out. If she saw him, she didn't signal back. Instead she lifted her hand and lit her cigarette.

Cigarette?

Paula doesn't smoke. Nick's stomach tightened. He hesitated, and then raced toward home.

The damp grass rubbed his ankles; in the distance crickets hissed. He could smell bog and wet earth; his mouth tasted sour.

All the while, the figure watched him.

A crackling sound to his left caused him to turn his head quickly and slow his gait momentarily.

Nothing.

When he looked at the house again, the window was empty.

Then he made out a figure standing on the back deck. Squinting across the darkness, Nick examined the form staring back at him, hunched slightly, feet crossed at the ankles. Lyra, of course.

So he wasn't paranoid after all. Who else but Lyra would follow and haunt him? He thought of how she'd dug the fork in his hand in the cafe, how she held the knife toward him in the motel room.

He had to deal with her once and for all, it was that simple. He would be firm. He would remind her of anti-stalking legislation that banned this kind of thing. A female professor once laughed at this very law, said people who stalked didn't listen to paper laws in the first place.

It didn't matter. He'd make her understand.

But when he got close enough he saw that it wasn't Lyra at all. It was Chloe.

He put both hands on the banister and pulled himself forward. "Chloe," he said. "Tell me you were just inside my house."

"I saw you run into the swamp." She folded her arms. "What was that all about?"

He hesitated. Tried to catch his breath. "Chloe, you weren't in the house?"

"No."

"I've got to get inside."

He jerked the door open and raced up the steps. Chloe followed close behind. "Nick, what're you doing?"

He inhaled the lingering scent of cigarette smoke. "Someone was in the house."

"You mean like an intruder?"

Outside the door of his apartment, Nick looked anxiously at the floor where he'd first discovered the book. "Smell the cigarette smoke?"

"No."

"I saw someone looking out this window, I tell you. A woman, she was smoking a cigarette . . . "

"A woman breaks into your house to smoke?"

"I'm serious, okay?"

Chloe shrugged. "You want to call the police?"

"Let's just look around."

They checked the downstairs and then the second level. Nothing appeared out of order.

"I guess no one's here," Nick admitted. "Or not now. I know I saw someone, Chloe. I know it."

"Well, there's always the attic," she added. "Why don't we look there to be sure?"

He licked his lips. "The attic." He had a sense that Chloe was humoring him, stretching out the dramatics. Even so, he was glad to have her with him, and wasn't that a cowardly thing to admit? What, you need a woman to save you from the bad genie?

"Sure," he said with false bravado. "Let's go."

The staircase that led to the attic was at the end of the hallway. There was a door at the top of the steps. It was closed. With one foot on the lower step, Nick balked. As if sensing his reluctance, Chloe gently nudged him.

"You'll feel better when you realize no one's here," she said.

He didn't answer. He *knew* someone had been here, might still be here.

"Nick, you seem really nervous."

You'd be nervous, too, he thought, if you were being chased by an evil genie —

Lyra's no more a genie than Chloe is a wizard, he corrected himself. *Only in Lyra's demented mind does any such nonsense exist.*

They climbed the steps. At the top, he pushed open the door and they stepped inside. He fumbled for the long string that hung from the ceiling. There was a little click and then stripes of dim light wagged over the floors and husks of furniture. Chloe's red hair seemed nearly black in the dusky light.

Chloe coughed into her fist. "When was the last time this place was cleaned out?"

"It's never used." He looked around, located an old red bike he'd used as a boy and a sewing machine that had been his mother's. There was nothing to suggest anything out of the ordinary. Still, the place gave him the creeps. He looked at the door to the far right, his mother's office. He remembered the family photos on her desk and the many stained coffee cups she'd leave around until Bruce, complaining, would collect them.

Nick hadn't been in there since she passed away.

Chloe touched his arm. "Your father kept everything the way it was when she died, didn't he?"

He nodded.

"We can check in there," she suggested.

"No, it's locked, has been for years."

Chloe glanced around. "See? No one's here. Feel better?"

"Yeah."

"Nick, you must release control."

"What?" His head snapped up. "What'd you just say?"

"I said let's go downstairs." She made a face. "Are you hearing voices now?"

"I'm sure you just said . . . " He threw up his hands and let them fall to his sides. "I'm tired, I guess."

Chloe laughed just as a maggot squirmed its way out of the cup of her eyelid.

Nick blinked and stared. And then lifted his hand and slapped her face.

chapter nine

"What are you doing?" Chloe shrieked and threw up her hands. Nick pointed to her face. The maggot burrowed and slithered deeper into her face. Why couldn't she feel it?

"I'm telling you, Chloe, there's something on your face!"

She stepped away and lowered her head, as if fearing that he might slap her again. Her red hair fell tangled around her neck. When she looked up again, it was gone.

Gone?

There was a red smudge below her eye where he'd slapped her, but nothing else.

Had he imagined the maggot? No way; it had been too clear, too real.

She touched her face, as though driving home the point that he'd slapped her. "What's gotten into you?" She glared at him.

He shook his head. He was sure he'd seen the insect. Sure of it.

"Chloe, I . . . " He shrugged. "You don't actually think I'd hit you? Hit any woman? Chloe, c'mon, that's crazy."

The attic door at the bottom of the steps squeaked open. Chloe stepped closer to Nick and grabbed his hand.

"Paula?" Nick yelled. "Paula, is that you?"

No answer.

Chloe whispered, "Nick, I'm afraid."

Nick expected to hear footsteps on the floor, expected it to scare the hell out of him. But when he didn't hear any noise at all, it scared him all the more. Expectation softens terror. It's what we don't expect that has more power.

"Paula?" he called again. "Are you there?"

"What'll we do?" Chloe asked, chewing on her thumbnail.

Oh boy. Why is it that women always expect the man to know what to do when there's a bump in the night? Still, he went along with the part. "Let's go downstairs. It was probably the wind. Or the bogey man."

"Be serious," she said, glancing toward his mother's office. "We could go in the office and call the police."

Nick shook his head. "It's locked, remember?" Even if it weren't, there was no way he'd go inside. It would be like visiting a tomb, disturbing something that was sacred.

They descended the steps slowly with Nick in the lead. Something touched his lower back; it was Chloe's hand. He reached back and grasped it firmly between his own.

He looked down at his sneakers; bits of damp swamp grass stuck to the white leather. The stairs cracked like old bones as they made their way through the dim stairwell. The door was slightly ajar at the very bottom and Nick pushed it all the way open. The hallway was empty.

"All clear," he whispered.

Chloe's eyes skittered from him to the hallway. "I don't like this kind of scene."

"And I do?" He flicked on the second hall light. That's when they felt the assault of wind.

A thick, inexplicable current of air flattened Chloe's bangs against her forehead; she squinted and leaned fearfully into Nick.

They shuddered against the cold wind that carried with it a trace scent of cinnamon. Nick thought about his Egypt dream again.

Instinctively, he glanced down at his feet, knowing that he'd forever associate the smell of cinnamon with scorpions, with *evil.*

The attic door slammed shut behind them just as the wind tore at Nick's wolf pendant, slapping it against his face. He grabbed at the chain to keep from having it ripped away.

"Let's get to the apartment!" Nick hollered out. "C'mon!"

But just then the wind died, as quickly as it had gathered, and they stood staring at one another and wondering what the hell had just happened.

In his apartment, Nick locked the door and immediately reached for Chloe. She seemed to melt against him.

"It's okay," he whispered, rubbing her hair. Would she ever forget that he'd slapped her?

"I don't understand," she told him. "Any of it."

"Neither do I. But Chloe, I'd never hurt you. You believe me, don't you?"

"I'm not sure what to believe."

Nick could relate to that. He thought about the face in the window. If it hadn't been Paula, then who? Lyra? Had she been here? Had she put the book at the top of the steps? And the sudden gust of cold wind? Was Lyra responsible for that, too? But how? A thousand questions . . .

"I really thought there was a maggot on your face," Nick said.

"That's pretty bad."

"I know."

She lay her head in the crook of his neck. "Where did the wind come from?"

"I'm sure it can be explained somehow."

"You think your house is haunted?"

"I think maybe Paula played a joke on us."

"You don't believe that."

He didn't. Not to mention the fact that Paula wasn't home, hadn't been for hours.

"I don't know what else to say." He shrugged. "There might've been a window open and some freak wind ripped through the house."

"The funny thing," Chloe added, "is that the wind nearly ripped off your wolf pendant — but not my locket."

It was true. He could even feel where the chain had chafed his neck. *The genie's only enemy is the wolf.* Nick shivered and forced a half-grin. "It must've been where I was standing, that's all."

The less he made of the freak wind, the better. There were a lot of unexplained and harmless events in life and this was probably just one more.

"C'mon," Nick said, taking a breath. "Let's just . . . make some coffee or something."

"Sounds like the best plan I've heard in ages." Chloe followed him into the kitchen.

Gerald peered down at the square of paper in his hand.

His very first friend.

Standing in front of the bathroom mirror, Gerald frowned at his smeared mascara. Tucking the paper beneath a potted plant on a small table near the sink, he scooped a glob of Vaseline and smacked it against his face.

It was important he do a good job taking off the make-up. What if a student noticed a smudge of lipstick or foundation along his chin line, after all? That would be horrific, yes indeed.

"Oh, Nicole." He plucked at his lashes to remove the mascara. "Sweet, sweet girl."

Tonight had been their second meeting at the Lizard Cafe. Only this time, she'd been exceptionally verbose. So much so that Gerald wondered briefly if she knew his secret.

They'd walked toward the old fortress that was called Citadel Hill, and Nicole had taken his arm. She talked about how important honesty was and how keeping one's word was akin to keeping one's clothes on. Gerald hadn't gotten the parallel but he'd agreed anyhow. The girls' club probably had lots of parallels and metaphors he wouldn't get right away.

Then Nicole had slipped and he'd instinctively moved to catch her. When he did, his hand had accidentally brushed against her breast. That wouldn't have been so bad, except that he'd pulled back and said, "Heavens, I apologize! You must think I'm perverse!"

It was the way she looked at him, as if telling him with her eyes: *I know what you really are.*

Nicole had wanted to go for a drink after that, but Gerald had declined. It had been enough embarrassment for one night. They agreed to meet again the following Saturday evening at the cafe.

But what would he wear? His female attire was somewhat limited. There was the blue one-piece suit but he wasn't sure he had the upper arms for such a thing.

Holly's red jumper!

Perfect!

It was one thing he would be forever thankful for, that he and Holly were practically the same size. He was slightly taller, but he could squeeze into her red jumper easily.

It would cover his arms and legs, thank God. And he had a red hat he'd purchased just last month. He and Nicole could go for another walk, maybe plan a shopping trip. It was obvious she needed new clothes; maybe he'd convince her to let him buy her something. Something other than that dreary black dress.

He turned from the mirror. Was that a car he heard in the driveway? He went to the living room window and looked out. He saw Holly reach into the back seat of her Dodge Neon and withdraw two grocery bags. The wind had picked up and it blew her coat open.

Gerald was shirtless, but he still wore the orange skirt and pantyhose and sporty underwear. In his haste to remove the hose, his fingers pushed through the thin fabric and he cursed and limped toward the bedroom just as the front door opened and Holly called his name.

He didn't respond. He needed the few extra seconds to get out of the clothes and hide them. It was only nine; she was early. Gerald certainly hoped this didn't mean an alteration in her schedule.

"Gerald honey, are you home?" The sound of crinkling plastic bags from the kitchen. "Honey?"

"Out in a sec, hon."

"Hungry?"

"Ah . . . nope."

Then she was coming down the hall, her tiny heels clicking against the tiled floor. Gerald was naked now and he stuffed the clothes beneath the bed. She opened the door and sniffed the air.

Could she smell that he'd been bad?

She frowned at his nakedness. "What's going on?"

"You're home early."

"Notice anything different?" She wiggled her shoulders.

"Ah . . . " Geesh, he hated it when she asked these kind of questions. He examined her closely: her blue waitressing uniform, black shoes, pearl earrings and necklace, bobbed brown hair, plum lipstick.

"Well?"

"Ah. Do something with your hair?" he guessed.

"You noticed. Good." She kissed him. "I like that. I got it cut, that's why I left early. Like it?"

"Cute, Toots."

He could smell grease from the restaurant on her clothes. "How was work?"

"Tiring." She sat on the bed, kicked off her shoes and massaged her feet. "What'd you do tonight? Besides undress and wait for me?"

"I was just about to shower," he told her. "Care to join me?"

This seemed to catch Holly off guard.

Gerald watched her closely. She was eight years younger and there were times he still wondered why she'd agreed to marry him. When they'd met, she was engaged to some electrician with arms the size of cannons. Gerald had intervened, suffered a bloody nose when the dumb jock got his feelings hurt, but won the prize: the lovely young Holly.

"Shower?" he repeated.

Holly pointed to the sink. "My mascara's out." She crossed the room; Gerald felt his heart jump. "So is the Vaseline. Were you using it?"

He'd left the jar open. "Ah. Yeah, I was trying . . . I used it to grease the kitchen door."

"Grease the kitchen door? Didn't know you could do that."

Holly put the square white top of the Vaseline back in place and dropped the mascara into the red make-up bag. "You're just full of tricks, Dr. Sampson."

"Sure am." He rubbed the hair on his chest with his palm. "I'm a regular clown."

Holly smiled.

They made soapy love in the shower and afterward fell sleepily into bed together. Gerald thought about Nicole and felt a wisp of guilt. He wished more than ever that he could share his secret with his wife. But would she assume he was having an affair? What would she say?

It didn't matter what she'd say, Gerald decided. Part of the fun was the secrecy. As long as he kept it innocent — and he would — there was no more harm than collecting porno mags and the occasional 1-900 call.

"You're amazing," she said across the pillow. "Shower was a good idea, Gerald." She yawned. "Real good."

Gerald nuzzled into Holly and closed his eyes.

He thought of his new friend's number tucked beneath the plant and smiled in the dark.

c h a p t e r   t e n

Chloe made a sandwich from leftover roast beef and stuffed it in the fridge for the morning. She made her way into the living room and flicked through the television channels — and wondered again why Nick had slapped her.

His explanation didn't make sense. A maggot crawling over her skin? Was that an excuse? She didn't think so. Nick could have a bit of a temper, but there'd been nothing to indicate he could be violent.

She had never seen him so jumpy, even paranoid. But he hadn't been himself tonight. In fact, Nick hadn't been the same since his trip to Montreal. Something happened there; she was sure of it.

"What'd you do there?"

"Not much. Kayaked a little, read, hung around the motel room."

Their conversation had been too vague, too unremarkable. Nick was a detailed kind of man. He loved to tell her the little things that made up a good story, but he'd scarcely said more than a handful of words about Montreal.

Chloe muted the noise of the television and leaned against the sofa. It was chilly in the living room and she yanked the patchwork throw from the back and wrapped it around her shoulders.

A woman.

Had Nick met a woman in Montreal, *been* with her? Did it matter?

No, not really. Sure, she and Nick were . . . well, exactly *what* she wasn't certain, but she had no claims on him, no real reason to be jealous.

A light breeze wafted over her feet.

She pulled the patchwork quilt tighter around her shoulders.

Calm down, Chloe. Not every breeze is a wicked wind . . .

Had she left a window open? It was Indian summer, but the evenings were chilly. She felt certain a draft came from somewhere.

Chloe checked the windows in the kitchen, dining room and bathroom only to find them locked shut. She was about to settle on the couch again when a rustling sound made her stand in the middle of the room, listening.

She thought of Hazel, the cat they'd had since she'd been a baby. The cat had died last year but Chloe still imagined she heard its plump orange body rubbing against the screen door at night.

Yawning, she decided it was just as well to go to bed. A good night's sleep did wonders for the unsettled mind.

In her basement room, Chloe flicked off the overhead light and before crawling into bed, turned on the small lamp so she could read a few more pages of her paperback, *Black Water Born*. Reading always relaxed her.

Only a few pages into the paperback, Chloe felt sleepy. Closing the book slowly, she rubbed her eyes and yawned. The house creaked above her.

She had just fallen into that surreal state between sleep and wakefulness when something tugged at her, some annoying presence that nagged and teased.

And then a thunking noise. Opening her eyes, Chloe realized the draft had been coming from her room all along.

The window above her bed was open.

Strange, she hadn't noticed it earlier. No, not so strange, she decided. The wind had come up, that's all, causing the wooden slats of the blind to slap against the frame.

Kneeling and then standing on the bed, Chloe pulled the gaping window shut with both hands and fell back into bed.

She slept immediately.

As Paula sat on Brad's couch, she realized two things: Brad's feet stank *bad*; and that it was nearly eleven o'clock and she needed to go home.

"Stay the night," he told her for the third time. "You don't need to answer to no one, babe."

It amazed her how Brad could think this way. She was sixteen, not old enough to drink or vote and he expected her to do as she pleased? She stood up. "Brad, I'm sorry, but I need to go home; I haven't even called."

He pulled his fingers through his beard, picking out bits of dried crust from the pizza they'd eaten for dinner. His dark eyes flickered over her and then away. "Maybe your brother is right. Maybe I am too old for you, babe."

"Don't say that." Her stomach began to churn.

"I want a mate, a partner, someone who goes against the grain with me, someone I can wake up with." He looked directly at her. "Ya know?"

"W-what are you saying?"

"Ah, babe, don't get that look in your face. Ya know I'm crazy about ya. Ya got me right here." He touched his heart. "It's like welfare of the soul, the way we are. Never enough, babe."

"I can't help it." Her face felt flushed and she dug her nails into her sweaty palms. "Brad, I won't be sixteen forever." He didn't respond right away. She didn't know if that was good or bad. Finally, he said, "We'll work it out."

She pulled on her coat. "Sure?"

"Yeah, I'm sure."

They drove in silence across town. When they passed a nightclub, a staggering man with a black trench coat flicked his hand toward the car. Brad slowed. "Mind if I take this guy, babe? Haven't worked all day, ya know."

She really didn't want him to do anything but take her home, but she said, "Sure, go ahead."

The man reeked of booze as he climbed into the back seat and gave directions for an area just outside of town. It was good for Brad, but bad for her. It would mean she wouldn't get home for another half hour or more.

"There's lots of you to go around, isn't there?" the man said, gesturing over the seat toward Paula with a chuckle.

She ignored the remark, as always. But ignoring it didn't make it hurt any less. She wished Brad would say something or kick the guy out. Did he need the money that much that he'd put up with having someone insult his girlfriend? At least Brad didn't laugh with him. That would be unbearable. Pressing her face against the cool glass, she closed her eyes and imagined she was far, far away — and very skinny.

When they arrived at her house, Paula asked him to park down the street so she could sneak inside the side door. She knew Nick would be watching for her.

The car idling, Brad plucked her against him. "Give ya man a kiss, a *squishy* kiss, babe." He laughed and kissed her with such intensity that it began to feel like she couldn't breathe.

Finally she pulled away, softly gasping for air.

"I know," he said. "Us kissin' does the same thing to me."

He patted her knee. "You feeling all right now?"

"Yeah, fine." She reached for the handle of the door and pulled it. The interior light came on. "I'll seeya, Brad."

"Sure thing." He blew her a kiss and winked. "Remember, babe, against the grain, okay?"

She closed the door behind her. "Yeah, against the grain. How could I forget?"

Nick found it hard to settle down, even after he knew Paula was okay. He'd watched her sneak in the side door, letting it bang shut behind her. He sighed. She'd never make it as a professional curfew-breaker.

A good brother would confront her about the time, but he didn't have the energy. Arguing with Paula about Brad and curfews would only put him in a worse mood. There'd been enough to deal with tonight.

He thought about Chloe, wondered if she were having a sleepless night, too. He went outside and peered at her basement bedroom window; it was dark.

He walked across the driveway and paused. He wasn't ready to go back in the house, not yet. Instead, Nick climbed inside his car and just sat there, enjoying the quiet.

He wished Chloe were with him.

Wished that tonight she might've stayed with him in his apartment. If only he could put Chloe and Lyra together —

No, not Lyra.

Lyra was good in bed, but there'd been nothing past that. He thought of how temporarily enamored he'd been of her. What if she hadn't turned out to be a basket case? What then? Would he have abandoned the eternal wait for Chloe?

Time. Isn't that what Chloe said? Give her time. Little did she know that time was the last thing he thought about when he saw many of his friends having *real* relationships.

"Screw you, time." Nick started the car and backed out the long driveway. "Screw you big time."

He drove aimlessly.

Fog rolled in off the sea, settling over the city. Nick liked fog, liked the feeling of being tucked away in a secret. He drove across town towards Ralph's house, hoping his best friend would still be up.

Nick parked the car in front of the house and gave the horn a little pressure, just enough to make Ralph cup his hand to the window and peer outside.

A few moments later, Ralph slid into the passenger side of the Toyota.

"You idiot!" Ralph scowled playfully. "What the hell you trying to prove?"

"I wake the roommates up?"

"Nah."

Nick flicked on the radio, hoping for music but getting only news. He turned it off again. "Want to go to Jinx's for a beer?"

Jinx's was a bar in a seedier part of Halifax that was just bad enough to be entertaining. Located in the basement level of what was once a hotel, the lounge was more like a cave than a bar. They sat near the back entrance. Ralph's face looked yellow in the sickly lighting.

"Hey, Nick. Know any Birds?"

Nick leaned closer. "What did you say?"

"Birds."

"What?"

Ralph's eyes slid downward mischievously. "Why don't I tell you about the girl I met."

"Her name is Bird?"

"Candice Bird. B-i-r-d." Ralph tore the edges from the beer label. "Great, isn't it? I met her a few days ago in Public Gardens. She was getting a fortune reading from the lady who does the card reading stuff. She asked me if I knew any places to buy ice cream."

"Sounds like she picked you up."

Ralph ran his tongue along the front of his teeth. "Yeah, I guess. You can meet her at the party this weekend."

"Party?"

"The one at Taylor's," Ralph said, rolling his eyes. "The one to celebrate Chloe's birthday. You can meet the new little lady then. She really is something else. Gorgeous and sorta mysterious, too."

Nick tapped his fingers on the edge of the table. He hesitated. "Mysterious? What's she look like?"

"Gorgeous! Man, I can't stop thinking about her —"

"She doesn't have . . . black hair, by any chance?"

"What kind of a question is that?"

"Does she?" Nick held his breath. "Black hair?"

"No, blond."

"Thank God."

Ralph made a face. "I think you need another beer. You're starting to act even weirder than usual. And that, my friend," he added, pushing away from the table with his hands, "is a very scary consideration."

After Jinx's, Nick and Ralph drove to the waterfront and walked along the boardwalk to Tim Horton's coffee shop.

Tim's coffee is famous for its strength, and by the time Nick slipped into bed at home, he was wide awake. It was almost one thirty. The morning would be cruel if he didn't get some sleep.

He tried deep breathing exercises. He read for a while. He counted various Jenns jumping on a trampoline. The latter only made him more awake.

Finally, he went to the kitchen, poured a glass of apple juice, made a slice of toast with peanut butter and took it back to his bedroom.

It seemed to do the trick. He slid between the flannel sheets with a sigh and closed his eyes. The momma-conscience within bickered that he should brush his teeth; he ignored it. Peanut butter and toothpaste just didn't go together, no matter how bad you wanted it to.

The party at Taylor's for Chloe was tomorrow night. Ralph would be bringing his new girlfriend, the Bird girl.

Surely she wasn't . . .

Nick danced along the edge of sleep. No, it wasn't Lyra. That wasn't possible. Lyra was far, far away . . .

Thinking of her led to dreams of her.

He dreamed that they were in the motel in Montreal again. At the end of the motel room was a door. Steam sifted from the line beneath the door.

Lyra smiled. "Let's go, Nick," she said, reaching for the doorknob. "C'mon, don't be shy."

"I don't want to go in there," he said, but then his legs moved, one after the other. He stared down at them, unbelieving as they moved seemingly of their own accord. He clenched his wolf pendant and shuffled toward Lyra.

The door opened and then they were falling.

His stomach wrenched and twisted and he clawed at the air. Like Alice in Wonderland, he thought, squeezing his eyes closed. *And I'm with the Chesire Cat, no doubt about it —*

With a jolt, they were plunked on their feet. Nick cursed and rubbed his ankle. He inhaled the scent of cinnamon and when next he looked up, saw that they were standing in the desert, just beyond the walled city.

"What're we doing here?"

Lyra wore a gown so white it glistened. Her long black hair was tied back and a few soft ringlets danced around her shoulders. She looked incredible. "You had such fun last time," she said.

"No, I didn't. It was anything but fun." He realized that he, too, wore a white gown, nothing as fancy as Lyra's, but just as heavy.

"Take me back," he demanded.

"Nick, don't be a baby." Black smoke sifted in the distant sky. She pointed behind Nick.

He turned to see a large cauldron, like the stereotypical witch's brew pot. Steam rose toward them. "You're just full of tricks," he said, stepping back.

Lyra curled a finger toward him. Her dress caught the light and sparkled silver. She lifted her brows reassuringly. "Now come, Nick. Come see what's in store for you."

chapter eleven

Nick said, "I don't like this, Lyra."

Lyra laughed and came to him across the sand. Birds sailed overhead toward the city. "Oh Nick, sweetness. Don't be afraid of me. Didn't I promise to cure that hurt thing?"

"That Hurt Thing," he echoed. "I threw the book away. Chucked it into the swamp. It's gone!"

She touched him and then he couldn't resist. Like a rag doll, he was pulled along by Lyra toward the cauldron. Sand got inside his sneakers — how odd he'd still be wearing his sneakers with such a gown — and he moved his toes uncomfortably.

A puff of steam made him squint. Whatever she was brewing smelled real bad. He turned away.

Lyra stood behind him, her hands moving over his back; he felt himself becoming aroused. What a brain-drain, to be repulsed by the smell and be so horny at the same time.

She pushed her lips close to his ear. "Nick, I want to heal that hurt thing, but only if you let me."

"What does that mean, Lyra?"

"Nick, Nick, don't fight me. All I want is you. All I need is you. Don't you see that yet? The way you were with me, so wild —"

"Was I really? I don't have that much experience . . . "

"I know," she told him.

"You could tell?" He looked at the ground.

"Not really." Her arms went around his neck. "You liked it, didn't you?"

"Yeah, I liked it."

She stood beside him. "You'd like it right now, wouldn't you?"

"No."

"Look into the pot." Her hands fell to her sides. "It's time."

At first nothing of what he saw made sense.

Hunks of pink plastic or Styrofoam bobbed in brownish liquid that reminded him sickeningly of sewer water. Steam curled toward him; he squinted.

"This," he announced, "stinks real bad."

Lyra just smiled.

And then suddenly Nick knew exactly what he was looking at. Flesh. Chunks of flesh.

He saw a part of a shoulder, a foot, a head. As terrible as it was, he found that he couldn't stop looking into the cauldron to see the hunks of human remains. The liquid churned the pieces of flesh like a dryer throwing clothes against the glass.

A head rolled to the surface then; before seeing its face, Nick knew that it was Chloe's.

Fire gathered at the back of his throat.

Chloe's red hair twisted around her chin and nose. Her eyes were open and they seemed to peer at him with such sadness that he fought the impulse to jump in and retrieve her floating, bobbing head.

Behind him, Lyra laughed.

Lyra's laughter pounded at him. He wanted desperately to make her stop laughing, but she had complete control over the situation. Maybe she'd had control from the very beginning. Even in Montreal. Even then.

What a joke he'd been with her.

Her company had never been a choice. She had spun her pretty web and he'd fallen like a crippled moth.

"Look at me, Nick."

Nick turned to see that she was naked.

His eyes went to the mole on her shoulder and despite the fury that boiled inside him, he *had* to look at her, even appreciate how well she was built.

It went beyond that. Lyra was one of those women that made men take a second look, a lingering look. It wasn't just that she was beautiful — for she was — it was an underlying tension that made men feel a hunger.

Lyra was dangerous.

Smiling, she moved toward him.

He turned away, looked longingly toward the city. If he could get there, perhaps he could hide. The boiling vat gurgled and bubbled. He glanced at it and saw once again, Chloe's head drifting to the surface and then disappearing into the oily liquid. Fury built inside him.

He made a fist and lunged toward Lyra —

Blackness.

Sweat.

Burning.

Nick blinked and peered through the darkness of his room. Instinctively, he glanced down to see if he still wore a robe. But no, he wore only his shorts.

It was a dream, just a dream. But a dream that made him grasp for the pillow to have something to hold on to.

The image of Chloe's floating head made his stomach tighten. The room was cool and he sucked at the air, hoping it would soothe the burning fear that throbbed inside him. He shivered in the dark room.

Rain splattered against the glass.

It was frightening, to think he couldn't evade Lyra, awake or asleep. What was happening to him, to his life? He wanted things back the way they were, before he'd found the book and went to Montreal, before he walked naively into Lyra's life.

Don't get carried away, now, he told himself. *You had an odd weekend with a bewitching woman, and it's still with you, that's all.*

And Lyra, is she still with me?

Nick rubbed his eyes. He was making more of things.

He stretched to ease the tension knotted in his arms and shoulders. His hand met with something warm. He flinched and pulled back.

Swallowing, he peered through the darkness to see a figure huddled on his bed.

He laughed.

Chloe.

He had touched the top of Chloe's head, her *connected* head, he added. She was asleep on top of his covers near the edge of the bed.

How long had she been there?

He moved his hand to her lips and felt her gentle breathing. The clock read quarter to four. It was surreal how time had passed without comfortable sequencing.

Touching her head made him think of the dream again, made him think of Lyra leaning over the cauldron telling him to peer into the future; Lyra laughing at him.

"Chloe," he said, peeling back the blankets. "Get under the covers."

She stirred and clumsily obeyed. She wore jeans and her pajama top, but her neck and arms were cold. Nick cuddled into her. "You're freezing."

She pushed her feet between his calves.

"I didn't hear you come in."

"You were sound asleep," she whispered. "I couldn't wake you."

"Guess I was dreaming." He wanted to ask Chloe why she'd chosen this night to visit him; had she sensed that he was lost in a horrific dream? But there was no predictability to the way she slipped across the driveway to his bed. More than likely, it was a simple coincidence.

"I'm so glad you're here," he whispered, meaning it more than she could realize.

"Me, too."

A blast of wind threw rain against the window. Thunder rolled in the far-off night sky. Chloe felt so soft and vulnerable in his arms. When she slept, her body took on a scent that was absent at any other time. Nick couldn't identify it exactly, but it reminded him of sweet fresh earth or plums. He pushed his face into her hair.

Chloe flinched. "I was afraid, Nick . . . "

Nick lifted his head slightly. "That's why you came over?"

"Yes."

He licked his lips. "Afraid of what?"

She shrugged. "I don't know."

Nick closed his eyes and hugged her, knowing that if he thought one more moment about fear and blackness and dreams he'd be awake the rest of the night. Maybe the rest of forever.

chapter twelve

"Red would be a dear color on you," Gerald said as he took his seat across from Nicole at the Lizard Cafe.

"Thank you. You think so?"

"Definitely, Nicole." Gerald put a finger to his lips thoughtfully. "If you don't mind me saying, that black dress is cute, but it's good to have some variety."

Her green eyes softened. "I'm glad we're friends and you feel you can say that to me."

"More coffee?" The waitress held a glass pot toward them.

Nicole extended the white ceramic cup and nodded. Gerald mimicked the gesture. When he did, he noticed hair snaking along the back of his hand. He wasn't sure how to handle that aspect of being a woman. If he shaved it, wife Holly would surely notice. He tugged on the edge of the sleeve.

"Want to have an adventure today, Holly?"

Gerald flinched. It was difficult to hear his wife's name. He should have chosen a name less related to his life.

"Adventure? W-what kind of an adventure?"

Despite Gerald's intention to join the girls' club, his eyes flickered over Nicole's legs and chest. Wow, she was built. Adventure, huh?

"Let's go to a sex garage!"

Gerald had never heard of a sex garage; would there be such a thing in Halifax? Halifax was a modern city and the European influence gave it a certain naughty acceptance, but a sex garage? "Ah, where is it?"

"I know where it is. Just leave it to me."

Gerald scratched his chin. He hadn't shaved closely enough; he could feel a nine o'clock shadow. "How long will this take?"

"Why? Mommy waiting up for you?"

She laughed at her own joke and hurried them out of the cafe. Gerald walked beside her, suddenly not so sure about this *adventure*. When he thought of adventure, he imagined necking in the back seat of his Explorer, or smoking a little weed along with a wine cooler.

"Nicole." He stopped on the side walk. "I'm too old for this. I'm just not sure."

"Then what do you want to do?" She looked disappointed, even a tad hurt. "I thought you were my friend."

"How about we go for a ride in my Explorer?" He forced a laugh. "We can go to Citadel Hill, watch the male prostitutes."

"I need money, Holly."

"Money?"

"Can you give me money?"

"S-sure." He reached into his purse and gave her a twenty dollar bill. She snatched it and glared at him, as if it weren't enough. Gerald swallowed. He thought about the hair on the back of his hands again.

"Where'd you park your car?"

Gerald pointed. "Two blocks that way."

"Let's go." She whistled a tune he didn't recognize and when they'd walked a few feet, poked him playfully in the ribs. Gerald giggled back, relieved that she felt better. He had a feeling his new friend could be pretty moody.

"Sorry the sex garage thing isn't what I'd be comfortable doing."

She shrugged. "Not every *woman* likes that kind of scene."

Gerald unlocked the passenger door. The way she'd said the word *woman* made him uneasy. Could she be on to him?

Settling behind the steering wheel, he adjusted the rearview mirror and said, "Well. Where shall we go?"

"Just drive." She flicked back her hair. "Anywhere, Holly. *Any*where."

Gerald drove out of the city toward the highway. "How about Truro? Quaint little town. Perhaps we could go there and have a drink, maybe a bite to eat?"

"Whatever. I don't care." Nicole looked out the window.

He turned down the radio. "W-what do you need money for?" he asked. "Are you in some sort of . . . trouble?"

"Do I look like a girl who looks for trouble?"

"That's not what I meant —"

"Do we have to talk about it, Holly? That's what girlfriends do, they just know when to leave well enough alone."

Gerald adjusted the rearview mirror again. "So, where do you live, anyhow?"

She seemed annoyed by this question. Was she getting moody again? "Wherever I hang my attitude, Holly. Mind if I smoke?"

"Ah, it's fine, I guess."

"Can you pull down that old road there?" It was a dirt road and Gerald wasn't sure where it led, if anywhere.

"I'd rather not."

"Why not?" Cupping the cigarette with one hand, she lit it. The flame of the lighter illuminated her face and Gerald let out a little gasp. She shot her head his way. "What the hell is wrong with you?"

"N-nothing."

A few miles later, he pulled the jeep to the shoulder of the road and turned in the direction of the city again. Truth was, for an instant, he swore Nicole's face had been that of a skeleton's. He ran his hand over the back of his neck. Girls' club be damned; his new friend was giving him the creeps.

"We going back?" Nicole said, blowing smoke his way. "What about quaint little Truro?"

"Well, I . . . I'm sort of exhausted tonight, so if you don't mind, I'd just like to go home."

"Party pooper."

"I'm sorry."

"So, tell me, Holly." Nicole leaned her arm along the back of the seat, almost touching his head. "Do you have a boyfriend?"

"Do I have a boyfriend?" he repeated, stalling for time.

"Yeah, a man. A man who does you good?"

"No." Gerald cleared his throat. "You can turn up the radio if you'd like."

"Perhaps we can double date sometime. Wouldja like that, Holly, huh?"

"That'd be fine." Gerald shifted in the seat. This conversation was making him uncomfortable. Not just the questions she asked, but the tone she used. A tone that had an edge of harshness, much like his own tone, he supposed when he taught disinterested students.

"I bet you're an old fashioned kind of gal," Holly continued, lifting her chin and blowing the expelled smoke high. "I bet you like to be wined and dined before you put out, am I right?"

Gerald just nodded and they drove for a way in uneasy quiet. When the lights of the city shimmered into view, Nicole put her hand on his leg. At first, Gerald ignored it. But then he felt her nails digging sharply above his knee.

"Please," he said.

"Were you hoping I'd be a dyke, that it?"

"Please take your hand away."

"Two hundred should take care of it."

He was silent for a few moments and then he glanced her way. "Take care of what?"

"It, my friend."

"What's *it*?"

"A tip would be nice, too. *Gerald.*"

Gerald bit down on his teeth so quickly he caught the edge of his tongue. Tears sprang to his eyes. He pulled to the shoulder of the road. "Get out."

She extended her palm and pointed to it with an index finger. "I'll tell sweet Holly. The *real* Holly. The real woman. Tell her what a freak you are."

"So . . . so this was a game?"

"Two hundred bucks, Gerald."

"You think I carry that kind of money —"

"Bank machine." She examined the nails on one hand.

"How . . . how did you know about me? You were a student of mine, weren't you?"

Of course. That had to be it. He had several hundred students over the course of a year; he never remembered them all. She could've been a bitter student, perhaps someone he'd failed or snubbed.

A fellow professor, Dr. Cassyn, once had a student who wrote him love letters. She'd leave them on his podium or slip them beneath his office door. Day after day after day. To protect himself, Dr. Cassyn reported the behavior and the girl was removed from his course. Good thing, too, for the student had already been starting rumors about the two of them being involved. It could've been disastrous for the professor. Gerald clenched his jaw. What would happen now? Was Nicole about to humiliate him publicly? He could only imagine the head of the chemistry department finding out that he cross-dressed and associated with young, beautiful women.

What had he been thinking?

"Listen, Nicole," he said evenly. He had to get the upper hand here. "If I did something to offend you in any way, I am deeply sorry."

She shook her head. "Don't flatter yourself."

"Please tell me. Were you a student, or are you now?"

"I got better things to do than sit in on your class. Any class —"

"You're not a college student?"

"No, I'm not."

"Then how . . . ?"

"Let's just call this debt repayment. Consider me a debt collector." She pursed her lips and blinked her eyes. "Without the harsh voice and low IQ."

"A debt against whom?"

"That's a secret, Gerald. We all know how you like secrets." She whispered the last word.

"You're insane," he told her.

And you're pathetic, Dr. Sampson. Not to mention flat chested and pretty boring. God, I hate boring people."

"I'm hoping we can work this out like civil people —"

"Who's civil? Money," she said.

Gerald drove to the closest bank machine, withdrew the money and set the bills on the seat between them. She counted it. "What, no tip?"

"This remains between us, right?"

She slid across the seat and kissed his cheek. "I'll take a cab from here, Gerald. You know, the sex garage would've been a hell of a lot more fun —"

"Get *out*!"

"Boring, boring, boring." She gave a little wave. "Bye, freak."

He pressed on the gas pedal and the jeep shot away from the curb. In the rear view mirror, he saw her blowing him a kiss. Damn her! She'd seen right through him. But how, oh how did she know so much about him, down to his name — and Holly's name?

Debt collector?

The only good thing was that he'd refused to go to the sex garage. God knows how much blackmail material that would've given her. He'd take comfort in that small blessing.

He drove home and pressed the remote to open the garage.

After tonight, he doubted he'd dress up for a while. This Nicole had really taken the wind out of him. It wasn't even the money; it was the game she played. Who knew how far she'd planned to take it?

The garage door stuttered open and Gerald drove inside and parked. He'd been so distraught he hadn't noticed Holly's car parked in the garage.

Holly was home?

Leaning against the seat, he examined her car. It wasn't time for her to be home. Not yet. How dare she alter her schedule? He picked up the remote again, pointed it, and then put it down again. It might attract more attention for him to leave. Surely she saw him pull in the driveway. Perhaps he could take off his clothes in the jeep and sneak in —

The door between the garage and kitchen opened.

Holly stepped inside.

Gerald wanted to die. He looked down and saw his spiky heels; his head shot up again. He clenched the keys tightly in his hand.

His mind raced for an escape. But there was nothing to do but face her, deal with the situation.

When he got out and came round the Explorer, Holly frowned, as if she didn't recognize him. "Gerald?" Her eyes went from his heels to the red hat. She bit her thumbnail and gestured with her chin. "What . . . what's this about?"

"Holly . . . "

"You frightened me. I wasn't sure who . . . " Her words tapered to nothing. "Gerald, tell me this is a . . . a joke. Tell me it's *something*."

"Why're you home?" It was a stupid question, but Gerald fired it anyhow. He needed precious seconds to figure out the right thing to say. Maybe she'd believe he was at a costume party. Or some silly variety show the college put on to raise money.

"I'm home. I . . . there was nothing doing." She poked at the fine blond hairs along the edge of her hairline. She still wore her waitress outfit, a blue and white checkered dress covered with a long blue apron. Her feet were bare. They looked cold against the dingy gray concrete. Her toenails were painted pink.

"Should I not have come home, Gerald?"

"Don't be silly, Holly."

"Then what's this about?" A fragile smile hovered, as if everything would make sense once he just explained.

"Talent show at the school. Can't believe I didn't tell you about it."

"You didn't."

"Sorry. You didn't miss much, believe me."

Gerald's feet were killing him and he slipped off his heels and pressed his toes against the cold floor. Holly watched closely.

"Talent show," she repeated. Her smile flickered and died. "Tell me. Tell me the truth, Gerald. I'm your wife —"

"For the love of God, you don't need to point that out."

"What's going on, Gerald?"

"I . . . I don't know."

"Yes you do."

He took a breath he wished he could hold forever. "Holly, it's just that . . . I like to . . ."

She took a step closer, blinked. "You like to what?"

"I like to dress up in women's clothes when you go to work."

There, he said it. It was out and he could never take it back. Not even if he wanted to.

She licked her lips over and over again. Her eyes glanced to the floor. "Dress up? What do you . . . mean, dress up? Gerald?"

"Isn't it obvious?"

He felt impatient. Impatient and tired and angry that he'd been taken for two hundred bucks and now had to deal with Holly's questioning. As happily married as he was, he had a fleeting wish for bachelorhood again, for the freedom it offered.

"I'm sorry," she said to the floor.

"Why are *you* apologizing?" That was one of the things that bugged him about women. Their incessant need to say they're sorry — even if they have nothing to be sorry about.

He touched her arm. She looked up; her eyes lingered at his mouth. Was his lipstick smeared? "Holly, I'm the one who's sorry —"

"This dressing up." She bit on her bottom lip, took a deep sigh. "Is this because you . . . you no longer find me attractive?"

Of all the responses Holly could've given him, this was the one he'd expected the least. Not find her attractive? Good God.

Holly was an angel, a lovely woman.

He shook his head. "No, *no*, Holly. It's nothing like that. Nothing."

She took a step back and looked away, as if she didn't dare believe him.

He moved toward her and she burst into tears.

Gerald stroked Holly's back as she lay slumped against him in bed. Her breathing was heavy and regular; he hoped she was asleep. The last few hours had been difficult — he'd expected that. What he hadn't expected was the resolution.

He'd held Holly as she cried, but then she'd done something that made Gerald wonder if anyone really knew anyone, even a spouse.

She rubbed him through his dress and before Gerald had a chance to really explain his cross-dressing activities, they'd fallen to the garage floor and done it right there, done it hard and desperate and loud.

It'd been better than any initiation into the girls' club. To think that Holly found it sexy that he dressed like a woman was, well, pretty arousing. She'd always been so conservative, almost timid. Wow. He thought of how she'd hooked off his panties with her thumbs. *Wow.*

"Gerald?"

"What, hon?"

"What do you do when you . . . dress up?"

"I go places."

"What kind of places? Nice places?"

He kissed the top of her head. "Not nice places. Thought you were asleep."

"I was thinking, just thinking." She played with the curly hair across his chest. "I think Dr. Sampson is bravest person I know."

"Brave, huh?"

"Oh yeah, Gerald. Real brave." She lifted her head. "I'd like to join you on your excursions. Is that too weird?"

Wow again. "Holly . . . I'm . . . so surprised by all this, by your reaction."

"I was upset at first, but more because you didn't feel you could tell me the truth. That you kept all the secrecy."

Part of the allure *was* the secrecy, but Gerald didn't tell her that. "Like a girls' night out."

She giggled. Her voice was still stringy from weeping. "Any men ever hit on you?"

"You kidding? No. God, that'd be awful."

"Any women?"

Gerald hesitated and thought about Nicole again and how she'd screwed him royally. Two hundred bucks! It would be a while before he could swallow that one without feeling his guts churn.

"Well, there was one woman."

"There was?"

"It was in a garage . . . "

She smirked. "That's not what I meant."

"Oh, Holly, you were wild." It was the truth. "Think the girls' night out can be as wild?"

She exhaled slowly. "Oh, I think something can be arranged, Dr. Sampson."

"Why does it turn you on, you think?"

"Not sure. It just does. Am I a freak?"

Gerald heard Nicole giving him a little wave. *Bye, freak.* He nuzzled into his wife's neck. "Maybe we're both freaks. But that's all right, too, Holly. That's all right, too."

chapter thirteen

Chloe's birthday party at her friend Taylor's was anything but a stress breaker, Nick decided. He'd had too much to drink, too early. Only an hour or so had passed. Not even enough time for Ralph to show up with the new girlfriend.

And God, the music.

What did they think classical would do for anyone right now?

"You okay, Nick?" Chloe asked. "You're kinda pale."

"I don't like the music."

She made a face as if she didn't understand, and then her focus went across the room. She waved to her friend Connie. "I thought you liked heavy metal, Nick."

"I do. *That's* the problem!"

"You're not making any sense. They're playing metal. Did you have a lot to drink?"

"What difference does it make to you?"

Chloe pulled her head back and frowned. "Why are you so touchy? And on my birthday, too, I might add."

"Sorry. I . . . well, we can sing Happy Birthday to you again if you want."

"That's quite all right. It was nice of Taylor to offer his house for my party, wasn't it?"

Taylor had dropped out of college to become a repo man — he had the build for it, that much was true. Still, it seemed odd, going from an English major to a repo man.

"Yeah, real good of him."

Nick shook his head to try clear it. He felt slightly disoriented, the way you feel when you first wake up.

"You okay, Nick?"

"I . . . I'm tired, I guess."

"You know your dad called me to wish me a happy birthday. Wasn't that sweet of him? I bragged about my locket, told him it matched your necklace."

"He's a great guy," Nick murmured.

Chloe tugged on the hem of her skirt. The gray skirt and pink blouse looked good on her. Too bad he wasn't in a better frame of mind to enjoy it.

"Hey, Connie's coming over," Chloe said. "Don't embarrass me in front of my best friend, okay?"

Nick shrugged. Embarrass her? Was he in *that* bad of a mood?

"Hi, Nick," Connie said, patting down her short brown hair. It was a common fact that Connie usually didn't go to parties, preferring instead to devote time to maintaining her straight A average. Nick had always found her a bit intimidating.

"Hullo," he said.

"Chloe, you all ready to look at the house tomorrow?" Connie touched Chloe's arm.

"Oh yeah, sure."

"House?"

"I told you about us renting a place, Nick."

"Right, right. You and the perfect one."

Chloe frowned. "Nick, that's terrible . . . "

Connie wasn't the least taken back by his remark, however. She snickered and said, "Yeah, guess Sampson's D took you out of my league, huh?"

Nick didn't respond. He simply nodded. Besides, he had to use the bathroom, real bad. But where was it? Surely Repo Man had a bathroom.

Then he saw it. Just past the kitchen and blocked by at least five girls. Why is it, he wondered, that women seem to congregate toward bathrooms?

Across the room, he pushed the balcony screen door open and stepped onto the large deck. No one was out here, great. It wasn't the most eloquent of moves but taking a leak over the edge of the deck sure beat wetting his pants.

Nick fumbled for his zipper but try as he might, he didn't seem to have the coordination to unzip. He counted the beers he'd had — only three that he could remember.

He managed to get the metal button on his jeans undone and after careful focus, got his pants down, but then they crumpled all the way to his knees. He took a step, tripped and fell head first into the wooden banister.

He pulled in a breath, exhaled vomit.

Retching over the side of the deck, he knew his white backside was exposed but for the life of him, he couldn't seem to do anything about it.

"Ewwww . . . ." came from behind him.

Nick didn't place the voice. He could only place the sarcastic tone.

Someone knelt beside him and giggled. "I can see . . . your ass."

"Then kiss it!"

Then he was alone again.

What was he doing here, anyway? He didn't know Taylor very well. It had been Ralph's idea. No, this was Chloe's birthday celebration. They'd sung to her; others had given her presents.

How long had he been here?

He couldn't be sure.

It hurt to think.

Chloe was right. He was really drunk.

But not so drunk that he didn't see the dark figure scuttling across the beach.

Closing one eye to focus better, Nick concentrated on who it might be. The air grew cooler around him. Nick took deep breaths to try to still the sense that he was going to throw up again. Wait, he told himself, wait . . . not just yet. Let me see what's happening . . .

It's Chloe!

Chloe?

Sweeping the sand with her feet, extending her arms upward, and lifting into flight —

Nick threw up again.

Between heaves, he tried to focus on Chloe . . . flying? No, that didn't make any sense.

He must have passed out then, for the next thing he knew, he was lying across Chloe's lap and she was wiping his forehead with a wad of damp paper towels.

He heard the words, "Couldn't wake him up," and lifted his head to see Chloe talking to Ralph.

"We can take him to the hospital . . . " Ralph was saying.

"He hasn't had so much to drink that he needs a hospital, I'm sure of it," she explained. "Give him a bit of time. It might be something he ate."

"No hospital," Nick whispered.

Ralph got down on a knee and clapped him on the shoulder. "Hey, buddy, you gonna make it?"

Nick groaned.

"I'll get you some water," Ralph offered.

"No, I'm . . . " His words dragged to nothing as he remembered: Chloe, flying.

"Wings?" he murmured.

"Shhh . . . ." Chloe cooed. "Try to relax. We'll leave soon, okay?"

"Okay," he murmured. And then, "Can you . . . fly?"

Chloe's face burst into an amused grin. "Why, yes, of course I can. Every genie can fly."

He just stared at her.

She ran a sharp nail over his throat. "Oh, Nick, if you only knew how vulnerable you are right now . . . "

Nick felt like he'd been sleeping on a bed of air and someone had slashed it with a razor blade.

Something told him he wasn't thinking straight. Why was it so hard to think?

"Think you'll have to go on home, buddy," Ralph said. "You'll have to wait to meet the woman later."

"Woman Bird, right?" Despite himself, Nick laughed.

When he inhaled to laugh again, he was home. In his own bed. Chloe stood with her back to him, staring out the window. She wore her coat. "You leaving?"

"Oh." She turned and went to sit beside him on the bed. "You're awake."

"What time is it?"

"Eleven."

Nick's head felt like a slug was trapped inside it. He pinched the area between his brows. "Eleven?"

"In the morning."

It seemed impossible that it could be morning already. "You took care of me last night, didn't you?"

"You remember anything of last night?"

"A bit, not too much." A dark memory tried to wiggle to the surface of his brain. Something that made him feel uneasy, like a feeling of dread. "Was I . . . difficult to handle?"

"Oh yeah." She put a hand on his chin and lightly scratched the new growth of stubble there.

"Did you meet Ralph's new girlfriend?"

"Where'd that question come from all of a sudden?" She glanced at her watch again.

"You have somewhere to go?" He didn't want her to leave. It seemed that she was always leaving him.

"Connie and I are looking at the house today. Don't you remember?"

"Oh yeah."

"You don't like Connie, do you?"

"She's okay."

"She'll make an excellent roommate," Chloe explained. "She's smart and tidy. You know she's working on a novel? One of her profs said her writing was like a diner sitting down to a buffet of words. Impressive, huh?"

"Impressive." Nick wondered briefly if Chloe compared Connie's success to his infamous D.

He sat up and leaned his head against the headboard. "Ralph's girlfriend. What's she like? Describe her."

Chloe swished her lips to one side. "Why?"

"It's Ralph," Nick continued, his voice calmer. "He gets so caught up in these girls that are no good for him. It's a guy thing to fall for beautiful women without thinking it through."

"Experience talking?" Her tone was light, but Nick heard the insecurity there.

"I fell for a beautiful woman, but Chloe, I've been thinking of us since we were kids."

She smiled and pushed her fingers through his. "If it'll make you feel better, Candice seems really nice."

"Hey." Nick touched her neck. "Where's your locket?"

Chloe glanced down and made a face. "I don't know." She felt around her shirt and looked to the floor. "It must've fallen off."

"Probably when you were asleep."

"That's weird. It had a safety catch on it. Will you look for it here?"

"Sure will."

Chloe stood up and smoothed the wrinkles in her pink blouse. "Well, I've got to get going." She giggled. "You know, last night you showed Connie your ass."

"Bet she enjoyed that," he added with a grin.

"The funny thing is, you didn't seem to have that much to drink." She shrugged and kissed him. "Who knows? Seeya later?"

"Yeah, later."

When she left, Nick tried to sleep again, but he felt too restless. That, and his head was pounding. He went downstairs, found some Tylenol, took two with apple juice. Just as he was putting the container back into the fridge, the phone rang. It was his father.

"So how was the birthday party?"

"All right," he said with a sigh.

"Son, can you come help me in the kitchen right away?"

Nick's stomach churned. The last thing he wanted to deal with this morning was dead people. He rubbed his eyes. "Can it wait?"

"It's a real mess, Nick. I've never seen anything like it. That, and I'm waiting for a phone call, too. I really could use you."

"Okay." Nick sighed. "Be there shortly."

"Oh, and do yourself a favor," Bruce added. "Wait until later to have breakfast."

chapter fourteen

There are various scents associated with death.

The smell of a body as it breaks down can be harsh, but not necessarily repugnant. There is one smell, however, that offends even the most seasoned mortician. That is the scent of liquor-induced death.

While some morticians call this foolish paranoia, others swear that when a person drinks himself to death, he carries to his grave a smell that can be likened to rotting meat.

Nick met that smell when he entered the *kitchen* of the funeral home. He pulled his head back and swallowed. "Dad?"

"In here."

Bruce was scrubbing his hands over the sink.

Behind him on the embalming table lay the body. Stats: white male about fifty, thick brown hair, large build. From his chest down, he was covered by a white sheet.

"Smell it?" Bruce gestured to the table.

"Oh yeah."

"Maybe the guy did himself a favor running headlong into a transport truck. Apparently, he'd have drunk himself to eternity pretty soon anyhow."

Bruce attached the candula — a hooked steel tube— to the rubber hose connected to the container that held the embalming fluid.

"Poor bastard lost both his arms in the wreck." He shook his head. "It's the strangest thing. There were two of 'em involved in the accident and they both lost their arms."

"There's more than one body here?"

"A lady was with him in his car."

"And they *both* lost their arms?"

Bruce rubbed at the back of his neck. "Both of 'em. At the same time. Told you, I never seen nothing like this."

"That *is* odd."

"We seem to be getting death pairs in here lately. First the two girls and now these two. It gets better. The lady in the car with him wasn't his wife."

"Oh, it's like that, is it?"

"I have a hunch. Mr. Felix's wife dropped off his good-bye suit, all upset, telling me what a good man he was. She thinks he was alone in the car."

Nick moved to the sink and scrubbed his hands. "We showing them at the same time?"

"We are. Different rooms, of course."

"Of course. Think you're up for the chore?"

"Yeah, guess so."

Truth was, Nick wondered if his stomach was up for the chore. During the best of times, he didn't care for this side of the business, though the sewing of limbs wasn't as difficult as it sounded. The arm or leg simply had to be attached enough to look good for the viewing. It was just a ghastly chore, knitting the skin together and ensuring the placement was correct.

"Okay, when we get them smelling pretty, you take the woman. Her name is Miss Jackson," Bruce instructed as he wound a green apron around his hips and tied it in back. "You can be the Avon lady, too, okay?"

Nick knew some would find it distasteful, the jokes his father made about the day-to-day duties of business. But Bruce meant no disrespect. On the contrary, his father considered theirs a noble profession.

'We're magicians,' Bruce would say. *'We give the families that last illusion of life. It's almost spiritual.'*

After the bodies were filled with embalming fluid and other preparations were made, Nick paused to drink from his thermos. Nothing like a hangover to make you feel dry.

In the smaller room of the kitchen, Nick lifted the sheet from the woman. She was a pretty woman and younger than Mr. Felix by at least a decade. Soft auburn hair fell past her shoulders and she had a cute, upturned nose that gave her a girlish appearance.

Her skin was plump and full and except for the arms missing below both elbows, Miss Jackson could almost pass for a robust woman sleeping. The clothes her family left for her included a pale blue dress, two rings — one a sapphire, the other an initial pinkie ring. Nick hoped her fingers weren't too swollen to wear them.

"Hey, Nick? Think you can handle these two on your own?" Bruce hollered out.

Nick stuck his head in the doorway of the larger room. "Why? What's up?"

"I just got the call. A family wants me to meet them at the hospital about arrangements. Be back to help as soon as I can. Is that okay?"

"Sure, go ahead. I can finish up here." The truth was, Nick's head was starting to pound again. But he didn't want to lean on an excuse as pitiful as a hangover.

When his father left, he took more Tylenol and drank the rest of his juice. He wheeled Mr. Felix's body into the back room beside the woman. It would make it easier to work on them side by side rather than running between the rooms.

Nick worked on the woman's limbs first. It was tedious work at first, but after awhile he found that his headache was completely gone and he actually enjoyed the task at hand. In fact, he felt sort of hyper, energized in a way that surprised him.

Before he realized it, Mr. Felix and his lovely companion had their limbs attached adequately for viewing and were *ready to go!*

Nick took the large cosmetics tray from the shelf and sat near the top of the man's head, in the same way a dentist might when staring down into a patient's mouth.

Mr. Felix's skin was bad and Nick mixed a little pink with the foundation to give him a bit of shine and color. Miss Jackson, however, needed little more than a dusting. Her skin must've been the envy of her friends.

Finally, the job was done. The bodies would be put in their respective coffins in the morning. Bruce would be pleased that he'd finished the job in such a timely fashion.

"Well," Nick said to the bodies. "Last chance for you two to be together. Enjoy your night." He chuckled.

He was about to close the door when he noticed that one of Miss Jackson's hands had fallen to the side. The hands were usually folded in the prayer position, but sometimes they didn't want to stay that way.

He lifted the cold hand and repositioned it. Gave it a little squeeze.

It squeezed back.

Nick's arm instinctively flailed out, making contact with the gurney. The table wobbled and the upper legs supporting it collapsed.

Miss Jackson's pudgy body spilled out and as Nick tried to catch her, they both fell to the floor. Nick landed first with Miss Jackson piling on top of him like a bad wrestling move.

Nick thought of her hand squeezing his. "Dad," he screamed. "Oh *God*!"

But of course, Bruce was gone and might not be back for the rest of the day.

Nick pushed against Miss Jackson. Her head nestled in his neck, that cold, waxy skin. Nick pushed a hand through her thick hair and yanked upward. Her head lolled and hovered above his, one open blue eye gazing down at him.

He went to slide from beneath her and dropped her head again. It smashed against his nose.

He tasted blood at the back of his throat. Assaulted by a dead woman, now who'd ever believe that?

How could she be so damn heavy?

It shouldn't be this difficult, Nick mused, to get her off him. He felt a new appreciation for the term *deadweight.*

He could smell the embalming fluid and some kind of cheap perfume from her clothes. It was an odd mixture.

Okay, Miss Jackson. Time to take control of the situation. One of his legs was free, and with a grunt of exertion, Nick kicked the leg up and jolted the rest of his body with the force. Miss Jackson slid down his body, her head landing directly in his crotch.

"Oh, gross," Nick murmured, pushing her all the way off him.

Now that he was upright, blood trickled down his face. He pinched his nostrils until he found a clean paper towel. He pushed it against his nose until the bleeding stopped. His head started to throb again.

When Nick gathered his composure, he managed to get Miss Jackson back on the gurney and fixed her hair and make-up again. He was sweating so much that his clothes stuck against his skin and his sneakered feet felt drenched and hot.

Nick replaced Miss Jackson's eye cap, a device to keep the eyes closed. How eerie it had been, to see Miss Jackson's one open eye peering down at him.

He shivered. Felt hot and cold at once.

She'd squeezed his hand; he was sure she had. He tried not to make too much of it, though. Maybe it had been something as simple as a muscle reaction. Some odd and rare occurrence that happens to newly dead people. He was sure if he told his father about it, Bruce would laugh and tell a similar story.

Only Nick knew he wouldn't tell his father.

Just in case. In case of what, he wasn't sure, but sometimes it was best to leave things alone that are not completely understood.

He glanced at Mr. Felix. At least he seemed to be behaving himself. What a crazy business this could be.

Nick stood back and examined both bodies again. They looked good. Still, he had the nagging feeling that there was something he'd overlooked, something not right.

Or maybe it was just that Nick didn't feel right. Let's not forget the correlation between the physical and the mental, he told himself.

"Hangover stuff," he told Mr. Felix. "You're lucky you'll never drink again."

Mr. Felix didn't answer.

Nick went directly to his apartment. When he pushed the key in the lock and opened the door, he heard the phone ringing.

It was Ralph.

"Hey, want to meet the woman?"

Nick hesitated.

"Well?"

He tapped the phone against his head lightly. What was the problem? Did he really think . . .

Too many things were happening at once. First Miss Jackson's hand squeeze and tackle, and now this paranoia that his best friend's new love was the crazy genie Lyra —

She's not a genie!

How many times would he have to hammer that into his brain?

Then why do I feel that she's near?

You're paranoid, O'Brien. Let it go.

"Nick?" Ralph's voice was impatient.

"Sorry. Course I want to meet her."

"Great. We're in your driveway. Be right up —"

"But now's not a good time, Ralph."

" — there in a coupla seconds."

Nick hung up and took a deep breath. Geesh, the guy could've given him time to shower the smell of death and sweat away.

Then he heard their footsteps coming up the back staircase. Ralph was saying, "Oh you'll love the guy," and a feminine little giggle followed.

Nick bit down on his lip. It was Lyra's laugh. Of course she was here, he'd sensed it, almost smelled her presence. Nothing told the truth like a gut instinct, nothing. He should never have doubted himself.

How to handle the situation, that was the issue. Should he just blurt out that he knew her? That he'd shared a wild weekend in Montreal?

Knocking at the door.

Nick watched the door, feeling almost paralyzed to move. He didn't want to see her, didn't want anything to do with her.

"Nick, gonna let me in or what?"

"Ah, just a sec." Nick went to turn the doorknob but his hand was so sweaty it slipped. Wiping his hands on his pants, he braced himself and then opened the door.

chapter fifteen

It wasn't her.

Nick closed his eyes, relieved. "Thank God," he whispered. "Not her . . ."

Ralph just stared at him. "What, man?"

"N-nothing." He gestured them inside.

Ralph's girlfriend was a petite blond with a high ponytail. She wore a bright yellow shirt and blue jeans. A pretty girl, but not nearly in the same class as Lyra.

Not Lyra.

Anything but Lyra.

"Nick?" Ralph pushed his lips together. "Nick, what's going on, man?" His tone was friendly, but they both heard the *what the hell is your problem*? there.

Nick didn't answer right away. He kept staring at Bird Woman, as if expecting that any second he'd see a sliver of evidence that proved that she was Lyra in disguise, fooling them all.

He didn't dare let down his guard completely.

"Maybe we should come back another time," she said.

Nick scratched his forehead and then ushered them inside. He forced an apologetic chuckle. "C'mon, come on in."

Ralph's expression told Nick that he was far from amused.

"This is Candice. Candice, my best friend, Nick."

"Hi, Candice." Nick shook her hand. "I'm sorry, it's just a bit of a crazy day. Have a seat."

Nick fell into the single chair and Ralph and Candice took the sofa. Nick tried not to stare at Candice. He ached for the paranoia to go away; he reminded himself again that this woman was not, could not, ever be Lyra.

"Hey, Nick," Ralph said. "You seem a bit spaced."

Nick knew he looked bad, sweaty and greasy and bloody. "Tired, is all. I was working."

Candice crossed her legs and squeezed Ralph's hand. Nick thought of how Miss Felix had squeezed his, and that one eye peering down at him —

Nick stood up quickly. "Want something to drink?"

"What happened to your face?" Ralph leaned closer. "There's blood on your lip."

Candice just stared and squirmed closer to Ralph.

"I . . . I fell . . . at the home, the funeral home. I didn't have time to shower before you showed up."

Candice leaned forward. "You work in a funeral home?"

He nodded.

"Wow." Her eyes widened and she flicked back her light hair with one hand. "Must be scary!"

"Not really." It was tempting to tell them about Miss Jackson falling on top of him, if for no other reason than that they could all have a big laugh about it. Humor was a great crutch.

"Do weird things happen?" Candice said, her eyes widening. "Weird or spooky?"

He sat down again. His head felt foggy; he blinked to try clear it. "Nah. So are you a student?"

"Yes, studying Psychology. I'm a grad student."

"She's doing her Masters," Ralph added, smiling.

Great, thought Nick. I bet she's enjoying analyzing me right now.

"I wonder what working with stiffs does to a person," Candice said. "You think it affects you?"

"Only when dead women squeeze my hand."

Candice blinked and threw an uneasy glance to Ralph. "I see," she said.

"Hey, Nick," Ralph added. "That's a weird thing to say."

"I know it," Nick agreed.

Maybe working in the funeral field wasn't right for him. Maybe it was affecting him in ways he hadn't realized until now. Maybe that's how insanity is. Maybe it's like a stalker that watches and waits for the right time, the precise moment when you're most vulnerable.

"I need to shower," Nick said, getting to his feet quickly. He knew he sounded less than hospitable, but he simply *had* to shower. Had to wash away the blood and embalming fluid and sweat and snot and tensions of the past few hours.

Ralph put his arm around the back of the couch. Candice looked down at her hands.

"Listen, a dead woman toppled out of her coffin on top of me and I can still *smell* her. I can't stand the smell . . . " His words rotted to silence.

"A dead girl?" Candice gasped.

"Not a girl, a woman," he corrected. "She landed right in my crotch. I was just relieved her arms didn't fall off since I'd just sewn them back on."

Ralph nudged Candice's knee with his own. "Maybe we'll go, Candice."

"No, I didn't mean —"

"Nick, forget it. Like you said, it's not a good time. I guess I didn't realize how true that really was." He stood up and pressed his lips together. "Nick, man, you're a mess."

Candice stepped toward the door, as if she were eager to leave. And why wouldn't she be? Anyone with two grains of sense would be wary of a man talking about the smell of dead women with sewn arms, falling into his crotch.

He opened the door and saw them out. At the bottom of the steps, he heard Candice say, "He's a bit *different*, isn't he?"

Nick closed the door and leaned against it. He felt like a jerk. But he'd told Ralph it wasn't a good time. Ralph deserved what he got. Didn't he?

He rubbed his eyes with one hand.

The phone rang again. It was a sharp sound and for a second he imagined it might be Miss Jackson calling to reprimand him for hassling her before her good-bye party.

It was Chloe. "I think we're getting the house!"

"Congrats," he said with as much enthusiasm he could muster.

"It's not far from the university. One of those row houses like I told you. Nice big windows."

"You coming over later?"

A little silence. "Is that all you care about? I tell you about the house and you just want me to come over?"

Nick sighed.

He heard Chloe cluck her tongue. "No, I'm not coming over, Nick."

"Geesh, Chloe. C'mon —"

"I just wanted to let you know." A pause and then, "Maybe the distance will do us good."

"Distance?"

"Me not living next door anymore." Her voice was thin and high.

Nick didn't answer. This talk of distance and space was like an old shoe, an old worn, uncomfortable shoe that needed to be tossed out — or burned.

"I'll let you go then, Nick."

"Chloe, it's just been a crazy day." He hoped this might soften her anger. "That's all it is."

"I've heard that before."

"Chloe . . . "

She hung up.

Nick gritted his teeth. "What a bit —" He fought the impulse to slam his fist into the wall. Instead he put the phone down with exaggerated politeness, and went to the bathroom. If he didn't shower soon, he'd be an environmental hazard.

The hell with Chloe and her nonsense. She wasn't the only one with news. *Dead woman falling* would be sure to make headlines all of their own.

Chuckling, he bunched the brown shower curtain in his fist, and scraped it open.

His smile disappeared.

Standing upright in the drain cover was a black tulip.

Identical to the tulip on the cover of *That Hurt Thing*.

As Holly Sampson drove toward the Lizard Cafe, she realized she hadn't been this excited since their courting days when Gerald would carry out the most delightfully romantic gestures. Once he'd made a heart out of Styrofoam and painted it pink and hung it in the front lobby of the apartment where she lived.

I love you, Toots! read the caption.

It had been just outrageous enough to be sexy, and oh how endearing. What Gerald lacked in other areas, he certainly made up for in unpredictability.

When she first met Gerald, she'd been dating Ernie, an electrician with enough charisma to power religion.

Ernie was built, oh was he built.

The man with a stomach like a slatted blind, had laughed when he became aware of the competition: suspender wearer Dr. Gerald Sampson. Ernie had called Gerald an egg. It was the closest he'd come to a witticism.

How many times had Holly wished that she could blend both egg and tool belt. Alas, it was not to be, and when Ernie said he didn't like books without at least *a few* pictures, she sighed and went to Gerald's bed.

From Gerald's bed to Gerald's house. Her status moved quickly from lover to girlfriend to wife. It was a comfortable fit, the two of them. Oh, the last few years had been a little, shall we say, bland, but Gerald was changing all that. She should have known he would.

His *dressing up* was as much an aphrodisiac as the day he'd wrapped himself in tinfoil. Oh, Gerald. Oh, oh Gerald. How lucky I am.

She spotted the Lizard Cafe and slowed. Gerald had said the place was eclectic. Did eclectic include a smashed glass front door and panhandlers not a block away? Her mood dampened. Was it even safe to walk in this neighborhood?

She pulled the car onto a side road and parked. Gerald would be at the cafe soon, just as they'd planned. It wasn't late, only about eight o'clock. She'd read somewhere that violent crime happened between ten and two a.m. Yes, she'd be fine, just fine.

It was difficult to walk in the black six inch heels she'd chosen for Gerald. For their first night out as *the girls*.

Holly would arrive first and later Gerald would show up as Loly — she'd chosen the sassy name herself. They'd make eye contact and she'd ask Loly to join her.

What happened after that would be anyone's guess.

Holly flicked the short hem of the black suede skirt against her thighs. The white tee shirt she wore was too, too tight. Her feet ached. She wasn't used to dressing this slutty, but it had been Gerald's request and maybe a little slutty did a marriage good.

Or is he setting me up to get attacked in this neighborhood? she wondered resentfully. Is that what the girls' night out is all about?

The cafe came into view and she quickly crossed the street toward it. She told herself not to sulk, not to let her discomfort ruin the evening. She recalled her initial excitement about this scheme. This *would* be a good evening.

Inside the cafe, she ordered a coffee — with cream — that's what Gerald told her. Order coffee with cream and sit at the table facing the door.

Only the table near the door was taken. A young woman with long black hair sat there holding a cigarette between her fingers and looking indifferent as beige.

The cafe was smoky and congested and for an instant Holly felt as if she were a ghost moving among the patrons, as unnoticed as cream when it dissolves into coffee.

Then the young woman with the cigarette patted the seat beside her. "You want to sit here?"

Holly hesitated.

Gerald wouldn't like it if he found her sitting with another woman; he might even be jealous. But what could she do, there were no other tables available.

"I'm waiting for someone . . . "

"Then sit until he arrives. I'll probably be gone by then anyhow." The woman shrugged and hauled on the cigarette. "But suit yourself."

"Thank you." Holly sat and sipped the coffee; her lipstick stained the edge of the white cup. She wiped at it with her thumb.

"Busy spot here," Holly said.

"Yeah. You want a cigarette?"

"No."

"What's your name?" She extended her hand. "I'm Precious."

Holly couldn't help but laugh. "That's your name, really?"

"Something wrong with it?"

"No, no." They shook hands. Precious' hand was cool and soft. "It's just different."

"Lots of things are different."

Holly agreed. And then, "How'd you know I was waiting for a man? You said, when *he* arrives."

Precious grinned. She had the prettiest eyes, so green and wide. "Just makes sense."

Then Holly remembered that Gerald wasn't a man. Not tonight. She cleared her throat. "Only I'm . . . not meeting a man. It's a woman. She's my friend, best friend. Loly."

"Loly. That's a different name, too."

"Yes. Different."

"He, ah, she's late, though. Not like Loly."

"Some women like to be fashionably late," Precious added with a sneer. "It makes them feel important or something to make others just *wait* around like the world has absolutely *nothing* better to do."

"I'm sure she'll be here soon," Holly said, feeling a little defensive. If she didn't know better, she'd swear this Precious was waiting for Gerald herself. She chuckled inwardly; yeah, like Gerald would have *anything* to do with a cheap girl named Precious.

The waitress stopped at their table and without asking, refilled both cups, her long saggy arm stretching past them.

Half an hour had passed. Holly began to feel angry.

"Sure this is the right place?" Precious suggested.

"The Lizard Cafe."

"Sure it wasn't the Wizard Cafe?"

"There's such a thing?"

"Sure is." Precious nodded. "On this street, too. It's a nicer place, actually. This place is okay, but a bit of a dive compared to the Wizard."

Of course! She should have known Gerald wouldn't want to meet at a spot such as this one. "On this street, you say?"

"This is a long street, though, and it's kinda tucked away. I'm not real good with directions. But hey, why don't I take you there? I was about to go there myself."

Holly thought about the suggestion. Leaving with a stranger was never a good idea and if Precious had been a man, she'd not for one second consider it. But really, how dangerous was this slip of a girl? More times than not, men were the predators of society.

Holly got to her feet, nodding. "Sure, let's go. We can drive in my car."

"Glad I can help. Too bad your best friend has to make things difficult."

Precious threw her cigarette to the floor and stamped on it with the heel of her shoe. "I really hate it when people make things difficult."

chapter sixteen

Gerald kicked the tire of the Explorer. "Hell!"

Of all the times for the jeep not to start. He glanced at his watch. Holly would've been waiting at the cafe for almost forty-five minutes.

He wished he were more mechanically inclined. More like jock Ernie had been, he scoffed.

He lifted the hood and stared down hoping that something might jump out like a loose wire or missing cap — or a jeep fairy pointing out the trouble, but all he saw was a bunch of unfamiliar wires and metal.

He slammed the hood shut and leaned against the Explorer. He went to scratch his face when he remembered his make-up.

Grabbing the cell phone from the holder inside the jeep, Gerald dialed Holly's cell phone. No answer. Just a recorded announcement that the customer didn't have their phone turned on. He thought of Holly again; he'd have to take a cab.

Which was risky, as he'd have to walk to the driveway and take the chance that the neighbors might see him.

He unlocked the door leading to the house and went inside. Holly's perfume still lingered in the air. "Sorry, Toots," he whispered.

The cab would be there in fifteen minutes, the dispatcher told Gerald. Gerald used the bathroom and then stood in front of the mirror. Tonight he'd pulled out all his tricks.

He and Holly had shopped earlier in the week, and together they'd chosen a complete outfit for him. Holly had exquisite fashion sense. She'd recommended a peach dress that fell in soft pleats to his ankles and a string of pearls to flatter the V-shaped neckline. He wore a floppy white hat that softened his features, and Holly had shown him how to apply lipstick so that it didn't bleed.

"You're a snaaaake!" he informed the reflection in the mirror. But this evening, his declaration didn't have the same sting. All he could think of was Holly sitting in the cafe in that grungy part of town. Sitting there drinking her coffee with cream and wondering where the heck he was.

He considered calling the cafe when the phone rang. He grabbed for it. It was Holly.

"Gerald, where are you?"

"Home. The jeep wouldn't start. I called a cab."

"You on your way then?"

"Be there shortly. I called your phone earlier."

"I turned it off, sorry." She laughed. "Want me to swing by and get you?"

"No, don't bother. The cab'll be here any sec."

"Just as well, I went to the wrong place. I'm on my way to the Wizard now."

Static broke the connection for a moment. "Toots?"

"Sorry, Gerald. I'll meet you there, okay? I have someone with me . . . "

Had he heard right? "Someone with you?"

"A nice young girl who's showing me how to get to the Wizard." Holly spoke to someone else for a moment just as he heard the cab's horn sounding in the driveway.

"Toots, you did say The Lizard, right?"

The phone crackled again. "It's dying," she hollered. "Love you."

Gerald rushed outside and folded into the back seat of the cab. He gave the address. The cab driver watched him in the rearview mirror. "Nice weather we got, eh?"

Gerald nodded and turned away. He thought about Holly again. It had been an odd conversation and he wasn't sure he'd heard or understood it correctly.

He knew it was risky, meeting at the Lizard Cafe where he'd had that horrible experience with Nicole. But the risk was worth it; what were the odds that she'd be there anyhow?

Past that thought was another more snug thought. If Nicole were there, she'd see him with Holly, beautiful Holly. It would be his way of saying, *See, this lovely woman is my wife. See, I* am *a good person . . .*

If she tried to confront them, Holly would take his side over that evil slattern. She'd understand. They were a team; he never felt more sure of anything.

Holly had said a nice young girl was helping her find the cafe. Now that he had a chance to think about it, that was rather odd, wasn't it?

What a coincidence that Holly should mess up the address and someone would be right there to help. Maybe someone who wanted a little fun —

"Dear heavens, no!"

The driver turned down the radio. "Something wrong?"

"You have a cell phone?" Gerald forgot to add his womanly voice. The cabbie frowned in the rearview mirror.

Gerald leaned ahead. "Well?"

"No cell phone, sorry."

"Just hurry!"

"We're just about there. You forget something?"

"No, I just remembered." He pushed his hand against his forehead. "I just remembered something very, very bad."

The car slowed and Gerald could see through the glass window that Holly wasn't at the Lizard Cafe.

He asked the driver to wait while he went inside.

"Was there a lady here?" he interrupted the waitress behind the counter who was about to take an order from two men. "Blond woman, so tall . . . "

"That could be one of a thousand people, *sir*."

Hearing the word sir made him realize that he was still dressed up. God, how he must look. The two men exchanged an amused look.

"It's important, please. She might've been sitting with a dark haired girl, pretty girl, smoking a cigarette —"

"Wait now." The waitress rubbed her flabby upper arms and tilted her head. A dark lop of hair fell across her face and she batted it back. "Sitting right by the door."

"Yes, that's right, by the door."

"They left."

"Together?"

"Uh huh.

Gerald cursed.

"Sir?"

Gerald left and climbed in the back seat of the taxi. "Take me back home."

"Home? That was quick."

Gerald didn't answer. All he could think about was Holly.

Nicole might do nothing more than scare Holly, or suggest they go to a sex garage, or ask for money, but Gerald wasn't taking any chances, not when Toots was involved. He'd call the police and have them track her car.

The cab pulled into his driveway; Gerald pushed a wad of bills over the seat.

The driver snatched them up. "Thanks. Good luck with your problem." He gestured to Gerald's dress. "And . . . uh, so is this like a joke or something?"

"Yeah, that's it." He slammed the door shut and sprinted across the lawn, his dress flapping in the wind. It was amazing how well he could run in his heels. "Just one big joke."

"Sing to me, Holly."

Holly made a face across the car seat toward Precious. "Sing?"

"I like it when people sing to me. Is that a bad thing?"

"I'm more interested in finding the cafe. We've been driving for a while now."

Holly tried to keep the irritation out of her voice. It seemed that Precious didn't know the way as well as she'd indicated. That, and the girl was getting on her nerves.

"We're almost there now. I feel it."

"You said that fifteen minutes ago."

"If you sing, I'll be able to think better."

Holly gripped the steering wheel. "I don't have a very good voice."

"Try me, Toots."

Holly swallowed. "What did you call me? T-toots?"

"Yeah. You just seem like a Toots. Ya know, cute and kinda innocent. Not a bit difficult."

"That . . . that's what my husband calls me."

Precious threw up her hands. "What an *absolute* coincidence! Now sing. A few bars and I'm sure the directions will suddenly come clear."

Holly cleared her throat. "Ah . . . 'You are my sunshine —'"

"Not that one! Something a little more sassy."

"Sassy?"

They stopped at a four way stop intersection. Holly wondered if they should turn or go straight, but it was obvious Precious was going to be of precious little help. "I don't know any songs like that."

Precious twirled a strand of her black hair between her fingers and let out a long sigh. "No naughty song, no directions to the Wizard."

Holly tried to think of a song that Precious might find naughty. "I don't believe I'm doing this."

"That's how people are. They do things they think they'd never do. Adventures." Precious giggled. "Think of it like a girls' night out."

Holly's hands began to sweat. She rolled down the window, grateful for the little wind on her face. There was a song she used to sing to Gerald when they were first married. Should she sing part of it?

"No," she decided aloud. "I'm not singing. How about I drive you back to the Lizard and I'll just find my own way?"

"That's not very adventurous of you."

"I'm not in the mood for adventure. I'm meeting my . . . my friend."

"Okay then," Precious said with a long sigh. "Have it your way."

"You'll show me the way now?"

"Sure, I can do that."

"Good." A chuckle. "I was beginning to think you were stringing me along."

"Okay, keep driving."

"Is it far?"

"Not really. A bit out of the way, is all." Precious slumped against the seat and looked out the side window.

They traveled in silence, which suited Holly just fine. Precious was an odd woman and just the sound of her voice made her uncomfortable.

She hoped Gerald hadn't been waiting long at the cafe. She pictured him sitting with his coffee, the long peach dress flowing around him. It was just the right color for Gerald. Oh, oh, Gerald, you are my original man.

"Should I be turning soon, Precious?"

"Yes. Soon."

"Thought you said it was on the same street as the Lizard Cafe?"

"I lied."

Holly chewed the skin along the inside of her lip. "Lied? Why'd you do that?"

"We were at the right cafe, all along, Holly. Holly Sampson."

They were stopped at a streetlight when Precious called her by name. When the car behind sounded its horn, Holly zipped through the intersection. "How . . . how do you know my name?"

"Because it's Gerald's last name and I know Gerald, Holly. I know Gerald real well."

Holly didn't know what to say. Precious knew her Gerald? Had Gerald . . . been cheating?

She looked at Precious, saw her in the eyes of any man, saw the tight skin and pinched waist and long legs. Holly felt her composure begin to crumble.

"Holly, see the old wheat factory there?" She pointed. "Drive behind it and we'll talk."

Holly did as she was told. "Suddenly you know where everything is in the city," she said blandly.

"Pass me your phone."

"I turned it off."

"Good. That's real good." Precious punched in a number and held the phone up to Holly's ear. "I'm calling your house —"

"Gerald's not home," she said.

"Oh, I have a hunch he is, Toots. Ask him if he knows a Nicole."

"Your real name."

"Clever."

Gerald picked up on the first ring. "Holly?"

"Do you know a Nicole?" she said right away. "A girl named Nicole?"

Gerald paused, one of those pauses that say too much within a marriage.

"Answer me, Gerald!"

"Holly, you've got to listen carefully to me right now —"

"Is it true?" She screamed into the phone.

"Yes, I know her and that's why I'm telling you to listen . . . "

Precious took the phone away. Gerald was still talking when Precious said into the receiver, "You're a freak, Gerald. Bye, freak."

She turned to Holly, put her hand over hers. "Park right there behind the grain house, Toots. And then I'll tell you what kind of a slime bag you married." She took a deep breath. "A slime bag that seduces girls half his age."

chapter seventeen

Nick stared down at the tulip.

"*That Hurt Thing*," he murmured between gritted teeth.

Surprisingly, finding the flower wasn't as upsetting as he would have thought. Maybe because the past twenty-four hours had numbed him and feeling *anything* would've been a challenge.

Crouching, he plucked the flower from the drain and felt the velvety black petals. It was a beautiful flower, as far as flowers went.

"Lyra!" he shouted. "Lyra, are you here?"

A knocking at the door served as an answer.

Standing quickly, Nick cracked the stem in half, stuffed it in the garbage can and answered the door.

He let Paula inside.

"Whoa, you look bad," she exclaimed. "Did I hear you talking to someone?"

"What do you want?"

She moved past him and looked around; she hunched her shoulders. "Something . . . weird here," she said.

"Yeah, *you*. Ah, c'mon, Paula. Don't give me that psycho junk —"

"It's psych*ic*," she corrected. "Then again, your apartment always gave me the creeps. Bad vibes or something . . . "

"So what do you want?"

"Dad's downstairs if you need to talk to him. He said to tell you, that's all."

Nick stood with the door ajar. He leaned on the doorknob and thought about Miss Jackson. "I forget to do something?"

"Not that he mentioned."

"Paula, I'm about to get in the shower."

Her focus went to the floor and up again. "It's Brad."

"I'm not following this conversation, Paula."

"H-he threatened to break up with me."

Nick's first reaction was to call it a blessing. Instead, he said, "Why would he say that?"

Paula crossed the room to the sofa and slowly sat down, her hands between her knees. "He said I'm too immature. That I don't . . . " She took a breath. "Go against the grain."

"Against the grain?"

"That I'm too normal."

"Paula, no offense, but you read Tarot Cards and your family's in the funeral business. I'd hardly call that normal."

She chewed on her knuckles. "You think I'm immature?"

"You're sixteen, Paula. Of course you're immature. And what's this going against the grain stuff? Is he into this odd free love and anarchy head space?"

"Yes, I think so."

Nick shook his head. "Paula, you're too smart for this."

"I'm not that smart. Not like you."

"Stop putting yourself down, okay?" He hated the way she did that, stomped all over herself.

She let her head loll back against the sofa. "What am I going to do, Nick?"

"Call his bluff. Tell him if he doesn't like you the way you are, then . . . " He held up his middle finger. "Give him the universal sign."

"Nick. It's just not that easy . . . " Her face wrinkled and then she sobbed into her hands.

Oh God. How to deal with this? "Paula, listen . . . maybe you'll work it out. Talk to him, see what's in his head."

What a hypocrite I am, he thought. I just want her to stop crying and leave so I can deal with the tulip that was stuffed in my shower drain.

Paula wiped her face with the back of her hand. "Is it because he drives a cab? That why you don't like him?"

"Partly," Nick admitted, leaning closer. "I don't think he's good enough for you. Don't you ever feel that way?"

"No."

"You're sixteen; he's nineteen and even you said he drinks too much."

"I know . . . but I love him, Nick."

Nick could never understand how women tolerated all kinds of crap with the *but, I love him* excuse. That was the stuff talk shows were made of. *Woman hung by thumbs by husband, comes to his defense at trial.*

She wiped her nose. "Maybe I'll call Chloe. Think Chloe will talk to me about it?"

"I'm sure she will." He patted her knee. "It'll all be okay, Paula."

"Thanks. For an annoying older brother, you're acting pretty nice."

"Don't get used to it." He winked.

Paula hesitated. "Is . . . is there something bothering you, too?"

He shook his head.

"You don't seem yourself lately."

"I'm fine." He gestured to the door with his chin. "Anyhow, you'd better try to catch Chloe before she goes out again."

"Right." She stood up. "You sure you're fine?" she said again.

"Yeah, sure."

When Paula left, Nick locked the door behind her, relieved to be alone. He thought of Paula's words, that he didn't seem himself. Was it true? Was he acting differently? Even Chloe had mentioned it.

Sure he felt strung out lately, but he was the same Nick who'd walk ten miles to stand in Chloe's garbage.

You slapped her, remember? You said there was a maggot on her cheek. And let's talk about Montreal — were you thinking of Chloe when you were in bed doing the nasty with Lyra?

No fair. If Chloe wasn't such a cold fish, I wouldn't have to . . .

The thought wouldn't permit itself to be completed.

No one forced him to sleep with Lyra. And now that he had, it felt like he'd spend God knows how long paying for it.

Like the freaky dreams, like the black tulip.

Maybe I should tell her about Lyra, he considered. *Tell her everything.*

As freeing as the consideration was, it also gave him fear. Fear that he might lose her. Like he'd lost his mother . . .

That's a peculiar thought, he noted.

And while he didn't know exactly where the thought came from, he did know that times like these he would've liked to had his mother to talk to, to advise him, to tell him that things would all work out.

Because he wasn't so sure anymore.

Things were getting more and more surreal. It was getting harder to explain the odd occurrences, like the black tulip for one. Just the fact that the book had shown up after he'd left it in Montreal was reason enough to question what the hell was happening to him.

Could it get any worse?

He didn't dare let his brain even try answer that one.

"So he seduced you, my Gerald seduced you?" Holly couldn't even think of it. She cut the engine of the car and leaned her head against the steering wheel.

"I'm afraid so." Nicole lit a cigarette and sucked at it greedily. "Of course, at the time I didn't realize he was married. He told me his wife had died."

"Died?"

"Pathetic, isn't it? Just goes to prove that you can only trust your mother and your dog."

Holly swished her tongue around her dry mouth. This evening had started with such promise. She glanced to Nicole, imagined that young, hard body beneath Gerald's, saw Gerald happily panting and sweating.

"So what happened?"

Nicole waved a hand. "Let it go, Holly. It'll just upset you. But I couldn't with good conscience let him get away with this kind of slime-ball activity. I had to tell you."

"But how did you even know who I was?"

Nicole's mouth quivered. The poor thing, this must be difficult for her, too. Gerald may be an egg, but he was kind and funny. Even young gorgeous women weren't immune to his charms.

"I knew it was you because . . . " She hauled on the cigarette and sighed as she exhaled. "He told me he was bringing you to the cafe. See, that was *our* meeting place."

Holly put a hand over her mouth. Could Gerald be this cruel? "But why would he bring his wife and mistress together?"

"Kink. Pure kink. He gets off on that sort of stuff. He didn't think I'd tell you. He . . . he threatened me. Threatened to . . . hurt me real bad. But when I saw you there alone, I knew it was my chance. My chance to make up for inadvertently — isn't that a big word? — hurting you?"

Gerald threatening violence seemed like a cartoon, a caricature of the man she'd known for so long, and she dared to consider that Nicole might be lying. Maybe she was a student of his and had fallen in love with him.

Holly turned to Nicole. "I-I just don't know what to think, Nicole, or if I . . . even should believe you."

Nicole's lips jerked into a half smile and she sucked in a quick breath. "*Should* believe me?" She fumbled for another cigarette. "You think I'd lie about a freak like Gerald just for kicks?"

"He's not a freak —"

"He wears pantyhose, a dress!" Nicole lit a match and hunched her shoulders forward to light the cigarette. "You think that's *normal?*"

"I . . . I don't know."

"Stupid, *stupid*!"

They were quiet for a few moments; Holly listened to the sounds of Nicole huffing on her cigarette and the cry of seagulls and the sloshing of the ocean against the shoreline.

She was suddenly aware of how isolated they were behind the abandoned grain factory. The buildings loomed in the black sky; an excellent divider between them and the city. A perfect hiding place — if they wanted to hide.

Holly felt a shudder along her spine. She touched the keys in the ignition, turned them.

Nicole's head jerked her way, black hair flicking across her shoulders. "What're you doing?"

"I want to go home."

"Not until we're finished. Don't you want to know about your husband?"

"It's not true, is it?"

"It's true. It's *true*."

"What's this all about?" Holly touched the gear shift, studied it. "Really all about?"

The car's engine died. Nicole held up the keys, wagged them between her fingers. "I said not until we're finished."

"Wh-what else is there to do?"

Nicole put down the window and flicked the cigarette out. They watched the tiny ember throb against the ground and die.

She turned back to Holly. "You're making it difficult. I don't like that."

"What else do you want? Could you want?"

"I made a promise to someone very dear to me. I take my promises very seriously —"

"Gerald didn't sleep with you, did he? Are you in love with him, is that it?"

Nicole made a face. "The guy's a dolt. A round, boring *nothing*. In love with him? Sick."

"You're not answering my question." Holly glanced at the phone on the seat between them. She slowly moved her hand toward it. "Nicole, I think something's bothering you. I can help you."

"Help me?" Nicole slapped her knee and chuckled. "That's pretty funny —"

"Let me help you. We can . . . be friends. Would you like that? Do you have many friends?"

Holly wished Gerald could hear her now. He'd be impressed by how she was getting the upper hand here. He always said she was too passive and sweet.

"I don't have any friends . . . " Nicole whispered. "You don't know how lonely it is."

"Oh, Nicole . . . " Her hand touched the edge of the phone. "I'm here for you."

"But what kind of a friend would you be?"

"Ah . . . a *good* friend, I suppose."

"You suppose?"

She grasped the phone. Nicole didn't seem to notice. "We can do things together, you know, coffee shops — not the Lizard though — and go to movies, walks along the Shubie Canal, even see an opera . . . you like opera?"

Nicole made a face.

"Give it a chance." Holly twisted the phone in her palm. She reached her middle finger toward the Talk button. Just a little further . . .

"Opera's . . . very passionate," Holly continued. "I think you might like it."

"I'm a little under-cultured."

Holly coughed and pressed the Talk button at the same time. She didn't want Nicole to hear the sharp bleep. "That doesn't matter," she said. "Doesn't matter one bit."

Her fingers fumbled over the number keys.

"Orchestra right."

"What?"

"Since you're making reservations." Nicole yanked the phone away and dropped it out the window. "Holly, Holly, Holly. What're you *doing?*"

"Okay, Nicole. Just take it easy, okay? Easy and nice and calm."

"Like friends?"

"Like friends."

Tears shimmered in Nicole's eyes. "You promise?"

"Y-yes, I promise." Her stomach burned.

Nicole pressed one hand against her heart. "I'm so very glad we're friends."

"M-me, too."

Nicole opened her arms and tilted her head. "Hug to seal it? Seal our friendship?"

Holly reached across the seat and put her arms around Nicole. She felt small and childlike in her embrace. Something like cinnamon met her nostrils. "There, there, isn't that better now —"

Her words halted when she felt something cool against her stomach. Cool and sharp and unexpected.

She went to pull back but Nicole clung to her, hugged her harder. And harder.

And harder.

And then Holly Sampson felt nothing.

Nothing at all.

chapter eighteen

The darkness was sweet and welcoming, as Nick folded into the flannel sheets and let his body relax with one full breath.

The familiar clunking of the furnace as it cut in was a reassuring sound. As was a soft rain that gently massaged the window pane.

He felt better.

Usually it would be depressing to be alone on a Saturday evening. But he needed a night to recover. He'd consumed only water since the morning; his stomach was thankful. Maybe that's why he felt so crazy lately; maybe he'd been simply exhausted and battling a flu bug.

If he were to get into medical school next fall, he had to be at the top of his graduating class. There was no more time to dilly-dally and worry about feeling crazy.

First period Monday morning was chemistry. He'd fallen behind there, too. He made a note that after this weekend, he'd pull himself together, pull his life together.

And the black tulip in the shower drain?

Nick hugged the pillow and took a deep breath. He couldn't figure that one out. There. He'd admitted it. He didn't know, might never know. He'd been so convinced that Lyra had followed him from Montreal, but now that seemed like a crazy, if not an arrogant, idea.

Nick closed his eyes and imagined that he was throwing the flower away, throwing it from the top of a high rock cliff. He saw it in his mind's eye as it floated away, far away, away from anything that could touch him . . .

Let it go, Nick. Let it all go . . .

His leg jerked as he hovered along the edge of sleep.

Then he was awake again.

Without knowing why. He lay on his back, his arms folded beneath his head, ankles crossed. The house was quiet and dark and peaceful.

He thought of the flower again, and that thought led to pondering how the book had been at the top of the stairs that day, even though he'd just told himself that the *how* didn't matter anymore —

That Hurt Thing.

Climbing out of bed, Nick went to the kitchen, opened the fridge door and squinted inside. He located the jar of juice and reached for it, then decided his stomach needed only water. He ran the tap and filled a glass.

His stomach gurgled from lack of food. Tomorrow he'd eat a big breakfast. Bacon and eggs, a bagel smeared with butter, hot coffee, maybe even a bit of fruit.

Yawning, he closed the fridge door and returned to bed. The muscles in his shoulders and back ached; he arched a shoulder and pushed it against the bed.

He felt himself relax again.

He was so tired . . .

Images flickered beneath his lids. Pleasant images; images of him and Paula as children running in the field behind their house; images of eating gooey candy apples at the summer fair — *"Master?"*

Nick's head snapped up like a puppet's. He sat up, fists clenching the sheets. He held his breath, waiting. Was he imagining things?

There, by the dresser. A black form staring back at him. But no, it was just his coat thrown over the corner of the mirror. He took a deep breath.

But then the coat moved, and Lyra came to sit beside him on the bed. "Master," she said. "You're going to be so very pleased."

Nick squinted in the darkness. It was so dark he could only make out her form, and the long black hair tumbling down her shoulders. He inhaled Lyra's scent, that musky cinnamon scent that even now tormented him. "H-how the hell you get in here?"

A giggle.

"Turn on the lamp," he ordered.

"As you wish."

Soft light fell over them and reached furtively toward the corners of the room. Despite himself, Nick's first thought was how lovely Lyra was. He stared at her.

She touched his arm. "Oh, Nick, it is good to see you."

When he didn't respond, she lowered her head and frowned. "Nick, this isn't much of a greeting."

"How'd you find me?"

"I know you."

She sat cross-legged on the bed. The black dress hiked up to her thighs; Nick intentionally kept his eyes focused on her face.

"Tell me how you got here."

"What does it matter?"

Nick scratched a hand through his hair. He'd forgotten how she evaded his questions, and how frustrating it was.

"Answer me."

"I took the bus, okay?"

"Genie cutbacks?"

Lyra frowned. "Are you finished now?"

"If you're a genie, why would you take the bus? Wouldn't it be easier to just . . . " He shrugged. "I don't know, transport yourself or fly?"

"Nick," she explained. "Part of being who I am is enjoying being human when I feel the need."

"I don't understand."

"I took the bus because I could. That's all. I have lots of earthly hobbies, just because."

"Hobbies?"

"Sure. I'm very interested in . . . " She ran a finger over her lips. "In medicine."

That had to be the craziest thing Nick had ever heard. Lyra, the genie, interested in medicine. "So let me guess. You're thinking of following me to medical school?" He laughed.

She just looked at him.

"Did you put the book at the top of the stairs?"

"Yes.

"And the tulip in the shower?"

"Yes."

"So you've been in Halifax for a while?"

"Yes."

"Why the wait? Why not come to me the moment you arrived?"

"Because until now I was unworthy."

Nick bunched part of the blanket between his knees. What kind of nonsense was this? "Unworthy?"

"I want to fulfill your every desire. And I will. One at a time. And then," she whispered. "I'll be free."

"That makes no sense."

"It will, very soon. I assure you."

Nick leaned forward. "Hey, is that dried blood on your shoulder?"

She pulled back and touched the line of her shoulder blade. "I scratched myself. Just a scratch." She threw back her head; her black hair rippled down her back. "Do you worry about me, Nick?"

She shifted from a sitting to a kneeling position, causing the dress to hike upward. Nick felt himself becoming aroused. Lyra's like a drug, he decided. An addictive drug. Just seeing her made him ache. "Lyra," he said. "This whole scene is just really weird, ya know."

"I understand how scary it must be." She drew a circle with her finger over his arm. "I really do."

"Do you? Do you know lately I feel like I'm going crazy? I thought I saw a maggot in Chloe's eye. Was that true, do you know?"

Lyra shrugged.

"I slapped her. Slapped Chloe. Of all the people in the world . . . "

"She makes you angry, doesn't she?"

"God, yes."

"She takes you for granted, edges you on, hot and cold and rarely in between."

"Yes!" Part of him felt guilty to be discussing Chloe — and with Lyra, of all people. But damn, it was good for the moment to hear someone else state the obvious, acknowledge what he was going through.

"Women don't like a man they can walk over, Nick. Let's face it, she's got you wrapped around her finger. There's no challenge there."

"So it's my fault?"

"You just have to understand women, my friend."

"It's easier to teach women to parallel park than to understand them."

Lyra smirked and then laughed. "I can't help but like your wit."

Nick, too, laughed. "Oh, Lyra. Everything is crazy."

"I know," she agreed. "But it'll all be okay. I promise."

Nick threw up his hands. "Sometimes I wish Chloe would just get with it, decide that yes, she wants me or no, she doesn't and just go away for good, leave me the hell alone."

Lyra touched his arm. "I'm sorry you're upset. Shall I rub your feet?"

He shook his head. Her hand on his forearm felt good, too good. He was falling into her spell again. He gently pushed her hand away.

"You have your family," she reminded him. "That has to count, Nick."

"Yeah, my father who may as well be a priest and my little sister who loves this . . . this absolute loser, this Brad." He made a fist and gritted his teeth. "I care about her so much and . . . hell, Lyra. I'd just like to smash the guy. Smash the life right out of him, and isn't that terrible to admit?"

"Nick, calm down. You're making yourself upset."

She smiled again and touched his hand. This time, he didn't remove it.

What was he doing, telling his problems to Lyra? But she was so easy to be around, so comfortable and exciting and attentive.

"How about you let me take care of you for a while?"

Nick imagined Chloe saying those words. It seemed so often in life that the wrong people said the right things.

"I'm fine."

"No, you're not. You've got so much on your shoulders. I see it. I'm here now, Nick. I'll help."

"Lyra. Listen, you should go back from wherever you came from —"

"Go back?" She chuckled and flicked back her hair. "But it's only just begun."

"You know it freaks me out when you say that."

"Oh, Nick, don't be so serious."

She touched both his arms with her hands, her soft, cool hands. His eyes closed and he took a deep breath. "Nick," she whispered. "Nick, I missed how *good* we are together."

"Lyra, I don't think —"

"Then don't. Don't think." Her hands traveled from his arms to the bareness of his chest; he winced with pleasure. God, he wanted her. Past reason, past sanity, he wanted to feel that lithe body beside his, wanted her to make him feel good again, important again, a man again in the way only she could.

Bad love. This is bad love . . .

He didn't care.

Nick pulled her into his arms and beneath the blankets. His hands groped her, gathered her closer, pushed between her legs.

"Release control," Lyra whispered harshly as she helped Nick peel her dress away. "Just let go, Master. Just *let go . . .* "

Nick welcomed the blackness, welcomed just letting go.

Just letting go.

chapter nineteen

When the alarm blared Nick awake the following morning, he saw that Lyra was gone and *That Hurt Thing* was propped open against the pillow.

His first thought was that of Lyra wading in the thick slimy swamp to retrieve the book. He grinned. She was nothing if not determined. Wiping sleep out of one eye, he reached for the book, laid it across his lap and wondered what creative foolery Lyra might have added this time.

He saw a picture, well drawn, too, of a naked woman lying on a bed of black tulips. The nude woman resembled Lyra in that she was thin and lovely, but this woman was on fire. Was the fire a metaphor for the heat of last night? Her way of saying good-bye?

He certainly hoped so. Last night had been wild and addictive, but still, Nick just wanted to have his life back to normal again.

He turned the page. Black. That's odd, thought Nick. An entire page made black by what seemed to be marker. The next page was the same.

And the next.

And the next.

He licked his thumb and was about to turn the next page when he heard the back door open and close and then a shuffling of feet across the floor.

He tucked the book beneath his bed and lay down again.

His blue boxer shorts lay crumpled on the floor beside the bed. Nick pulled them beneath the covers and closed his eyes as if he were asleep. He could still smell Lyra on his skin; had she returned for one last *celebration?*

Only it wasn't Lyra.

It was Chloe.

She put one knee on the bed and shook it with her leg. "Nick, wake up. C'mon, wake up. We need to talk."

"I'm awake." Nick propped the pillow behind his head. "What's so important that you've got me up on a Sunday morning?" His voice could be friendlier, he supposed, but it felt good for once, not immediately deferring to her.

Chloe glanced about the room. Nick felt himself growing nervous. He'd been careful to flush the evidence last night. Still, he clamped down on his back teeth and said, "W-what're you looking for?"

"Nothing, I guess. Can I sit down?"

"Let's go in the living room," he said, pulling on his bathrobe. "We can make breakfast together. Would you like that?"

She agreed.

While he added coffee to a paper filter and poured water in the back of the coffee maker, Chloe made toast and put a bottle of strawberry jam on the table.

It was the regular routine so many mornings. Him making the coffee; Chloe burning the toast. The familiarity between them was comfortable — a comfort he'd come to count on.

"So . . . you talked to Paula, that was nice," he said. "How is she?"

Chloe licked a smear of jam from her finger. She had tied her hair back and Nick thought of Anne of Green Gables. Anne with an *'e'*. "She'll be fine. She's planning on going to see Brad, though."

"I can't understand that girl."

The coffee bubbled into the glass carafe, the fresh scent filling the kitchen. "So, what did you want to talk about?"

"Us."

"Us?" Nick's stomach did a flip. This could be very good or this could be very, *very* bad.

He poured two cups of coffee and sat at the table beside her. Downstairs he could hear someone moving about. He took a bite of his toast; it felt dry in his mouth and he swallowed it down with a gulp of coffee.

"Do you remember when we were kids and I was fooling around and pushed you in the swamp?"

"Yeah." He nodded. "I cut my foot on a piece of glass."

"You didn't tell your mother that I pushed you. You said you tripped. You got grounded for walking around in bare feet, and I went to the fair without you."

"Boy, I was mad at you."

She pressed her lips together. "That day, I realized what a good friend you are. I never forgot that."

She looked down at her hands. "Nick, when Connie and I went to see the house, I thought of not living next to you like I have all these years and . . . "

Her blue eyes lowered. "When I thought of not being with you, I . . . well . . . Nick, do you still . . . want to try?"

It took a moment for Nick to understand what she was telling him. He put down his cup quickly. Coffee spilled onto the place mat. "You mean . . . Chloe, you're saying —"

"That's exactly what I'm saying." She laughed and flicked her ponytail over her shoulder. "Exactly."

He looked past her to the bedroom to where a few hours ago he'd been doing the nasty with Lyra.

His mood darkened.

If Chloe knew —

She doesn't know, he corrected himself. *And if you want this, boy, you make sure she doesn't know.*

Nick got to his feet and he hugged her. "Chloe. I'm shocked."

"I can tell. Why do you keep looking around? Expecting someone?" She winked.

"N-no, of course not." He forced a chuckle. "What a notion. What a crazy, crazy notion."

He hugged her again, hoping against hope that Chloe couldn't detect the scent of cinnamon on his skin.

After Nick showered and dressed, he went to the funeral home to help his father with the respective showings of Mr. Felix and Miss Jackson.

Bruce had recently hired a new assistant part-time. Sam was what Chloe would call an original man — rugged, good with his hands, a hard worker.

"Hullo, Nick," Sam greeted him when he entered the office. "Your dad's not in yet."

Nick glanced at his watch. The guests would be here in less than half an hour. "Did he have an errand to do?"

Sam pulled on the hem of his jacket. He looked uncomfortable in a brown suit and tie, so much so that Nick found it painful to watch him squirm.

"Yeah, think that was it. Said he wouldn't be more than five minutes late."

Nick turned away. "I'll go check to make sure the guest book is there."

It was. Sam was nothing if not thorough. When Nick moved toward the office, he saw a woman in the front lobby. With both hands, she lifted a plastic cap from her curly hair. She wore a long navy coat that hung open. Beneath the coat was a modest black dress with a string of shiny pearls around her neck. She was striking, with deep blue eyes and perfect posture.

"Mrs. Felix?" Nick said.

"Yes?" She squinted over her glasses.

Nick shook her hand and offered his condolences about the loss of her husband.

"Thank you. It's been quite a shock to lose Howie like this. But you've all been so very helpful."

"Would you like a cup of coffee or tea? There's some time before the guests arrive."

"Yes, thank you."

Nick led her into the small reception area where Sam had placed tea, coffee and round oatmeal cookies on a silver tray.

Mrs. Felix perched along the edge of the blue plush seat, her teacup held daintily between her hands. "Well, these things are never easy, are they?" Steam rose from the tea and for an instant, fogged her glasses.

"This is always a difficult day," he agreed.

"Howie was a dear man. We were very happy, you know. So many marriages are shams, nothing but theory." She sipped her tea and then wiped a lipstick stain along the ridge of the cup with her thumb. "We were real, Howie and I. I just hope he'd have been pleased with the arrangements."

Grief was an odd emotion, Nick had come to realize over the years of helping his father. People respond differently to death but a common element is the overwhelming indecision about the funeral process. A good funeral director appeases that confusion.

He patted her hand. "I'm sure he'd be more than pleased, Mrs. Felix."

Bruce appeared then and announced that some of Miss Jackson's family had arrived. He asked Nick if he'd be so kind as to greet them.

The other viewing room was at the opposite side of the building, offering privacy for both families. "Certainly. Excuse me, Mrs. Felix."

Nick had just stepped into the Jackson viewing room when a piercing scream caused him to flinch back.

"What the . . . "

The scream came from a tall red-haired man who stood over the casket wringing his hands and shouting, "Evil has been here. Oh no! Evil!"

"Sir?"

He threw up his arms; his lips shivered as he squeezed his eyes shut. "Savior help us with this curse!" A woman beside him, wearing a long green dress, pulled at the man's arm. He shook her away.

"Is something the matter?" Nick touched the man's sleeve. "Sir?"

Just then another scream was heard from another part of the building, and the dozen or so people in the room stopped to listen.

Nick clenched his jaw. What was going on? He turned back to the tall man. "Sir, please, you need to calm down —"

"Evil, I tell you!"

The woman with the green dress pointed to the casket, then covered her face and began to sob. Her long silver earrings dangled and shivered.

"*Evil has been here!*" The man whispered now, leaning over Miss Jackson's casket, gripping the sides desperately. "Oh, merciful God . . . "

"Sir," Nick said, "please, *what is wrong?*"

He slumped to his knees, his head against the smooth wood. His shoulders trembled. "Merciful God . . . *merciful God . . .* "

Nick looked down at Miss Jackson but didn't see anything out of the ordinary.

Not at first.

Then he saw it, saw what everyone else saw.

Miss Jackson, in all her pretty splendor, wore the arms and hands of Mr. Felix.

chapter twenty

As horrific as it was to see the pale Miss Jackson with hairy arms and ruddy hands, Nick pushed a hand tightly against his mouth to stifle his laughter.

He stared at her, afraid to meet the eyes of Miss Jackson's mourners, afraid he'd say something inappropriate and worsen the situation — if that were possible.

How had this happened?

He skimmed the notes of his memory. Had he inadvertently confused the two bodies, put the wrong arms on the wrong body? Could he have been that stupid and inattentive?

He remembered the two rings her family had left for Miss Jackson and how he'd pushed them on her fingers, cutting one ring in the back so it would fit over her swollen middle finger.

If his memory about the event was so clear, how could this be explained? Nothing seemed to make sense of the situation, no matter how he examined it.

He heard more shrieking in the distance and recognized Mrs. Felix's voice. It was a bitter noise.

"What the hell is going on here?" a voice crackled behind him.

Nick opened his mouth to speak and then closed it again. He glanced around, saw how everyone stared at him. And why wouldn't they? They deserved an explanation.

Only Nick couldn't give one.

He quietly walked to the other viewing room.

Except for the initial scream, Mrs. Felix hovered quietly over her husband, shaking her head. The other family members watched, obviously lost as to the proper etiquette in this situation.

Bruce stood beside Mrs. Felix. He glared at his son, as if demanding to know how this could have happened. Nick lifted his shoulders to indicate that he didn't know. He simply did not know.

If the sight of Miss Jackson was odd, with Mr. Felix it was tenfold. To see such a large man with tiny white hands bearing the dainty rings was . . . well, funny. And the fact that there was tremendous pressure not to laugh made Nick want to all the more.

Mrs. Felix blew her nose and then turned toward Nick and his father. "I don't understand what this is about." Her tears seemed to harden into anger. "You've made a complete mockery of my husband."

Bruce nodded. "I'm very sorry, Mrs. Felix. But this can be fixed —"

"Fixed. How? Tell me how."

Nick knew that wasn't a question his dad had counted on answering. He opened his mouth but no words came forth. After an unbearable silence, Bruce cleared his throat and said, "May we speak to you in private?"

In the hallway, Bruce put his hand over Mrs. Felix's arm in an attempt to placate her. "Your husband lost his arms in the accident. They had to be reattached." Bruce took a breath. "Another person that day also had their limbs reattached and I'm afraid, somehow, they got confused."

"Confused?"

"Mixed up," Nick added.

The horror on Mrs. Felix's face was unmistakable. She stepped back, her hands flitting to her neck. "So you put another person's, a *woman's* arms on my husband?"

Across the building, the sobs of the Jackson family reached them.

"Is that . . . ?" Mrs. Felix sniffed and gestured with her head. "Is that the other party involved?"

Bruce nodded.

"Are you telling me that by pure coincidence, two people who died separately on the same day both lost their arms?"

"Yes, as odd as that may sound."

"Who handled these details?"

"I did," Nick offered. "It's my fault —"

"I'd like to see where my husband's limbs went."

Bruce swallowed and dragged a hand through his hair. "Ma'am, I don't recommend that you . . . "

"Show me now, please." She took a few steps in the direction of the sobbing. "Or shall I find my own way?" Her voice was without uncertainty.

When they stepped inside the Jackson viewing room, all turned their way. Mrs. Felix kept her head high as she went to the casket and grasped the hairy arms that stretched out from Miss Jackson's sleeves. The tall man who'd been screaming about evil cautiously approached her. His lips quivered as he touched Mrs. Felix's shoulder. "I'm sorry," he whispered.

Mrs. Felix ignored him at first. And then she said to the room, "It's simply a mockery. A *mockery!*"

Then she calmly walked across the room, lifted a hand high and slapped Nick's face.

The slap in the face from Mrs. Felix had been the easiest part of the ordeal, Nick decided, as he made his way through the halls of Dalhousie, to chemistry class the next morning. His father threatened to fire him, and went as far as to question Nick's mental stability.

"*If only you could give me an explanation,*" Bruce had pressed.

But Nick was unable to give any explanation. Might never be able to give one.

He considered that Lyra might've had a hand in it, but how would she have gotten inside the home?

The same way she got inside your apartment.

"Let's just hope this doesn't end up in court," Bruce had warned. "Surely it'll mean the end of our family business."

And it's all my fault, thought Nick.

A headache throbbed behind his eyes; he pinched his forehead as he took the steps leading to the second floor. Outside the classroom, he spotted Dr. Sampson attaching something to the door and then recognized it as a cancellation notice.

"No class, sir?"

Dr. Sampson shook his head and then glanced toward Nick. Nick sucked in a tight breath. Dr. Sampson's eyes were swollen, and his expression, blank, as if his face were a slate that had been wiped clean.

"Sir, are you all right?"

"No." He offered no further explanation and then pushed past Nick toward his office and curtly shut the door.

Despite his dislike for Dr. Sampson, Nick wondered if the man was okay. He contemplated knocking on the office door but what would he say? If Dr. Sampson were upset, Nick would probably be the last person he'd want to see.

Still, he couldn't help but wonder what had happened for the seemingly cool professor Sampson to be so upset.

Gerald closed the office door and slumped in the black leather chair. He stared ahead without seeing anything. He felt detached from his body, as if it continued to exist despite him.

Holly was gone.

He swallowed the horrific realization, let it burn deep in his gut. Time would be measured from this point onward as *Life before Holly* and *Life after Holly*.

Even before the police had called on Sunday morning, he'd known Holly wouldn't be coming home ever again. The officer, a Constable Clubb, had danced around the words before stating, "Your wife is dead. Foul play is suspected."

Of course foul play is suspected, he'd wanted to scream. When he'd called to report her missing on Saturday evening, they'd not taken him seriously. Only afterward did they take an interest in how he'd known something terrible had happened to his wife.

"I felt it," was all he could say. "Felt it deep in my bones."

Holly had died with only a small life insurance policy, just enough to cover funeral expenses. Gerald couldn't help but wonder if that eased their suspicions about his possible involvement in her death.

It was Nicole's doing. He'd told the police that, too. He'd given her name and description and said that she'd been his mistress. The lie would help explain why she'd be so intent on destroying him, snuffing out the life of his precious Holly.

They'd questioned him from a hundred different angles and in the end, seemed satisfied — for now — that he hadn't been involved in the murder of his wife.

As if he'd hurt Holly. As if he'd harm a single skin cell that was hers. She was his *life.*

And now his life lay in a funeral home while they went to work fancying her up, hiding the rip in her gut. Hiding how Nicole had plunged the blade into the soft flesh of her belly with such force that it pierced vital organs and tore a hole in her the size of a beach ball.

The police said it wasn't practical to even suggest a woman could have had the strength to inflict such an injury.

Gerald knew different.

Oh, poor Holly. How she must have suffered . . .

Gerald's head fell into his hands; his teeth chattered. He thought of Holly's sweet belly and how many times he'd kissed her navel, how they used to imagine their unborn children some day nestled there, safe and protected.

"You're a freak, Gerald. Bye, freak."

Gerald wished he knew more about Nicole. Oh she'd played him well, left no traces of anything identifiable. For all he knew, Nicole wasn't even her real name. Maybe nothing about her was real. Maybe *she* wasn't real.

The police found it odd that she'd be his mistress and yet he knew so little about her, not even an address. He'd explained that it had been an odd sort of relationship, meetings in coffee shops, sex in the back seat of his Explorer.

It *was* odd. The whole situation was odd — why would Nicole murder his wife? Hadn't it been enough to play with him, taunt him, stiff him for two hundred dollars?

He thought back to the night when Nicole had wanted him to drive down the deserted road outside the city. Had she been planning on killing him that night? Part of him wished that she had; she may have spared Holly.

Then again, maybe she wouldn't have.

Maybe she wouldn't be satisfied until she killed everyone who mattered to him.

Gerald wiped damp tears from his face.

When he looked up again, he saw the small leafy plant that Holly had placed in the window of his office. *Water it every other day*, she'd told him. *And think happy thoughts; plants suffer when you don't.*

He stared at the plant, gathered the brown clay pot between his hands. Tears fell down his face, but this time he didn't bother wiping them away.

Outside, the wind howled.

Nick heard the news from his father when he stopped by the funeral home that evening to pick up his paycheck: Dr. Sampson's wife had been murdered.

He thought of how the professor had awkwardly stumbled past him to his office. Nick would never have guessed. And murder?

Good God.

"Let me work on his wife, Dad."

"No." Bruce handed over a white envelope containing his pay. "You know that's not possible. After what happened with the Felix family . . . "

They were standing in Bruce's office. Nick glanced to the bulletin board where the work hours were posted. He didn't see his name.

"Dad, am I really fired? That's it, then?"

"Not fired, Nick. Just . . . well, it's like I already told you. We need to let a little time pass. Nick, it was the only way to maybe stop the families from suing us. I told them you'd be . . . suspended. I didn't say for how long. Look, you're stressed and —"

"And what?"

Bruce just shook his head. After a moment, he said, "Did you know her, Mrs. Sampson?"

"No." He sighed. "I barely know Dr. Sampson, really. We have a mutual D, that's about it."

"Son," Bruce said. "You've got to forget about that one lousy grade."

"Yeah." Nick did up the zipper on his coat. "After what happened to his wife, it seems pretty insignificant. Is it bad, the condition of her body?"

"It's bad."

"Dad, let me help you with her —"

"No."

Nick let out a long breath. "Okay. Well, I guess I'll go."

"Son, it'll all work out for the best," Bruce added.

"Right," Nick said as he closed the door behind him. "Right."

Nick drove toward his apartment. Chloe was coming over later. She'd be moving some of her belongings into the new house and would be by after that.

As he pulled into the driveway, he imagined losing Chloe in a similar fashion. A terrible image.

He pushed the key in the door, heard the cl-clunk of the dead bolt as it swung aside. Pushing the door open, he went inside, kicked off his sneakers and inhaled the incense.

Incense?

He looked down at his sneakers.

And then saw the Oreo cookies.

Rather the *trail* of Oreo cookies that led to his bedroom.

"Lyra," he whispered.

chapter twenty-one

Nick picked up the first cookie and popped it whole in his mouth. He loved Oreos, always had. Still, he couldn't help but dread what he'd find at the end of the trail.

He rounded the corner of the kitchen into the hallway. He paused at the bedroom door and then pushed it open.

Chloe.

Chloe dressed in a black and white silk nightie that fell to the top of her thighs. An Oreo nightie.

Chloe stretched out on his bed, her legs and shoulders looking silky smooth.

Chloe smiling.

Chloe, waiting for him.

"Hey, Dr. Love," she cooed. "I'm in need. I ate too many sweets and I hurt. I hurt for you."

Nick just stared, afraid to move, afraid to blink for fear that he'd discover this was a hopeful mirage. Surely Chloe wasn't lying on his bed in such a sweet way, and looking at him with a certain *warmth* in her eyes. Surely not.

He moved toward her, touched her hair. It felt warm beneath his hand. "The cookies, nice touch."

She smiled up at him. Despite himself, he felt nervous.

Chloe kissed his hand. "Hi."

"Hi."

He lowered himself onto the bed and folded her into his arms. It didn't seem real, the lack of hesitation he'd become accustomed to sensing in Chloe. Then again, nothing seemed real today. He briefly thought of Dr. Sampson again. Chloe's touch was comforting; perfect timing.

Nick pushed his face into his hair. She smelled good, real good. He stroked the back of her neck; his hand trembled. Truth be known, he'd be content right now just to hold Chloe. Dr. Sampson's death had shaken him more than he wanted to admit.

As if sensing his reluctance, Chloe pulled back and smiled kindly. "I know about Dr. Sampson. I'm sorry, Nick."

"I don't deserve condolences. I'm just shocked, is all."

"It's unbelievable. What do you supposed happened?"

He shrugged.

Chloe gestured to her Oreo nightie. She looked almost embarrassed. "Nick, this isn't a good idea . . . I see that."

He put a hand along her thigh. "It's *good*. It's an excellent idea."

She grinned. "Think so?"

Nick pulled her against him. "Yeah, I think so."

Their loving was as delicious and rich as the cookies that had led Nick to this sweet lair, to Chloe, to the beginning of *them*. Afterward they held hands in the dark. Nick couldn't believe how good he felt inside.

"Chloe?"

"Yeah?"

A soft chuckle. "I'm never going to look at Oreos the same way again."

She laughed softly. She touched his arm, smoothed it. He could feel the tips of her fingernails near his elbow.

After a little silence, she said, "You working on Dr. Sampson's wife?"

"You kidding? Dad wouldn't let me anywhere near her."

"Does Dr. Sampson know your connection to the funeral home, I wonder."

He shrugged. "Who knows? I won't be working at the home for a while so it doesn't matter."

Chloe snuggled closer to him. "Your father will get over the limb confusion. Just give it some time."

"I hope so. I need my job."

"It'll all work out. Promise."

"What bugs me is how he thinks I'm going crazy or something," he told her.

"You do seem really stressed lately," she admitted carefully.

"I do?"

"Yeah. Just not yourself."

"How so?"

She shrugged. "Sometimes you just seem like you're a million miles away. You . . . slapped me, remember? And Taylor's party, you weren't yourself at all."

Nick didn't respond right away. He could feel himself getting angry. Of all the people in his world, he wanted Chloe to understand, to believe in him.

"I wouldn't hurt you intentionally."

"I know that, Nick."

Nick didn't want to talk about Dr. Sampson now. He wanted to hang on to how wonderful it felt to be here with Chloe. He wanted the world to be a million miles away.

He sighed. "Hey, can we find another topic?"

"Sure. Cookie?" She picked one off the floor and dangled it in front of his lips.

He nipped it with his teeth and let her feed him playfully. He told himself that she wasn't judging him, she was just being concerned. Like any girlfriend would.

Girlfriend.

What a lovely, lovely title.

They talked late into the night, no longer about Gerald Sampson but rather of happy things, the kind of things Nick had dreamed of talking about with Chloe. They discussed plans for Christmas vacation and maybe a biking trip that summer and finally they fell asleep curled together.

Nick was sure life couldn't get any better.

So when he awoke at four in the morning with an urgency that made him leave the warm comfort of Chloe, Nick revisited the feeling that his life was spiraling out of control.

He left the apartment, hoping he'd complete what he had to do, long before Chloe woke to find an empty bed.

The first thing Paula heard coming from Brad's apartment was loud music. She recognized Mick Jagger's voice hailing out that he couldn't *get no satisfaction.*

Her mouth felt dry as she lifted a fist to knock on Brad's door and then stopped the motion in midair.

What am I doing? When she'd discussed coming to see Brad with Chloe, it had seemed like a good idea. Now she wasn't so sure.

Especially since Brad hadn't called her in several days. She'd followed Nick's advice and informed Brad that she was fine just the way she was. If he didn't like it, he could be like the birds and flock off.

He'd done just that.

Would her coming here seem like she was begging, crawling on hands and knees to him? She didn't care. She wanted to make amends.

She knocked on the door three times for good luck.

The music died and then footsteps. Her pulse quickened.

The door opened a crack, paused and then opened all the way. Brad stood there in track pants and a stained white tee shirt and bare feet. She could smell beer and sweat.

"Hi, Brad."

"Babe, it's you. C'mon in."

He closed the door behind them. "You're lookin' real good, ya know."

She'd gained ten pounds in the last week and a half and her skin had broken out from too much chocolate and stress. Still, she said, "Thank you." A compliment from Brad had to be a good sign.

"So . . . " He rubbed his hands together. "What brings you to my door?"

She hadn't expected him to be so direct. As if he didn't know what brought her to his door. As if she might be selling Avon or Mary Kay or doing a survey on carpet cleaners.

"I just thought . . . " she stammered with a shrug. "Dunno. Maybe we could talk."

He sat down, plunked his feet on the coffee table and folded his arms. "Talk? About what, Paula?"

It was obvious he enjoyed this toying with her. Maybe Nick was right, maybe he wasn't good enough for her. She felt stronger then. And just as insulted that he planned to grind her integrity to nothing by dragging this out.

This is how a skinny woman thinks, she thought joyfully.

"Never mind, Brad." She stood up. "I just wanted to say hi, really."

"That's cool, babe." He took a drink of his beer. "You want somethin' to drink, a brewsky?"

Brewsky?

"No, it's a school night."

She saw the disapproval in his expression and tried to pretend it didn't matter — but it did. It still did. She felt her strength slipping away.

"I better go."

He put the beer bottle on the table and quickly got to his feet. "Hey, hey, babe. Don't go rushin' off." He shoved his hands in his pockets and rolled his shoulders forward. "Paula, I agree, we should talk."

"Talk about what?" She hoped those words sounded familiar.

"I been meanin' to call ya."

Paula wanted to believe him. "That true?"

He nodded quickly. "I would've. Sooner or later."

"Later could be next year."

"Not next year. Maybe next week." He crossed his feet at the ankles and leaned one hand along the wall. "Look, ya as much as told me to go to hell. What's a guy s'posed to do?"

Paula didn't see it that way, but Brad seemed so sincere, she didn't want to argue the point.

"Look." He grabbed a piece of white paper from the coffee table. "I been writin' you a new song." He took a breath, as if he were about to deliver a speech. "Babe, don't I miss you, Babe, ain't I sad," he read. "Babe, you're a squishy kisser and I love ya like your dad."

"Squishy?" Paula smiled.

He nodded and gestured to the couch. "Can we sit and talk, Paula? Talk it out?"

Hope welled inside her. She had so few friends and spent so much time alone. Brad gave her a way out of that. So he wasn't perfect. So he was possessive. It didn't mean they couldn't try to make things right again.

"Can I have a blanket? It's a bit cold here."

Brad agreed. "I'll pull one off my bed." He kissed the top of her head and left the room. "Gotta water the lilies, anyhow," he hollered over his shoulder.

Alone in the room, Paula pushed back her hair and applied a little lipstick. The apartment wouldn't be so bad if Brad cleaned it up some, invested in a plant or two, got some decent curtains. He'd placed a white sheet over the window and pressed thumbtacks along the top of the pane to keep it in place. The sheet wasn't quite wide enough and there was a wedge of black where night peeked in.

Paula tugged at the sheet and peered outside. She could see a backyard swing set and a child's wagon. The swing rocked in the wind. She thought of the swing set she used to have. It had a small slide attached to it and Nick would stand at the bottom, his arms outstretched to catch her —

A black blur zipped across her vision.

Paula jerked her head back. What in the heck was that?

She followed the line of the swing set past the wagon and beyond to a white fence. She spotted a gate, saw that it was open. Had she seen a dog? Yes, perhaps so. A black dog or cat or maybe a fairy. The *tooth* fairy.

The last thought amused her, took away the odd sensation that someone was watching. Watching her watching them, equally amused.

Paula turned from the window with a shrug and then went to see what was taking Brad so long.

chapter twenty-two

The scent of disinfectant and floral carpet cleaner met Nick as he let himself into the funeral home. It was nearly four o'clock in the morning, and he shouldn't be here. He should be home in bed with Chloe before she woke up and wondered where the hell he was.

He'd only waited, oh . . . half his life for Chloe to return his affections, and here he was, not hours after she'd declared her love, sneaking away to a funeral home to stare at his professor's dead wife.

Not to mention how angry his dad would be to find him here.

Nick slowly locked the door and dropped the keys into the front pocket of his blue jeans. He'd never been here this late before. The silence felt damp, as though it seeped through his skin and chilled him.

He reminded himself that he wasn't doing anything wrong.

His mission was simple: to see Holly Sampson. He would disturb nothing and no one would ever know he'd been here.

Why he wanted to see her was another matter — and truth be known, he was still figuring it out. Part of him was curious as to what kind of woman would've married suspender-man Dr. Sampson and he captured a flickering image of a pudgy woman with glasses and bitten nails.

The rest of *why* went deeper, like an itch that wouldn't go away until he scratched it.

It was cool in the building; Nick zipped up his jacket. He wasn't sure which viewing room held Mrs. Sampson. There was a sheet taped to the back of the door in the office that outlined these details, but Nick didn't want to go in there. The office was where his father spent much of his time and he feared that if he went inside, Bruce would later *sense* it. Sense it the way people did when you touched items on a dresser, or opened a drawer.

The first room was empty. Nick moved through the building toward the second, the largest viewing room. It was his favorite room, painted a pale blue with stained glass windows. He was glad to think Mrs. Sampson might be in there.

Only she wasn't.

Of course, the chapel. Sometimes they used the chapel if it was requested by the family, or if the other rooms were occupied.

Nick opened the thick oak door and squinted through the darkness. He didn't see anything right away, and then his eyes adjusted and he made out the casket and the outline of a body. He moved inside and scraped his hand over the wall for the light-switch just as the door slammed shut behind him.

His jaw snapped shut.

Complete blackness choked him.

He inhaled a hint of the formaldehyde, which was unusual. Once the embalming fluid entered the body, it pretty much dissolved all noticeable scent.

God, he hoped something hadn't gone wrong involving Mrs. Sampson. They didn't need another horrific incident.

Why had the door slammed shut behind him?

Nick scrubbed his hand over the wall. His hand was sweaty and it made a squeaking noise that spooked him.

Where was the damned light-switch?

He imagined Mrs. Sampson getting out of her casket to help him find it. Saw her staggering toward him, her cold, cold hand reaching to touch him —

He found the small plastic lever, flipped it. Yellow light filled the room. Nick slumped against the wall, his breaths hard and rapid.

Mrs. Sampson lay passively in her casket, not saying a word.

Nick sucked at the air. When he raked a hand through his hair, he realized that he was trembling.

He had to calm down. The door might've closed because of a loose hinge, or a draft, or maybe it closed like that all the time and he just hadn't noticed.

It was no big deal.

Just his imagination running away and dragging him along for the bumpy ride.

Wiping his hands on his jeans, he went toward the coffin and peered down. She was a lovely woman, Mrs. Sampson. Though he couldn't see her eyes, he imagined them to be a sparkling blue. A complete contrast to what he'd envisioned. Younger, too. A real lesson in stereotypes.

Nick touched her hands affectionately. "I'm sorry you got hurt," he whispered. She had quite the rock of a wedding ring, too. Good ol' Dr. Sampson had more taste than he'd ever given him credit for.

The more Nick eyed pretty Mrs. Sampson, the more he felt the loss of her. Someone had purposefully snatched her life. God, it wasn't fair. Maybe nothing was fair anymore.

"I'm so sorry . . . " He leaned forward and kissed the top of Holly's head. Her yellow hair smelled clean, minty, and for an instant he had an image of Dr. Sampson making love to his wife, running his hands through her hair.

Nick's eyes closed and he took a deep breath.

When they opened again, he noticed the necklace lying gently at the base of Mrs. Sampson's pale throat.

He blinked and pulled his head back. It looked very familiar, the heart-shaped locket with the letter C engraved on the outside.

"No . . . "

He flipped it open and stood back, blinking in shock, in disbelief. On the inside was an N.

Chloe's necklace.

The one he'd given her.

What in the name of God was Chloe's necklace doing around a murdered woman's neck?

His fingers fumbled around the locket. Thoughts floated like dead goldfish through his mind. *Chloe's* necklace. Had his father found it and put it there, thinking it would be a nice touch? But no, Bruce would never do something like that.

He plucked at the chain, saw how the pressure made tiny marks along Holly Sampson's neck. He kept waiting for something to explain how this could be, some rational thought that would make sense of it all. None came.

Nothing except a tiny whisper that told him he wasn't seeing it. Still wasn't seeing it.

Nick closed his fist around the locket and heard movement behind him.

His first thought was a sinister one. Nick read a story once about a demon who avenged those who stole from graves. This demon would exchange a pound of flesh, just like Shylock in Shakespeare's *Merchant of Venice*, for every item taken.

"But I'm not stealing . . . " he whispered. You couldn't steal what was yours —

"Nicholas Gary O'Brien."

Bruce. Nick couldn't remember the last time he'd been called by his full name — maybe when he was a child and had been caught putting oatmeal in the fish tank.

Bruce's eyes went to Nick's closed hand. "Just what are you doing to Holly Sampson's body?"

I should shower more often, Brad thought as he dried himself off with his one blue towel. He felt like a new man. Showers were overrated and society too concerned with hiding natural scents which were really quite beautiful. Still, the indulgence was special; he felt relaxed, invigorated.

He wished Paula were here to share the indulgence.

It didn't seem right that they'd make up and then she'd go home. But, what could he do?

Paula reminded him to think of the future, when they could be together all the time. He tried to consider this, but it was hard when he missed her.

He remembered reading of a society where men danced all night with apple slices taped to their armpits and would later present these delicacies to their lovers who would eat them as a gesture of love.

He wondered if Paula would eat an apple taped all week to his armpit. Somehow, he doubted it. He laughed at himself in the steamy mirror and rubbed the towel over his dark beard.

In the living room, Brad plunked on the sofa with a long sigh. Still wearing the towel around his waist, he uncapped a beer and let his head loll back on his shoulders.

This is life, he told himself. This is relaxation.

If only Paula were here, there'd be nothing else to want for.

As if on cue, there was a knock at the door.

Brad felt warm all over. She'd come back! He and Paula had, like, this psychic connection; she just *knew* he needed her.

Taking a swig of the beer, he smoothed his beard and tightened the towel around his waist. He considered answering the door naked but he wasn't sure how Paula would react. After all, who knew what offended women anymore?

He swung the door open to reveal a woman who wasn't Paula.

No sir, not Paula.

"Hullo?" He glanced down at his partially covered body. Half-dressed or half-naked, which would it be?

She was gorgeous, this creature who'd knocked at his door. Long black hair and a sexy black dress, she looked sort of wild and sort of innocent and sort of everything good and naughty all swirled together.

"I'd like to come in," she told him.

Whoa, momma! "Ah . . . " he stammered, hating himself for being so thankful that it wasn't Paula at the door. "Ah, sure, sure, come in."

She perched on the edge of the sofa and flicked her hair back with one slender hand. Brad watched her, regretting that the towel didn't offer much *concealment* as to how happy he really was to have such a babe in his apartment.

He crossed his legs and hugged a pillow to his lap. She still hadn't said what she wanted. Maybe she was a saleswoman or someone doing a survey or census. He hoped she wasn't one of those Jehovah's Witness folks. One time two men had come to his door and asked Brad if he knew of Jehovah's Witness and he'd replied that he hadn't even seen the accident.

Though they hadn't appreciated his joke, they kept coming back for months until finally, he'd posted a drawing on his front door of a middle finger pointed upward, and below the finger, two words: Witness *this!*

Nick scratched the back of his head. "So . . . what can I do for you?"

She extended a hand. "My name is Paula —"

"Paula?" He smacked a hand to his forehead. She stared as if she didn't understand his reaction. "My g-girlfriend's name is Paula," he explained. "Odd coincidence."

"Paul-*ette*," she corrected. "I said Paulette."

"Oh." He felt himself blushing as he shook her firm hand. "Okay." He bet she was a saleswoman with that handshake.

"You're wondering why I'm here," she stated simply.

He agreed.

"Business." She smoothed her bare knees with both hands. She had great legs, toned and long. "We have some business to discuss."

"So you're selling something, right?"

"In a manner of speaking. Only for you . . . " She ran her tongue along the front of her teeth. "It's free."

"I don't follow you." He shrugged. "Well . . . ah. You want a beer or somethin'?"

"Somethin'."

"Huh?"

"I'm here to seduce you, Brad."

Brad felt his eyes widen. *What* had she just said? And how the hell did she know his name? He thought of Paula, put her aside, thought of her again.

"I'm not dressed," he mumbled. Holy smokes, what a stupid thing to say. He got to his feet, took a long drink from his beer.

"You have objections?" she asked.

He didn't answer right away. He thought of Paula again.

Something didn't feel right. She was beginning to spook him. But not enough that he didn't look her over and imagine sliding his hands all over her, from top to bottom and the middle . . . oh yeah, definitely the middle.

He took another drink, let the beer froth over his tongue before slowly swallowing.

"I don't . . . don't know you," he told her.

"You're absolutely right." She stood up and smiled. "This must seem like a weird dream, a woman such as me showing up and telling you that I want to do things to you. *Bad* things."

Brad groaned.

She smiled. "Well, I don't want you to compromise yourself. It's your call entirely."

Call was a good word, Brad decided. This gal was a call girl. Scouting out business, offering free samples, a test drive. Paula was right when she warned him about moving into this neighborhood.

"And if I say no?"

"Then you do."

"Not that I would. Or wouldn't, you know." He was rambling now, buying time, trying to decide.

Eenie, meenie, miney mo . . .

He saw a mole near her shoulder, imagined how sweet it would be to roll his tongue over the dark spot. He loved moles on women, always had.

"Maybe it would be wrong to sleep with me, a complete stranger," she continued. "For all you know, I could be a real animal. Into all kinds of weird and wonderful things that might blow your mind."

She examined her fingernails. She may as well have been talking about trying a new dish at a restaurant. "But you look like a man who likes to go *against the grain*, isn't that right?"

"Against the grain," he repeated. "Yeah, that's right. But, how . . . why me?"

"Why not you?" Her eyes moved over him. "Let's not analyze this too much,

Brad. Thinking too much is bad for your heart."

She walked across the room and touched his arm. Her touch was powerful and he felt himself being drawn to her, pulled along like tissue that sometimes sticks to the bottom of a woman's shoe.

He sighed.

And followed her into the bedroom.

The funny thing was, she seemed to know exactly where it was.

"Well?" Bruce repeated, "what are you doing to Holly Sampson?"

Nick swallowed. "Dad, this is serious stuff."

"I know."

"No, look." He uncurled his hand. "It's Chloe's necklace. See, the initials C and an N? I gave her that necklace. Don't you remember? For her birthday."

Bruce shook his head and said very slowly, "Nick, there was no necklace on Mrs. Sampson."

"You think I'm making this up?"

"I think you're suffering from . . . something lately." His tone was smooth, as if he were talking Nick down from a window ledge. "I'm worried about you."

"Dad! I swear, I found this on the body!" He shook his fist holding the necklace.

"I asked you not to come here," Bruce reminded him. "Though I had a hunch you would."

"Dad, if you didn't put Chloe's necklace on the body, then who did? Huh? Someone has been obviously sneaking in here and playing tricks. Maybe it was the same person who mixed up the arms . . . "

"I think it was the same person, yes."

Nick glared at his father. "It wasn't me!"

"Son, it's okay. I'm not angry —"

"Why are you talking to me like that? What, you really think I've lost it?"

"You're under a lot of pressure at school, and maybe working here hasn't helped."

"It's my job!"

"Son, I'm going to have to ask for your keys."

Nick had had keys to the funeral home for years since he'd been a boy. This was ridiculous.

"Nick," Bruce said.

He quietly handed them over. When Bruce pocketed them, he let out a sigh that sounded much too much like relief.

Nick swallowed. There had always been an easy trust between him and his father; the smallest request of asking for his keys had torn something away.

"You did a good job on Mrs. Sampson," Nick said as he moved past his father.

"I'm glad you took so much care."

"Thank you. She's beautiful, it was easy."

Their casual conversation was like theater of the surreal, thought Nick. His guts churned. "So, guess you want me to leave, huh?"

Bruce didn't respond right away. And then, "When you're ready, son. Just don't think of it as being kicked out. Don't take it personally."

But when Nick left the funeral home, he heard the definite sound of his father swinging the dead bolt shut behind him.

chapter twenty-three

Why is it we do most of our thinking in bed? Why not when we're having breakfast or walking the dog or sitting on the pot? So pondered Nick the next night as he flung one leg over the blankets and willed himself not to think about finding Chloe's necklace on his professor's dead wife. Think on it tomorrow. Or the next day. Or never — that might be a consideration, too.

But try as he might to put the thought away, it lingered. He *needed* to make sense of it, it was that simple. And beyond that, Nick had a sticky sense that clogged deep inside him. A sense that all of these events were building to something bigger than everyone involved.

He closed his eyes and took deep breaths. He imagined he sucked in good, calming air and expelled the tension from his body. He'd left the blinds open so he could see the maple tree outside as its leaves brushed against the glass.

He yawned. The deep breathing and discipline of the mind was working, it really was. Nick dared to give himself a little pat — but no, it might be bad luck to brag about yourself to yourself.

Instead, he stretched and his feet met with hardness along the bottom of his bed. Hard like a casket.

Opening his eyes, he saw that it *was* a casket.

Mrs. Sampson sat up just as he did.

Nick was too afraid to move.

He simply stared ahead, ignoring the twitching of his bladder, terrified and yet amazed at how real Holly Sampson appeared — after all, this couldn't be authentic, could it? — and wondered what she could possibly want with him.

She pointed a finger his way. "You have my necklace." Her voice wasn't at all how he imagined a ghost's would sound. It wasn't crackly or mottled, but clear and firm and *angry*.

"It's n-not yours." My God, was he really arguing with a dead woman? "It's Chloe's. I gave it to her —"

"You need to give it back."

"Why? Why do you want it? What could you possibly want with . . . " His words went to nothing when he saw Mrs. Sampson's tears.

Or what he thought were tears.

Blood.

Hot steamy bubbling blood that glinted from the street light outside as it poured down her face. Nick bit down on his lower lip. If he lived to be a hundred, he'd never forget the image of Mrs. Sampson's face with the bubbling, trickling blood.

"The necklace," she said between sobs. "The necklace . . . "

"I left it at the funeral home. My father has it. Mrs. Sampson, you have your funeral tomorrow and —"

"*Necklace*," she demanded, her voice getting higher and sharper. "Necklace!"

"I don't have it!" Nick took off his wolf pendant in one jerked movement and let it dangle from his fingers. "Take this one, please. Stop crying. There's no need . . ."

Holly reached for it but then at the last second, pulled her hand away and the wolf pendant fell to the floor. She let out a sob and wiped at her face with her wrists. The funeral director in Nick wanted her to stop; she was messing up all the hard work, ruining her dress and make-up.

"I'm afraid." She put both hands against the sides of the casket and pushed as if she wanted to get out. It was weird enough that a casket lay on his bed holding a conversing Mrs. Sampson, but to have her get out was simply beyond what Nick could take.

She struggled and sobbed. "Where's Gerald? Tell me where he is."

"I don't know."

"Is he at the Lizard Cafe? With his pantyhose? I loved that peach dress." Her words ran together. "Where is he?"

Pantyhose? Nick took a breath. She wasn't making any sense. Then again, she was dead; why should she?

"Tell Gerald I'm alone here. It's awful to be so lonely in this dark, dark place . . ."

Nick just stared. "Tell me who did this to you," he whispered.

She opened her mouth to speak and then it seemed that she looked past him. She shuddered and shook her head. "Am I dead? Is that it?"

"Mrs. Sampson . . . "

"Am I dead?" She clasped her hands in front of her, the possibility seemingly terrifying. *"Am I?"*

Nick nodded. "Y-yes, you are."

Mrs. Sampson pointed a finger toward him and screamed.

Was this how she screamed when she fought the lost battle for her life? Nick put his hands over his ears, needing to block out the shrill, piercing sounds of her screams that seemed to go on forever while her bloody tears rained down and her hands clattered at the casket as she tried in vain to get out —

"*Nick*!"

Lyra stared down at him.

Nick's bladder released in one sharp thrust; he felt the warmth pool between his legs.

"Oh, now you've had a little accident," Lyra said.

Holly Sampson was gone. His ears still rang from the sound of her cries. He pulled the covers into his lap to hide the growing stain of urine. Blood rushed to his face from embarrassment.

"Oh God . . . " He tasted the salt of tears at the back of his throat and swallowed them back. "I'm going crazy. I'm actually going crazy . . . "

"Oh, Nick." Lyra moved closer and flicked an indifferent hand. "Don't be so dramatic. It's not becoming."

"I *am* going crazy, aren't I? Maybe you're not even real. Maybe I just get all kinds of visitors at night. Maybe that's just the way it is when you're nuts. *Nuts!*"

"I love you," she told him.

That was the last thing he expected to hear. It didn't help his anxiety; it only annoyed him. "Where's Holly Sampson?"

Lyra shrugged. "She just wanted attention. Such a little *whiner.*"

Nick stared at the foot of the bed. Had he only imagined Holly's coffin there? It had seemed so real. He shifted his legs; the urine-soaked cotton stuck to him.

"Lyra . . . I . . . thought you were going away."

This seemed to surprise her. "Going away?"

"Yeah, after last time, that was my impression."

"I would never abandon you." She pinched his cheek with her thumb and forefinger. "Oh, Nickie darling, I've only been making myself worthy of you, fulfilling your desires. Three wishes until I'm free, remember? I'm almost there."

This again. He sighed. "Almost?"

"The third will take a little more time."

"How about I just tell you that you can go? You can be free! I don't care."

Lyra pulled her chin into her chest and looked up at him with wide eyes. "Nick, is this how you show your appreciation of me?"

"Look, I need to . . . ah, put some clean shorts on and . . . change the sheets. Mind leaving the room?"

"As you wish."

Nick balled up the sheets and shoved them to the back of his closet. He wanted to shower, but didn't trust to leave Lyra alone. Instead, he dried himself as best he could with a shirt yanked from the laundry hamper and then pulled on a pair of flannel sweats and went into the living room.

Lyra had been busy. She had arranged the sofa cushions on the floor and struck a seductive pose alongside. His one candle burned at the center.

She lifted the corners of her mouth sweetly. "Feel better?"

He didn't respond.

"I hope so, Nicky darling. Tonight is a celebration."

"I'm not in the mood to celebrate."

"Master, but tonight is —"

"Is what? Where you lay on your back to make up for being so psychotic?!"

He hadn't meant to sound so harsh. But he couldn't take it anymore. He wanted his life back, his sane, predictable life. Lyra had to understand that. She had to go away, stay away. He no longer cared if she ended up living on the streets. She was a sick girl and needed the kind of help he couldn't possibly give.

"Lyra." He knelt beside her. "Listen. This was entertaining, but it's . . . over."

"Are you too tired tonight to celebrate?"

Nick sighed. She wasn't hearing him. Simply wasn't hearing him. What would it take to make her understand? A flashing neon sign on his forehead that blinked, *Lyra, stay away, Lyra, stay away*?

"Look," he continued. "I could have you arrested for breaking into my apartment. For a lot of things. I didn't because I felt sorry for you. I mean, c'mon here, it's not normal that a woman follows a guy around, sneaks in his house and . . . "

"And makes love to him?" she finished his sentence.

"That was a mistake —"

"A mistake you seem to keep wanting to repeat."

"Chloe and I are together now, okay?" He stabbed the air with his finger. "It's got to stop. You've got to leave me alone."

She laughed. "You think Miss Holy Chloe will stick around? Oh, that's so funny!"

"Lyra, you're a pretty girl. You can find some other guy without a problem, I'm sure. Find some married guy to mess with —"

"How *dare* you?" She glared at him. "You make fun of the love I lost? Don't you know how much hell I went through, all because of your —"

She stopped and pushed a hand against her lips.

"Because of my what?"

She shook her head. "Look, you summoned me, that wasn't my doing."

Nick raced to the room and found the book beneath the bed where he'd hidden it from Chloe. "Take it then." He dropped it in her lap. "I didn't mean to summon anyone. So here. Find another master. I don't want it. I don't want *you*."

"You don't understand, Nick." She slowly smoothed the cover of the book with her red fingernails. "I *have* to fulfill your three wishes. I've fulfilled two."

"I didn't make any wishes! I refused to play this stupid game right from the start."

"Are you so sure?" She examined her nails. "Think back. Mess up your professor real bad, is one."

Nick's knees felt weak. "*You* murdered . . . his wife? You did that?"

"What better way to mess someone up *real bad?"*

"Tell me that isn't true." But already, Nick knew it was.

"Lyra, why . . . how could you do that? Don't you have any dignity, any sense of right and wrong? Does human life mean that little to you?"

He was shaking, he was so angry. He couldn't believe it; Lyra talked about murdering poor Holly Sampson as if it meant nothing. He threw out a hand, "And . . . Chloe's necklace, the one I gave her. You took that, didn't you? Took it and put it on dead Holly Sampson."

Lyra gave a long stretch and yawned. "Oh, Nick . . . now why would I do such a thing?"

"You tell me, you sick piece of —"

"Nick, stop. You're getting ahead of yourself. "First of all, you must realize that I like Chloe. I really do. You should've left the necklace where I placed it —"

"But why? Why would you put Chloe's necklace on Holly Sampson's body?"

She rolled her head from shoulder to shoulder, as if she'd been sitting too long. "Remember what you said about Chloe the last time we were together in our most delicious and special way?

Nick shook his head. He couldn't remember much of anything except for the obvious.

Lyra rubbed the side of the white candle with her thumb. Wax brushed the top of her fingernail. "You wished she'd go away somewhere and never come back."

"I'd never say that."

"Oh yeah, you most certainly did."

"This is crazy! I was probably mad. Anything I might say, you try to make true?"

"Careful what you wish for, Nickie." She rubbed the warm wax on the back of his hand. "You just might get it."

He winced from the heat. "You're evil, you know that?"

"As you requested, Nick, I wanted to send Chloe away. Send her to prison for the murder of Holly Sampson. I didn't want to hurt her —"

"You didn't hurt Chloe, did you?" He grabbed her wrists. "Tell me you didn't."

"Relax, lover boy." She yanked her arms away. "Not a single hair on her head." She rubbed her wrists. "There's no need to try to bully me."

"I'm going to the police about you, Lyra. I'm going to tell them everything. You won't get away with murder. You can't keep threatening me and screwing up my life. There are laws —"

"Nick, *Nick*." She put up a hand. "There's no need to make anything difficult. You won't go to the police," she informed him. "You won't."

He glanced at the cover of *That Hurt Thing* glinting in the candle light. If only he'd known all the evil repercussions resulting from what had started as a curious lark.

He'd call the police tonight. They'd probably offer some kind of protection. After all, they'd probably be more than happy to take a murderer off the street.

"Lyra, how could you do it?" He tried to keep his tone matter of fact. "How could you kill Holly Sampson?"

Lyra stretched like a cat kneading a blanket. She skinned her lips back into a grin that revealed her teeth. "Nick, all this, I did for you."

"For me? You killed people for me?"

"Only those who you wished dead. You *wished* it, Nick."

She glared at him, as though she were truly shocked by his reaction. Nick tried his best to keep his expression neutral. "I don't want you to hurt any more people," he told her, taking a step closer. "Listen to me. You can't keep going like this. It's only a matter of time before the walls crumble in."

He stroked her hair kindly. Not that he wanted to touch her, but rather, he wanted to give her support so that she might give herself up. Surely it had to be scary for her, too. "Lyra, you're not well. That's obvious."

"Is it really?"

He nodded. "You don't have to make this worse for yourself. If you . . . well, give yourself up, it'll go easier for you. You do want to make it better, don't you?"

"Y-yes, I suppose I do." She lowered her eyes and took a small breath. "Nick, I just want you to always remember something. Everything I do, I do for love."

She pushed the sofa cushions to the floor and patted them. "Please, let's talk."

Nick sat on the floor beside her. With only the bathroom light shining into the living room, Lyra's features were softened. It really was a shame, her instability.

She sat beside him and laid her head against his shoulder. "I really made a mess of things, didn't I?"

"Just tell me what happened."

She kissed the inside of his wrist; he pulled back. "Lyra, let's not go there..."

"I'm sorry," she said, but then Nick felt her tongue along the inside of his arm. She clutched it and pulled it toward her. "Lyra, no."

She bit him.

"Hey! What the hell you doing? That hurt!"

"Yes, it's supposed to." She kissed the tip of his nose and got to her feet. She held the needle to the light of the candle. "Heroin has a bit of a sting, this is true."

Heroin?

Nick looked down at his arm, saw a tiny round bulb of blood on the surface of his skin.

He hoped this was a joke, one more of Lyra's little sick games. Like kissing his feet in the diner at Montreal, or leaving a tulip in the shower drain.

"Why for . . . now that?"

Nick shook his head. He'd meant to ask Lyra what was happening, but his words weren't going along with the rest of him.

Oddly, Nick's disorientation felt familiar. Like realizing how much you missed someone only when you are reunited.

Lyra stood with her legs spaced apart, hands on her hips, staring down at him. As if she were examining a painting or piece of sculpture. "Nick, does it all make sense now?"

It did, but he didn't know why it did.

"First in your apple juice."

Apple juice? What did that mean?

He knew he should be afraid now, but he wasn't. He was completely relaxed; in an odd space. So much so that he saw flashes of color when he pulled his eye muscles to the left or right. It was amazing, even warm. He couldn't be afraid, not even if he wanted to.

Apple juice?

"LSD does wonders when you drink it. Perfect. Colorless, odorless, tasteless, even when you . . . " She made a face. "*Inadvertently* drink it."

Nick watched her. She'd been spiking his apple juice with LSD? And now she'd shot him up with heroin? "Why . . . " he whispered.

"Oh, Nick darling, let me explain. First off, did you think you're creative enough to imagine a maggot in Chloe's eye? Or any of the other trips you've been taking?"

She laughed. "Even my genie power can't go inside your head and make you hallucinate. I needed a little help with that. And, it was fun. I like needles. They're so . . . sharp." She giggled. "And this way, the drugs will show up in your system and everyone will think you're just like all the other druggies who happened to *overdo* it."

"No . . . " he murmured. "Please . . . "

"You know, Nick, this was never about you." She reached down and swiped a fingernail over his throat. "That probably doesn't make much sense, does it?"

She pinched his cheeks and shook his head for him. "No? Well, let's just say that I had the right house, but the wrong *room*."

Nick went to throw up his hands but they fumbled against his sides. "Too much . . . "

"Oh Nick, that's the point. LSD did wonders, but I need something far more potent for tonight. Now you just lie back and enjoy the ride, because you're on your way to *hell!*"

Time passed.

Passed with color and texture.

I'm going to die, Nick thought. He was sure he could hear the angels of death whispering to him, talking to him, *about* him, plucking at his clothes, his hair, his feet.

He saw Chloe watching from a distance. Standing beside Mrs. Sampson. Holly Sampson tried to speak, but then Dr. Sampson threw a large black blanket over them all. Chloe screamed.

Then he was in Egypt again.

Standing in front of the execution pedestal. The man who'd turned away from Lyra before she'd been burned alive was beside him. He was naked. "Serqet," he said to Nick. "We are each other."

He embraced Nick tightly.

"I know you?" Nick said.

The man nodded and pointed into the sky.

Chloe stared down at him, her body slowly taking on the appearance of a cloud, stretching out and drifting.

"I'm going to die," he hollered up to Chloe.

Only he didn't die.

He came round.

His eyelids felt weighted as he opened them. His head hurt. Lyra was curled up in the rocker watching him.

He said her name.

She rushed toward him and kissed him on the mouth. A pink halo seeped from the top of her head. "Oh, Nick. Coherent so soon." She tutted. "You're making this difficult."

I'm funny that way, he told her with his eyes. *I've always been difficult when someone wants me dead . . .*

She kissed him again. "Well, it can't wait any longer, I suppose. Don't you know love awaits me?" And then she withdrew her knife and brought it across his wrists.

Nick watched her, as if watching from another dimension. He saw the skill in which she drew a line with the tip of the blade across one wrist and then the next.

The pain wasn't as bad as he believed it might be.

He saw a hole in the ceiling and from the hole, a ladder plopped out and dribbled to his feet. He edged his feet toward it and then they were entangled and he was being pulled, up up and away. Like a zipper being plucked upward, he felt himself slide away from Lyra, from the blood, from himself.

He heard music, soft music that seemed to breathe and then the angels rushed toward him, laughing and calling to him, telling him it was over, *lover boy.*

And maybe that was for the best. For it all to be over.

Over and done and this is the end of the line. The end of it all. Ralph laughed and slapped him on the back.

Harder.

And now there was pain. Pain so real it made Nick cry out. Only he couldn't cry out. He could do nothing but flinch each time Ralph's fists slammed into his shoulders.

Chloe screamed. "Nick, don't go!"

Paula said, "Didn't think he'd do it."

His father added, "I might've known."

A buzzing noise that filled each and every pore drowned out their voices. A buzzing that whined and got darker.

Lyra was moving him now.

Jolting him, doing God knows what to his body. She probably wasn't satisfied with slashing his wrists and drugging him. She probably needed to do the full meal deal, chop him into little bits, feed his liver to his father.

The book *That Hurt Thing* danced in his brain. Danced in perfect time to the whine and the music, the whump, whump, whump that was probably his heartbeat — or lack of. The angels toasted him, lifting their silver goblets. "Apple juice," they sang. "So good, so clevah!"

Nick forgave them for their impertinence.

"That hurt thing," he said their way. "That hurt thing."

Nick squinted at the pale beige walls. The ceiling was tiled, that institutional chalky white tile with reams of brighter white intersecting large flecked squares.

He struggled with a vague memory of being carried on a stretcher. Another memory surfaced of hearing his father's voice.

His wrists. Bandaged. Another Band-Aid was taped across the back of his hand, as if there'd been an IV inserted.

A hospital, of course.

A yellow curtain was closed most of the way around his bed. It wasn't a private room as he could see the very end of another bed, but there was no movement or noise from that side.

I'm here and I'm alive . . .

Apple juice, hallucinogens, and Lyra. She'd confessed to spiking his apple juice with LSD, probably for months, probably since Montreal.

She'd confessed to a lot of things. The murder of Holly Sampson for one. And then she'd promptly decided to shoot him full of heroin and slash his wrists.

He needed to call Chloe or his dad. Maybe they didn't know he was even here.

"I think the nurse took my pills again."

Nick flinched. "Hello?"

So he did have a roommate.

"Hello," came the reply.

"You have a phone on your side?"

"I can't use it."

What kind of an answer was that? Nick tugged across the curtain to see a man sitting up on the bed. Stats: male, about 40, black greasy hair, small squinting dark eyes, large shelf of a chin, sunken cheeks, wearing sloppy sweat pants and baggy white tee shirt.

Nick glanced to the night stand. No phone. Not much of anything, for that matter. Not even a television. Spare.

"I think the nurse took the phone," the man said.

Nick smirked. "That nurse takes a lot, doesn't she?"

"They all do. They hate me, see."

A woman entered the room then, wearing a thick green sweater over a flowered dress. She stopped at the end of Nick's bed and smiled. She played with gray ringlets, tucking them behind her ears. She reminded Nick of a large chubby dwarf. "Dear little angels, aren't they sweet?"

The man in the other bed shook his hands toward her. "You won't be stealing my feet!"

Nick reached to press the call button for the nurse. There wasn't one.

The woman said, "You wouldn't hurt 'em, would ya?"

Nick shook his head, but said nothing.

That's when another woman entered the room. A nurse. Thank God. She patted the edge of the bed and said, "Morning, Nick."

"How long have I been here?"

She checked his bandages. She was a young nurse, a stout woman with red hair that reminded him of Chloe's. She was so pale that her red mouth seemed exceptionally large.

"Here? A few days."

"I don't remember coming in."

"That's typical. It was late when you were transferred and you were still groggy."

"Transferred?"

"Don't worry, you'll need to see Dr. Genter today."

"Who's Dr. Genter?"

The woman with the gray curls left the room. They could hear after her, "Dear little angels, aren't they sweet?"

The nurse pointed to the man in the other bed. "This is Andy. You're going to be roommates for a bit."

Nick frowned. "A bit?" Nick felt his stomach churn. "What hospital is this?"

The nurse fluffed his pillow and hesitated.

Nick knew then. Knew without asking. He was in the psychiatric facility. "Dagnorth General?"

She nodded. "You were in pretty sad shape. That's the way it is when you hit bottom."

"Hit bottom?"

She gave him a look that said, *Don't play me for a fool.*

"I was drugged," he told her. "This is all a big misunderstanding. I don't need to be here."

"Of course you don't." She lightly slapped the bed. "Your father brought in some clothes for you and they're in the closet. You'll be seeing Dr. Genter and he doesn't like to be kept waiting."

She was right about that, Nick later decided when he was ushered into Dr. Genter's office and immediately told to take a seat.

Stats: white male, late forties, too-big mustache and glasses for his long face, thin pinched lips, tall, maybe six feet with a gut that bulged over a black belt.

He held a pen and flicked it toward the seat, as if Nick were taking too much time in getting there.

"Tell me why you tried to kill yourself, Nicholas."

"I didn't."

Dr. Genter nodded curtly. "How do you explain your wrists?"

Nick glanced down at the bandages. Hard proof like this was going to be difficult to explain. But he had to try. Dagnorth General was infamous for sucking people in and not letting them out. It was rumored that there were patients here from the sixties' free-love scene.

Nick put his hands in his lap. "Someone else did this to me. A woman —"

"A woman?"

"A woman who . . . " Nick paused. Should he include the fact that she thought she was a genie? From a shrink's perspective, that may make *him* look even more crazy than Lyra. Crazy people hung out with crazy people, wasn't that the deal?

"Yes?" Dr. Genter said.

"A woman who's been following me around."

Dr Genter's expression was serious. "Is this someone you know?"

"I met her in Montreal and she followed me to Halifax. She's stalking me."

"Stalking you? Has anyone else seen her?"

"Well, see, for a while she hid away and just did weird things to freak me out."

Dr. Genter pinched his lips together. "What I'm hearing is that she stalked you from a *distance?*"

"Yes. Her name is Lyra. I spent some time with her in Montreal and then —"

"Were you and Lyra . . . intimate?"

Nick pulled his head back. "I don't think that's anyone's business."

Dr. Genter nodded and scribbled in the chart. He wore a square gold watch and a single initialed ring. His glasses slid down his nose.

"There is one other person who met her." Nick squirmed in the seat. "And I'm sure after I tell you, you'll want to call the police."

Dr. Genter looked up from his notes. "I'm listening," he said.

"Dr. Gerald Sampson's wife, Holly Sampson . . . she met Lyra." Nick paused. "At least for a little while. See, Lyra . . . murdered Holly. She told me herself. That's why we need to talk to the police."

Dr. Genter's expression was still. "Tell me about your drug use."

Didn't he hear what I just said? Nick couldn't believe that the shrink wouldn't be the least bit curious about a murder. Was the man brain-dead?

Nick sighed and let his shoulders slump. "I don't do drugs. Lyra had been spiking my apple juice. She sneaked in my house. I thought I was having hallucinations, going crazy. And the night she wanted to kill me, she stabbed me with a needle that was full of heroin. But listen, what's more important than all is about my professor —"

"So what I'm hearing is that you feel you had no choice in taking drugs?"

"Yes, no —"

"We tested you . . . " He skimmed the chart. "Nicholas. We tested and found evidence to suggest a history of drug abuse."

"I'm not a drug addict!"

Dr. Genter wrote in the chart again. The office was stuffy and sterile. The one window was small; dark brown curtains were pulled tightly shut. Fluorescent lights overhead hummed and occasionally blinked. A bookcase behind the psychiatrist held only a couple of thick books which led Nick to believe this was perhaps one of many offices the man used. He was probably a traveling shrink, going from one loonie bin to the next like Alice in Wonderland traveling from one neurotic adventure to another.

Nick laughed.

"Is something funny, Nicholas?"

"This whole thing is funny, actually."

Dr. Genter looked up. He pushed his glasses up his nose. "What's the whole thing?"

"Look. If you contact my dad, I'm sure he'll tell you that there's nothing wrong with me."

"Why do you think there's something wrong with you?"

"Well, I'm in *here*, aren't I?"

"Nicholas, life is a process, a roadway. Sometimes life takes us to paths that make us happy, sometimes it leads us to paths that make us ill."

"Am I ill?"

"What do you think?"

"I think that you answer questions the same way Lyra does."

Dr. Genter just stared at him. Nick wondered if the doc had to take a special course to maintain that *beige* expression. He tried to imagine the man having a good laugh over something, or breaking wind, or picking his nose — and couldn't. Absolutely couldn't.

Maybe he's a robot, Nick contemplated. Not even real. A simulated psychiatrist created when medical cutbacks were imminent.

"You don't believe a word I'm saying, do you, Dr. Genter?"

"What makes you say that?"

If I were anywhere else, you would listen. But in here . . . no one has any credibility. I don't need to be here."

"You sound angry, Nicholas."

Nick put his head in his hands. "I *don't* need to be here."

"Don't you want to get well?"

"I don't have a drug problem and Lyra *is* real." He shook his bandaged arms. "She did this to me. You've got to believe me."

"Tell me about your mother, Nicholas."

"My mother?" The muscles in his shoulders tightened. "She has nothing to do with this."

"She died when you were young. Does Lyra resemble your mother in any way?"

"No." He pulled at his lower lip with his fingers. "My mother was kind and sweet. I loved her; I hate Lyra. There's no resemblance."

"And did you hate your mother when she died? Did you feel abandoned?"

"I don't know. God." Nick shook his head. "Of course I was upset. Don't need a degree to figure that out."

"Sounds like it was traumatic."

"Of course it was! She was my *mother*. Wouldn't you be upset if *your* mother died?"

"I think if I were young Nicholas O'Brien and my mother died, I might feel pretty angry with her."

Nick thought of how good it would feel to leap across the desk and shove those big glasses up Dr. Genter's nose.

"Are you upset, Nicholas?"

Nick took a deep breath. If he were to prove to this quack that he was sane, he needed to stay in control. There was a paperweight on the desk, a triangular block of dark wood. Nick studied it.

After a few minutes, he said, "When Mom passed away, I was more concerned for my sister, Paula. She was a toddler. My father and I raised her together. I helped him."

Nick raised his chin. "But if you're insinuating that I've invented Lyra to deal with unconscious anger toward my mother, then you're wrong. It's not so difficult to figure your theory, Dr. Genter. Making an evil woman a safe focus for my hatred toward my mom. But there was no anger or hate in the way you suggest. There is none. Lyra is *real* and she drugged me, tried to murder me and murdered my professor's wife, Holly Sampson.

Dr. Genter tilted his head and nodded, as if impressed that Nick would be capable of such thought.

"This name, Lyra. Isn't that the name of a star?"

"A constellation," Nick corrected.

"How did you know that?" Dr. Genter's tone was gentle, that of a parent telling a child to go to sleep so the good tooth fairy can come slip something real nice under your pillow.

Nick shrugged. "I just knew. Why?"

"I find it ironic that the name Lyra is a place in the sky. Where we often think of heaven being."

"I didn't give her the name so I really can't answer that."

Dr. Genter leaned back in his chair. He pinched the tip of his nose in thought. "Nicholas, I understand that you have a girlfriend."

"I do."

He cleared his throat. "Are the two of you engaging in sex?"

"Whatever we *engage* in, doctor, is none of your business."

"Nicholas, I can't help you if you won't cooperate."

"It's private."

"I want to help you."

"How does knowing who I've banged, help me?"

Dr. Genter didn't react, or not outwardly. The beige expression flinched for an instant, and then he cleared his throat again and said, "Time's up."

"Can't I at least talk to the cops? Tell them what I know? Don't you have some kind of ethical legal clause about murder?"

Dr. Genter scribbled in the chart. "I'm designing a treatment program for you, Nicholas. You'll see me about once a week.

"Once a week? Surely I won't be here —"

"You're very ill right now, Nicholas," he said, over-enunciating Nick's name. He didn't look up from the chart.

"Ill with what?"

"You're depressed. You've a lot to deal with. Please close the door behind you."

Nick put his hands on the edge of the desk and stood up. "Listen. I'm afraid my girlfriend's life is in danger."

"Yes, I'm sure you are."

"Dr. Genter, please. Can I make a phone call? Aren't I entitled to one call? Even in prison they get one call."

"Close the door behind you, please."

"Don't you have someone you love? You can't be all textbook!"

Dr. Genter glanced up, sighed quickly, but didn't speak.

Nick threw up his hands. "Fine."

"Close the door, please —"

Nick ignored him. If the good doc wanted the door closed, he could lift his heavy ass from the chair and close it himself.

chapter twenty-five

Nick took his time getting back to his room, if only that it would kill another five minutes or so. Time stretched forever in here.

His ward offered little freedom. The rooms revolved in a circular pattern around the nurse's desk; behavior was closely monitored. By the nurse's desk, the angel lady trotted back and forth. "Dear little angels, aren't they sweet?"

This place would make you crazy, Nick thought as he entered his room. Andy was on his bed, sitting in the exact position as when Nick left. "I think the nurse took my blanket," he said.

Nick pointed. "It's on the floor."

"You take it?"

Nick ignored him and slumped on his bed. The pillow smelled like bleach; he sat up again. The door was open and he saw Dr. Genter walk to the nurse's station and put a few files on the counter.

"How's that golf swing?" the nurse asked as she slid the files into a square basket beside her.

Dr. Genter winked. With his big glasses and thin lips, he reminded Nick of a fly looming over the small nurse. "Getting too cold for much golf, but I do try."

She giggled. "All you can do, doctor. All you can do. The newest patient being transferred?"

He shook his head. "New meds. It's in his chart. Well, I'm outta here, folks. Gotta run by the clinic."

Dr. Genter walked to the large double doors past the desk. There was a small keypad on the wall. He typed in four numbers and then pushed the left side open. He left and there was a moment's delay when the door closed in little stutters behind him.

Nick pounded his fist against the pillow. Still a threat? How could he stand it here much longer? A week in a place like this and he'd *need* a place like this.

He had to talk to Chloe.

He had to make her understand the danger she was in. Convince her to talk some sense into his father. Surely, Bruce could get him out of here if he really wanted to.

Why hadn't anyone visited him?

He guessed that was Dr. Genter's doing, too.

He thought of a movie he'd seen about Frances Farmer and how her mother had committed her to a mental ward. She'd ended up with a lobotomy before she was released. Would that be his fate, too?

"Dr. Genter does bad things to me," Andy added. "He steals things that are mine." Andy rocked back and forth, his greasy hair flicking like black string. He grinned to show three missing front teeth, two upper and one lower. "He did this, he did."

"You're really nuts, you know that?"

Andy just rocked.

The meds cart came around a short time later, and Nick was given enough medication to knock out a horse. Strangely enough, it didn't affect him as harshly as he would have thought. *Thanks to Lyra for letting me build up some immunity.*

In fact, it felt rather good. The nagging pain from his wrists mellowed; he mellowed. It would help the time go by, he supposed. God, what had he come to?

When Nick had been there a few days, Dr. Genter decided that Nick could take his meals in the main dining room. The nurse hinted that transfer to another ward might be happening soon and wouldn't that be so very exciting?

The main cafeteria was where the social lives of various wards converged. Friends who'd been separated when one or the other had been transferred to a different ward, sought one another out. There were awkward exchanges of hugs and social adjusting of seating, not unlike, Nick noted, that of high school.

Andy shuffled behind Nick in the lineup, his trembling hands holding tightly the orange food tray. Tonight's slop was turnip casserole, liver with onions and some beige bumpy stuff they called surprise pudding.

"Just a little," Nick told the staff as he held up his plate. "Not very hungry."

Andy, on the other hand, held his plate to be filled high.

Nick wasn't sure where he should sit, so he waited to follow Andy, who shuffled to a table near the door. Three other people were already seated, a skinny black man with a walrus mustache, and two women who sat together holding hands.

"Hi," Nick said.

The two women smiled and turned back to their own conversation. The black man didn't acknowledge him.

"This where you always sit, Andy?"

"Yup. They don't steal nothing from me here and I can watch the cooks. Sometimes when they want to give you seconds, it's cuz they poisoned the seconds."

Nick took a forkful of the turnip and grimaced. "I think they already did." He swallowed harshly. "Andy, I'm curious. Why would they poison us? If there were no people to feed, they'd be out of a job."

Andy clanged his fork against the side of the plate. The two women huddled together. "They're dirty *rascals*!" He picked up his fork again and pushed a big slice of liver into his mouth.

Nick decided to abandon the logical slant with Andy. He focused instead on managing to get some of this slop into his stomach.

"Nicholas," the nurse said the next morning, "you have a visitor."

Nick was lying with a pillow stuffed under his chest. He turned over and sat up. "Who is it?"

He hoped it was Chloe, but no, it was his dad.

Bruce stood at the foot of the bed, his arms crossed. His eyes were bleak and his blond hair looked like it hadn't been washed in days.

The nurse hovered over them. Surely she wasn't about to stay for the whole visit, was she? Nick turned to the nurse. "Can we have some privacy?"

The nurse glanced at her watch. "The first visit is supposed to be monitored. But I suppose it's okay. I'll be at the desk."

Andy said, "Dr. Genter does bad things to me."

Nick had intended to stay cool when his father visited. But when Bruce put a hand on his arm, he felt his composure weaken.

He rolled his eyes. "Dad, you need to get me out of here. I don't belong in here."

Bruce pursed his lips and held them rigid. He pointed to Nick's bandaged arms. "Look what you did to yourself."

"It wasn't . . . " Nick wanted to tell his father about Lyra. Wanted to warn him. Who knew what crazy stunt she'd pull next? But he doubted his dad would believe him. Instead, he said, "How soon can I get out?"

Andy whistled and slapped his knee. "You ain't gettin' my feet."

"See?" Nick shook his head. "I *have* to get out of here."

Bruce scratched the back of his neck. He glanced at Andy and then brought his focus back. "Well, Nick, it's that Dr. Genter is concerned —"

"What does he know? He's so textbook. God, dad. There's nothing wrong with me."

Bruce had been standing near the edge of the bed and now he sat beside his son. His blue eyes narrowed; it was obvious he wasn't dealing with this well.

"Nick, you've not been *right* for a while." His voice was hushed, the same tone he used so many times when talking to bereaved families. "But it's not your fault. I think it's stress, or maybe you never really got over your mother's death . . . "

Not this again. Did everything in psychiatry deal with the mother? "It has *nothing* to do with Mom. I'm telling you, it doesn't."

"Okay," Bruce said. "Okay, son."

Neither of them spoke for a time, which was just as well. Nick couldn't remember feeling so helpless. Here was his father, the one person who might be able to influence the happy shrink to let him free, and Bruce might as well be on another planet.

"Can you bring in my school books?" Nick asked his father. "I'm going to have a lot to make up."

"Son, don't think about school right now. Just think about getting well."

"Forget about school? Dad, this is my last year. I'm applying to medical school."

"Oh, Nick. Do you think that's wise?"

"I won't give up, Dad!" Nick felt tears at the back of his throat. His father expected him to forget about medical school? It didn't seem real.

Bruce gave a little smile. "Dr. Genter said you might be transferred to another ward. A better ward with more freedom."

Nick grabbed a handful of hair and squeezed. "Dad, please listen to me. I need to come home. I can't take it here. People are *nuts in here*."

Bruce filled his cheeks with air and slowly let it out. "Nick, I'm sorry."

"You won't help get me out, will you?"

"Son, I . . . I just can't help but think this is all my doing, somehow."

"All your doing? Don't be ridiculous."

"I can't help but think . . . if I'd been better to your mother, maybe this wouldn't have happened." Bruce looked away. "Before her death, we'd been having some problems, Nick. You may as well know. I can't help but think those problems made her . . . do what she did."

Nick just stared at his father without speaking.

"I did some things that I regret. Will regret the rest of my life." Bruce's voice choked on the last word. "It's like throwing a stone in a pond and watching the ripples. First your mother, and then you . . . "

"What are you talking about?"

A nerve jumped in Bruce's lip. "She was . . . thinking of leaving me."

Nick pushed his shoulders back. It didn't seem possible. His parents had seemed so happy. Why was his father confessing these things now? The timing was a little off, after all.

"Dad, I don't understand."

"Lynn's research was very important to her, as you know. I started to feel ignored . . . "

Bruce took a deep breath. "I started going out more, telling her I was at work. I think I wanted her to be jealous, but she wasn't. Isn't that ironic? Things got worse. Finally she said she couldn't take it anymore and hell knows I couldn't blame her. Not a month later, she killed herself."

Nick felt like something was missing in his father's story. "She wanted to leave you because of what exactly? That you were going out a lot? Dad, that doesn't make any sense."

He agreed. "It's rather complicated, son."

"So this is why you won't date anyone?"

Bruce nodded.

"Punishing yourself . . . " Nick wished he could convince his father that none of it was his fault, not what was happening with him; not his mother's suicide.

"Dad, what else happened with you and mom. You may as well tell me everything. I feel like I'm not getting it."

"Oh, Nick." Bruce knuckled his chin. "Okay, when I —"

"Mr. O'Brien?" It was the nurse.

Both Nick and Bruce looked up.

"Bruce O'Brien," she clarified. "There's a phone call for you. You can take it at the desk out here."

Bruce left the room and returned a few moments later

"Who was that?" Nick asked.

"No one, son. Just business, is all. But, I've got to be getting back —"

"Dad. What about . . . what you were telling me; please don't go."

"I have something for you," Bruce said, ignoring his pleas. He reached into the pocket of his blue dress pants and withdrew the wolf pendant. "You're not supposed to have jewelry on this ward, so don't let them see it. I think once you get transferred, it'll be okay."

Nick slipped it over his neck and tucked the wolf's head inside his shirt. The hood on the sweatshirt hid the base of his neck and would hide the necklace. He hadn't owned the wolf pendant very long, but when it settled around his neck he felt strangely renewed — as renewed as possible in a mental ward. He thought of Chloe telling him about the wolf being the genie's only enemy.

"I guess you found this when you found me that night, eh?"

Bruce pressed his lips together. "Yes. It was on the floor next to your bed."

"Dad, since we're being so honest, I need to tell you something, too. Please stay and listen; it'll only take a few moments."

Bruce glanced at his watch, but said, "Okay."

"Dad, I'm being stalked. A girl I met in Montreal followed me back here. Her name is Lyra and no, don't look at me like that. Dad, she murdered Holly Sampson. I know it. She told me." He turned his wrists up and shook them. "*She* did this to me. I didn't try to kill myself."

"Nick . . . "

"No, listen. Why would I? Think about it. I'm perfectly sane and you know it. I'm really worried Lyra is going to hurt Chloe, or Paula. Or you."

Bruce strained his head forward, but said nothing.

"Dad, I know what I'm saying makes me sound like I belong in this nut place. But it's *true*. You've got to be careful, keep a close eye on Paula. And get me out of here!"

"Son, you need to rest —"

"I'm telling you!" Nick grabbed Bruce's sleeve. "Remember the mix-up with the bodies? It was her. That, or she gave me something to make me space out so I'd do something like this. LSD. She's been putting it in my juice. She put Chloe's necklace on Holly Sampson, too."

Bruce pulled his head into his chest. He sucked in a wet, teary breath.

"Hell, what . . . " Dear God, his father was crying.

Only one other time had Nick seen his dad cry and that had been at his mother's funeral. He could still see the way his father's shoulders had trembled as he tried in vain to hold it all in, to be the strong man for Nick and Paula.

Part of Nick wanted to comfort his father — after all, this had to be hell on him. But more than that, Nick felt angry. Why couldn't his father just believe him? Believe *in* him?

"Nick." Bruce said after a few moments. "Nick, it's so much . . . " He wiped his eyes with the back of his arm and sniffed back his tears. "It's more —"

"I know it's hard to see me here . . . "

" — than that." He squeezed his eyes shut and opened them slowly. "Nick . . . the police need to see you."

"See *me?* " Nick let his feet slide off the bed to the floor and he stood up quickly. "About what?"

Bruce put his hand on his son's shoulder. "About the murder of Holly Sampson."

chapter twenty-six

Nick heard the words his father spoke, but none of it seemed to register. The police wanted to talk to him about Holly Sampson? It was ironic that Nick wanted to talk to the police, too — about the same issue.

"They think I murdered her, don't they?" Nick said simply.

"Gerald Sampson," Bruce said. "You hated him since he gave you that bad grade."

"I wouldn't kill his wife over it!" Nick felt like a weight was slowly pressing down on him. Pressing him further and further away from anything that resembled reality. "So I'd do in his wife? You don't believe that? I know you don't! Dad?"

Bruce just stared at him.

"It was Lyra. I wasn't anywhere near Holly Sampson. I'd never met her until . . . I saw her in the casket. Where'd the police get such an idea?"

"The . . . blade that murdered her," Bruce said as he pinched the tip of his nose, "was the same one that you used . . . on your wrists."

"Not true. It's not true!"

"Dr. Sampson's secretary gave a list to the police of any students she felt didn't like the professor. You were on the list, so when you were taken to the hospital, they examined your apartment. The knife had Holly Sampson's blood on it. The knife you used."

"Dad," Nick said calmly. "I did not kill anyone. I'm not made that way. Dad, you know it."

Oh, Lyra was keen; she'd planned it all so very carefully.

"You're not in your right frame of mind, son. They know that. It'll help. No one wants to put you away."

"They just want to convict me of murder."

"Nick," his father continued. "No one's going to question you about either event for a while yet. Not until you get better and Dr. Genter thinks —"

"Is that supposed to comfort me, what Dr. Genter thinks?" He folded his arms and slumped face-down against the bed. The white cotton was warm against his forehead and for an instant he remembered his mother tucking him in at night, her small hands smoothing his head and her little laugh that was full and sweet.

For the first time in years, he missed her. His mother would have believed him, he was sure of it.

"Dad, I'm not crazy, not a killer." His voice was muffled. "Just get me out of here so I can defend myself."

"I can't get you out, Nick. It's not up to me. Under the circumstances, Nick . . . "

"Wait a second." Nick sat up. "You said *either event*."

Bruce looked away.

"Either event. Dad, what does that mean?"

Bruce glanced at his watch. His shoulders hunched forward. "Nick, the nurse said this was a quick visit. And I really have to go."

"Is Chloe okay?"

Bruce nodded. "She's fine."

"And Paula?"

Bruce hesitated. "Fine."

"She still hanging out with the loser?"

Bruce looked away. "Uh . . . no, no, she's not."

"Dad, what is it?"

"Nothing, nothing at all."

Nick folded his arms and clenched his fists. Maybe he really was losing it just like everyone thought. He was being paranoid again, reading more into his dad's words. Or was he? He scanned Bruce's expression, but could see nothing except pain and confusion.

"Why didn't Paula come with you? Or Chloe? Or do they think I'm a *murderer*, too?"

"I didn't say you were a murderer, Nick. They'll be in. Dr. Genter wanted to wait a few days first."

"Keeping me from my girlfriend and sister?" He shook his head. "Does that make sense?" The more he saw and heard of this shrink Genter, the less he liked him. He thought of all the horror stories he'd heard about Dagnorth General. Little did he ever think he'd experience it first hand.

The nurse entered then, carrying a little plastic cup and a blue water jug. Pill time. She took a Styrofoam cup from the night stand and filled it. "Here you go, down the hatch." She tapped her watch. "Mr. O'Brien, it's getting near that time, I think."

"Yes, I have to leave anyhow."

Nick didn't want his father to leave. He wanted desperately to hear more about the police's crazy notion that he'd hurt Holly Sampson. If only he could talk to Dr. Sampson. Maybe he'd listen to him, take his side. "Please. Can my father stay a little while longer?"

The nurse shook her head. "Not today." She gave a little smile. "A sapped boy's not a well boy."

Bruce clasped his arm around Nick's shoulder. The gesture was awkward and functional. God, what had they become to one another?

"Tell Chloe I love her, would you do that?"

Bruce nodded. "I sure will." He stood in the doorway, biting his lip. "I'll talk to you real soon . . . and don't worry about anything. It'll all work out. Promise."

"Yeah, Dad. Sure."

When Bruce left, Nick pulled the pillow over his head. Across the room, Andy said, "A sapped boy's not a well boy."

The next day Nick was transferred to what the nurse called ward L. He didn't know what the L stood for, but loser or loonie might be an idea. He was led into a room that held two beds. The room was larger than the previous one. On the puke-yellow wall, a painting of blue flowers was bolted into place, and on each bed, a checkered red and white quilt was folded across the end.

The nurse counted the rules on her fingers. Smoking only in the smoking room at the end of the ward; meals in the main cafeteria, but you can make toast or tea in the small kitchenette; no physical contact with the other patients, and, oh yeah — if you try to kill yourself again, you'll be sent back to the first ward. One more thing: try to sign up for a few options like art or music therapy and of course, you'll see Dr. Genter once a week and group therapy is a possibility; any questions?

"No roommate?"

"He's out and about. His name is Dander."

Dander? That's quite the name, thought Nick when he was alone in the room. His room caught the morning sun and threw striped shadows across the floor. From the barred window, he could see Halifax harbor. A tanker floated past his vision flying an American flag.

I'm like that tanker, he thought. Life is passing me by while I rot in this messed up place.

What bothered Nick the most was missing school, a selfish thought but there it was. Dr. Sampson had lost his wife and all he could think of was ruining his shot for medical school.

He told himself he could finish the term later. He could apply later. It should've comforted him, but it didn't. It only made him more determined to get the hell out of there.

"What's the capital of Somalia?"

Nick turned from the window to see a tall man march into the room. Stats: white male, early fifties, six feet tall, 200 pounds, silver hair, white mustache, blue pants with a white daisy and polka-dot print, and a pink tee-shirt, and quite a sight, oh yeah, quite a sight.

"You must be Dander."

"That would be me." He saluted and said, "The capital?"

"Uh . . . I don't know."

Dander smoothed his long white mustache and grinned. He was the oddest looking man Nick had ever seen. "Young people, don't know enough to make a hole in the ground. Mogadishu, that's the capital."

Dander extended a hand to shake it and then plucked it back and laughed sharply. "Gotcha!"

Nick sat on the edge of his bed. He'd had enough of fruitcake people to last a lifetime. Why on earth would a man who looked like a retired football player dress in such feminine colors? He reminded Nick of art students who dressed and acted outrageously for the sake of being different.

"Capital of Canada?"

"Ottawa," Nick mumbled out. That was too easy.

"Wrong. It's a C. Ha ha!"

"Here's one for you, then." Nick said. It was odd to be going along with this charade but it wasn't as if he had a booked afternoon. "Columbia?"

"Bogota!"

"Mexico?"

"Mexico City!"

"Germany?

"Berlin."

Dander made a dramatic circle with one finger and pointed it. "Next?"

"I dunno. I don't want to play anymore."

"Ah, such a poor jelly-belly who lost his marbles." Dander grabbed the loose material of his pants and squeezed with both hands. "You'll have to be quick to live here with me. Last guy, ha! Didn't even know the capital of his own destiny. He simply had to die."

"Die?"

"I smothered him with his *own briefs*."

"I wear boxers."

"Ah, so you are quick." Dander whipped a hand through his silver hair. "But. Do you know the capital of your destiny?"

"I said I don't want to play anymore."

"Poor jelly-belly."

"Why do you dress like that anyway?"

Dander grinned and smoothed his mustache. "Like what?"

"Like . . . " Nick gestured to the pink shirt and polka dotted pants. "Like *that!*"

"Because I'm a freak."

"A freak?"

Why am I even arguing with this nut-case, Nick wondered.

But there was something about Dander, like the hint of a rich room past a shabby foyer. Maybe he doubted the sincerity of Dander's insanity. Or maybe he wanted a little entertainment.

"I refuse to obey the gods, see?" Dander continued. "You, however, with the designer goods, play right into their hands."

"Hollywood," Dander stated. "We emulate the slugs of Hollywood, we make them our gods. What they wear, we wear."

"I don't know if it's contagious or not, but that makes sense," Nick couldn't help but admit.

"So what's the capital of your destiny, jelly-belly?"

Before Nick could try to answer, Dander put up a hand and went toward the doorway. "I'll leave you to think about that. Cuz if you don't know the answer to that, jelly-belly, then nothin' else don't mean squat. Nope, don't mean squat a'tall."

Despite himself, Nick found himself wondering about that, too.

chapter twenty-seven

Paula answered the phone on the fourth ring. She'd fallen asleep on the sofa, and during those first few seconds of waking, had forgotten — and hoped it might be Brad calling.

"Hello."

Brad would not be calling again, ever. His days of *going against the grain* were over.

"Is Nick there, please?"

Paula cleared her throat. "Sorry, he's . . . " She sat up. Yawned. What could she say? "He isn't here. Message?"

"Ah, yes, it's Dr. Sampson calling from the Chemistry Department at Dalhousie University. Do you know when he'll be in?"

Paula knew the name was familiar. Dr. Sampson. Oh yeah, the professor dork who gave Nick the D. Then she remembered why else he sounded familiar. His wife had been murdered, and the police suspected Nick, which was wrong. She knew Nick would never hurt anyone, and especially not over a bad grade.

She supposed that was why Dr. Sampson was calling now. He probably blamed Nick, too.

"Hello? Is anyone there?"

"I'm here," she said curtly.

"When will Nick be back?"

"I don't know."

"He hasn't been in school for some time now; I'm concerned."

Dr. Sampson's quiet breathing was muffled in her ear. She hadn't ever met him, but his voice reminded her of a bald man with long scrawny fingers who walked hunched over, probably scouring the floor for lost pennies.

"Dr. Sampson . . . Nick didn't . . . he didn't hurt your wife."

"I know," came the unexpected answer.

"Oh." Paula rubbed the bridge of her nose. "The cops think he did."

"That's unfortunate."

"Think you can tell the cops what you think?"

"I already did, but you know . . . what is your name?"

"Paula. Nick's sister."

"Paula, they have to carry out their own investigation regardless. Ask people in my work and personal life, questions. I'm sure in the end your brother will be found innocent."

She scrunched her toes against the carpet. "I hope so."

"I'm sorry about your boyfriend's death, Paula. I hope the investigation into his murder is fruitful."

Paula swallowed. "Thank you."

She felt herself warming to this professor dork. She didn't want to, either. To do so felt like she was betraying her brother.

"Please just tell Nick I called. I guess I wanted to tell him that I know it wasn't him. And I've been saving notes for him so he can catch up in class. Can you pass along that message?"

Paula wondered if she should tell Dr. Sampson that Nick was in Dagnorth General. But her dad had warned her to keep that information quiet. She guessed that he was embarrassed, though she didn't know why. It wasn't like mental illness was contagious.

Instead, she said that she'd pass on his message.

"Give yourself time to grieve, Paula," Dr. Sampson added. "Losing the one you love is like peering into an endless dark cavern. At first. That's what I keep telling myself."

Paula wanted to tell him that she was sorry about his wife, but she was uncomfortable. It felt like he was confiding in her; she hated it when adults did that, poured out their hearts to teenagers and expected them to know what to say.

"Good-bye, Paula. Nice speaking with you."

She hung up and thought about his words. Peering into an endless cavern. That summed it up pretty good. She'd thought a lot since Brad's death. Thought about things she'd never really thought about before. She'd been too little to remember her mother, or her death. Except for photographs that showed the dark-haired woman who seemed to always wear lipstick, she had no idea what her mom had been about.

In a way, Brad was like the first death she'd experienced.

"Oh, Brad," she whispered. She missed him bitterly. When they'd broken up last time, she'd put any reminders of him in a box in the attic. Now she wanted those things around her again. Only thing was, she couldn't bring herself to do it. It was too painful to hold the teddy bear with 'World's Best Girlfriend' written on it; to look at the pictures of the two of them cuddled up and smiling; to read all the letters and poems he'd written her.

But soon. Real soon.

The phone rang again.

She considered not answering it. It might be Dr. Sampson calling back with something he'd forgotten to say. But then she snatched it up and said hello.

There was a buzzing noise that made her lift the phone away from her ear for a second. A buzzing like bees or electricity. "Hello? *Hello?*"

"Carry that thought, babe . . . "

The voice was dim and she could barely hear it. Babe? She yanked in a breath. No it couldn't be. Couldn't be — "Brad?"

"Babe, *theoabic . . . "*

"What?" Her voice choked. She began to tremble. Was it really Brad, or someone playing a sick joke? She couldn't be sure. Of anything.

"I can barely hear you," she whispered, sobbing into the phone. Her fingers felt sweaty. "Who is this?"

" . . . babe, it's me."

"Brad?" No, it couldn't be. How could it be? Still, she said, "Brad, oh Brad . . . I miss you so much, Brad . . . "

More humming and crackling.

"Are you okay, Brad?"

Maybe that was a silly question. But she needed to know. Needed to know he wasn't suffering in the after-world, if that were even possible..

" . . . much time . . . " His voice was breaking up again. "Daabbic!" he whispered.

"What? The attic? Is that what you're saying? Brad, I can't hear you. You're fading . . . "

A surge of static and then the dull drone of the dial tone.

"Brad?" she yelled into the phone. *"Brad!"*

Slowly she hung up, hating to do so, as if it were the last tie to her dear Brad. She mopped at her tears with the sleeve of her tee shirt. Had that really been him? And the attic? Why would Brad want her to go there? She smiled. He wanted her to look at their photographs, of course.

That was her Brad; always wanting to be her hero.

Then it occurred to her. She should've asked Brad who'd murdered him. Unless it hadn't been Brad after all. For all she knew, it could've been some boys at school, maybe the same ones who called her names like piggo and wide load.

But he'd called her babe and talked about the attic. Then again, it didn't take a rocket scientist to figure out their large house had an attic. You could probably figure that out by looking up at their home.

But just to be sure, she'd go to the attic soon.

Real soon.

Why not now, babe?

Well, what would it hurt? It didn't make a lot of difference whether she looked through the box marked "Brad" now or later. She had to face it sometime.

She climbed the first flight of steps and paused when she saw the door leading to Nick's apartment. Poor Nick. Locked away like some rabid dog. It wasn't fair. No matter what anyone said, he didn't belong in a mental ward. There wasn't anything wrong with him.

She wished she could've gone with her dad to see Nick today. But Bruce wanted to make sure Nick didn't find out about Brad's death. Bruce didn't want Nick to be any more upset than he had to be.

Down the hallway she paused again by the door that led to the attic stairs. Brad wants me to go up there, she told herself — and boy oh boy, now that she thought of it, it was eerie in a big way — getting a phone call from your dead boyfriend. Eerie and sad.

She reached for the doorknob and then yanked her hand away with a sharp cry. The handle was hot — so hot that it brought tears to her eyes; she shook her hand out and blew on it.

Her first reaction was to flee, run to the safety of the living room, maybe even call her dad to come home from work. She knew doorknobs weren't supposed to be hot, no matter what.

She watched the doorknob carefully, reached out a tentative hand, hesitated. She didn't want to disappoint Brad, just in case it really had been him on the phone. But surely Brad wouldn't want her to burn herself. She could come back later, with her dad. All she had to get was a single box. It would take no more than a minute or so.

A nerve in her arm jumped and she reached to scratch it.

Her skin came away beneath her fingernails.

"What the —"

Ants.

Not skin, but ants.

She felt them in the collar of her shirt, in her hair, at the waistband of her jeans, down the legs, wiggling inside her socks. Wiggling and squirming and *biting*.

For an instant, Paula was too stunned to move. She could only wonder how it was possible to be suddenly swarmed with ants. She glanced to the floor to see if there was a trail, some nest she'd disturbed. But nothing.

And then fear kicked astonishment out of the way — and Paula screamed. She batted at her head and tried to whip her shirt over her head, but in her panic, she only managed to get one arm out and the shirt ended up twisted around her neck.

She clawed at herself, her frantic yelps sounding far away.

She tried to call out to her father, but it didn't matter. He was at work. He was *always* at work.

She had to get her clothes off. If she got them off, she could rush to the shower and wash the little bastards down the drain. But it was hard to think straight with adrenaline surging through her; it was hard to stop wrenching her hands and arms like a macabre dance step.

"Ahhh . . . "

She had no idea that ant bites could hurt like this. She'd never been bitten by an ant. They stung, that was the thing; stung like a quick burn.

She stumbled across the hallway, hitting her elbow against Nick's apartment door. She swatted an ant near one nostril, knocking the ant away, but giving herself a good smack in the meantime. Her eyes blurred. She felt the little legs digging into her scalp, wiggling into her ears and eyebrows, even in the crack of her backside.

"God, oh God . . . *oh God* . . . help . . . *help!*"

She'd managed to get her shirt off and she used it to try to flick the rest away. A few ended on the floor, only to scuttle back to Paula's body like people racing toward the exit of a burning building.

The ants made a crackling noise, almost like a war chant or laughter. Paula slammed her foot on a couple, delighted in smashing the life out of the tiny creeps. She'd killed only about half a dozen, but it gave her encouragement.

She concentrated on the staircase that descended to the first level. Her breath wheezed; she was getting tired. As heavy as she was, it was difficult to maneuver, let alone battle an army of ants at the same time.

Now at the top of the staircase, she paused. It was getting harder to breathe and she felt sick, like she might throw up.

One step at a time, babe. C'mon, concentrate.

She bit down on her teeth. Lifted a foot, dropped it. Now the other. One. Two. Two and a three. Pause. Three and a four —

"What a hideous sight!"

Startled, Paula whipped her head to one shoulder. Who said that? Was someone in the house with her?

Her stomach burned. Her tongue felt big in her mouth. "Who . . . who . . . help —" she blathered out. She couldn't finish the sentence. She stumbled and caught herself on the railing, wobbled, and then fell headlong down the staircase.

Her knees hit the wood first, and then she somersaulted as if something had lifted her up and chucked her.

Chucked her like she was fifty pounds.

Nick raced to the visiting area where he was told that Chloe waited to see him.

And there she was. Standing in the doorway, arms crossed, looking mildly uncomfortable.

"Chloe!"

She turned and rushed toward him. She put her arms around his neck. Her familiar perfume made him ache. "Nick, are you okay?"

"I am now." He kissed her mouth. "Here, let's sit down."

The plastic sofa squeaked as they sat together holding hands. It seemed there was so much to say that they didn't know what to say, where to begin.

Nick soaked up her presence. He'd been in Ward L for three days, and seeing Chloe reminded him that he could indeed feel something other than rage and resentment. "I love you," he blurted out.

She smiled. "I know. I love you, too."

"The nurse told me you were coming. I've been on pins and needles all morning."

Nick had played this scene in his mind many times over the past few hours, and hadn't come to any conclusions. But having Chloe here now, he knew — he had to tell her about Lyra.

But, if he told her everything, she'd probably break up with him — and who could blame her? Unless he told *almost* everything. He wondered what made him a bigger bastard, sleeping with Lyra, or denying that he'd slept with Lyra.

"Chloe, how you doing?"

"I miss you." She licked her lips. "But I'm all right, I guess. I've moved into my new place and . . . how much has your dad told you?"

"He told me about the police wanting to question me." He swallowed. "Chloe, you know I'd never hurt anyone like that, not even Dr. Sampson's wife."

"I know." She ran a finger over his nose and jaw. "It's all a big mix-up."

"It's so good to hear you say that." He kissed her again. "I'm going to get out of here. I don't belong in here."

"But you . . . " She touched his bandaged wrists. "Why?"

"I'll tell you everything, but you have to promise to believe me."

She nodded. "Your dad said you're very depressed."

"Listen, Chloe, nothing is as it seems. Okay?"

"Okay."

"Chloe? Why do you have an odd expression on your face?"

She shrugged. "I don't."

Nick watched her. Why did he have the feeling that something wasn't right? Of course it wasn't. Chloe was visiting her boyfriend in a mental hospital. He fell back against the seat and rubbed a hand over his hair. "Being in here is making me paranoid —"

"No, it's not." She chewed on the edge of her thumbnail. "You're not paranoid at all."

He just looked at her. "Chloe, is there something —"

"Brad's dead."

"What did you say?"

"Brad's *dead*."

She closed her eyes. "It's true. I haven't been here because I've been with Paula at Brad's funeral." Her voice went to a whisper. "He was *murdered*, Nick."

Nick shook his head. Brad, murdered? "That's why I felt Dad wasn't telling me something. But I would have never guessed something like that. How's Paula?"

Chloe pushed her hand into his. "Pretty shook up."

"Who . . . "

Not that he needed to ask. This was Lyra's doing; he *smelled* it.

"We don't know what happened. Not yet, anyway."

"I wish I could see Paula."

"Your dad doesn't think she's strong enough right now."

"Of course," he said bitterly. "Don't let her near the fruitcake." He sighed. "Do you know anything of what happened?"

"Not the full story. Just that someone broke into his apartment. Paula didn't hear from him for days. She thought he was ignoring her. Then . . . " She dabbed at her eyes. "One of the neighbors complained about the smell."

"That's bad."

Chloe frowned. "Nick, he was found in bed, hacked to pieces." She chewed on the top of her knuckle. "Why is all this happening? I thought things were getting better. I got my new place, new roommate. You and I got together. Paula and Brad seemed to be working it out. I thought life was good."

"It's terrible what happened to Brad." He kissed her face. "Which is why, Chloe, you've got to listen to me."

"You look so serious." Her lips hovered into a little hopeful grin, as if she dared to believe that surely, whatever he was going to say couldn't be *that* bad.

Nick grabbed her hands and squeezed. "Chloe, I'm not insane or depressed and the part of you that loves me realizes that. God, Chloe, if I don't have you on my side —"

"I'm on your side," she told him. "Whatever it is you have to tell me, I'll believe you. I will."

"Where do I start? Chloe . . . it's like this. When I went to Montreal that weekend —"

"*Chloe-toes!*"

Chloe's head flicked up and she smiled. Nick followed the gaze, annoyed that now that he'd gotten up his nerve to divulge the story, he was being interrupted . . .

Wait a second. Who would interrupt him here?

Lyra, that's who.

Smiling, she made her way toward them, her black hair flicking over her shoulders, her smile wide. Chloe stood up to greet her.

"There you are," Lyra said with a giggle. "There you are, Chloe." She tilted her head and thrust out a hand to Nick. "And you must be the boyfriend I've heard so very much about."

chapter twenty-eight

Chloe saw the shock in Nick's eyes.

"Nick," Chloe said, "this is my new roommate, Becky Farm. She came with me today; I was a little nervous. Hope that's okay."

Nick didn't answer. Nor did he accept Becky's outstretched hand. Chloe didn't understand. Why was he being so rude?

Maybe Nick was embarrassed that she'd brought along a friend, a stranger at that. But Becky had promised that she'd wait outside. Why hadn't she done that? While Chloe supposed there was a good reason, she felt annoyed, too.

"Nick." She smoothed his arm. "Didn't you hear what I said, this is —"

"You *bitch!*" Nick slapped Becky's hand away and pointed a finger in her face. "You stay away from Chloe. You —"

"Nick, stop!" Chloe yanked Nick's hand down and held it between hers. His lips were pressed so firmly together that it made a white rim around his mouth. She couldn't believe what she was seeing. What did Nick think he was doing?

"You don't know who she is, Chloe. I was just about to tell you about her. She's part of what you need to be aware of. Becky Farm?" Nick cackled. "That's rich. Rebecca of Sunnybrook Farm."

"No, this is my roommate, my *friend*. She's been waiting outside for me."

"Chloe, listen to me. This girl isn't a friend to *anyone*. She murdered Holly Sampson, and Brad, too, I'm sure of it. She's sick. She thinks she's a genie!"

"A genie?"

Becky put a hand over her mouth, as if she were curtailing laughter. "I'm . . . sorry . . . it's just that . . . *me*, a genie?"

For the first time, Chloe wondered about Nick's mental state. Surely this behavior wasn't normal. A genie who murdered Mrs. Sampson and Brad? She remembered Nick asking about genies that night she'd helped him study for his Shakespeare exam. Was that when he began to get ill?

"What happened to Connie?" Nick asked. "Thought she was your new roommate."

"Connie got sick," Chloe explained. "Some bad flu or something and then all of a sudden she didn't want to move in. I met Becky on campus and she was looking for a roommate, too. It worked out perfectly. It's a *good* thing, Nick."

"You listen to what I'm saying, Chloe. This girl is evil. Her name is not Becky. Her name is Lyra and you have to stay away from her. She killed two people and . . . you're next, I'm sure of it."

"Nick, please —"

"I know it sounds crazy, Chloe," Nick continued. "But I swear on my life! You said I wasn't the same since Montreal . . . well, *she's* the reason why —"

He stopped short. "Tell her, Lyra. Tell her!"

Becky's eyes went from Nick to Chloe. She hesitated and took a step back. "I . . . I don't know what to say. This is the first time I've ever seen you. Perhaps you've mistaken me —"

"She's lying. She followed me to Halifax!"

"Why would she do all that?" Chloe hoped common sense might bring him around. "Why?"

Becky tilted her head, as if she wanted to hear the answer, too. Poor Becky, to have to see Nick in such a state. She'd told her such good things about her boyfriend, too.

"She's in love with me. We . . . " Nick's nostrils widened and he swiped his hand over his head to the back of his neck. "We slept together."

His shoulders fell and he let his mouth hang open. "I'm sorry, Chloe. But it's the truth. I wasn't going to tell you. It was stupid and wrong, but Chloe . . . it was a long time ago, long before you and I . . . "

His words dragged to nothing. His posture slumped; he looked old, if that were possible. Exhausted and old. Why would he make up stories about Becky? Or maybe he really believed he'd been intimate with her.

Which was worse, she wondered.

Becky shrugged and said, "Chloe . . . ah, I should've waited outside. I'm sorry."

"It's all an act," Nick continued. "She can make herself look innocent, just like she's doing now, trying to fool you. That's what made her so attractive in the first place. The way she plays you, makes you feel like you're the only person in the world."

Chloe's stomach churned. This isn't Nick speaking, she told herself. It's his sickness.

Becky cleared her throat. "Chloe, perhaps I'll go back outside." She glanced warily at Nick. "It seems I've *inadvertently* caused enough trouble."

Nick bolted to his feet. "You hurt Chloe and I'll kill you! Kill you, you hear? Keep Chloe out of this. Haven't you done *enough?*"

"Nick, keep your voice down," Chloe said harshly. The nurse at the counter turned her head.

Nick pointed both index fingers in Becky's face. "I'll get you. So help me God!" He was shouting now. "I'm warning you to leave her alone, leave her out of this!"

"My goodness," Becky said evenly. "There's no need to be difficult."

"You *bitch!*" Nick grabbed Becky's arms and pushed them over her head. She managed to squirm out of his grasp, but then Nick grabbed her around the waist and turned her toward him. Chloe screamed to the nurse, who immediately picked up the phone and spoke into it.

"I'll *kill you!*" Nick put his hands around Becky's throat. Becky's eyes widened as her nails slashed Nick's face. A thin line of blood oozed from the wound.

Chloe tried to pull him away, but it was no use. "Nick, stop it! *Stop it!*"

Becky lifted a knee and smashed it between Nick's legs. His head jutted forward with the pain, and his hands loosened. He staggered backwards.

So this is the rage he used on Dr. Sampson's wife —

No, don't think that way; Nick is innocent.

Or is he?

Chloe didn't know what to think. Moments ago, she believed him when he said he didn't belong here. She'd been ready to stand by him through this illness. But now . . . now she was afraid. Afraid of him.

Even in pain, Nick staggered toward Becky, tried to put his hands around her neck again, but fortunately, he lacked the strength. Becky shifted away from him just as two security guards rushed toward them.

"Visit's over for today," one said, jolting Nick's arm behind his back and pushing him forward. "C'mon, Nicholas, time-out."

"Chloe, listen to me," he shouted over his shoulder. "She's *evil!*"

A nurse helped a coughing Becky to the sofa. Poor Becky, such a small girl, too. It was terrifying to think what would've happened had security not acted so quickly. Would Nick have killed her?

"You . . . all right, Chloe?" Becky rubbed her reddened neck and chin.

"Don't worry about *me*. Are you okay?"

"Yes, fine. A bit shaken, I think."

"I'm so sorry. I had no idea anything like this would happen. If I had . . . "

Becky put up a hand. "It's not your fault, Chloe."

"It sure feels that way. I just can't believe Nick would act like this. It's not like him, really, it isn't."

Becky smiled. "Let's just put it behind us. Sound like a plan?"

"Yeah," Chloe agreed. "Sounds like a plan."

"Don't try to pick me up," Paula told her father when he found her at the foot of the stairs. "I can stand." His face was ashen and his eyes skittered from his daughter to the stairs, as if he couldn't believe she'd fallen all the way.

"What in the blazes happened?" he asked. "Did you trip?"

Paula stared up the dim stairwell. She remembered the ants crawling over her. "I . . . I don't know."

Bruce put his hands under her arms and with a grunt, he helped her to her feet. "Good thing I came home, that's all I can say. You must have fallen."

Paula forced a shallow chuckle.

No, she hadn't fallen — she'd been *pushed*. Not that she'd admit it to Bruce, lest she end up in a bed beside Nick, but it was true. Some force had jolted her so hard that she went whizzing over the steps like a paper plane.

That force had meant business.

It had meant to kill her.

"You got bruises along your neck and arms," Bruce said. "Let's take you to the hospital just in case."

She brushed herself off. "I'll be all right."

She hated the pitying way Bruce looked at her, as if he worried she wasn't competent enough to even walk down a flight of stairs. "You might've given yourself a concussion, Paula."

"I'm fine. Really I am. I think all my fat cushioned me. Let's wait and see how I feel? Some ice on my knee, be as good as a new penny."

Paula thought about the ants again. Had she *imagined* them? No, they were real, as real as the bruises and the cut across her knee. "I really didn't mean to scare you, Dad." She examined her knee. That was the worst of it, a bloodied scratched knee. She knew she'd be sore later, like she'd done an aerobic workout — not that she actually knew what an aerobic workout was like.

"Go clean up," he told her. "And . . . if you're sure you're fine, then . . . hey, why don't we order a pizza for supper, huh?"

Paula's first reaction was anger. Was he only offering food for comfort because she was fat? Then again, fat or not, she had to eat supper. *I'm overreacting. Again.*

She smiled. "Sounds great. Pepperoni and double cheese?"

"If you like."

"Chocolate shakes, too?"

"Shakes and pizza?" Bruce made a face. "Together? Now that's an odd combination."

Paula glanced up at the stairwell again. It was a miracle she hadn't been killed during the fall. "That's just it, Dad. Sometimes you need to take chances. Sometimes ya just gotta go against the grain."

Becky's arm came around Chloe as she handed her a cup of tea over the back of the sofa in their townhouse an hour later. "Chloe-toes," she said. "I'm so sorry about today. I didn't mean to make trouble."

"You did nothing wrong, Becky. I . . . I just didn't realize that Nick was so . . . troubled."

"That's the sad part about mental illness. We never know for certain. There's probably hundreds of people around us as sick as boogers and we have no idea."

Chloe drank her tea in silence. She kept seeing Nick reaching out to her, pleading with her to listen to him, to believe in him. He'd sounded so sincere, it was hard not to believe him.

"Well, let's hope he gets better soon," Becky added.

"Yeah, hope so." Dr. Genter told Bruce that Nick was suffering from depression. And beyond that, some kind of disorder that made him act in extremes. Dr. Genter believed it stemmed from his mother's suicide.

Chloe thought back to Lynn's death. Nick had been upset, yes. That was to be expected; he'd lost his mother, after all. But he hadn't fallen apart. In fact, he'd seemed more concerned about Paula than himself.

"How does this feel?"

Becky. Still behind her, massaging the muscles in her neck. "Great. Sure Nick didn't hurt you today?"

"I'm sure. It was so quick, you know. I felt more for *you*, to be completely honest. To hear your boyfriend say he slept with me . . . wow. That musta been *bad*. You think he was attracted to me, some deal like that?"

"I . . . I don't know . . . "

"Is he good that way, Chloe?"

Chloe looked down at her hands. She didn't know what to say.

"Listen to me here! I'm sorry, Chloe-toes. What am I saying! I can be such a big mouth when I just want to help." Becky's hands stilled for a moment. "I've invited some people over tomorrow night . . . "

"I'm not sure I'm ready for that."

"Oh, but Chloe, you need your friends around you, especially now."

"I can't have a party while Paula's grieving over Brad and Nick's in the hospital. It wouldn't be right. Feels like my entire life is going to hell." Her voice fell. "I . . . I feel so alone . . . "

"Oh, sweet Chloe." Chloe felt Becky's chin against the top of her head. "Let me take care of you. It'll all be fine, I promise."

Take care of me?

"I . . . I need to get up," Chloe said. Surely Becky was simply being kind, but something about her mood or behavior spooked her. Nerves, it was probably all nerves. "I think I left the milk out earlier."

"Here, I'll check." Becky gathered their tea cups and brought them into the kitchen. "Thought you might like to see Ralph, too," she hollered from the kitchen.

"Ralph? How do you know Ralph?"

Silence followed by a little giggle. "He called for you. Caller ID's a wonderful invention. I phoned him last night."

"Oh. So you already planned this party? Confirmed it?"

Becky came into the living room holding a red dishcloth in her hands. The color matched her lips. Chloe didn't know anyone with such naturally red lips. She pouted. "Oh, Chloe, I'm sorry if I've made a boo-boo in planning this little party." She pronounced the last word as *pahtee*.

"Look, I'll call everyone back, tell them you're in no mood to see anybody just now. I'm such a fool sometimes. I was trying to help, is all."

"It's okay." I'm being too sensitive, Chloe thought. Becky is trying to help me and I'm being ungrateful. "Would just an hour or so be fine?

"Absolutely," Becky told her. "Absolutely, my dear. Do you think we should buy a new plant for this place?"

"What?"

"A plant?" Becky waved the red cloth toward the window. It was an old townhouse with old blue carpet and chipped window panes. "You know plants cheer you up *inadvertently.* Isn't that a big word?" She laughed.

Chloe just stared at her.

"Plants are natural healers, Chloe," Becky added. "And life is short enough as it is, sweet Chloe-toes. Short enough as it is."

Nick fluttered in and out of consciousness.

They'd put him in a straitjacket; in his naiveté he had believed that Dagnorth would surely have caught up with the rest of the world and abandoned the ancient tactic. But no, they'd forced the jacket on, drugged him and chucked him into a room alone like a naughty felon. They hollered that they'd be back later when he was calm, when he was ready to be *sensible.*

Sensible. What a word. There was nothing sensible about this situation. This was hell and crazy in one. Lyra was slowly but surely destroying him and had that been a wish? Had he said to her, *Ruin me, please, that's what I wish?*

She'd stalked him from Montreal, drugged him, murdered his professor's wife and then his sister's boyfriend and was now living with his girlfriend.

Sensible?

To hell with sensible.

To hell with it all.

There was nothing to do but ride the tide of dreams and sudden but incomplete wakefulness. And consider, during those brief instants of lucidity, about how he would break out of this loony abode and protect Chloe.

Of that there was no choice.

Nick didn't know how he could pull it off, breaking out — after all, the ward was locked and security was tight. But there would be no time to wait until Dr. Shrink said he was free of his mommy-issue. By that time, Chloe could be dead.

Just the thought of Chloe's death made his guts feel like a turnip in a blender. But his denial of how dangerous Lyra was had surely contributed to Holly Sampson's death —

I'd like to smash him, smash the life right out of him.

Nick moaned. Now it made sense and Oh. My. God. That's what he'd said about Brad the night Lyra came to his bed. He'd complained about Paula being mixed up with a loser and then he'd talked about how he'd like to do him in.

As you wish, Master.

She'd taken it as a wish.

"I didn't mean it," he whimpered. "I didn't."

The drugs made it hard to think; he was being pulled into unconsciousness again. And Chloe . . . how long before Lyra tired of toying with Chloe and murdered her, too?

Three wishes. Two deaths so far . . .

From beyond the room, a loud scream shredded the air; despite the drugs, Nick flinched. His nose itched and he wiggled it in a desperate ache to ease the discomfort. He was hot in the straitjacket and his legs and mouth felt numb.

"Chloe . . . " he whispered.

He imagined that he could lift from his physical body and soar past skin and bone. He imagined his soul floating through the city, through Public Gardens and Spring Garden Road and honing automatically on Chloe's townhouse. He imagined her seeing his ghostly image and reaching curiously toward him . . .

He thought of Chloe's Oreo cookie trail, and how she peeled an orange, and how she smelled and the way she held her red hair at the nape of her neck and how scared she'd been today . . .

A thought rose to greet him, a thought that tried to tell him something about Chloe.

It was a hollow image, like a drawing in a child's coloring book just waiting to be colored in. Nick struggled to fill it, but it continued to evade him.

Sleep snatched him again.

c h a p t e r t w e n t y - n i n e

Chloe's house made Ralph uneasy and he didn't know why. Located with a sweet view of the waterfront, it was an ideal city location. The house was roomy and old with high ceilings and a fireplace. Chloe had hung her Degas print near the entrance; it spoke of come on in, relax.

But like those friends who are friends in theory — *oh yeah, let's get together, been thinking of ya, yeah, give me a call sometime* — Ralph didn't feel right in letting down his guard.

To make matters worse, Candice couldn't make it. Or wouldn't make it, more than likely. Well, no matter. When he thought about it, it wasn't like he was so hot about her. Not really.

"Ralph, have another drink."

"Okay, Becky. Thanks."

He accepted the long flute glass of champagne. Across the room, Chloe sipped from her glass, not saying too much. Not that Ralph could blame her. The poor girl must be worried sick about Nick.

"So how's Paula doing?" he asked her.

Chloe gave a tiny smile and rubbed her thumb over the base of her glass. "She'll be okay."

"Poor kid."

Becky added more champagne to Chloe's glass. It was quite generous of this Becky to plan a social event to help cheer up Chloe. She'd gone to a lot of trouble, buying champagne and making little ham sandwiches without crusts.

He watched her give a little stretch on the couch beside Chloe. Geesh, she wasn't hard on the eyes at all, no sir, nuh uh. He tried to decide what was prettier, the eyes or the way her mouth turned up at the corners. He bet that mouth could be pretty talented.

And that dress, wow. Becky sure filled it well. A brave dress. Black and sparse and short. A dress only a confident beauty would wear.

"Yes, Ralph?"

She'd caught him staring. His eyes jerked to her legs and then away. He drank his champagne. "N-nothing." The intercom sounded; relieved, he jumped to answer it.

It was Connie and Paula. Paula dragged behind Connie, the epitome of a little girl lost. Poor girl, to lose her boyfriend and have her brother committed to a mental institution in the same week.

"Hi, Paula. How you doing?"

She nodded. "Connie convinced me to get out a bit." She wiped at her nose and shrugged.

"My Lord!" Chloe said. "What happened? Your face!"

Paula explained how she tripped and fell down an entire flight of steps. She had a pretty nasty shiner there, too. Ouch.

Paula hugged Chloe. Her pudgy arms reminded Ralph of swollen sausages as they went around Chloe's shoulders. He reprimanded himself for the callous thought, but there was no denying that Paula O'Brien was one big girl.

Becky put three logs in the fireplace. "The fire will be comforting." She ripped a strip of newspaper and lit the end before tucking it beneath the logs. It didn't catch. Of course it didn't. She needed kindling for a proper fire, or at least smaller bits of wood. You couldn't just touch a big log with a little flame and expect it to burn. City girls.

"Want me to do that?"

She glared at him. At first. And then she smiled in a way that made him feel warm, very warm.

Becky was right about the fire being comforting, Ralph decided. It soothed the nerves so that soon Chloe and Paula began to talk about nothing in particular. That was a good sign, when women did that. A silent woman was not a good thing, no indeed.

He made his way into the kitchen and found some more of those tiny ham sandwiches. The bread was crusty along the edges; he picked up two, squished them together and pushed them into his mouth.

"I saw you watching me."

Ralph swallowed harshly.

Becky.

Standing in the doorway, her right arm extended high and leaning against the frame. Her long hair fell straight and shiny down her back. She let her right hand fall lazily to the top of her head.

Ralph looked past her to the living room. "Good sandwiches."

She giggled. "You do amuse me, Ralph."

"Oh yeah?" He wasn't nearly as casual as his voice made him out to be. Then again, Becky probably knew that. He had a pretty strong hunch that she wasn't just another pretty face.

"This was a good idea," he told her. "To help Chloe."

Becky nodded. "I do everything I can for those I'm obligated to."

"You're obligated to Chloe?" He hoped she hadn't planned this party out of pity or a resentful obligation to roommate etiquette.

"Chloe's a sweet girl." Another giggle. She walked past Ralph to the fridge. "Don't you think so?"

"Ah, yeah, I think so."

Becky withdrew the third bottle of champagne. "More?"

He shook his head. "I feel giddy already."

She smiled and gestured for him to open the bottle. "I like a giddy man. You have a girlfriend?"

"Ah, yeah."

"Too bad." She caught his eyes and held them. "I was hoping you could take a few moments to appreciate the womanliness of me."

While Ralph didn't fully understand what that meant — the womanliness of her, he knew he wouldn't mind appreciating her and a few moments would be a keen, keen start.

He flipped out the cork of the bottle too quickly; bubbly liquid burst over his hand. Keeping her eyes on his, Becky slowly licked his palm. Ralph couldn't believe it. He felt a rush of arousal. God, what a woman.

He went to touch her and she pulled away. "Not here. Later."

"I'll come to your room?" he whispered.

"No, somewhere else." She pressed a key into his wet palm. "This is the key to Nick's apartment —"

"How'd you get that?"

"Shhh . . . never mind." She winked. "When everyone leaves, you leave, too. I'll meet you there."

"I told Chloe I'd stay here tonight and take her to see Nick in the morning." He couldn't disappoint Chloe. That, and he hoped to see Nick, too. They all had to pull together at a time like this. And then there was Candice to think of —

She smoothed two hands over his chest and nuzzled his throat; he felt the edge of her tongue. "Ralph, I want to make you *cry*," she whispered.

Ralph started to speak but it came out a raspy groan. He cleared his throat. "I can't drive . . . too much to drink," he told her.

She touched his cell phone, in the leather holder attached to his belt buckle. With a little sigh, she removed it and put it against the counter. "Call a cab," she breathed. "I'll make it worth your fare."

Then she moved away, threw back her hair, grasped the bottle of champagne and left the kitchen. Ralph fell against the counter and closed his eyes.

He knew he should go far far away from this Becky Farm, but for the life of him, he knew he wouldn't.

He wouldn't.

"What time is it?" Nick said as they lifted him from the cool floor. His legs were wobbly when the nurse and security guard placed him on his feet; he staggered.

"Take it easy." The guard gripped his arms. "There, steady now, steady."

"What time is it?"

The nurse flicked a look to her watch. "Eight o'clock. You've been out for a while." She frowned. "You were pretty outlandish today. Here, let's get you out of this room and into bed."

"Eight in the evening?"

"Why, you got somewhere to go?" The guard chuckled at his own joke as they led him back to his room. Dander was sitting cross-legged on his bed and he nodded when they entered.

Nick took several deep breaths. The drugs they'd pumped him with had left him strung out. He put one hand on the wall and steadied himself.

"Nicholas," the nurse said, "any more foolishness and you'll be put back in the jacket, okay? Dr. Genter wants to have a quick word with you. He's on the ward."

She left with the guard and Nick fell across his bed. His arms ached and he stretched them out with a yawn. "Hello, Dander. Miss me?"

Dander curled the ends of his white mustache. "Capital of The Netherlands?"

"Amsterdam. Listen, Dander, I've got to get outta here. Tonight."

Dander smiled. He'd exchanged his pink tee shirt and polka-dot pants for a yellow blouse and pajama bottoms. He looked like a human dandelion. "Belgium?"

"Brussels."

"You need to go?"

"Yeah. Can you help me?"

"No." He threw out his hands. "We're sealed in here. Picked peas in a can."

"You ever been in love, Dander?"

Dander sighed and his face softened. He moved closer to Nick. "Ya know, it's hard to believe but once I was a welcomed member of society. It was Girt's fault. She broke me. Broke me down to wind and bone. After that, not much meant nothing anymore."

"My girlfriend's in danger. Real bad."

"Girt loved danger, that was her problem. Once, we wuz in a restaurant and she dared me to eat off a plate on the next table. If I didn't, she said, she would.

"Before I could say a word, jelly-belly, she up and grabbed a hold of this woman's turkey leg and hump! Down the gullet just like that! The poor woman near had a fit."

Dander rubbed his hands together. "Leave it to a woman to get me to love her and then she goes and eats a turkey leg off a plate without me."

"Yes, that's interesting —"

"There's no way outta here," Dander announced. "It's as good as a prison."

Nick opened and closed his hands, trying to regain full sensation in them. He thought about Dander's words. Maybe there wasn't any way out. And even if there were, did he have the strength to get all the way to Chloe's house?

He hadn't even been there. He knew approximately where it was from what she'd told him; knew the row of apartments across from the waterfront, not far from Citadel Hill. But how would he get there? He had no money for a taxi or a bus. He sunk into the bed again, and closed his eyes.

"Ya think about the question yet, jelly-belly?"

He didn't look up. "What question?"

"The capital of your destiny."

"I don't have a destiny, Dander."

"Sure you do, sure you do." He pointed across the room. "It's right in front of you."

Nick sat up. "The wall?"

"Ah, you see a wall, do ya? That's the thing, jelly-belly. Ya gotta see it everywhere. See it blinking and grabbing at ya. In *every*thing, *every*where."

He didn't have time for this nonsense. "I've got to get out of here!"

"Why?"

"My girlfriend is in danger."

"Why?"

"You wouldn't believe me if I told you . . . then again, maybe you would."

"Try me."

"A psycho woman who thinks she's a genie —"

"Thinks?" Dander scratched his belly. "How do you know she isn't?"

"Genies are mythological." Nick sighed. He should've known better than confide in a mental patient. "They're not real."

"So, jelly-belly, you're saying there's nothing bigger than us peon humans? That's it?"

"No, that's not what I meant."

Dander threw out a hand. "If you knew the capital of your destiny, you'd not give me this crap. You'd face the truth, the reality that you create."

"So I created *this?*" He gestured around the room. "Being locked up *here* while my girlfriend, maybe my whole family is being stalked by a freak, a *genie*? Messing up my chance for medical school! Messing up my *life*!"

"What's the capital?"

"I don't know! I don't care! I've got to get out —"

"Say, *I will get out.*"

"I will get out."

Dander touched the back of Nick's head. "There's hope for you yet, jelly-belly. Now listen. Walk Dr. Genter to the door when he leaves the ward and —"

"Nicholas."

Dr. Genter entered then, clearing his throat. He looked tired and rushed, anything but a man who wanted to talk to a misbehaving mental patient.

Nick watched him. It was incredible how he could have such loathing for a man he barely knew. The only other person had been Dr. Sampson. *And look where that got you, Nick . . .*

"Nicholas, I hear you had some friction today."

Nick smirked. "It was the alien living inside me."

Dr. Genter scratched the side of his nose. "Can we talk seriously now, or perhaps this should wait for another day?"

"I wouldn't mind waiting," Nick answered. It was true. He'd rather peel his own toenails than talk to the good shrink.

"Very well." Dr. Genter pushed his glasses up his nose. "In the meantime, no more visitors. I think it's more than apparent that you aren't yet ready."

Nick just nodded.

"One more thing, Nicholas. Why did you attack that girl today? Did she provoke you?"

"She's been provoking me since I slept with her."

"An old girlfriend?"

"Actually, she's a genie." Nick no longer cared how he was perceived by Dr. Genter. "A genie who lives in a book."

"She visited me, too," Dander interrupted. "She told me bad stories. She's a wily coyote woman, she is. Oh yeah!" He bucked his hips back and forth and laughed aloud. "Oh, Mama!"

Dr. Genter frowned. "Something funny, Mr. Jonas?"

Dander licked his lips. "You've got a pinched bum, doctor."

Dr. Genter blinked and the lines around his mouth deepened. Nick put a hand over his mouth, but it was impossible to curtail the laughter.

"Nicholas," the psychiatrist said, "your outburst today was unacceptable."

"Thought we weren't going to talk about this until later," Nick reminded him. "If you don't mind, I'd like to call it a night. Been a hard day at the office. I'm sure you understand."

"I'd eat a turkey leg off your plate, Doctor," Dander added.

Dr. Genter's face reddened; he sniffed and lifted his shoulders. Nick enjoyed the discomfort he saw. Like watching the end of a good movie, he tried to stretch it out, savor it.

"Goodnight, Nicholas."

"You leaving the ward now?"

"Yes, I'm going home."

"Do you have a wife?" Nick asked.

The question seemed to catch the doctor off guard. "Ah . . . no. No, I don't."

"Children?"

"No."

"A cat?"

"Nicholas, why all the questions?"

"Why not?" He twisted his ear lobe for affect, hoping it made him look a tad crazy. Why he was badgering the shrink, he wasn't sure. But it felt good, damn good.

"Good night, Nicholas."

"Doctor?"

"Yes?"

"Can I walk you to the door?"

"If . . . if you like."

"I'm sorry about everything. I do want to get better."

Dr. Genter gave a quick smile and smoothed his mustache. "Of course."

They walked together through the ward. It really was a depressing place. In the quiet of night, the growls and moans of the patients and shuffling of slippered feet moving across tiled floors were easily heard.

Nick knew he'd never last in here. He had to get out, before the place claimed him, sucked him down into the abyss, made him one of their own.

"How do you do it, Dr. Genter?" Nick whispered. "How can you keep coming here?"

"Here's a place to make people better, to improve lives." He pulled at his tie, loosened it.

"I'm not sure I believe it," Nick countered. He saw no evidence of improvement. An hourly talk once a week with a shrink and drugs so strong you couldn't think straight? How did that help? How?

"You know," Nick added, "straitjackets aren't used anymore. Except in here."

Dr. Genter sighed. "I'm aware of how that must look, Nicholas. But as a private hospital, we are keen to hold onto older, *effective* traditions." He cleared his throat. "I hear you had plans to enter medical school, Nicholas?"

"I *have* plans."

Nick strolled slowly; it was still difficult to have full coordination. He tried to act and sound casual, but in reality, his heart was beating so hard and fast, it made him dizzy.

"Do you know the capital of your destiny, Dr. Genter?"

"I beg your pardon?"

"Forget it."

Nick watched the long double glass and screen doors at the end of the hallway. A gold rod at the top of the glass held flimsy white cotton curtains in place. A homey touch. Beside the doors was the keypad for the coded exit.

Nick wasn't sure what would happen, if anything, when they reached the exit. He thought of Dander telling him to walk Dr. Genter out. But why? And who knew just how crazy Dander really was?

They passed by a room with an open door; a woman not much older than Nick, sat propped against the pillows, her eyes half-closed and mouth hanging open in a big O.

A place to make people better? Nick sighed. Yeah, right.

The door was closer now.

At the doorway, Dr. Genter paused and pushed his glasses up his nose. "I'll see you next week, Nicholas."

Nick knew the shrink wanted him to turn away so he wouldn't see the numbered exit code.

He did so. "Goodnight, Dr. Genter."

He heard the beep beep beep beep as the door swung open.

It was followed by shrieks coming from the nurse's station. Dr. Genter paused, held the door ajar with one hand. "What is going on *now?*"

It all happened so quickly, like swiping a castle made of playing cards. There were the screams from the nursing staff and the rush of security and orderlies. There was Dander who'd taken off all his clothes and held a nurse — the same nurse who'd lectured him about his behavior — by the hair. In his other hand, Dander held a bedpan and he repeatedly smacked the nurse over the head with it. His white backside glistened. A pinched bum? Despite all that was happening, Nick let out a long shrill belt of laughter.

And then there was the last long beep of the door and the disgusted expression on Dr. Genter's face. He looked from the door to the nurse's station.

Nick swallowed and lunged toward Dr. Genter. He hit the doctor full force with his body, knocking him aside. Dr. Genter cursed and grabbed Nick's shoulder just as Nick pushed toward the door that was slowly closing in little stutters.

Dr. Genter held him back, mere inches away from the gaping door.

chapter thirty

Dr. Genter held Nick securely by the shirt collar.

It was over that fast.

Nick didn't have the strength to fight him. He looked past the open doorway toward a long hallway. It was a sickly sweet sight. So close and yet so far.

"We're going back," Dr. Genter said. "Nicholas is not behaving himself at *all* today."

Nick sighed, but didn't resist.

"Hey! What's the capital of your destiny, jelly-belly?" Dander screamed as he slapped the nurse on the backside with the bedpan. "Hey, jelly-belly, *hey?*"

Nick watched him, amused. What *was* the capital of his destiny? Chloe, he supposed. Medical school, his family, friendship, love, laughter, life.

Life!

Something moved inside him then, something uncomfortably hot, like the painful burn a wasp leaves when it stings. Dr. Genter's hand pinched his shoulder blade tightly. Nick felt a sudden revulsion for the slimy moist hand. It wasn't just the hand, it was what the gesture stood for — the loss of freedom, the loss of *self.*

The loss of life.

Nick snapped his head up and twisted it to the right. His teeth found the flesh between the shrink's thumb and index finger. He pressed his teeth together.

The psychiatrist was clearly not expecting the assault.

He let out a cry that sounded feminine and desperate, and yanked his hand away.

Dander yelled, "pinched bum, ho hum, *yeah, jelly-belly!*"

Nick twisted with ease out of the shrink's grasp. He bolted toward the door.

"Nicholas, you come back here!"

Without looking back, Nick held up his middle finger over his head. And then raced to catch the door not a second before it closed.

In the long hallway, he glanced back to see the door stuttering to a complete close. He'd made it!

He raced down the hallway. He wished he'd paid more attention when he was transferred from the first ward. It was a fairly small building, however. Surely it couldn't be that difficult to find his way outside.

He followed the hallway toward the back of the building until he saw shadows that danced along a wall toward him. He stopped abruptly.

Security. Of course they'd be rushing to find him; that was to be expected. He flattened himself against the wall and heard the clattering of boots getting nearer. But then the sound disappeared and he wondered if he'd heard it at all.

After a few seconds, Nick moved down the hallway until he came to a large

Coke machine. It hummed and flickered light over the walls. On the other side of the machine was a foyer with a glass door that led outside.

His muscles burning from the sudden rapid movement after being sedated for days, Nick stumbled toward the door and then he was outside and it was so real and true he could have cried. He paused to catch his breath, his hands on his knees. He was tired; it'd be only too easy to slump to the ground and just collapse there.

But he didn't collapse.

He abandoned his fatigue and broke into a shuffled jog until he met with the main road. There, he slowed to a rapid walk toward the heart of the city. He hoped Dander was kicking up enough of a fuss to divert security for a few moments longer.

It still didn't seem real, the sequence of events that had led to his getting away. If there was one true miracle in his life, surely it was the perfect timing that permitted his escape.

He stepped into the street in line with a cab that whizzed past him. Cursing, Nick turned up a side street. If he kept using side streets until he got to Spring Garden Road, there'd be little chance — or so he hoped — of security finding him. He supposed the hospital had called the police, too. Especially since the cops wanted to question him about the murder of Holly Sampson.

His legs were wobbly and when he paused, he felt as if he might topple over. The air refreshed him, but he was cold. He didn't know if it was the medication or the fact that he wore only jeans and a white sweatshirt.

Finally he reached Spring Garden. For a Sunday, the streets were full of people and color. Nick had always liked Spring Garden, liked how it reminded him of London though he'd never actually been to London.

He passed the string of coffee shops, glimpsed people inside, their heads bowed together as they chatted and laughed. The dark smell of coffee was enticing; Nick yearned for a coffee and a bagel with cream cheese.

Someday, he promised himself.

Someday real soon.

The thought was cut short when he saw the police car coming toward him.

Chloe lay on her stomach across her bed. Too much champagne left her sleepy and flushed. She let the darkness of the room soothe her.

"Chloe-toes?" Becky opened the door softly. "You okay in there?"

"Yeah."

"I'm just cleaning up. Have fun tonight?"

Chloe grunted affirmative. She wished Becky would leave her alone. She wasn't pleased with the way her roommate had acted tonight.

Chloe had passed by the kitchen and Becky was smoothing Ralph's chest and the two were hunched together, whispering.

Becky's expression had been sleezy, aggressive. Shocking, too. Becky presented herself as so innocent, almost naive. To see her drooling over Ralph had been alarming.

Maybe she didn't know her roommate nearly as well as she had believed.

Becky came inside the room and sat on the edge of the bed. "Am I keeping you from getting to sleep?"

"Well, yeah, actually."

Her tone was harsh, Chloe knew. But it didn't seem to affect Becky — that was the other annoying thing about her: she never seemed to get the point. She never seemed to get angry, either. It was as if Becky were a blank paper waiting to be drawn upon.

"Chloe-toes is a stressed girl," Becky said. "Poor Chloe-toes . . . "

"I'd just like to sleep now, if you wouldn't mind."

Becky put a hand on the lower part of Chloe's back. Chloe flinched ever so slightly. She didn't want Becky touching her. Not right now; maybe not ever.

"Let me give stressed Chloe-toes a wee massage," Becky said with a mock Scottish accent. "So tight, so *knoht-ted*."

Becky's hands felt strong as they kneaded the muscles on each side of Chloe's waist. It was unreal that she could have such strength in her hands, maybe even a little scary. With this power, you'd think she could've fought off Nick pretty easy yesterday, Chloe thought.

As if peering into her mind, Becky said, "It's a real shame about Nick, I know." Her hands made a wide circle and then paused. "He's a real sicko, isn't he?"

Chloe bit down on her lip, but said nothing.

"I'm sorry, did I offend your delicate senses?"

Chloe lifted her head. Was this sweet Becky sounding so . . . well, so horribly hateful?

Becky's eyes caught the light of the hallway; they seemed almost silver. Her shiny lips parted. "Chloe," she whispered, "in the morning, it'll all be new."

Chloe wished Becky would stop watching her so intently. Chloe thought of Edgar Allan Poe's story 'The Telltale Heart', about the man with the one evil eye.

Becky moved her hands upward and pressed her thumbs along the ridge of muscle near her shoulder blades. "You have such smooth skin, you know. Milky white. I bet it's really white *everywhere*."

Chloe wasn't sure how to respond to that.

"I bet Nick thinks about your milky smooth skin, Chloe. I bet he thinks of it all the time." Her voice was raspy and thin. She seemed to breathe the words.

Becky's hands patted the back of her neck and then they slowly lifted the weight of her hair away. Chloe held her breath. She was uncomfortable now. Even nervous. She wished Ralph hadn't changed his mind about staying the night.

"I'm . . . I'm tired now, Becky —"

"*Relax*, Chloe-toes," Becky insisted. "You've been through a lot lately; you need some TLC."

"Thanks, but I'm fine, Becky —"

"Re*lax* and let me put you to sleep in my own special way." She cradled a hand around the back of her neck. "I'm very good at that, you know. Good at putting people to sleep. A deep, deep sleep."

Nick's first instinct when he saw the police cruiser was to run, but no, that might bring attention to himself. Instead, he kept a steady pace, just a regular guy taking an evening walk.

The car slowed. Inside, the cop, a young guy, stared up at Nick. And then the car stopped.

Nick froze. He stared back at the officer, his hands tight by his sides.

The cop pressed down on the horn and gestured with his hands. Then Nick realized why; he was standing facing a crosswalk. His heart pounding, Nick quickly crossed the street.

When the police car went out of sight, Nick ducked into the foyer of a nightclub. A woman at the door looked up and then away. She seemed to sense that Nick didn't want to go inside. Nick waited for a few minutes and stepped into the street again.

Chloe's place was less than ten minutes away. She lived in one of several row houses facing the harbor. Passing by the main library, a street kid asked Nick for change; Nick just shrugged. Two punk-haired girls played bad guitar on the front steps. They giggled as he walked past them.

And there they were, the row of brownstone houses.

Nick paused, afraid.

Afraid that he would fail. Chloe was counting on him. She just didn't realize it yet. He remembered the way Lyra had thrown an arm around Chloe's shoulders at the hospital; she had no idea of the danger she was in.

Finding the right houses shouldn't be too difficult, he surmised. All he had to do was walk along the back of the houses and peer through the windows. Surely it wouldn't be that hard to find something that spoke of Chloe.

And when he saw her, then what?

Would he quietly get her attention and gesture her outside? Would she listen? He wished he knew the phone number; calling would be easier and simpler. Then again, he didn't have a cent to his name.

A cat scuttled between his feet as he crossed the road, startling him. He stopped in the middle of the street, swallowed harshly, continued to the back of the houses.

There were eight houses huddled together. The windows of the first house were dark; the second held a white sheet to the window as a curtain. No way Chloe would use a sheet as a curtain.

The third, fourth and sixth houses were all lit from within. Nick moved closer, trying to appear as casual as possible considering that it was eleven at night and he was skulking about, peering into windows.

Nick had to be quick about this peeping business. All it would take was one call to the police and he'd be carted back to Looneyville with the charge of voyeurism added to his mental profile, and wouldn't Dr. Genter love that?

A man passed by the fourth window and stared directly into Nick's face.

Nick froze. But no, the man didn't see him. There was too much glare. Nick was safe unless the guy got close to the window or turned off the light.

The man poured a glass of water and uncapped a pill bottle. He looked sleepy, not really with it. Then the lights went out and he hollered out to someone that he was coming back to bed.

That left two lighted apartments, considering of course that Chloe's apartment would even be lighted.

He slid to the next window, and immediately saw Lyra.

Standing in the kitchen. Flicking the air bubbles from a syringe.

chapter thirty-one

Nick dashed closer to the window, overestimated the distance and crumpled against the glass. In that second before his left side smashed into the window, one thought became clear to him: that needle had Chloe's name written all over it.

Lyra's head flicked up at the noise.

She frowned and squinted toward the glass. Nick knew she couldn't see him, or not well. Still, he flattened himself against the side of the house and peered from beyond the shadows.

There was a champagne bottle on the small island at the center of the kitchen. So they'd been having a few drinks. Of course. Chloe was probably asleep in her bed, without a single thought that she was about to be pumped full of heroin.

Nick pulled in a dry breath.

Lyra put the needle on the kitchen island and took a step toward him — and then snapped her head in the opposite direction.

Ralph entered the kitchen.

Ralph?

Lyra seemed just as surprised to see Ralph there. Her eyes went to the window and then she gently covered the needle with a paper napkin.

Seeing Ralph did Nick a world of good. If there was one person who'd stand by him, it was his best friend. Nick lifted a fist to knock against the window when Ralph threw his arms around Lyra and kissed her.

Nick's hand stopped in midair. Lyra and *Ralph?*

Was this a new development? He couldn't be sure. Lyra's hand draped down Ralph's back all the way to his backside and up again; Ralph's fingers threaded her black hair. They kissed with such abandon it was embarrassing to watch.

What're you doing, Ralph? God, don't be so stupid.

But he couldn't blame Ralph. Not really. Lyra was an erotic leech that sucked all sense of time and place. Even now, it was only too easy for Nick to remember.

Poor Ralph.

Finally, Ralph pulled away and smiled into her face. " . . . didn't show . . . Nick's . . . "

He wished they'd kept a window open so he could hear more of their conversation instead of these useless shards. Why would Ralph be saying his name? And *'didn't show?'* What did that mean?

" . . . some fun?"

Nick bit down hard on his lip. Lyra, using the same sweet voice on Ralph that she'd used with him.

"So pretty," Ralph said as he plucked Lyra into his arms and kissed her shoulders and neck.

Nick turned away with a shake of his head. He pushed away from the house and went around to the front. There was a mat beneath their door that said *Friends Welcome.*

Nick went up the steps and shook the doorknob. Unlocked.

Perfect.

Gently, he opened the door and stepped inside. From the kitchen, Lyra's giggles mingled with Ralph's hardy laugh. As sickening as it was, Nick was grateful to Ralph for distracting Lyra.

The steps were covered in blue carpet and muted the sound of Nick creeping upstairs. There were three rooms at the top level, each with a closed door. He guessed the middle room was probably a bathroom. He picked the door to the right and opened it.

The musky scent told him immediately that this was Lyra's room.

The room was practically bare, just a single bed and a bureau. Nick opened the closet door; empty except for a pair of white sneakers. Didn't she have any other clothes but that one black dress?

He turned to the bureau, opened the first drawer. Empty. The second drawer held a green towel. Nick touched it and heard a rattling noise. He removed the towel to find a dozen or more little bottles and syringes. Of course, the trusty drug supply — working materials for every genie.

Downstairs he heard the fridge door slam and then Ralph asking where the corkscrew might be. *That's right,* Nick encouraged, *Have a drink, keep her busy; that's it, good buddy, you're my pal.*

He pulled open the third drawer. Another green towel. (Had there been a sale on green towels?) He picked it up, let it unroll in his hands.

He gasped.

It was *the* doll.

The doll he'd found stuffed in the grate of his house a day before he'd found the book. The doll that his wolf pendant had been wrapped around.

Good God. Lyra had stolen it?

Nothing should surprise him about Lyra, but this did.

Why had she stolen it? Had she planned on doing some kind of sick voodoo spell against them? It didn't make any sense. What was the tie between Lyra and the doll?

"Nick . . . "

Chloe was calling to him.

She instinctively knew he was near. *This* is real love, he decided as he stuffed the doll back inside the drawer. Real love is knowing your mate will be there when you need them.

He bet Lyra never experienced anything close to what he and Chloe had. She was too selfish, too delusional. Even her obsession with the married guy was probably a farce.

Nick could feel sorry for her and her delusions.

But he didn't feel sorry for her.

He hated her.

Hated her in a way that twisted inside him and scraped bone and tissue. Hated her in a way that could destroy him, if he let it.

"Nick . . ."

Closing the drawer, Nick followed the sound of Chloe's sleepy voice. In her room, she lay curled on the bed, the comforter wrapped around her feet. There was a framed photo of them on the night stand, taken last Hallowe'en. Her fuzzy blue slippers lay toppled on the mat beside the bed. She'd had those slippers for years. A Christmas present from some aunt who lived in Oklahoma.

Nick kissed her hair. "Chloe, wake up, hon."

She stirred and with a little frown, opened her eyes. Nick put a finger over her lips. "Chloe," he whispered, "we need to leave the house right now."

She sat up quickly. "Nick. How'd you get out of the hospital?"

"Never mind that now. We have to get away from Becky."

"Becky?" She took a quick breath. "Oh, Nick."

"She's busy with Ralph in the kitchen, and we're leaving. Now, do I have to drag you out of here?"

Chloe pulled her head back. It was obvious she wasn't used to hearing him speak so harshly.

"Downstairs quietly. And right out the door, without any noise. Let's go."

Chloe folded her arms. "Nick, you need to go back to the hospital —"

"Chloe." Nick put his hands squarely on her shoulders. "Listen to me. We're leaving here; I don't want to hear an argument, do you understand?"

Wide eyes stared back at him.

"I'm sorry . . . oh, Chloe." He let his hands fall away. "Don't tell me you haven't wondered about your new *friend* just a bit?"

Chloe didn't answer.

"You know you have. You feel it, too, Chloe. I see it in your face. You know something's not quite right about her. She spooks you, too, admit it!"

"I . . . I don't know."

He grabbed a fistful of his hair. "Chloe, do you think I'd go to all this trouble if I wasn't sure of what I'm saying? Why do you think I got so upset at the hospital, huh?"

She touched his face. Nick hated the pity he saw in her eyes. "Chloe, just trust me!"

"Okay, I'll go with you," she told him. "But we're going right back to the hospital, okay?"

"Agreed," Nick lied. He pulled her to her feet. "Now let's go quietly. Not a sound."

Chloe pushed her feet into her slippers with a yawn. At the top of the stairs, she paused and whispered, "It sure sounds quiet if Ralph is here."

She was right. Especially if Ralph and Lyra were making out. Nick remembered Lyra's dramatic noises only too well. The muscles in Nick's shoulders tensed, as if they knew something he didn't.

As they descended the steps, Nick kept his eyes focused on the door. A dozen steps, a quick turn of the doorknob and they'd be free.

He glanced back at Chloe, who gave a little shrug. He could smell a trace of alcohol on her breath. "Right out the door, okay?"

Chloe nodded.

They reached the last step. The kitchen light was off. The wall lamp in the foyer cast fuzzy shadows along the hall way. It was so quiet they could hear the soft thunking as the furnace cut in and warm air seeped out of a grate near their ankles. So maybe Ralph had taken Lyra back to his place for a little more privacy. God, he hoped Ralph was okay.

Nick reached for the doorknob. His hand was sweaty; he grasped it tightly. The back of his neck felt hot.

It just didn't seem real that he could get away from Lyra this easily. Not even when he swung open the door and the cool night air swept in, lifting Chloe's hair. Nick peered up at the black slab of sky and said over his shoulder, "Okay, let's get the hell outta here —"

Lyra stepped into the doorway.

Her black hair billowed out and settled around her shoulders. "Well, well," she said. "Are we going somewhere?"

chapter thirty-two

Chloe leaned back with a startled cry. "You scared me half to death, Becky." But there was no fear in her voice. On the contrary; it was as if she were relieved to see her roommate.

"I went for a little walk," Lyra said. "It's such a beautifully starry night. Van Gough would have been proud."

She turned to Nick. "So what's this, the mental patient, out roaming the city?"

Nick said, "Get out of our way. It's *over*, Lyra."

The corners of Lyra's mouth turned up ever so slightly; just enough to declare her amusement.

Nick wished Chloe didn't seem so unaffected. She wasn't helping their cause one bit. Especially when she said, "Becky, I'm taking Nick back to the hospital."

"In your slippers?"

Chloe giggled. "That must seem pretty silly, I guess."

Lyra cocked her head and pinched the tip of her nose. "Tell ya what, Chloe-toes. I'll go with you." Her voice was sugary sweet and Chloe was falling for every sickening crumb. "This isn't something you should face alone, after all."

Nick felt himself beginning to sweat. He had to think this out, find a way to turn things around. Obviously, Chloe still believed in the goodness of Rebecca of Sunnybrook Farm.

"Chloe," Nick said, clearing his throat. "I'd prefer just the two of us . . . this is kinda embarrassing, you know. Please."

Chloe shrugged. "Nick, I'm not sure . . . "

Nick touched her hand. Things were falling apart. He took a breath. "Well, can I talk to you outside alone, Chloe? Just for a moment?"

Before she could answer, Lyra twisted the dead-bolt into place and flicked on the hall light; Nick squinted at the brightness. The furnace cut out with a loud *clunk*. "Are you making things difficult?" she said.

"Get out of the way."

"Tell you what," Lyra continued. "I'll put some coffee on and we'll talk, huh?"

"So where's Ralph?" Nick said. "I saw you with him in the kitchen."

Lyra blinked and ran a finger along her chin. "Why . . . he went home, of course."

"I saw you kissing him!"

"Oh dear." She pouted. "I guess that makes me a bad, bad girl."

"Nick, please," Chloe said.

Nick threw up his hands. Even now, when they were *this* close to getting away, Lyra was making an ass out of him. He pressed down on his back teeth. He had to change tactics.

"Let's walk up the street to The Second Cup and have coffee there." He did his best to keep his tone neutral. "Like you said, *Becky*, it's a beautifully starry night."

"No," Lyra interrupted. She gestured to Nick knowingly. "Your're going nowhere."

Nick glanced to Chloe. "You going to stop us from leaving, is that it?"

Chloe was quiet, as if she, too, wondered how her roommate would respond.

"I . . . I just think we should talk about this." She folded her hands and tilted her head toward Chloe. "After all, Nick isn't . . . isn't well. I didn't want to say this, but . . . Chloe, I'm afraid to leave you alone with him."

"C'mon, Chloe," Nick ordered. "Let's go."

"No." Lyra's hand fondled the dead-bolt, as if she wanted to ensure it was locked. "He's sick, Chloe. I can't let you leave with him."

"Get the hell out of the way!" Nick hollered.

Chloe touched his arm. "Maybe she's right."

"It's a trick," Nick insisted. "She's playing you. Listen to me, I . . . I found that weird voodoo doll in her bureau, the same one my wolf pendant was wrapped around."

"Voodoo doll?" Chloe turned to Lyra.

Lyra shifted uncomfortably and gave a tiny laugh that didn't sound nearly as confident as she might've liked. "I don't know anything about a voodoo doll. He's really crazy."

"Go look," Nick encouraged. "Third drawer. Wrapped in a green towel. I'm surprised it doesn't have pins in it yet. Or a *syringe*."

Lyra rolled her eyes. "He doesn't even know me, Chloe."

"Then what about the scorpion tattoo just above your backside, huh?"

Chloe's focus went from Nick to Lyra and back again. "Tattoo?"

"There's no tattoo," Lyra said.

Nick pointed a sharp finger. "If she didn't break into my motel room in Montreal, if we didn't spend the weekend together, how would I know about the tattoo? Think about it, Chloe. I'm not psychic."

"Do . . . do you have a tattoo?" Chloe asked.

"Of course not!"

"Then show us, Lyra. *Show us.*"

"You're a sick bastard," Lyra hissed out. *"You always were!"*

A stunned silence interrupted them. Chloe's face paled. "*Always were?*" she repeated. "Were you in Montreal . . . with Nick? The two of you . . . together . . . "

Lyra shook her head. "Chloe-toes, I wouldn't lie to you. You know me better than that —"

"It's the truth," Nick insisted. "You feel it, Chloe. You know it."

Chloe shrugged, but Nick saw the hesitation there. It was time to turn up another card. "Like I tried to tell you before. This sick roommate of yours thinks she's a genie in a book."

Chloe smiled uneasily. She moved closer to Nick and before Lyra could offer an explanation, she added, "You know, a coffee might be a good idea after all."

But Lyra didn't move away from the door. Not even when Chloe reached around her and turned back the dead-bolt so it was no longer locked. "We won't be gone long, Becky . . . and uh, can you move out the way, please?"

Lyra's eyes ticked between Nick and Chloe. She brought her mouth into a deep frown and turned toward the bookshelf beside the door. She pulled out *That Hurt Thing* and presented it across her open palms. "Chloe, I'm sorry," she said. "I even liked you a little bit."

Chloe glanced at the door. "Your name isn't Becky, is it?"

Lyra shook her head. "No." She glanced to Nick. "It's not even Lyra."

Chloe just stared at her. "I . . . I don't understand what this is all about . . . "

"I'll explain everything," Lyra said. She opened the book and held it toward Chloe. A light seeped from the book, a hazy light the color of ash. Chloe lifted one arm protectively and stepped back, blinking, as if she couldn't believe what she was seeing.

Clumps of smoke unfolded, thickening and darkening, and then began to take form. First a mouth that curled and shifted into a frown, and then long, twisting hair and black, black eyes that shifted and blinked and focused. A smell permeated the room. A smell that reminded Nick of the cauldron in his dream, and the oily human stew.

Chloe gasped. She reached for the door, frantically twisted the doorknob. It didn't move. Even though she'd unlocked it.

She trembled and turned back toward Lyra. "W-what the hell is going on?"

Not the least distracted by Chloe's attempt to escape, the form lifted a fist and slowly the fist uncurled to show three outstretched fingers. "Three," Lyra explained. "Three wishes." She turned to the figure dancing above them, changing form again — this time, to resemble Lyra.

"Number one: Mess up the good professor. Two: Smash the life right out of Brad."

"And three . . . " Lyra stared at Chloe, who stood huddled into Nick. "Make Chloe go away and never come back."

"W-what's this?" Chloe said uneasily. "Make me go away?"

When Lyra threw her head back in laughter, Nick grabbed Chloe's arm and pulled her along with him toward the back of the house.

"Is this really happening?" Chloe whispered, her voice high and frantic as they rushed toward the back exit.

Nick grabbed at the door handle, but it didn't budge. Of course not. Had he really expected it would? Chloe couldn't open the front door; this would be no different.

Lyra's laughter filled the room. Smoke curled along the floor toward them, rising and falling like a black wave and Nick was reminded briefly of being a child and playing tag with the waves at Lawrencetown Beach.

"Stand back," he said, thrusting a foot through the window. The glass shattered; Nick immediately began to widen the hole.

"Hurry!" Chloe said beside him. "*Hurry!*"

The smoke that snaked toward them faded and disappeared just as Lyra entered the room. She didn't appear to be alarmed by what she saw. If anything, she seemed rather relieved, as if she'd known all Nick would try to kick out the window.

"When you're ready," she said simply with a nod and left again.

Ignoring her, Nick stepped on glass, heard it crunch under his feet as he pulled his sweatshirt sleeve over his hand and tried to break off a long slice of remaining glass. His stomach growled, reminding him that he hadn't eaten since a bad lunch of *something* soup.

"C'mon, hurry up, Nick."

There was a snapping noise and then the pieces of glass on the floor shifted and spiraled upward — and flew back into place, like the construction of a jigsaw puzzle shown in rapid speed, or a fast rewind.

"I don't believe it," Chloe whispered.

Nick put his hand against the smooth glass. Incredible.

*In*credible.

When you're ready . . .

"Listen to me, Chloe. Is there another way out or somewhere to hide?"

"There's a pantry." Chloe pointed down the hallway off the kitchen. "Door at the very end. It . . . it has a lock."

"No, that'll just be a trap."

"There's nothing else." A pause. "I don't hear anything, Nick. Where is she?"

"A phone? Is there a phone?"

"Don't have it hooked up yet." She licked her lips nervously. "Nick, I don't hear her."

"That means nothing," he said impatiently. "C'mon." He pointed toward the front of the house. "Let's try to get upstairs."

"What for?"

Nick wished she wouldn't ask questions, especially questions that needed logical answers. "I . . . I don't know. You have a better suggestion?"

"No." She looked down at her fuzzy blue slippers. "But the bathroom upstairs has an unfolding ladder from the window."

"Well, there's your reason. Let's go."

The silence was a mockery, Nick realized as they advanced to the front of the house and passed Lyra sitting at the dining room table, leaned back in the chair, casually smoking a cigarette.

She'd lit a candle and studied the flame, as if she might be meditating. The only contrast to the peaceful scene was a long knife beside her. It was simply a kitchen knife, but hell, a can opener would be dangerous in Lyra's hand.

Her stance reminded Nick of the first time he'd seen her in the motel room at Montreal, that casual cockiness that had annoyed the hell out of him.

She didn't speak or do anything as they passed by. It was as if she didn't even see them. But Nick knew not to trust that she'd had a change of heart about letting them go. More likely, she was just getting her breath, gearing up for her next move.

In the foyer, beside the bookshelf, Lyra had thrown down *That Hurt Thing*. Impulsively, Nick grabbed it up. Lyra hummed behind them. The foil cover glinted from the wall lamp.

"What are you doing?" Chloe said. She put one foot on the lower step. "C'mon, Nick!"

"I . . . I don't know . . . "

He felt a shudder move through his arms; the tips of his fingers were prickly, hot. He tried to shake the book out of his grasp, but he no longer had control.

"Nick!"

When you're ready . . .

His stomach growled again. He tried to speak, but couldn't.

"Nick, come on. Drop it!"

When you're ready . . .

"I . . . I can't . . . "

Nick felt his thumbs spread against the thick pages and with a deep breath that seemed to come from somewhere else, some*one* else, he peeled open the book.

Despite the champagne Paula consumed at Chloe's party, she lay in bed, unable to sleep. She was wide awake and missing Brad so much she wondered if she'd ever feel normal again.

And beyond that, she was spooked. Things happen in threes, wasn't that the truth. First Brad's phone call — God, it was odd to say that: Brad's phone call. As if he might've picked up a phone in heaven and explained to the big G. that he needed to get a message to his girlfriend.

Then the attack of the ants, and following that, being thrown down the stairs. Both of these events happened when she tried to go to the attic. Was there a connection?

Was there an unseen force that didn't want her there?

The attic, Paula . . . don't be afraid.

Paula scrunched her eyes closed. She didn't want to hear Brad's voice. She wanted to move past this time, this pain. Even if that made her selfish. Even if that made her a bad girlfriend —

"I'm *not* a girlfriend!" she screamed so loud that her throat hurt.

You're dead, Brad . . . Her sobs were shrill. *You're dead, so just let me —*

"*Paula?*"

She gasped.

"Paula, you all right in there?"

"Dad?" She bit back a rising sob. "Come . . . come in."

Bruce's head broke a vertical line of light thrown from the hallway. Paula squinted and sat upright.

"I heard you scream." He stood at the base of her bed. "Nightmare?"

"Yeah," she told him. "Well, no."

Bruce reached a hand back to open the door a little more. "Paula, you having a hard night?"

"Dad, do you believe in ghosts?"

"I'm . . . not sure. Why you ask?"

She went to tell him about Brad's phone call, and stopped. With Nick in Dagnorth General, it would only add to her father's worry list to hear about her long distance calls from the other side. Instead, she said, "I just feel like Brad's with me."

"Oh, honey," Bruce told her, "he *is* with you. He'll be in your heart forever."

"Do you feel like that? About your wife?"

"My *wife*? That's an odd way of referring to your mother."

Paula agreed. Her eyes were adjusting to the light and she examined her father. His hair needed to be washed and he stood slightly hunched, as if life were pressing down on him.

"Mom's like a stranger to me," Paula admitted. "I was too young, I suppose."

"You're so much like her." He sat along the very edge of the bed. "And yes, she's with me. Sometimes when I see someone staring at me from a car in the next lane, or at a doctor's office, I imagine it's her, that she's taken on the form of another person so she can visit me. Isn't that weird?"

It surprised Paula to hear Bruce talk like this. Maybe I don't really know him, she wondered. Maybe I don't know him at all.

"It's not weird," she told him. "I think it's beautiful."

"Your mom was an incredible woman. I like it when I feel her around me, like she's forgiving me for all I did wrong."

"Did wrong?" She chewed on the edge of a torn hangnail. "What do you mean?"

Bruce's shoulders lifted and fell slowly. "Just life stuff, Paula." He stood up. "We always hurt the ones we love, maybe most of all." He kissed the top of her head. "If you want, you can sleep with me in my room."

"Dad, I'm too old for that!"

He smiled. "You're never too old to take comfort. Goodnight, sweetheart."

When Bruce left, Paula snuggled down in the covers. She felt better now, maybe even a tad sleepy. Tragedy can bring people closer together, she realized. Even with people you think you know inside and out —

The attic, babe! The attic!

"No . . . " she groaned out. Not again. *Go away.*

The attic! Now!

But why?

Go now! Oh, babe . . .

Brad's voice was like a buzzing whine or a distant tin whistle that wavered with changing frequencies. She wanted to reach toward the sound because it was Brad, and yet, she wanted it to stop, wanted it all to just go away.

She didn't want to go into the attic.

She was afraid. Afraid of what would happen if she dared defy whatever was keeping her out. Afraid of ants that had scuttled into her ears and nostrils and down her pants, and let's not forget the wonderful lunge down the stairs.

She would abandon the teddy bear and the other souvenirs of her time with Brad — forever, if it meant she didn't have to go up into that dark, cold, smelly place during this lifetime.

But with all that said, Paula knew that she would go to the attic. *Tonight.*

After she went to the attic, it would be over. Their real good-bye. She would move ahead and Brad would, well, he'd be at peace.

I'm taking care of business, babe. Now hurry!

"Yes, okay, Brad," she whispered.

Without turning on the light, she dressed in her jeans and floppy brown sweater. She was careful not to disturb her father, though a part of her hoped he'd come upstairs again and stop her. Or maybe go with her.

But she knew that wouldn't be acceptable. She had to do this alone.

Slowly, she opened her bedroom door and closed it behind her. It seemed all too soon that she stood in front of the open door that led to the attic steps.

Had she left it open?

She didn't think so. She remembered how hot the door knob had been, how it had burned. For the door just to be open like this was eerie.

It was almost too easy.

Like walking into a trap.

Unless it was all fine now. Unless Brad somehow had made it all right.

When she thought of it like that, she realized that maybe she'd made more of things. Maybe there really had been ants and maybe she'd really tripped at the steps in such a way that had sent her flying.

She had to take her grief into consideration, too. Grief was like stress, it could make you a little crazy. That's what her teacher Mr. Shawn had told her. He used to be a counselor in the military, so he knew his stuff. He told her of a man who thought crows were chasing him, sent by his wife who wanted a divorce.

And Brad's orders to go to the attic?

Paula couldn't explain that. And it didn't matter anyhow. She was getting the one box of her things and getting out of there.

She took a deep breath.

And then climbed the steps that led to the attic.

chapter thirty-three

Lyra's cackling laughter reached them just as Nick's hands flicked open the book and with a loud popping noise, it flew from his hands to the floor where it writhed on the floor like something alive. Writhed and squirmed while Nick and Chloe scuttled back until they met with the staircase.

Nick cursed his own stupidity. Why had he touched the book? He should've just left well enough alone.

Chloe gasped and pointed. "Nick, look . . . ."

Scorpions. Dozens upon dozens of black, huge scorpions that squeezed from the book, clacking and rattling toward them, tails arched high, ready to strike. It was chilling, these slick black creatures at their heels, following them up the steps without hesitation.

Near the top of the stairs, Chloe faltered as the scorpions clenched her pant leg with their claws, causing her to stumble backward. Nick grasped her arm, but it was no use. She slid — bump, bump, bump — down the steps and then they were upon her, black tails snapping.

"Nick . . . .oh, oh, Nick — Oh help!" She screamed and batted at the scorpions, at herself. It was a horrific sight, the scorpions tearing at Chloe's skin, flipping their tails to inflict the venomous sting, clinging to her clothes, her hair.

Nick dashed toward Chloe, but flew back, as if thrown, hitting his head against the handrail with a dull thud and landing harshly on his backside. The front door opened and slammed shut, and a wind sailed past them, rattling the windows.

Nick sat dazed, until the sound of Chloe's screaming brought him back to the moment.

Grasping the handrail, he pulled himself to his feet, went to help Chloe — and found that he couldn't move. It was as if he were paralyzed from the waist down.

"Lyra!" Trying to force his feet to move, he called over the sound of Chloe's screaming. "God's sake, Lyra!"

Lyra slowly walked toward them. She ran a tongue along her lower lip with a smile, but said nothing, not even as the scorpions tore at Chloe's throat, sharp claws snipping the soft skin while she screamed and pleaded. Blood gurgled from the corners of her mouth, oozing down her face and into her hair.

It was surreal, these giant scorpions attacking Chloe while he was helpless to help. Nick pulled at his legs and feet with both hands, but it was no use. They were as good as cement. He couldn't even feel them. "Lyra," he repeated, "stop it, c'mon, stop it!"

"Oh, don't whine," Lyra said.

And then Chloe's screams ebbed to a low moan; her eyes rolled back and closed. Nick shook the handrail, making it tremble. "Lyra, stop!"

Lyra waved her hands and the scorpions disappeared, their snapping noise dragging to a whispered silence. "I'm the king of the castle," she said, mocking the children's game where you hold your side of the seesaw down and made the other playmate, suspended in the air, promise a myriad of treasures.

The sensation returning in his legs, Nick rushed to Chloe and pulled her into his arms. Her blood dampened his arms and hands. "Nick . . . " she whispered.

Nick glared at Lyra. "You . . . stupid bi —"

"Don't be a dirty rascal," she said in a sing-song voice.

She laughed at her own joke, her expression eager, even joyful. If not for the fact that his girlfriend was slumped in his arms because she'd been attacked by giant scorpions, and there was a sick genie threatening them, this could be a bad comedy.

"Why are you doing this?" he asked simply. "Why?"

"Oh, Nick." She gave a little playful snort and wiggled her shoulders. "For love, of course."

Nick stroked Chloe's hair. She didn't look good. She didn't look good at all. "You love me so much you wreck my life?"

Lyra giggled so fiercely that her pale face flushed. "It was sown before you were big enough to dance your way across my sheets. But you know . . . " She flicked back her long hair. "It really has nothing to do with you, Nick."

Chloe's mouth fell open and she drooled. Nick hugged her closer. She murmured something too low to understand.

"Nick, bring your girlfriend all the way down the stairs." Lyra gestured with her chin. "You're making quite a mess."

Nick hesitated.

"I said," Lyra repeated, "bring her down the stairs. Now."

He didn't move.

She said, "Don't make me mad, Nick."

Nick advanced slowly, reluctantly. When he reached the lower step, Lyra nodded her approval. "Now put her down. Yes, that's right. On the lower step, just like that. We need to talk, Nick. And it's much easier if you're not holding up a dying girl."

"She's not dying!"

Lyra lifted a brow. "Move away from her now . . . yes, that's a good boy."

Nick leaned a hand against the wall in the hallway, Chloe's blood smearing the white paint. "What do we have to talk about?" he said bitterly.

Lyra examined her nails. "I simply need you to understand."

"Understand what?" He gritted his teeth. "That you're a psycho?"

"Oh, Nick. Hear me out; it'll be good for you. I know it will be. You're of a naturally curious nature; I understand that very well —"

"Spare me the bull, Lyra. Just tell me."

"Well, it's like this. I needed to make you believe in me before I got you out of the way. Got you *all* out of the way."

"All? What does that mean?"

"Well, I did need to grant your three wishes first." She glanced to Chloe. "I'm almost there. She won't last much longer."

"Chloe's innocent. This is between you and I."

"No, it isn't, Nick. That's just the thing. You're a side-dish. You merely got in the way."

"In the way?"

"When you found the doll in the grate along with the necklace, you freed me. I had been bound, you know."

"Bound . . . by who?"

"By your *mother*."

"My mother?" Nick shook his head. He took a breath and cleared his throat. "You knew my mother?"

"Oh yes." She snorted. "I knew all her tricks, too. I bet she's turning over in her grave, knowing that her own son *inadvertently* undid all her hard work. Quite ironic, really."

"I . . . I don't understand."

She hauled on her cigarette, then threw back her head to expel the smoke. "Lynn was clever, that much I have to give credit for. She bound me to keep me away from her family. Good thing, too, for I had full intentions of smiting the lot of you. But you see, Nick, there's one thing you need to understand. To offer protection to others, you must first make yourself vulnerable."

She pulled her lips into a thin line. "Your mother was such a sacrificing kind of gal that way. So she blocked me from hurting you and your sister, but before she could protect herself, I interrupted the process —"

"You *murdered* my mother?"

"Well, yes and no. Oh, it was quite a scene. Her desperately trying to bind me while I hacked away at her . . . "

Nick shuddered. He didn't want to hear more, but yet he had to know the truth.

Lyra continued. "She won, essentially. She had rendered me powerless. Sent me back to the book, in simple terms. You know this whole scene occurred in what is now your apartment. Isn't that a nice touch?"

"What are you saying? My mother was still alive when she bound you? How is that possible?"

"I didn't have time to pull out all my tricks. You see, time was running out. She'd protected her children, and immediately began to do the spell that would bind me again to the book . . . I tried to stop her, but she was driven. I had a few moments between the time that she initiated the binding spell and when it fell in place. It always takes the universe a few moments to recognize directed energy."

"And so . . . " Lyra smiled. "During that time, I slit her wrists to make it look like suicide. I didn't want anyone to think she was murdered. And that was my mistake. I took too long, was too careful in planning her demise. Here she was, bleeding, literally to death . . . and she kept going just like a trouper. She carried out the spell to the bitter end."

"My mother would've done anything for us," Nick snapped.

Lyra flicked the cigarette to the floor and twisted her shoe over it. "The only consolation I have is that she died alone."

Nick's eyes stung. All this time, he'd been so bitter, thinking his mother had killed herself. He couldn't bear to think that he'd been intimate with his mother's murderer.

He pushed his fists against his eyes. Tears slid down his face. "Why?" His voice shook. "Why would you hurt my mother? She was my *mother* . . . "

Lyra glared at him. "So I could have your father."

Nick's head flicked up. "What did you say? My father?" He swallowed. "My father . . . the *married man* . . . "

He wanted it to be a joke. It was too bizarre, too *wrong* a consideration. Bruce was a good man; surely he wouldn't have had anything to do with the likes of Lyra. Then again, he bet few men, under the right circumstance, could resist her.

"Bruce and I would've been together," Lyra continued. "But your mother found out about me. See, long ago, your father came across the same book you did. He was my master."

Her voice shivered. "We fell in love. Or rather, we continued our love from centuries ago."

"Centuries ago? How can that be?"

She looked to the floor. "You dreamed it, Nick . . . "

"The dream about you being burned alive?" He shook his head. "No, I don't buy into that whole past life stuff." Still, he bit his lip and added, "So that man, the one you were caught with, you're saying that was my *father?"*

"Yes, Nick, it was. Much later, in another time and dimension, Bruce found the book. I knew he would, of course. I knew it was just a matter of time before he freed me and we could love again. That is, until your mother tried to destroy us."

"How did she find out about you?"

"Bruce told her, the stupid man. He was going to leave you all, but . . . your mother pleaded. 'Think of the children,' she whined. 'You can't do this to your children.'"

She rolled her eyes. "And he fell for it! I decided to have my own little chat with this whiner, your mom. I followed her to a grocery store, waited in the parking lot for her to come out. I told her who I was; I told her that I wasn't about to give up on Bruce, no matter how much she tried to make trouble."

She took a breath. "I can still see the way she looked at me. She sensed something. For after a few moments, she said, 'What are you?' I laughed and said I was a genie, just for show, really. I didn't expect that she'd take it seriously. But seriously, she did."

"She was brilliant in her field," Nick said sharply. "I'm not surprised she saw through you."

"That's how she knew, I suppose, how to deal with me. How to get me out of the way. But I wasn't about to let her bind me without a fight."

"I can't believe you murdered my mother," Nick said aloud, as much to himself. *My dear, loving mother . . .*

"It's funny, you know," she added. "How everything always works out for the best. I was so bitter, believing all my plans had decayed. But then you found the wolf pendant. Fate, really."

"And then I found the book."

"Well, the book found you, Nick," she corrected. "See, once you'd freed me, I simply put the book where I knew you'd find it. I knew you'd be my master, but only until I granted your wishes. Then I knew I could finish my plan and return again to Bruce. A small sacrifice."

"Do you think he'd want you, knowing you killed his wife?"

"He doesn't know." She rubbed her hands together. "And he never will."

"Why didn't you just kill me before now? Why drag it out like this?"

She sneered. "You were protected."

"Protected? How?"

She smiled but didn't explain.

"You could've killed me that night you cut my wrists. Why didn't you?"

"I left you to die, Nick. It's just luck that you didn't." She pressed her hands together in a prayer sign and batted her eyes mockingly. "Guess someone was looking out for you."

"You cut my wrists so it'd look like suicide. Like you did with my mother."

She agreed. "I didn't want your father to be upset any more than he had to be. And like I told you that night, the LSD and heroin helped my cause, too."

"That's kind of lame considering what you're capable of. All those genie powers and you resort to street drugs?"

"The heroin was to add to the suicide story. Oh, Nick. I thought I explained all this that night I failed to . . . send you to your death." She sighed. "No matter how strong my powers are, I couldn't go inside your head and make you hallucinate, nor could I hurt you in any significant way, so I played a little mischief. I like mischief. I wanted to throw you off balance. That, and it would help your father believe you killed yourself if he knew you'd been taking drugs for a while. He did begin to suspect, you know."

"Why didn't you go to my father before now?"

"Nick, haven't you been listening? I had to deal with you first, and handle this protection business. Besides," she said with a grin, "I wanted it to be perfect. I wanted him to be needing me, suffering from the suicide of his son and then the accidental death of his daughter. She's such a big fat tank of a girl. Tripping on sharp objects, choking on burritos, falling down stairs . . . "

"You haven't —"

"Not successfully. Not yet." She smirked. "I suppose I could've just let her eat herself to death."

Nick inhaled deeply. All his life, he'd believed in things he could see and touch; he was the epitome of the Science Man. To think life could hold such a myriad of alternates was . . . well, terrifying. He had a new respect for his mother, who'd known all along about these aspects of existence.

"Now then, Nick," Lyra said, clearing her throat. "Enough chitchat. It's time. Take off your pendant . . . and throw it down."

Then it hit him. Of course, the wolf pendant was what offered him protection! Crazy not to have figured it out before now. "You must think I'm stupid," he told her. "I had taken it off that night . . . my necklace, the night Holly Sampson visited me . . . or that was you, wasn't it? Of course it was. Pretending to be her, getting me to take off the necklace." He shook his head. "So I take it off now, and you kill me? I'm not crazy."

"Clever," she admitted. She tapped her lips with an index finger. "But how about I offer a little compromise?"

"Such as?"

Lyra gestured to Chloe. It was hard to see her there, lying so still and pale, covered in blood. "You take it off, and I'll let her go. She doesn't have much of a chance, but if you agree, I'll let you call an ambulance."

"You're lying! What about the third wish, to make her go far, far away?"

Lyra tutted. "Nick, your wish meant to make her go far away from *you*. Your death counts as a fair enough distance."

Nick swallowed and looked down at Chloe again. "I don't believe or trust you," he said.

"Okay, then we just wait it out. Look at her, she's not even moving; she's lost *a lot* of blood."

Nick gritted his teeth, but said nothing.

"Well, Nicholas, I guess you've got a big decision to make now, huh?" Lyra dragged a finger along his chin. "Your life, or your girlfriend's. So what's it gonna be, lover boy?"

chapter thirty-four

The attic was dusty. Paula coughed into her hand.

She'd made it there with as little fuss as it takes for an overweight woman to climb a long flight of stairs. There'd been no ants or burnt hands or voices or sudden falls, either.

Peachy keen, she supposed.

She rarely came up here. Not only because it was dirty and she expected mice and all manner of insects to scurry over her feet, but because of the locked room at the far corner of the attic: her mother's office.

Her father had left things exactly the way they were when her mom died. Then he'd locked the room away, as if he could somehow preserve her memory.

Her mother was like a shadow, a ghost that lurked among their collective memories. Truth was, it spooked Paula, and what a terrible thought, to be afraid of your mother's memory.

Paula glanced at the locked door and quickly looked away.

Instead, she located the box holding the few last memories of Brad, and went toward it. The teddy bear Brad won at the fair hovered near the top, as though greeting her. She pushed it against her face.

"Oh, Brad . . . "

The bear smelled faintly of the attic. She sniffed into the toy, the memories of him suddenly all encompassing. Would Brad be the last boy who'd ever love her, love the fat girl with the strange family, the mortician dad and nutty brother?

The box also held several of Brad's letters. Tucking the bear beneath her upper arm, she lifted the bundle of letters held together with an elastic band.

She pulled one from the stack and opened it.

Dear Paula,

This man loves you very much, and you are the center of his world. Here's a poem: Paula is my babe, oh yeah, and when I get paid . . . I'll take my honey-boo to the zoo . . .

Paula smiled, Brad's messy penmanship endearingly familiar. She'd always found it sweet and odd that he referred to himself in the third person.

She picked up another letter, and read: *When we go against the grain we are real cool. Brad loves you!! Be strong, babe.*

"Brad, I miss you so much . . . " she whispered to the letter in her hand. "So much —"

Paula frowned. Was she seeing things?

The door to her mother's office. It was open.

It had to be the angle; her father would never unlock it. She walked toward the room cautiously and saw that, yes, it was indeed open. Holding the teddy bear and the two open letters tightly against her, she whispered, "Hello?"

She pushed on the door; it opened easily, not like a door that hadn't been used in over a decade. To her surprise there was a light on inside.

Paula hesitated, and then entered. The light was from a lamp sitting on the desk. Her mother's desk. So this was where her mom had sat writing her parapsychology articles.

Who turned on the light? She stared at it. Her father; it had to be.

It was a cluttered room. The desk held stained coffee mugs, a stapler and tape dispenser, a dictionary and thesaurus and a pile of old magazines. There was a chair in the corner and that too, was filled with magazines.

There was a cot in the corner where she supposed her mother had taken naps, though that seemed an odd thing to do when she had a perfectly good bedroom downstairs. Beside the cot was a small night stand which held a small dish and a plant.

A plant?

It had to be fake, Paula decided; plants couldn't live without care for that long.

It was cool in the room and suddenly Paula didn't want to be there anymore; a cool draft sifted over her feet. She glanced down and swallowed. Her scalp felt hot. Things were going to start going *wrong* again; she could feel it.

Paula went toward the door. This place even smelled evil. Mother or not, she wanted no part of her, no part of anything that resembled what Brad would've called *black energy*.

She was about to close the door when she saw a photograph that had fallen behind the desk. Crossing the room, she grasped the edge of the photograph and picked it up.

She gasped.

What was her father doing with his arms around Chloe's roommate, Becky Farm?

Paula found her father talking on the phone in the kitchen. She knew right away that something was wrong.

"That's right," he was saying, his hand curled into a fist and pushed against the counter. "He's not here. No . . . no, I have no idea. Sure . . . yes, I'll let you know if I think of any."

He slammed the phone down.

"Dad? Is it Nick?"

He rubbed a hand through his hair. "He got out of the hospital somehow. You know Chloe's new address?"

"I was there tonight, remember?"

Bruce nodded. "Let's take a drive over. You can show me the way."

Paula thought of the photograph of Becky with her dad. Maybe now wasn't a good time to ask about it. But if not now, when? "Chloe has a new roommate, you know." She took a breath. "Her name is . . . Becky Farm."

"I see. Let's go." Bruce grabbed up the keys.

Why hadn't he responded to Becky's name, Chloe wondered. While they drove across town, she thought about the picture again. In the photograph, Bruce had been wearing an old fashioned striped suit and his hair was real short.

That confused her. In the picture, Becky wore the same black dress she'd worn at Chloe's party; the picture had to have been taken recently? But if so, how could her father have grown out his hair so quickly?

"Dad?"

He put on his blinker and turned right, giving the engine a shot of gas. "What?"

Paula bit down on her lip. "I . . . found something today. Something that . . . I'm not sure what to make of."

She stared out the window. They were approaching Spring Garden Road now. Bruce slowed to let a group of noisy teenagers cross the street.

"What is it?"

"I went to the attic today, just a while ago." She paused. "I . . . I went inside Mom's office."

Bruce didn't seem overly alarmed by her admission. Surprised, perhaps, but not upset. "Honey, can we talk about this later? I'm preoccupied with —"

"I found a photograph," she blurted out. "Of you . . . and Chloe's roommate."

He frowned and glanced her way. "A photograph of . . . *what?* What did you say?"

Was he angry? She hoped that he wasn't. Then again, she'd been snooping in her mom's office and found things that weren't any of her business.

But surely her dad was her business, wasn't he? "Don't be mad. I just . . . didn't know you knew her."

Bruce slowed not far from Chloe's house and pulled into a parking space. He turned to face her. "Now tell me again what you're talking about."

"You and Becky," Paula told him. "I found a photograph of the two of you. But . . . how do you know her? I'm sorry, but I don't really like her. I think she's weird, and why was she wearing the same black dress?"

Bruce's face went white. He twisted his hands over the steering wheel; the engine idled. Paula swallowed. What had she said wrong? "Daddy?"

"New roommate," Bruce whispered.

Oh, how she wanted her dad to say something, tell her why he was acting so funny, explain to her how in the world he knew Becky Farm.

"Daddy? Daddy, *what is it?*"

Bruce turned off the ignition and stared in the direction of the row of townhouses. "Oh, dear God," he said, closing his eyes. "She's still here."

"Still here? What does that mean? What're you talking about, Daddy?"

"Paula, what's the number on Chloe's house?"

She told him. "Why?"

"Listen to me carefully. I want you to stay here, Paula. Stay here and do not come into the house, no matter what, do you understand me?"

"But why —"

"No questions."

"Daddy, what's going on?"

"Just give me your promise."

Paula hesitated.

"Promise me!" Bruce shouted.

"Okay," she said, drawing back against the seat. "I promise."

Nick watched Lyra.

There was no debate here. He had to get help for Chloe. And fast. But it didn't make sense that Lyra would let him call an ambulance. Surely an ambulance would put a kink in her plans of murdering him, wouldn't it? Then again, it might only take a moment or less — all she had to do was wave her hands or whatever she did, and poof! he'd be history and she'd be out of here in seconds. As it was, he didn't have many options.

"Well, Nick?" She blinked impatiently.

He nodded. "I'll do it."

"Good for you." She smiled. "You're a good man, Nicholas O'Brien. Just like your mother, a real martyr, a *slave*."

Nick reached for his pendant, lifted it slowly from his neck. Lyra watched with obvious delight. Behind him, Chloe softly moaned.

He raised it until the chain brushed against his forehead. Then he dropped it back against his chest and lunged toward Lyra.

She wasn't expecting the motion, for there was a look of astonishment and she raised her hands to ward him off, but too late, Nick slammed his body into hers and they both tumbled into the living room. Nick knew the pendant would offer some protection; he wasn't sure just how much. Perhaps it only prevented her from outright murder. But whatever it offered, he'd take. If it meant she was defenseless, that would be all right, too.

They scuffled together in a dangerous waltz and for an instant, Nick considered that he might gain the upper hand. But then, as if she'd been merely teasing him, she cackled and he was thrown harshly across the room.

His shoulder hit the table, jolting the knife and candle; the candle wobbled and fell against a knitted throw.

"Oh, now look what you've done," Lyra said. "My meditation candle."

Like watching a frame by frame scene, Nick observed how the candle simmered into the woolen checkered blanket and then heard a soft whoosh as the flame was pulled into the material.

Lyra didn't seem frazzled at all. She threw a glance toward the flame as it crawled from the throw to the thick curtain above it — and laughed.

The flames touched the hem of the curtain and flickered. Nick eyed the knife on the floor. He scrabbled after it just as it sailed out of reach — toward Lyra.

"Quite a mess you make when you don't focus, Nicholas," she said, grabbing the knife in one sure gesture and moving toward Chloe. She held the weapon over Chloe and smirked. "Now are you ready to cooperate?"

Nick stepped closer. "You like Chloe," he reminded her. "You said that."

"You should know my personal feelings can't enter into this," she said, tightening her grasp on the knife and leaning closer to Chloe. "And do I look like the sentimental type?"

"Okay, take the pendant." Nick ripped it upward, catching the chain on his ear and then struggling to free it. "Take it!"

Nick felt sick. His teeth chattered; his legs trembled. He remembered the fumbling way Lyra had held the knife in Montreal, as if it were a cigarette. It had all been an act. She was an expert at using a blade. An expert *at death.*

Lyra gave a tiny cough, tossed back her shiny black hair and took a step closer to him. She was all business now. She pointed to the pendant. "Throw it down," she said.

Nick grasped the wolf pendant and yanked upward. As he did, he could have sworn he heard the sound of a choir, something that reminded him of Gregorian Chant. It startled him and he paused.

"Well, Nick?"

Nick shook his head. It seemed that a lifetime had passed since he had knocked over the candle, though it had been only a few minutes. He pulled the chain over his head and let it swing freely between them. The eyes of the wolf flickered. Lyra's face beamed; her entire body shivered with delight.

The necklace clattered to the floor and Lyra immediately kicked at it. It sailed through the open door and over the doorstep like a paper plane.

"There now," she said. "Was that so terribly difficult?"

As she got closer, Nick instinctively threw out a fist, but it fell impotently. His spirits darkened. He was no match for Lyra; he never was.

"You said I could call an ambulance for Chloe."

"Oh, Nick." Lyra grinned. "Look at the fire; there's no time.

It was true. Fire licked the ceiling now and smoke unfolded against the walls. The fire was like a living thing breathing down upon them. As it was, none of them would survive much longer in here.

Or maybe that was what Lyra wanted. Maybe she had some kind of suicidal notion that made her careless and fatalistic. For all he knew, maybe she'd planned the fire, too.

If only he could make it to the door. Then again, he no longer wore the wolf pendant and he was certain the open door was simply a mockery, another way of torturing him.

She neared him, smiling, rubbing her hands together. Her eyes flashed gray with hate, the color of cement.

She blew Nick a kiss. "You take a deep breath, baby," she said, "because you ain't coming up for a long, long time!"

chapter thirty-five

Nick felt himself lifting from the floor.

Lifting higher and higher until he looked down at Lyra, who stood watching him, amused and content.

"What the —"

She pointed both index fingers, as if he were a puppet and she, the puppeteer. She directed him in the direction of the fire; Nick flailed his arms in a futile attempt to try control what was happening. "Let me down!" he screamed and coughed.

"Excuse me in here?"

A woman stood in the doorway.

Lyra's head snapped toward her.

An older woman — possibly a neighbor — with a white blouse and a large strand of beaded pearls, squinted inside. Nick knew she didn't see him right away, and when she did, her long hand flittered up to her throat and she took a gasped step backward.

"I'm sorry . . . I smelled smoke and called the — " She looked at Nick's body hovering in mid-air. "Uh . . . I'll leave." She turned her body toward the doorway so quickly that the string of pearls swept out from her chest and settled again.

Lyra was not so easily evaded, however. She jerked her head toward the neighbor and then quickly away; the woman flew across the distance, slamming into the wall with such speed and force that there was a sudden pop, and when the woman's lifeless body slid down the wall, thick blotches of blood smeared the wall above her.

"Love thy neighbor," Lyra said, tutting, as if reprimanding her for wearing fake pearls.

Nick pressed his toes into his shoes — and then he realized that he was touching the floor. Glancing once more at the poor neighbor whose mistake was simply being in the wrong place at the wrong time, Nick raced toward the back of the house. There was no logic to his actions; it wasn't as if he really believed he could outrun or outwit Lyra. He recalled Chloe telling him about the pantry off the kitchen; it was one more untried option, though Nick wasn't sure just what he'd do — if anything, once he found it.

Limping across the kitchen, he rummaged through drawers for a weapon. A knife was a pitiful defense against Lyra, but he wouldn't give up; he couldn't. He was the only thing between Chloe and her death. Maybe if he hid in the pantry, he could catch her unaware and show her what it was like to be intimidated.

Just as he yanked open the drawer and grabbed a knife, he spotted something even better — a phone. Ralph's cell phone.

Had Ralph left it here? More likely, Lyra had tucked it away during their *session*. He bet she wouldn't want something like a phone to distract her.

Flipping the cover open, he pressed 9-1-1, and almost cried at the sound of the rings going through. He heard Lyra's footsteps then, and shuffled down the back hallway, the phone cupped between his chin and shoulder.

He found the door at the very end pushed it open. The pantry, it had to be. Bolting inside, Nick slammed the door behind him and faced Ralph.

He gasped and turned away; the phone went dead.

"God . . . "

Pinned to the back of the door by a long iron post that pierced his throat, Ralph slumped unnaturally, his large arms swollen, one hand lifted slightly where he may have protested feebly against his fate.

Blood still seeped from the throat wound, painting the door in long irregular stripes. One sneaker had fallen off. Nick realized Ralph's sock as one of a pair he'd loaned him some months ago when he'd stayed overnight at his apartment.

Nick touched Ralph's sock. He shuddered. The single dangling bulb swayed overhead, throwing down jagged shadows that flickered and staggered.

He punched the phone numbers again, though he knew it was useless. Ralph's open eyes looked numbly past him.

"Ralph . . . " Nick swallowed to try ease the lump that climbed from his stomach into his throat. "God, Ralph —"

The door swung open abruptly then; Ralph's body thudded against the back of the wall with the motion. Lyra's hair crackled around her face; her lips blushed red, her eyes peered in excitedly, the color of air.

"You think you can *hide*?"

Nick said nothing. He glanced at Ralph's loose sneaker on the pantry floor. Ralph had liked to burn the tips of his laces; he said it preventing them from fraying.

He shook his head, feeling, for an instant, a bland nothingness that was oddly soothing. He let his head loll back on his shoulders and drew in a deep breath.

A flurry of sound caused his head to snap up, and a burning in his chest made Nick shuffle a few steps back.

Nothing made sense right away. Not until he coughed and felt the movement of metal shifting — and realized that Lyra's blade stuck out of his chest like a toothpick from a slice of ham.

Strange, he hadn't felt the assault — not that he had much of a reference point for knife attacks. All he knew is that he suddenly felt weak, rubbery. Panicked.

Nick stumbled in the small pantry, hitting a shelf containing cans of food. Tins thudded from the shelf to the floor. Grasping a large tin of peaches — Chloe's, Nick bet; she loved peaches — he made a forceful arc with his hand, making lucky contact with Lyra and she gasped and staggered backward. When she did, the metal shelf collapsed and toppled on top of her.

Nick heard her wild cursing as he shuffled out of the pantry. Gritting his teeth, Nick plucked the knife out of his chest. The pain was incredible and for an instant, he felt as if he might faint.

Throwing the knife down, he limped toward the front entrance. Fire had now engulfed the living room and made its way into the foyer where Chloe still lay slumped at the base of the steps.

He saw the bloody neighbor along the wall, the pearls around her neck slick with blood. Nick turned away. There was nothing he could do for the woman now, the poor woman.

Lyra shouted out his name over the roar of the fire. She sounded mad, real mad. He'd pushed the limits of her patience, that much was obvious.

He shuffled over to Chloe. She was barely breathing. He tried to draw her into his arms, but he was too weak and she rolled back with a tiny groan. The front of his shirt was saturated with blood; it mingled with Chloe's. He pressed a hand against the knife wound, it felt like a small, wet mouth. He shuddered.

"I'm sorry," Nick whispered to Chloe. "So sorry, hon."

Lyra's footsteps clicked toward them. There was no hesitation in her movement or stance. Her expression reminded Nick of a sprinting horse somehow, flared nostrils, concentrated focus, as she rushed to them and lifted the knife high. Nick threw his body over Chloe's, and in that thin veil of time before he would feel the shock of Lyra's knife, he hoped it would be quick and merciful —

"*Serqet*!"

The voice seemed to come from far away and near at once.

Nick's shoulders hunched forward; he waited to feel the cold metal piercing his skin and he drew Chloe closer to him.

"*Serqet*!"

His father's voice? Yes, his father. Looking up, he saw Bruce standing in the open doorway, staring down at them, blinking. His eyes flashed to the neighbor, moved over Nick and Chloe, and then settled once again on Lyra.

From Bruce's hand dangled the wolf pendant.

Lyra tilted her head, and the hand holding the knife, settled by her side. What was it his father said? *Serqet.* Why did that sound familiar?

Of course. The dream. The dream of Egypt. The man who'd spoken to him in English when Lyra was about to be burned. He'd called her Serqet. And the man; had that been his father? Could that be possible? Nick turned the thought away. Surely life couldn't have so many dimensions.

Lyra stared at Bruce. Her expression softened and she whispered something under her breath.

Bruce looked to the floor to see *That Hurt Thing*. He picked it up slowly, turned it over in his hands, traced the cover. Lyra smiled. "Oh, Master, have you come for me? Please say that you have." Her voice was sweet, like that of a child's. Bruce dropped the book and opened his arms. Lyra let the knife clatter to the floor and folded into his embrace

"Bruce," Lyra cooed. "So many lives have passed while I've waited . . . "

Lyra's back was to Nick as she nestled into Bruce's arms. It was as if no one else existed for either of them. She kissed his chin and then his mouth.

It was a hard scene to observe. Lyra had caused them so much pain. She'd taken his mother's life and torn their family apart. And yet Bruce held her warmly against him. It was a bitter taste.

Bruce caressed Lyra's back with one hand. His face was sad as he kissed Lyra, kissed her in a way that made it clear that whatever had happened between them, a part of him still cared for Lyra, would always care for her.

And then, just as Lyra tilted her head toward him again, Bruce slipped the wolf necklace over Lyra's head.

Her head snapped up when she realized the betrayal.

She opened her mouth to scream, but it was as if she had a mouthful of water and the only sound was a moan that was lost in the whine of fire-trucks and the roar of the flame.

Lyra's eyes were big as they rolled about and she looked so innocent it was hard not to feel compassion for her. Her hands clawed at the air. She tried to cling to Bruce and stumbled back.

The skin of her face began to melt to expose layers and layers of tissue and tendons and veins as the flesh peeled away from the bone. It was a hideous sight, her body twisting and melting before them, long strips of ruddy muscle dripping and oozing.

And then it was over except for a pile of sand on the floor between them.

Bruce wiped sweat from his forehead. "Let's get outta here," he whispered.

"Dad, I need help . . . " Nick gestured to Chloe. With a quiet nod, Bruce gathered Chloe in his arms and the three of them moved toward the door.

In the doorway, Bruce paused and looked down at That Hurt Thing on the floor beside the shelf.

Closing his eyes, he kicked the book into the fire. And then, with a final glance toward the pile of sand, Bruce closed the door behind them.

When Nick first awoke, he had a sudden moment of panic that he was back at Dagnorth Hospital. But when he saw the bright cheery walls he realized with relief that it wasn't Dagnorth General, but rather, the Queen Elizabeth Health Center.

Thank God.

His next thought was of Chloe. Was she okay?

And then there was Ralph.

Not that he had to wonder how Ralph was. The image of Ralph hanging suspended from the door would haunt him for a long, long time.

Bruce was asleep in a chair beside his bed, his head leaning into his hand, his mouth hanging open, dried saliva across his chin. For a moment, Nick just watched his father, and in the quiet of his room, thought about the events that had led to Lyra's demise. It was unsettling, to think there was more to life than could be held in your hearts or your hands.

Nick sucked in a deep breath and winced. His chest was strapped and the movement tore at the bandages. So much had happened; how would they put it all behind them?

"Nick?" Bruce said, waking with a stretch and getting to his feet. His checkered blue shirt was wrinkled. Dark circles ringed his eyes. He covered a yawn with a fist. "How you feeling?"

"Dad, is Chloe all right?"

"She's going to be fine, Nick, just fine."

They stared at one another for a few seconds, and then Bruce moved to the beside and hugged his son tightly. "I'm so sorry," he whispered.

"Dad, it's not your fault." He glanced down at his hands. "But . . . well, you . . . you found the book then, years ago? *That Hurt Thing*?"

Bruce slowly nodded. "On a bench in Mic Mac Mall. I really didn't think it would work, the instructions."

"Either did I," Nick admitted.

Bruce rubbed his eyes with one hand. He seemed so vulnerable, almost afraid. "The whole situation quickly got out of hand. I tried to break it off, but Lyra wouldn't leave me alone."

Bruce sunk into the chair, his hands clenching the wooden arms. "Still, when your mother died, I never for one second believed Serqet was responsible."

"But Dad, she's brutal; it's obvious? How could you be so naive?"

"She made me feel like . . . " He hunched his shoulders and let them relax. "Like nothing I've ever felt before. Like a drug. I felt like I'd known her all my life. She told me she was a genie; I thought it was cute, like a lover's game. But then she seemed to really believe it."

"Did you believe her?"

"Not until it was too late." He closed his eyes briefly. "Nick, is it all right if we talk about this later, or never?

"Dad, just tell me, how did you know to put the wolf necklace over Lyra?"

"It's strange, but Chloe told me."

"Chloe?"

"Remember Chloe's birthday when I called her? Well, she talked about the locket you gave her. She said you now matched, both having silver pendants. Then, laughing, she said, 'Yeah, it's Nick's genie protection, the wolf.' At the time, I didn't think too much about it — or I didn't want to, perhaps. Who knows what goes on in our subconscious?"

He sighed. "I'd like you to think I'm a hero, but it really didn't occur to me until that final moment at Chloe's house. I found the necklace outside on the porch and I thought of your mother, though I don't know why — almost like she was talking to me. Then Chloe's comment rushed at me, and . . . I wondered if it might be a possible way of dealing with the situation."

"Excuse me, Mr. O'Brien?"

A nurse appeared in the doorway then; both Nick and Bruce looked toward her.

She was a young woman, almost too pretty to wear the stiff white uniform and clinical thick soled shoes. "Nick O'Brien?" she clarified.

"Yeah?" Nick said.

"There's a police officer here to see you."

Were they here to arrest him? After all, the little matter of Holly Sampon's death had never been concluded. Dr. Genter had kept the cops away at Dagnorth General, but here and now, he was fair game. The police visit was inevitable, he'd known that all along. Still, the knowledge did nothing to ease the knot in his gut.

A short man wearing wrinkly beige Dockers and a dull white sweater stepped inside the room. He reminded Nick a little of Dr. Sampson — without the suspenders. He had clear blue eyes; a contrast to the frumpy appearance and ruffled brown hair.

"Johnny Mack, with the Homicide Department." He shook Nick's hand and then Bruce's. "I'm here about the death of Holly Sampson."

Bruce put up a firm hand. "Shouldn't we call a lawyer?"

Johnny Mack put a hand on the end rail of the hospital bed. "That's just it," he said. "There's no need."

"No need?" Bruce stood up, his chest lifting. "No need?"

"Mr. O'Brien, your son is no longer under suspicion. That's what I came here to say."

By God, Nick hoped this wasn't a dream. Bruce slumped back in his seat, the plastic chair squeaking beneath him.

"I don't understand," Nick said. Someone pushed a noisy cart past the open door.

Mack hesitated, glancing toward the noise. He rolled his tongue along the inside of his cheek. "Dr. Sampson came forward again. Gerald Sampson. He was insistent that you were innocent. To make a long story short, we did a search in his jeep and found black hair. The same hair we found at his wife's murder scene, and in your apartment."

"How does that prove anything?" Bruce asked.

Nick frowned. He didn't want his father to say anything lest Mack realize he'd simply overlooked something and take back the conclusion. He wished he didn't feel so insecure.

"Hair from the same person is significant. And the knife found in your apartment? It had your blood, sure, and Holly Sampson's. But," he said, pushing his head forward, "there was just a speck of another person's blood. The hair and that speck of blood had the same DNA, from the same woman."

"Surely that's not enough to let me off the hook," Nick himself added. "Lyra's blood on the knife. I could have used her knife, couldn't I?"

It was Bruce's turn to glare at his son, his eyes telling him to shut up.

"That's why I didn't exclude you right away," Mack explained. "Not until this morning, actually. Not until I saw the photos taken at the hospital."

"Photos?"

"When you were brought in, the police took photos of you, of your wrists, routine stuff, but these cops weren't from Homicide, see. More like shift workers, though I'd not repeat that anywhere else. They filed the photos along with the doctor's reports that says you slit your wrists, suicide attempt."

He pinched an earlobe in thought. "When I got the DNA report, I requested the file. Had a look at the photos. Nick, it's obvious you didn't cut your own wrists. Things like this aren't always spotted at the ER. In their defense, their priority is keeping you alive."

Mack tapped his own arms. "When a person cuts his own wrists, there are what we call hesitation marks. And since you're right handed, there would have been a difference in your right and left arms. Not to mention that there was no evidence of your being with Holly Sampson when she died." Mack threw out his hands. "Simple math, really."

"You can't know how happy I am to hear this," Nick told him.

"Well, you're not completely off the hook," Mack said. "We need to find this woman, and that's where you can help. Have you any idea where she might be?"

Nick thought back to Lyra's demise. He could have laughed at Mack's suggestion. "I don't know where she is . . . but if she contacts me, I'll let you know."

"Great." Mack slapped the bed. "Well, I promised the good nurse that I wouldn't take up too much time just now. I'd like to come back later ask you some more questions."

"Anything I can do," Nick repeated.

They talked a little more, and then Mack left. When the door closed behind them, Bruce let out a shout of relief and Nick fell back on the bed, grateful and exhausted.

"Doesn't seem real," Nick said to the ceiling. "Dad, I don't believe it! It's really over."

Bruce shook folded hands upward. "Thank God."

They were quiet for a few moments and then Bruce said, "Tell you what, let's go see Chloe. Tell her the good news. Shall I get a wheelchair?"

"No, I'm okay." Truth was, Nick wanted Chloe to see him walk toward her. Being pushed in a wheelchair was hardly a reunion.

In the hallway, Nick slowly put an arm around his father's neck and for a moment, he was serious. "Dad, you sure it's really over? About Lyra. She won't . . . "

Bruce lifted a stern hand. "Nick, I promise. She's gone. We've got to move on now . . . promise me that you will?"

Nick hesitated.

"Son?"

Nick nodded. "I will, I promise."

When they reached the elevator, Bruce pressed the round button with his thumb. A janitor moved past them swiping a damp mop over the tiled floors; a citrus scent met them. "Nick," Bruce said, his voice unsteady, "Do you . . . well, do you think worse of me? For how I acted during my marriage? And for not standing by you like I should have during all this?"

"Ah, dad, you did the best you could," he said. "Though I was really pissed when you fired me. But now, I'm just grateful it worked out. Someone up there must be watching out for us. Someone with a real big heart."

"Someone who'd do anything to protect her family," Bruce added.

The elevator opened with a jolt and an older couple stepped out. Inside, Bruce pressed the numbered button and then clapped his son's arm. "Now c'mon, enough of this serious talk. It's making me neurotic. Besides, I'm sure Chloe's dying to see you."

"*Waiting* to see me," Nick corrected with a half-grin.

Bruce chuckled in agreement.

Nick leaned against the wall, and thought about Dr. Sampson. Even days ago, Nick would have never believed he'd be thankful for the professor's stubborn need to stand up for what he believed to be right — the same ironic need, he mused, that had given him the infamous D. Tomorrow, he'd call Dr. Sampson and thank him. And right after that, he'd call the registrar's office and see about making up the term over the summer.

The elevator doors opened then, and they both stepped outside. A nurse and two attendants rushed a stretcher past them, carrying an unconscious man about Nick's age toward an area marked 'Surgery'. The IV bag rattled swung back and forth on its metal bar; a tired male attendant wiped sweat from his forehead without breaking their rapid pace. Blood interrupted the sterile whiteness of the sheet that covered the man from the chest down.

Nick and Bruce exchanged a knowing glance, but said nothing.

Quietly, Nick followed his father to Chloe's room.

She smiled when they entered.

e p i l o g u e

Dylan Charles picked his way through the shelves of Halifax's Regional Library. The library had just started their winter schedule and he was grateful for the longer hours. He loved books, loved the new worlds they let you enter, loved them maybe more than he loved his new wife Janice, though he'd never admit that to her.

Janice didn't like to read much and that disappointed Dylan. Maybe if she read a little, she might be a little less possessive, a little more logical. He chuckled as he added a Will Burnhap book to the growing bundle on the nearby table.

No one could plot like Will Burnhap, and the way he used humor to decorate the plot. He briefly considered that Janice might like to read him and decided that no, she'd only say he was trying to change her.

He wondered if other married men hid their books in the bathroom and read while they attended to matters so their wives wouldn't feel ignored.

Maybe his mother had been right about Janice. The girl's clingy, a control freak, his mother had said. *She'll give ya permanent hemorrhoids, that's what, Dylan.*

Chuckling, Dylan leaned on his haunches to check out the very last row. That's just what he told Janice about why he spent so much time on the pot.

Hemorrhoids, darlin', gotta take it nice and slooooowwww . . .

Oh, he liked Janice all right. But part of him was hungry. Hungry for something bigger and better than his life — and wasn't that pitiful to say after only ten months of marriage?

God, it ticked him off, the way she bitched and nagged and whined.

I wish she was easier to deal with, he said to himself. I wish . . . *wish she was dead!*

Oh my, that wasn't nice, Dylan.

His anger surprised him. He wasn't a man prone to anger; even impatience was a rare appearance.

Get your books and go home and grow up.

He sat on the floor in the aisle. One more book. Then he'd forget about his neural tantrum and behave himself.

His fingers ran over the books. It was a shame that good books could get missed just because they weren't at eye level —

Now *that's* an odd book.

What's the cover made of, some kind of foil?

Pulling it out by the spine, Dylan let the book flop onto his knees.

That Hurt Thing.

Interesting title. No author. And the cover, a black tulip slashed into two parts and a scorpion curled between the parts. Well, well, well . . .

He opened it and skimmed the first page. Those stains, were they honest-to-goodness blood? He glanced around to see if anyone saw the needy way he clung to the book.

Then he read:

Do you dare summon me, Oh weak and weary of soul?

Do you long to taste the wolf's blood gone cold ?

Be certain, for the scorpion goddess knows only rage,

For those who hold mockery upon my page.

Well, now.

What kind of an opening was that? Not even Will Burnhap had that kind of lead. Was it an invitation?

He swallowed. Felt a thirst inside him, a needy ache. A *new* ache.

Follow borders two from your place of birth,

Come willingly with courage and merry mirth.

Careful what you wish for I will grant it to thee

Without thought or pause or mediocrity.

Dylan began to sweat. He ran his tongue along the front of his teeth and licked his lips.

Once you arrive you will await my form,

And dark and light will mingle with storm.

Be worthy of disturbing my sleep and time,

There is no turning back once I make you mine.

Make you mine?

Holy Schmoly.

If the other supervisors down at the plant knew he'd found something like this . . . But he wouldn't tell them. No, this was his secret alone. His *adventure.*

Dylan stripped off the magnetic sticker along the spine and shoved the book to the bottom of his briefcase and hurried out of the library. In the parking lot, a blast of wind flattened his hair against his scalp as he bustled toward his car, the briefcase cradled tightly in his arms.

In the distant night air, he caught the pale scent of cinnamon.